REACHING RETRIBUTION

THE PROPHESIZED SERIES

KAITLYN HOYT

Cover Design by Victoria Faye
www.main.whitandware.com

Formatting by Inkstain Interior Book Designing
www.inkstainformatting.com

Editing by TCB Editing
www.tcbediting.weebly.com

DEDICATION

For the readers:
This book is for you. This whole series would not have been possible if I didn't have amazing readers like you standing behind me and supporting me through this entire process. Thank you for everything.

OTHER KAITLYN HOYT BOOKS

THE PROPHESIZED SERIES

BlackMoon Beginnings

Scorching Secrets

Descending Darkness

Reaching Retribution

Eternal Endings

STANDALONE NOVELS

Redeeming Lainey

REACHING RETRIBUTION

CHAPTER ONE

COLTON

"YOU KILLED HER!" I YELL again. Tom bends down and picks the man off the ground. I'm not sure what he's going to do, but I've never seen Tom look this angry before. The man is a mage— that much is obvious. I try to push away from Bragden and Liam again, but they tighten their grip. Blood is dripping down the man's chin from his split lip because of Tom's earlier punch. He killed my soulmate; I can't just stand here. She's dead because of him.

The man glances down at Ryanne before he speaks. "It wasn't supposed to hit her." A menacing look crosses his face before he narrows his eyes on Incendia and points. "It was supposed to hit her!" Bragden lets go of me and walks toward him. Recognizing the look on Bragden's face, I stop struggling. Liam lets me go and I move back and sit down next to Ryanne. She can't be gone. This isn't real.

It can't be real.

Seeing the feral look in Bragden's eyes, Tom steps out of the way. Bragden takes one look at him and punches him. Emma and Natalie gasp and flinch when the sound of his nose breaking echoes though the room. He slumps to the ground unconscious. With taunt muscles, Bragden stands over the man, fists clenched, trying to control his anger. A few seconds later, everyone turns and looks at me, crying next to the dead body of my soulmate.

It wasn't supposed to end like this. I lean back against the edge of the bed, trying to control my breathing. It feels like I can't get enough air into my lungs—like I'm slowing suffocating under pain. I just got her back and now she's gone. Just yesterday, Travis rescued her from Dravin's compound—broken and bloodied, but alive. Less than twenty-four later, she's dead.

Incendia falls to her knees on the ground next to me. "I'm so sorry. It was supposed to be me. She shouldn't have done that. I was supposed to die. Was that what she saw in the vision? Me dying?"

Bragden walks over to me, "Probably. That's kind of Ryanne's thing. You're meant for something bigger. That's why she saw that vision."

"But she's the girl from the prophecy! I'm nothing more than an average mage."

"And *Ryanne* thought you were worth saving," I tell her emphasizing Ryanne's name. She's more than the girl from the prophecy. Tom walks over the unconscious man and closes the door. We don't need to attract any more attention right now.

"Incendia, do you recognize this man?" Tom asks quietly. I don't look up at him because I don't think I can handle seeing the sadness in his expression.

"He's Mr. Garrowen's son, Enrique," she whispers. "I didn't know he was a mage." When Incendia's eyes start to water, Bragden reaches over and pulls her to him. She turns and starts crying into this shoulder.

"She saved me twice today. Why would she do that? She doesn't even know me."

"Ryanne would rescue a stray cat." I lean back against the bed. We all turn and look at Kyril sitting with Olive. "She *did* rescue a stray cat."

Even Olive looks upset. This shouldn't have happened. I was supposed to have a future with her. Claire told me that everything was going according to plan. This was not part of the plan. What changed? The last thing I told her was a lie. The last words I'll ever speak to her weren't true. I didn't even get to tell her that I loved her too.

I push myself up. "We need to find Dravin." Dravin is the man responsible for all of this, and I can't just stand here while I know he's out there causing another person or family pain.

"Colton," Tom starts.

"You don't understand. Literally a couple hours ago, she asked me not to stop fighting. She said if something does happen to me, you have to continue with this fight. You have to push forward; otherwise all of this would have been for nothing. Don't let it be for nothing, Colton," I quote her. "I have to finish this, Tom. For her." My voice cracks at the end and hearing that, Emma stifles a sob. I glance across the room at her and see silent tears streaming down her face. David is trying to comfort her, but yet again, this is one of those situations where nothing seems helpful in the moment.

The room gets quiet when Liam starts coughing and leans against the wall to support himself. "Liam, what's wrong?" Natalie asks. A layer of sweat glistens on his forehead, and an expression of pain crosses his face as he leans his head back against the wall and grabs his chest, gasping for air.

"It's Ryanne," Bragden explains. "He's supposed to protect her. She didn't get to complete what she was destined to, and he needed to protect her until that moment came. His body is reacting to losing their bond."

"Will he be okay?" Natalie asks.

"I don't know. His symptoms could fade over time or they could get worse."

"What do you mean they could get worse?" Natalie says—her voice an octave higher than usual. She's staring at Bragden with wide eyes waiting for his response, but instead of answering, he shakes his head. He doesn't have to say anything. The meaning behind his words is obvious. We could lose Ryanne and Liam within a short time period. No longer able to support his weight, Liam slides down the wall and sits on the ground.

"This whole situation just sucks," Incendia says.

"You can say that again," Emma hiccups.

"This whole situation just sucks."

I couldn't have said it better myself.

I HESITATE IN THE DOORWAY for a few seconds before following Claire. I don't know what is going on right now, but Claire does. Hopefully, she has the answers that I need. I hate always wandering around confused. Just when I think that I'm finally doing something right…I end up here.

"So I'm not really dead?" I inquire again.

"Not exactly," she answers but continues walking. I pick up my steps until I'm standing beside her.

"What the heck does that mean? Am I in a coma? Will I wake up? What is going on?"

"One question at a time, my dear. Magic has a way of complicating things," she tells me as she pushes the down button for the elevator. "It makes the simplest of things infinitely more difficult, while making the hardest things in life much easier. It all depends on how it's used." The elevator dings open and Claire walks in and leans against the wall, waiting for me to enter before she hits the lobby button. "I have the answers you need, honey," she says when I don't enter the elevator right away.

With a loud sigh, I walk in. I don't understand what's going on, but I've already come to the realization that I need to do whatever Claire tells me. She's right when she says that she holds the answers. I'm in the dark right now.

Giving me a small smile, she pushes the button. When the doors close, she looks back to me and says, "Technically, you're physically dead, but there's a chance that you will come back from this. Your body is back at the hotel with everyone else, but your soul is stuck in limbo. You weren't supposed to die today. This isn't how things were supposed to end for you or for anyone else. Your death will propel everyone forward into action, but what about afterwards? Colton will fall into depression because a part of him is missing. Liam and Natalie's story won't play out, because your death ultimately brings about his death. Bragden and Incendia will never get together, because Bragden is distraught at yours and his brother's death. David and Emma will fall apart, because David has to help his brother. Tom takes to drinking because he wasn't able to help you and couldn't help either David or Colton. Logan falls into a life of crime, frustrated that his magic failed him, and Larkin and Kyril get captured and killed by Dravin. They need you there, Ryanne."

"How?" I ask. "How do I go back?"

"I can't tell you. You have to figure that out on your own. You'll know what to do when the time comes."

"What can you tell me then?"

"You are the strongest girl I've ever met, Ryanne. Your life hasn't been easy, but you've risen to the challenge every time something new was thrown at you. This second chance doesn't happen for everyone. Few get the opportunity to turn back time and erase irreparable damage, but you've been given this for a reason."

"That's it? That's all you can tell me?" That didn't give me any of the answers I need. "What am I going to have to face? What lies ahead? Can't you give me anything more?"

"I'm so sorry, but I can't tell you more. Just know that mages aren't the only magical beings in the world and a handful of them impact the course of history. They have a lot riding on this war. This task isn't going to be easy, dear. Most people aren't successful. It'll be challenging and difficult, but I have faith in you. You're fully capable of doing this, but trust your instincts. You'll know what you have to do. Don't let something simple cloud your judgments and everything will be fine."

"What happens if I can't do it? What will happen to Dravin if I can't do this?"

"If you aren't successful, everything will move forward on this altered path. Dravin will defeat mages and reign over everyone. Many mages will be slaughtered for their magic. The world will be forever changed. Humans will be forced to work as his slaves. He'll be the most powerful dictator the world has ever seen."

My mouth drops open at the seriousness in her tone. Everything will take a turn for the worst, and that's saying a lot considering things are already bad. "Oh, no pressure," I mumble as the elevator opens.

"When does this start?" I ask as we walk out of the elevator and into the lobby which, like every other room in this forsaken hotel, is empty.

"Right now," she walks forward and gives me a hug. "I was in love once, Ryanne. I know that feeling you're experiencing. The all-encompassing, I'll do anything for you, feeling. Use that feeling to get back to your soulmate. You can do this. I've never known anyone stronger than you. Have faith in your powers and follow your heart."

"Thank you, Claire."

"Not everyone or everything is as it seems. Please remember that." Claire fades away, leaving me standing in an empty hotel alone. I don't really know what to do. I just know that I have to be successful. I can't let this future play out. The previous one was scary enough. There's no way I can let everyone face Dravin by themselves. The future Claire described sounded horrible. I can't let them experience that. I can't let my Avengers group fall apart. Oh my gosh, what about Jane? Have they already told Jane? I hope not.

I wonder what everyone is doing right now. Is Colton okay? Is Liam okay? Claire mentioned that Liam will die because of me. Is he experiencing symptoms already? How soon will those symptoms start to appear? I need to make this quick. There are too many things I don't know. I hope that nothing happens to Incendia. I didn't get to put a protective enchantment on her, but Bragden will protect her. I'm sure of it.

I cross my arms and continue walking toward the front door. I'm not sure where I'm going. I feel a little pull in my gut telling me to leave the hotel. What I need to do won't be found here. The answers I need are somewhere outside. They're not here. Nothing is here. Just me. Alone. Again.

"Some guidance would be nice!" I yell at the ceiling. This whole ordeal is just frustrating. How the heck am I supposed to get back if I have no idea what I'm supposed to do. Pushing the cold metal on the door at the entrance, I walk out of the hotel. There's nothing out here either. The whole town is deserted. I walk until I come to the road. Looking both ways, I expect to see tumbleweed roll across.

Nothing happens. Well that's depressing.

"What's going to happen to me?" I ask.

Silence. Who was I expecting to reply?

"Waiting for you is like waiting for rain in this drought. Useless and disappointing," I mutter. "A Cinderella Story. Point for Team Ryanne." Is craziness a side effect of dying?

"Talking to yourself doesn't change the fact that you're dead." I instantly tense when I recognize the high voice behind me. And here I thought dying would be the worst part of my day. Hesitantly, I turn around and face the girl who tormented me in high school. Please tell me that I'm not supposed to work with her.

"What are you doing here, Lily?"

"You think you're the only one who gets a second chance?" she places a hand on her hip as she watches me.

"You're dead?"

"Apparently," she snaps. "Otherwise, I don't know why I'm here." Her voice isn't as harsh as I remember. I watch as her eyes flicker around us, before I too glance around, finally getting a good look at our surroundings. I'm no longer standing outside of the hotel. I'm back in my hometown, standing in front of the high school. How did I get here?

A warm feeling spreads through my stomach. Dang it. I bet someone somewhere is laughing at this turn of events. Claire said that I would know when I had to do something, and I'm guessing that this is what she meant. Keeping my groan inside, I turn toward Lily and put on a neutral expression. "How'd it happen?" I ask her.

Lily crosses her arms and looks up at the sky. Biting her inner lip, she tries to hide the tears in her eyes. "Why? It doesn't change anything."

"Look Lily, obviously we're supposed to help each other. If you want to get out of this situation alive, we're going to have to trust one another," I tell her.

She tears her eyes away from the clouds above and looks down at me. I watch her for a few seconds, but she does nothing. Fine, I'll find my own way out of here. I turn and walk away from her, knowing that she'll call after me if she's serious about surviving this.

"Wait, Ryanne, I don't know what to do! I have no idea where to go. I'm scared and confused and I need help!"

"You're not the only one dead here, Lily! I want to get back too. I have a soulmate and a protector waiting for me. If I don't get back, my protector will die, my soulmate will become depressed, and a crazy man will rule the world, enslaving humans to fulfill his every need."

"Who the heck are you?" she asks when she catches up to me. I look at her out of the corner of my eye, but continue walking.

"You don't want to know."

"Yes I do. That's why I asked."

"Well, I asked how you died, but you didn't tell me. You have your secrets. I have mine."

We walk a few more steps in silence before she speaks. "My step-dad," she whispers.

"What?" I stop walking and face her, making sure I heard what I think I heard.

"My step-dad killed me," she repeats.

"What?"

"He got drunk and beat me." I may not be Lily's biggest fan, but she didn't deserve that. "I instigated it. He hit my mom, so I yelled at him. He didn't mean to kill me. He doesn't know how he acts when he drinks."

"What did your mom do?"

"She tried to stop him, but he knocked her out. I don't think she's dead." Technically, her mom could be dead, but I don't tell her that. Lily's here because it wasn't her time to die. She's getting another chance.

"I'm sorry," I tell her.

"What about you? How'd you die?" she asks me. I turn away and continue walking. We're heading somewhere, but I'm not quite sure. I bite my tongue to keep from talking, but for some reason, I want to tell her. She just shared her death experience with me, and right now there's really no point in keeping it in. I don't see what it could change.

"I walked in front of a flying dagger," I mumble while staring down at the ground.

"A flying dagger?"

"A man targeted someone near me and I tried to push her out of the way. He threw a dagger, and I got hit. End of story." There's actually much more to the story, but I don't know how much I can tell Lily. She doesn't know about mages, and even if we both get out of this alive, I'm not sure what we'll remember.

"What happened to the guy who threw the dagger?"

"I bet someone beat the crap out of him. I hope someone did," I say even though I'm not sure if I actually mean that. We're heading toward Pearl Village, the neighborhood of all the old rich homes in our town. Of course Lily lives there. I try to stop walking, but can't. My feet are moving without my permission.

"Are we heading to my house?"

"I think so," I tell her. "I don't really know how all this stuff works. Last time I died, I didn't have to do this."

"You've died before?"

"You don't want to know," I tell her as we stop in front of an older home. She doesn't live in one of the larger, ritzy houses. The house in front of me is a one story home. Deep red bricks are offset with beige shutters surrounding the windows. It looks like we're now in present time. There's a man walking his dog across the street, but he doesn't look in our direction.

"Can anyone see us?" Lily asks while looking around; her eyes landing on the man and his dog.

"Umm, I don't really think so." Before I finish, we start walking. It's weird not being in control of your body. We're obviously supposed to see something inside of the house, but we don't have to open the door. We literally walk right through it. "That's so weird."

I stop inside the door. A small living room with a box television and stained couch is directly to my right. Small pictures of a young Lily clutter every available surface. "Lily, why did you torment me in high school?" I've wanted to know the answer to that question for a long time now, and I don't know if I'll get another chance to ask it.

She turns toward me and grabs onto the ends of her dark hair. "I don't know, Ryanne. I didn't want to, but Adam threatened to break-up with me if I didn't. I didn't believe his story about you. You always seemed like this really sweet, shy girl. I knew it was him. I was afraid that if he broke up with me, I wouldn't be popular anymore. I was afraid that if I didn't go along with everything he said, everyone would find out that I come from this. I'm not the stuck-up rich girl everyone thinks I am, but I worked so hard to build this reputation that I just couldn't turn back. I had a role to fill, so I went along with everything."

"You never thought that more people would like you if they knew the real you?"

"No one would have liked the real me." She motions to the room around her. My eyes scan the area, but I don't see anything wrong with this house.

"I would have. I think this Lily is so much better than the one that I knew in high school."

Still clutching her hair, Lily looks down at me and frowns. "I'm really sorry for everything I did to you, Ryanne." She seems sincere. "I know that an apology doesn't give you back anything, but it's all I can do."

I glance up at her, but she's no longer looking at me. Her eyes are glued onto the entryway of the kitchen. "I forgive you." Nodding, she steps away from me and moves toward that area. A few seconds later, I follow after her. I try to hold in my gasp, but I can't when I see the scene in front of me.

An older woman is lying on her back in the doorway. She's breathing, so Lily's right about her mom still being alive. My eyes move toward the center of the room. A man is leaning back against chipped cabinets, silent tears running down his face.

Lily is standing near her mother, watching the scene. He slowly moves toward Lily's body lying in the middle of the floor. Her body is laying at an odd angle in the middle of the kitchen floor with blood dripping down her face from a head wound. Her arms are covered in deep purple bruises. He did that to her?

Her step-dad crawls over to her body. I can hear sirens in the background. Someone must have heard the commotion and called the police. "I'm so sorry, Lily," he sobs. "I'm so, so sorry." He kisses her forehead and leans back. Lily's staring down at him with sadness in her eyes. She's not angry at him for killing her. She's upset. Why?

"He's not necessarily a bad guy, you know? He was abused by his father when he was a kid. It's all he knows. My mom thought she could change him. Some people can't change," she explains to me. Turning to her step-dad, she crouches down in front of him. Police break the front door down and storm into the house, weapons drawn and ready. Lily looks over at her step-dad and briefly glances at me. "I forgive you," she whispers.

Lily gasps and her real body begins to shake. The police rush past me and yell at her step-dad to put his hands in the air. He willingly lets the cops cuff him and escort him out of the house. The Lily I was standing with fades until she's no longer with me. Paramedics rush into the kitchen with two stretchers. Lily's mother is placed onto one while two other paramedics move toward Lily.

"She's alive!" a female yells. I back out of the room. The paramedics are doing their jobs to ensure that Lily survives. I'm no longer needed here. Lily's need was to apologize to me and forgive her step-father. Now what am I going to do? There's no one to help me here. I still don't understand what is going on right now. I don't know the man that killed me. Honestly, I'm not really upset with him. I wish that he didn't throw the dagger, yes, but I don't have any previous problems with him.

Walking through the front door, I head down the driveway and back to the street we just walked on. I wonder if Lily will remember any of this afterwards. Will I remember any of this? I really need to figure out what I'm supposed to do. How long have I been dead? How long do I get before I'm officially considered dead?

As I turn right, I feel something pulling me back toward the entrance of the neighborhood. I follow the road until I end up back in front of the school again. Where am I going? I walk past the school and continue moving through town. It feels strange to be back here. I've been away for so long. Even when I was here, I didn't go out too often. When I get toward the edge of town, I instantly know where I am going. I try to bury my feet in the ground. I don't want to go any further. I start shaking my head as my hand moves forward, without my permission, and opens the gate.

Walking past the rows of tombstones, I head to the back lot of the cemetery. Tears are streaming down my face before my feet stop moving. I bite my lip and look around. I'm alone—alone with the dead. Falling to my knees, I look at the gravestone in front of me.

In loving memory.
Maureen Nicole Arden
April 30 1968 - July 17, 2012

A hurricane of emotions crash into me as I sit on the cold, damp ground. Despite not having my powers, the sky darkens and the temperature cools, seemingly matching my emotions. It becomes difficult to breathe. I try to control my feelings, but it's been so long since I've let myself feel this much. I've tried to close this part of me off. I've tried to forget about that day and push everything back. I lean forward and rest my head on the grass at the base of the tombstone, letting my tears soak the earth. "You left me," I whisper. "You left me here alone."

"I had to, Ry-Ry." I jump and fly backward when I hear my childhood nickname.

"Mom?" I start shaking as another sob racks through my body. She runs forward and wraps her arms around me. I know this isn't real, but it feels like it. She still smells like the familiar vanilla scent she always wore. I lean into her arms and cry on her shoulder. She runs her hand through my hair like she used to. It's like nothing changed. This was how she would comfort me when I was sad—when she was alive.

"I'm here."

"I don't know what I'm doing here."

"You're not supposed to be here, Ryanne. It's not your time yet," my mother tells me. I'm not letting her go. I don't know how much time we have.

"I can't go back. I have to do something here. I don't know what though. Claire couldn't tell me much."

"You have to talk to me. Admit everything that's going on in that brain of yours. Everything that you've locked away. All the secrets you've been keeping. You need to get everything off your chest. Then, and only then, can you go back." That doesn't seem too difficult.

I get out of my mom's arms and sit down against her grave. Tears are still pouring out of my eyes, but it's not as uncontrollable anymore. Hiccupping, I start. "I don't know what I'm doing. Not just right now, but all the time. When you died, I wouldn't let myself get close to anyone. I pushed everyone away. I locked my heart away."

"That's not going to get you back into your body. You have to dig deeper than that." I bite my lip and look back at my mom. I don't know what I'm supposed to say. "Say what's in here," she points to my heart.

"I'm mad at you."

"Good, keep going."

"I was supposed to die in that accident. Not you. Me! Do you know what that does to someone? I woke up after the accident, strapped to a bunch of IVs, alone in a hospital room. I had no family to go to. I had no friends to help me. I had no one. I was suddenly more alone than I've ever been in my life. Do you know what it's like to have no one? No one wanted me. And the whole time, I had to live with the fact that the only person who loved me was dead because she saved me.

"I should be grateful that you saved me, but I'm not. That car was headed for me, mom. You looked me in the eyes right as you jerked the car in a different direction. I watched the world blur outside the window as the car flipped. Do you know how many times I walked into Jane's bathroom and thought about how easy it would be to swallow a bunch of pills and make everything better? I thought about suicide, Mom!" I lean back and wrap my arms around my legs. I've never revealed that to anyone before.

"Now, I have Colton. I love him so much that it scares me. He's makes me feel desired and knows how to comfort me when I'm upset. He can make me laugh when I'm sad or angry. He's always worrying about me, which is annoying but nice at the same time. He's too good for me. I'll never be enough for him. He deserves someone who can focus solely on him, but I feel like I have to live up to this prophecy thing or everyone will be so disappointed.

"Sometimes I feel like I'm spread out too thin. I can't give Colton what he needs, because I'm so focused on everyone else. Someday he's going to realize he can do better and leave me. He's going to want someone who can be there for him when he needs it. He's going to want someone who can control her magic and is always in control of her life. He's going to want someone else."

"There's more."

I look at her. She looks the same as she did when she was alive. Her chestnut hair is still cut in a short bob. Deep blue eyes look back at me. We look nothing alike. I apparently take after the doctor in that department.

"I'm afraid that I'm going to screw all this up. Claire's dead because of me. Colton died because of me. What if someone else dies? I won't be able to live with that. Every day, I want to run away from all this. I want to grab Colton and run off. I want to live without fear. I'm tired of being surrounded by violence and death all the time."

"You have to let it out, honey."

"Fine," I stand up. "You want me to let it out? I hate that I have these powers. I hate that I'm the chosen one. I hate that dad was never there. I hate that you left me last year. I hate that I feel like I'm never going to be good enough for anyone. I hate that I can't stop worrying about those around me. I hate that Liam gave me this stupid pendant, because if I actually die today, he does too. I hate that Dravin is always one step ahead of me, and he has a plan while I don't. I hate that I get these visions. I hate that all I see is death, and I hate myself for attracting so much trouble and endangering everyone I love."

Mom just stares at me, knowing there's more I have to say. I start pacing back and forth, trying to collect my thoughts. I feel like there are so many things running through my mind right now that I don't know what to say.

"Despite all that hate, I wouldn't change anything, because I love all those people. I love everyone I've met since I've become a mage. I finally have a family again. Every day I wake up and miss you, but I know you had to die to give me something to fight for. I want to make you proud, and I'm afraid that I haven't done that yet," I whisper that last part.

My mom smiles at me. "There you go." She moves toward me and wraps her arms around me again. "Now, you have to admit that you are good enough for that boy who loves you more than life itself. You have to admit that you are strong enough to do this. You have to tell me that and believe it yourself."

"I can't," I whisper.

"Then you can't go back."

I could always tell when mom was lying to me and right now, she's being sincere. "But I'm neither of those things."

"Why can't you see what everyone else sees in you, honey? Your soulmate thinks *you* are too good for him. Everyone else thinks you two are perfect for each other. Tom is so proud that Colton found someone like you. I'm so glad that you found someone like him. You two are meant for each other. They wouldn't give you a soulmate who was too good for you. You're each other's perfect half, and you are more than strong enough for this. How many times have you been captured? How many times have you been beaten and broken? How many times have you come back from all that? How many times have you said I'm not going to give up?"

Everything she's saying makes sense, but I still don't want to believe it. It's hard to let go of so many insecurities. It's not like a switch that you can just move over to make everything better. "Can I tell you that I think that I could someday be good enough for him and that I have the potential to be strong enough for all this?"

"Do you honestly believe that? With all your heart?"

I know Colton loves me, and I know I love him. Maybe once all this war stuff is over I can feel more confident in us. I can finally be good enough for him. Yes, I do believe that part. Am I strong enough? At the moment, I don't think so, but everyone else seems to believe I am. I can't let their faith be misguided. I've already proven myself in training and in actual combat. With a little more practice and skill, I do think I can be strong enough.

"Yes," I whisper. My mom tightens her arms around me. I feel weird. My body starts to vibrate. What's going on?

"I'm so proud of you, Ryanne. Don't ever question that. I'll always be here for you. All you have to do is ask, and I'll listen. I wouldn't change anything that has happened. I love you so much."

I gasp as pain shoots through my body. I close my eyes and pray for this to be quick. This is the end. As darkness envelopes me, I feel my body being pulled in every direction. I must be going to Hell, because this pain is unbearable. If I could, I would be screaming, but my mouth won't cooperate.

"Don't fight it."

CHAPTER TWO

COLTON

"COLTON, STARING AT HER ISN'T going to bring her back," Emma says. I tear my eyes from Ryanne and look up at Emma. Her blue eyes are glossed over from her own tears. She has red splotches under her red, puffy eyes from crying. Ryanne was her best friend, but right now, she doesn't understand.

"She can't be gone," I shake my head and clench my jaw, trying to stop the tears again. "She can't be." Emma crawls over to me and rests her head on my shoulder, comforting me.

"She changed the course of history, guys. Don't you understand that?" Incendia says. "She's supposed to be here at the end. She's supposed stop Dravin. I've never seen anyone do what she did earlier. She fought all the men that we'd been fighting for hours in like ten minutes! No one else can do that."

"We are not going to try and find someone to replace her," I growl.

"There's no one to replace her," Incendia says. "I was supposed to die; not her."

"Incendia, Ryanne saw that vision for a reason. She was supposed to stop your death. Be thankful you get another chance. Don't dwell on what can't be changed," Bragden whispers to her.

Don't dwell on what can't be changed. Does he understand how difficult that is? It feels like my heart is literally breaking. I feel like part of me is missing. Ryanne filled a void that I didn't know I had before I met her. She broke down all barriers and filled my life with laughter, happiness, love…she filled the void with her love. Now that it's gone, I'm left with nothing but grief and pain.

I look across the room at Liam, who's sitting with his head against the wall and a hand across his chest. He can barely breathe. Natalie is frantically trying to calm him, but without Ryanne here, there's nothing she can do.

Ryanne was the glue in our group. She kept everyone together. I can already feel a rift forming between us. Tom's angry. Bragden's a bundle of emotions. He's upset over Ryanne, mad at Enrique, confused over Incendia, and worried about his brother. Larkin and Kyril don't know what to do. Larkin's pacing the room, trying to remain calm. Liam's dying. Natalie distressed, trying to help him. Emma won't let David console her. Logan's frustrated that, yet again, he couldn't save her when she needed it.

Me? I can't feel anything. It's like my body has shut off and refuses to let me know my soulmate is dead. Liam gasps loudly and leans forward. We all turn and look at him, confused at the sudden change.

"Something's happening," he grunts. My eyes move back to Ryanne again. She's lying on her back in the middle of the hotel room. Her dark hair is fanned out around her head messily from the fall. The contrast between her pale skin and dark hair is more apparent. The streak of blood that dripped out of her mouth has dried. The wound on her stomach is still bleeding onto the carpet.

Liam takes a deep breath. We all turn and look at him. He can breathe? He crawls away from Natalie and moves toward Ryanne. Something is obviously going on. When he nears her, Ryanne's body begins shaking. What? Everyone takes a step forward, wanting to know what is happening. Her body seems to inflate with oxygen. She gasps and sucks in air and then starts coughing. More blood comes out of her mouth. She's alive? The room is silent around me. How is this possible? Black liquid starts oozing out of the stomach wound. Logan pushes past everyone and tries healing her again. His hands give off a faint glow as he tries to close the wound.

I shoot up when I see the skin start to close. It's working. I move Ryanne's head so I can see her, but her eyes are closed. She still looks like death. I push her hair away from her face. Logan pulls his hands away and looks her over. She hasn't opened her eyes, but she's breathing. Small shakes still take over her body. How is she alive? She gasps again as her body goes still. I stare at her waiting for some sign of movement. Her chest begins to slowly rise and rise with each breath. She's alive.

"I guess she really is too stubborn for death," Emma says.

Tom hands me a wet washcloth. I move Ryanne toward me and clean the blood of her face, turning the white washcloth red. We'll have a lot of explaining to do when we check out of this room. I lift Ryanne up and lay her down on the bed. She's still so pale. Her body looks so fragile right now.

Turning around, I look at the room. "How is this possible? She was dead. You all saw it. Logan couldn't heal her. How is she alive?"

Mr. Howick pushes off the wall and looks at me. "I've heard stories about when a person dies before their time, they are given another chance. In every person's life, there is something they want to change, say, or do differently. Ryanne wasn't supposed to die today, so she got another chance. I don't know where she went or what she did, but she had to do something. If she wasn't able to do it, she would have died permanently."

"You couldn't have mentioned that before?" I ask. It would have been nice to know that there was a small chance that she could come back from this.

"There was no point. It wasn't a given that she would return. There was always a possibility that she wouldn't have come back. Not a whole lot of people are willing to change that late in the game."

"So what do we do?"

"Wait for her to wake up. There's not a whole lot we can do right now," Tom suggests.

"I hate waiting."

OPENING MY EYES, I ROLL over onto my side. I'm back at the hotel room. Alive. With a gasp, I shoot up. I'm alive. Colton jolts awake and gets into a defensive stance. When he sees me, he reaches out and jerks me to him, more forceful than necessary. However, that's exactly what I need right now. I bury myself in his arms and cry into his shoulder. I did it! I made it back. His arms tighten around me when he feels my tears on his chest.

Burying his face in my hair, he starts murmuring something. I can feel his lips moving against my skin, but I can't understand what he's saying. Leaning back, I look up at him. "What?"

"Don't you ever do that to me again, Ry. I love you so much. Don't you dare scare me like that." Before I can say anything, he crushes his lips to mine. I lean forward and kiss him back just as passionately. I know that I look like crap and don't feel much better, but I don't care. I almost died for good. I would have never seen him again. I thought that I would never get to see him again.

When I hear the sound of a door opening, I pull back and look around the room. "It's okay. It was just David and Emma," Colton says.

I turn back and look at Colton. He's watching me. Normally, I would squirm under his gaze, but today I don't. I lean forward and kiss him lightly again. "I'm sorry."

"I love you too. I'm sorry I didn't say it back before." Colton wraps his arms around me and pulls me against his chest. I curl into this side. I can hear his heart beating in his chest—the heart that belongs to me. He holds my heart and I his. I wrap my arm around his waist and pull him closer to me. "There was nothing I could do, Ry. I watched you die right in front of me again, but I couldn't do anything this time. I couldn't," he choked. I roll over and prop my arms on his chest.

"I couldn't let her die, Colton. She's Bragden's soulmate."

"What?"

"James told me. I was given that vision for a reason which means that Incendia has a bigger role in all this. We need her alive."

"We need you alive too, Ryanne," he tells me. "You're *my* soulmate."

"Which is why I'm here," I say.

Colton reaches forward and tucks a loose curl behind my ear. "How *are* you here?"

"I overcame some things," I vaguely say.

"I understand," Colton says. I'll reveal everything to him one day, but for now, I think that I should keep it to myself. I start to crawl out of bed, I really do need to take a shower, but Colton pulls me back. "Just let me hold you for a little bit."

I lean back down and rest against his chest. I'll never walk away from him again.

Never.

After my shower, I call everyone back into the hotel room. They are all sitting around waiting for me to start talking. I'm trying to ignore the large blood stain in the middle of the carpet. I don't need to be reminded that I died recently…again. However, my eyes keep landing on it. I died in that spot. In that exact spot…I pulled a dagger out of my skin.

I tear my eyes away from the spot and move toward the door. Before my gaze gets there, I meet a pair of grey eyes staring at me. Without thinking, I run across the room and launch myself at Liam. Wrapping my arms around his neck, I hug him too me. A second later, I feel his arms wrap around my waist and my feet are lifted off the ground.

"I'm so sorry," I whisper to him. I don't know what he went through specifically while I was…preoccupied on another plane…but I know that he was probably affected. Claire told me that if I didn't make it back Liam would have died.

Putting me back on the ground, Liam crouches down so that he's at eyelevel with me. "Please don't put us through that again," he whispers. I'm aware that everyone is watching us, but I don't care. "There are too many people here that love you, and none of us like witnessing that." I can see the sadness in his eyes. My eyes move back to the bloodstain on the floor again, but Liam grabs my chin and makes me look at him.

"I don't care what happens to me, Ryanne. I accepted the consequences when I gave you that pendant, but look around you. Look at all these people that just watched you die." When Liam lets go of my chin, I glance around the room. Like I suspected, everyone is watching us—all with relieved looks on their faces. "You keep this group together," he whispers to me. I return my attention to him, and bite my lip, trying to keep my tears down.

Stepping forward again, I hug him. Liam always knows what to say and what I need to hear. He's amazing like that. I pull back, but before

I step away, I place a small kiss on his cheek. He gives me a surprised look, but stands back up and moves beside Natalie.

Trying to lighten the mood, I give him a small smile. "At least I still haven't gotten shot again."

"Don't jinx it," he mumbles, but I see the small smile he's trying to hide.

I start to head back to Colton when someone else grabs me and hugs me. Instantly recognizing Bragden, I hug him back. Because of me, he almost lost his brother. I apologize to him like I did Liam, but he instantly starts shaking his head. He doesn't say anything though. He doesn't have to. I can read everything I need to from his expression.

Letting go of me, I finally make it across the room and back to my soulmate. "Ok, I think we need to leave here. We need to get back to finding other mages. We need to go back to the plan."

"Ryanne, you just died," Emma says.

"And now I'm alive. I've died before, you all know that. I'm back, it's all good. Let's move on from that. We need to stick with the plan."

"You don't want to rest?" Tom asks.

"No, I don't need to rest. I've slept long enough. I'm fine. My magic is healing me as we speak. We need to get a move on. Claire told me what would have happened if I actually died, and I am not going to let that happen, so we need to go and put the future back on its intended track."

"You spoke with Claire again?" Tom asks me.

"Claire, Lily, and my mom, but that's beside the point."

"Lily?" Colton asks, "Lily's dead?"

"No, I helped her. She wasn't supposed to die yet either. She's probably in the hospital right now. Anyway, stop distracting me. The point is I know what will happen if we don't continue on the intended course. I'm not going to mention specifics, but you won't like it. Like Incendia said before I…stepped in front of the dagger, we need more mages. We need more help."

Everyone continues to stare at me. They all expected me to sit down and rest for the next couple days. I promised my mom that I'd try to get over my insecurities and I'm trying to. I don't think I'm strong enough yet to accomplish this task, but I can feel my magic coursing through my veins. I can feel the power flowing through me, and every day, my magic grows. Every day, I'm getting stronger. I'm getting closer and closer to the mage I need to be, but I know I'm not going to become that mage by sitting down and resting for days. I need to move. I need to do something purposeful. I need to start accepting my responsibilities and do what needs to be done.

"Oh, and I need to put the protective enchantment on you, Incendia," I tell her.

Still no one talks. I know what they want to know. "You want to know what happened to me while I was…dead?"

They all nod. Taking a deep breath, I look up toward the ceiling and begin, "I woke up in this hotel room alone. You guys were gone and everything looked perfect. Claire came and told me that I wasn't supposed to have died and that there was a way to get back, but she couldn't tell me anything. I left the hotel. Pretended to see some tumbleweed. Ran into Lily. Walked away from Lily. She caught up to me. Told me how she died. I forgave her. She forgave her step-dad. Poof, she's alive. I walked to the cemetery. Cried. Boo-hoo. Tears. The whole she-bang. Then I promised to overcome some insecurities and viola, here I am." I rush through the explanation because I don't want everyone to dwell on it for too long. I don't want to have to explain anything in more detail. I'm not ready for that yet. "You guys good?"

They all continue to stare at me. Thankfully, I feel the familiar pull of my magic. Since everyone is sitting and I am standing, I know that there is no way anyone will catch me. I close my eyes and fall to the ground, going into a vision before I feel the physical pain of landing on the floor.

CHAPTER THREE

COLTON

INSECURITIES? WHAT INSECURITIES COULD BE so bad that she would have to overcome them in death? I'll have to ask her about it later. Ryanne bites her lip and looks around the room, waiting for everyone's reply. She spoke really fast, so I'm sure everyone is trying to catch up with her words. They all look surprised. I know that Ry left out a lot of information. She doesn't want to tell us everything.

She sighs and opens her mouth to speak again, but freezes. "Travis," I warn as Ryanne starts to sway. There's no way I can make it across the room fast enough to catch her. As she starts to fall, Travis jumps forward and catches her right before she hits the ground.

"Dadgumit. That was a close one," he says as he sits up, adjusting Ryanne on his lap. "Does she always just fall like that?"

"She didn't use to. When she first got her magic, she would have enough time to warn us before she fell. Now, it just happens so suddenly that she's unable to say anything," I explain.

Tom moves forward. "She's right though. We do need to get a move on. We're sitting ducks right now. Ryanne's enchantment seems to be working since Dravin wasn't able to detect the magic in her, but we can't just rely on that. We can't stay in one place for too long. We attract too much attention as it is."

"Can we discuss on this when she wakes up?" I suggest.

"Colton's right. She could be seeing something that changes everything," Liam says.

"I'm not," Ryanne mumbles as she sits up. Travis helps her. Ryanne turns around and thanks him.

"What did you see?" I ask.

Ignoring me, she turns and looks at Larkin. I hate when she does that. She knows that it annoys me. I see the small smile she's trying to hide. Stubborn girl. "Come on, Larkin. We gotta go."

"Go where?" he asks when Ryanne stops in front of him.

"You're not going anywhere," I tell her. Still ignoring me, she puts a hand out to help Larkin up. Larkin grabs onto her extended hand and stands. She leans up and whispers the location in Larkin's ear. He looks over her head at me, but grabs onto her arm and transports them out of the room.

"He does it because he knows it annoys you, Colton," Emma says.

"Wouldn't you get annoyed if you just saw your soulmate die? Claire told me not to let her out of my sight because she's in danger, and I can't even do that."

"She's not in danger, Colton. She knows what she is doing…usually. She didn't look like she was hiding anything too serious. I think she didn't tell you because she knows you'll make her stay here. I know she doesn't like upsetting you, so she wouldn't do it on purpose," Emma says.

"We weren't given the visions. She's the only one that sees what's going on outside of this room. She's the only one that can change anything," Kyril says, "and Larkin just likes making you mad, so he goes along with it."

"Well he needs to stop doing that," I say. Leaning back against the bed, I try to remain calm while I wait for my soulmate to come back.

Larkin transports back into the room holding an unconscious girl in his arms. She has bruises all over her body and her head is wrapped up in gauze. "Lily?"

"Ryanne said she needed our help," Larkin explains as he places her down on the bed and transports back out of the room. We all turn and look at the girl who's completely out lying on the bed. Logan tentatively stands up and walks over to her.

"Am I supposed to heal her?"

"Yes," Ryanne says when she and Larkin reappear. "We'll need her."

"She's a human."

"Not completely," Ryanne says as Logan begins to heal her.

"What do you mean?" I ask her.

"Like me, Lily's real dad left when she was a baby, so she never knew him. However, her real dad was a mage, so Lily is half mage. She has magic in her."

"How do you know that?" I ask her.

"She's right," Incendia confirms. "She does have some magic in her. I don't think she's come into her powers though. It's not very dominant yet."

Logan reaches down and places his hands on either side of Lily's face, focusing on her head injury. I walk over to Ryanne and pull her away from Larkin. "I need to talk to you," I whisper to her.

She grimaces and shakes her head. "I'm good. I think I'll just stay here." I start pulling her toward the door, "Colton, you know I can stop you."

"But you're not going to," I tell her as I open the door and pull her into the hallway.

"How do you know that?" she asks as she leans back against the door.

"Why do you do that?" I ask her instead of answering. "Why won't you just talk to me? Tell me what's going on instead of leaving like that? I just lost you, Ryanne. You were dead! I can't watch you just leave like that without knowing where you're going. Do you know what it does to me?"

Ryanne bites her lip and looks up at me. "Because..." Because? That's all she can give me. No explanation. No reason. Just because?

"Because why?"

"Because I want to protect you," she whispers.

This girl. Shaking my head, I step forward and place my hands on her cheeks, framing her face. "I need to be able to protect you too, Ryanne. Claire told me to stay with you because you're in danger. I *have* to protect you. Don't you understand? My mind wanders every time you disappear. I can't stop the images that flood through my head. I watch you die over and over again. Thousands of different ways. I don't know if I'll ever see you again. I've watched the life drain from your eyes twice. I've seen come close to death countless times." She bites her lip harder, trying to stop the quivering. I brush my thumb across her bottom lip. She sighs and looks back up at me. "What's going on, Ry? What are you not telling me?"

Ryanne opens her mouth to speak, but a teenage boy exits his hotel room and walks down the hallway. She watches the guy as he moves past. "Get a room," he mutters.

"We already have one, but thanks for the suggestion," Ryanne politely tells him. I lean forward to hide my smile in her neck. When I can't hear his footsteps anymore, I lean back and look at Ryanne again. "Please Colton, give me some time."

Her voice shakes at the end. I don't want to wait, but I know that it'll be hard to force it out of her. I'll give her some time, but I can also be pretty persuasive when I need to be.

Standing tall, Ryanne only comes up to my mid-chest. With my arms on either side of the door beside her head, I realize just how small she actually is. Why does it have to be her? I lean down and kiss her forehead, enveloping myself in her warm, floral scent. Sighing, Ryanne steps forward and wraps her arms around my waist, resting her head on my chest.

"Everything is going to get worse before it gets better, Colton. When the time comes, you're going to be needed somewhere else. I'm not going to be beside you, because I'm needed elsewhere. You just have to trust me. Sometimes, I know what I'm doing. Sometimes, I just make it up as I go—like Jack Sparrow. He usually gets out of sticky situations. Think of me as Captain Jack. Trust I have a plan even when I don't."

"You want me to think of you as Johnny Depp dressed as a pirate?" I ask. "I happen to find you much more attractive."

"I don't know. Johnny Depp is pretty hot," she says as she smiles up at me. I lean back and cross my arms. As Ryanne's eyes slowly move down to my chest, a slight blush rises in her cheeks. What is she thinking about? Clearing her throat, she looks up at me. "Please trust me, Colton."

"I'll try to trust your fake winging-it plans, but if you get yourself killed again, I'll..." she raises her eyebrows, waiting for the end of my threat.

The door she was leaning against opens, and Ryanne falls backward into Travis before I can finish it. He reaches out and catches her as she starts falling. "We're going to leave here soon. You guys should get ready." He looks down at Ryanne. "I've only known you for a day sunshine, yet you keep falling for me. What is it? My incredibly handsome face? Southern charm?" Travis pauses for a moment before saying, "It's the belt buckle, isn't it?" Ryanne opens her mouth to reply, but doesn't say anything. He does manage to get a blush out of her. He laughs at her reaction and steps to the side, letting her pass. Ryanne looks at me and starts giggling as she walks back into the room.

"SO TELL ME ABOUT THIS next family? Who did Dravin kill, and will they want to cause me harm because of it?" I ask.

"No, you won't have to defend yourself or Colton against these folks. They're friendly enough, but they are neutral right now. They don't want to be a part of the battle. Mr. and Mrs. Prowler used to work for Dravin, but they left before he started all of this 'Stop Ryanne,' stuff, so you'll just have to persuade them to come to our side," James explains.

"Do they know about the prophecy?" I ask.

James nods. I figured as much, but it didn't hurt to ask. "Ryanne, everyone knows about the prophecy," Emma says as she finishes packing her suitcase.

"I didn't know about it," I retort.

"Because you weren't born a mage, honey. You were a human for eighteen years." My eyes follow James as he leaves the room before I turn back to Emma.

"I'm still a human, Emma. It's not like being a mage makes us aliens or anything. We're technically still human. We all share the same characteristics. We all have dreams, goals, and drives. We all laugh, fall in love, and experience grief. The only thing that makes us different is that we have magic. We have powers that can be used to help said individuals."

"Look, sweetie, I love you, but I'm not the one who needs hear the speech. I'm already on your side," Emma leans forward and kisses me on the cheek and walks out of the room, laughing at my shocked reaction.

"Come on," Colton says as he throws my duffle bag over his shoulder pulls me out of the room too. I never unpacked, so it didn't take long to get everything ready.

"I can carry that." I try to grab my bag from him, but he holds it above my head, laughing. They always have to pull the short card.

"Nope, I got it," he says as he closes the hotel room and starts walking down the hallway. I run after him and jump onto his back, wrapping my legs around his waist and arms around his neck.

"Well then mister, you can carry me too," I say as I kiss the back of his neck. Colton laughs, but carries me through the lobby. We get a few strange looks from the concierges, but I don't care. Tom laughs when he sees us, but no one says anything.

"Hey, what happened to the man with the dagger?" I ask Colton as he puts our bags into the back of the car.

"He's been taken care of," he answers cryptically. I catch his glance toward Bragden, but I'm not completely sure what the look means.

"Oh." I don't think I really want to know what happened to him. Colton stops outside of the door, "Unless you want me to sit in your lap, this is your stop."

I jump down and wait for him to get into the car. Before I step in, Tom comes up to me and wraps his arms around me, pulling me to him. "It's good to have you back, Ryanne. Please be a little more careful though." His chest rumbles as he speaks. I wrap my arms around his waist and promise him that I'll try. With that he releases me, and I crawl into the car.

Since we have two more people, Emma and I are back to sitting in laps. Colton pulls me onto his as Tom starts the car. Lily is sitting in the back, between Incendia and Logan. "You okay?" I ask her. She seems a little scared, but hasn't complained or questioned anything.

"So, that was all real?" she inquires.

I instantly know that she is referring to what happened when we were both dead. "Yeah, that happened."

"I don't understand. Why are you helping me now?" She turns toward Logan. "Why did you heal me? How did you heal me?"

"I think we should start from the beginning," Logan says. For the next few hours, we explain everything to Lily. Like me, Lily had no idea that magic existed, so it took a while to explain everything. We all showed her our powers. I read her mind. Colton went invisible. David made her cell phone levitate and Incendia produced a ball of flames. We then told her about everything that has happened recently. Tom added in details when Logan forgot something.

"So, you had a vision of me dying again in the hospital?"

"Yeah. I get these visions because I'm supposed to change something. You're meant for something bigger, and now you're not stuck recovering in a hospital for the next couple of months."

"What about my mom?" she asks. I bite my lip. There's really nothing we can do for her mom. Logan's magic only works on mages. His magic combines with theirs to increase their naturally fast healing times. Lily's mother doesn't have any magic in her. Logan explains to her about how our magic works, telling her that technically there is nothing he can do. She nods, but the sadness is obvious in her expression.

"What now?" she asks me.

"That's a very good question, Lily. A very good question."

CHAPTER FOUR

"WE'RE HERE," TOM ANNOUNCES AS we pull up to a small two story house along the coast. I turn and smile at Colton. I've always loved the coastline. The waves are quietly hitting the shore and even though all the car's windows are up and the doors are shut, I can hear the sound of the ocean outside. Without saying anything, Colton leans forward and kisses me on the cheek, bringing me back to my immediate surroundings. A simple peck increases my heart rate and causes a slight blush to rise. Seeing this, Colton laughs and reaches past me to open the vehicle door. Tom extends a hand to help me up which I gladly accept. As everyone piles out of the car, I get a good look at the house.

Oh my gosh. Colton walks up behind me and wraps his arm around my waist. "Why did you just gasp?"

"Look at the house," I whisper. He looks at the house, but doesn't react like I did. I step out of his arms and walk to the back of the car. Opening the back, I search for my duffle. All of our bags look exactly the same. Finding my bag underneath all of them, I reach inside and pull out my old sketchbook.

Closing the back door, I flip through the sketchbook looking for the house I drew when I thought I was going to die the first time. The Prowler's house is the dream house I drew. A Victorian home with a wraparound porch, peeling white paint, and a wooden swing sitting on the edge of the porch. My drawing is an exact replica of the house before me. The beach in the background looks the same too. There are sea gulls flying around, small shells line the beach, and foam from the ocean is hitting the shoreline. Everything is exactly the same.

I smile up at Colton. "We're on the right track. We're supposed to be here. I knew we would somehow end up here." Tom walks behind Colton and looks down on the drawing.

"Interesting," he mumbles.

Hearing the front door open, we all turn and see a man standing in the doorway watching us. Oh my goodness, that's a big man. From where I'm standing, he appears larger than Bragden and more intimidating than James.

"What's going on here?" he shouts out to us. His voice seems amplified. He's not in a defensive stance, but his body seems prepared for an impending attack. I flinch as I sense the suspicion rolling off of him. Wait...I can sense his suspicion? Colton takes the sketchbook from my hands and places it back in the car.

"Mr. Prowler, I'm James Stapleton. We're here to talk to you about the Gadramicks."

"I don't want to hear about them. I want nothing to do with the Gadramicks. You're on your own," he says as he starts to close the door. I run past Colton and bound up the front stairs to stop him before the door shuts.

"Mr. Prowler, will you please just hear us out." I flinch again as Colton's anger hits me. The sound of footsteps on the gravel echoes behind me, and I know that if I look back, Colton will be right there.

That's why I remain looking ahead. Mr. Prowler towers over me as he stares at me from inside the house.

"It's you. You're the one." He didn't say it as a question, so I just nod. His suspicion starts to disappear as curiosity takes over. I'm not what you would expect for the girl who's supposed to stop a magical war. He looks over me at all the mages in the driveway. I hear someone walking around the inside of the house.

"Honey, who's at the door?" a feminine voice yells from inside. A tall brunette woman walks up to the door and looks out, eyes widening as she sees everyone standing in her driveway. "What's going on?"

"My name is Ryanne Arden, and I need your help."

"Dan, calm down. Let's hear what she has to say," Mrs. Prowler says. When she places her hand on his arm and pulls him back, Mr. Prowler steps away from the door and motions for us to come in. Colton grabs my hand and enters the house first. After assuring that it is safe, he pulls me in after him. He's still angry with me, but now he's the suspicious one. He is worried the Prowlers are up to something.

"Not everyone is out to get me, you know," I whisper to him as we walk into their living room. Colton looks down at me, confused as to how I know about his concern, but doesn't question me. Mr. Prowler glares at me as we enter into the living room. My steps falter with the anger that is again directed at me. Colton's grip on my hand tightens, and he pulls me to his side to steady me. Everyone else walks into the room and stops, confused as to what is going on. I grab my chest as it tightens inhibiting any air flow. I can't breathe. There are too many emotions flowing into me for me to do anything but panic.

"Ryanne, what's wrong?" Colton asks. I close my eyes and lean into him, trying to coerce oxygen into my lungs. My knees give out and arms wrap around my waist, keeping me upright. Confusion and worry trump the anger as my body starts to shake.

"What's going on?" Emma asks.

"Everyone calm down. Control your emotions. She's going to be fine," Liam says. "Ryanne look at me." I shake my head vigorously. I can't. "Trust me," he pleads with me. His voice sounds very close. The arm around my waist tightens as I try to stand on my own.

Slowly, I open my eyelids and look up at my protector. The waves of emotions increase. I whimper and stumble back again. Liam crouches down like he did earlier and places his hands on either side of my face, forcing me to look at him. "Push them to the back of your mind. Think about how you control the thoughts. Their emotions are no different. Push them into the background and lock them away. I know you can do this."

Closing my eyes, I look for their emotions. Right now, the feelings are just swirling around my mind. I can't gather anything. They're too jumbled. My thought box has cracked open and now those are seeping out as well. I can't even tell which emotions belong to whom. "I can't."

"Think about everything you're feeling. Compartmentalize all those feeling into similar categories. You can do this, Ryanne. You are so strong and capable of doing this. I've seen you do some pretty amazing things. Like I said before, you're Ryanne freaking Arden." I can hear the smile in his voice as he speaks.

His encouragement flows through me, giving me the support that I need. The emotions seem to be categorized with colors. Confusion is a blue green. Concern is a dull gray and anger is red. I push everyone's emotions into groups based on their color and stack the colors onto one another, creating one tall stack of varying color blocks. Mentally, I push the emotions into the back, visualizing them being locked into a box. I hear a single click of a lock being turned and slowly open my eyes now that I'm no longer being bombarded with emotions.

"Thank you, Liam." I don't know how he knew about the emotions, but I'm glad he was here.

"Anytime."

"What just happened?" Emma asks me.

"I think I can sense emotions too. I don't know. All of the sudden, I started getting all these feelings. I knew Mr. Prowler was very suspicious of us, and then he got very angry at me. Colton was really mad at me for walking away from him, and then he got really suspicious of Mr. Prowler. You guys all got worried and confused at the same time. It became really hard to breathe because I was overwhelmed with all your emotions at one time."

"You got *another* power?" Emma asks.

I wince as her jealously courses through me. When she sees my expression, she tries to hide it, but I felt enough. "I'm so sorry, Emma."

"It's not your fault, Ryanne. There's nothing you can do." She means it. She doesn't blame me, but it upsets her that she hasn't come into her magic yet. If I could give her some of mine, I definitely would.

"Mr. Prowler, could you please direct your anger somewhere else?" Liam asks him. I glance up at Colton, who's watching me intently, making sure that I'm okay.

"I'm fine now, I promise."

"What are you doing here?" Mr. Prowler asks us.

Instead of waiting for Tom or James to reply, I step forward. "Mr. Prowler, I'm sorry that we're intruding on your home, but we need your help. Dravin is getting more and more confident in his abilities. He has a plan that, if put into action, will make humans his slaves. He doesn't think that we should be able to help each other. He thinks that since we have powers, we should be able to rule over them. According to him, mages should stand above humans and dictate them. He's already killed so many of those who stood against him while looking for me. I'm not going to run and hide anymore, but I'm not stupid enough to believe I can do this on my own.

"Dravin is building an army. He's recruiting mages to do his bidding. They are killing off anyone who stands in their way. I'm not going to let him kill anyone else because of me. I can stop him, but I need help. You two were once working for Dravin. You know how he thinks; how he acts. You know him and what he is capable of. Whatever he was capable of when you knew him though, is nothing compared to what he is capable of now. If you don't want to help me, I understand, but don't think because you're not fighting this doesn't involve you. Whether you like it or not, mages are rising. Power is shifting, and a battle is ensuing. The end is near, and I hope you're ready for it." I step backward until Colton wraps his arms around me again. Mr. Prowler and his wife are both watching me. I don't sense Mr. Prowler's anger anymore. I'm not sure what I'm sensing right now.

Mr. Prowler stands up and walks over to the fridge. Getting out a bottle of beer, he turns around and watches me again. "You don't look like a mage," he states around the bottle as he takes a drink.

Colton growls and steps forward. I place my hand on his forearm to calm him. "I wasn't born a mage. My parents were humans."

"But you have magic."

"Yes, I have magic," I say.

"Just like the prophecy states," he mumbles.

I step away from Colton again as Mr. Prowler walks back into the living room. "Look, I know I don't look like much, but I've been through hell and back. I've fought off Dravin and his men countless times, and I'm still standing. Granted, I've actually died, but I'm still here. I'm here for a reason, Mr. Prowler. I'm supposed to do this. If I don't have your help, fine. I'll go find others more willing to help, but I need more people on my side. Dravin is building an army, and I can't stand up against him alone. You once fought for him. You left because you knew of the evil in his heart. Now, he's worse. He doesn't think with his heart. He doesn't think about others. He thinks about what is best for him and what can benefit him the most. I need to stop him, and I'll do it with or without your help. Now is not the time to be scared and hide. Now is the time to fight and stand for what you believe in."

"We're not hiding!" he yells at me. I try to keep my fear hidden from him. His anger crashes over me in waves. Instead of letting them dwell in my mind, I keep them flowing into the box. From behind me, I'm hit with Colton's anger. I hear whispers of those around me, but I don't acknowledge them.

"Then prove it, Mr. Prowler," I say calmly as I take another step toward him. I may be way smaller than him, but size doesn't mean anything. I can be just as intimidating if I want to be. "Prove that you're not afraid. Prove to Dravin that you're not going to stand by and watch him take over the world. *Prove it.* Retribution is coming whether we are ready or not."

I'm standing less than a foot away from him now. He's staring down at me, curiously. He doesn't know what to think about me. I know that I don't look like the typical mage, but that shouldn't mean anything. I can fight. I can defend myself. I can do anything these guys can. I'm not some helpless damsel always needing rescued...well I'm not helpless. Usually.

"You're not afraid of me?" he whispers to me. He looks behind me. "The girls behind you all flinched when I yelled." Mr. Prowler is no longer angry. He's actually slightly amused.

"I've had my share of large men yell at me. I'm pretty good at attracting trouble."

Mr. Prowler moves away from me and looks down at his wife, who is still sitting on the couch and waits for her reaction. She sighs and gives me a small smile. Nodding, she says, "We'll help."

CHAPTER FIVE

EVERY DAY AFTER THAT, WE visited mages. Some were easy to convince while others took more persuading. I was able to convince most to join our cause. A couple were persistent in their views and weren't willing to change. They didn't want anything to do with Dravin. Because of my new power, it made deciphering people's feelings on the subject much easier. When someone was mad, I channeled that anger and yelled at them. When someone was hesitant, I turned into Miss Nice Girl and politely convinced them.

I can keep the emotions flowing into the emotional box in the back of my mind. Sometimes I can take the feelings from those around me, give them a different emotion, effectively calming them. It's easier to control this emotion power, but it definitely has it side effects.

Because we've been so busy, Colton and I haven't had any alone time. We stay in hotel rooms, but we have to room with someone else or if they are nice enough, some of the people we visit let our large group stay with them. It depends on the day. We had just finished talking with Mr. Thalland and were heading back to the car, when Colton grabs my hand.

"I'm so proud of you," he whispers in my ear as he opens the door. Letting everyone else get in first, I look up at him.

"Why? What did I do?" I ask.

"You're handling all of this so well," he tells me as he gets into the car. Crawling in after him, I sit down on his lap.

"I don't really have a choice," I say.

"Girl, if any of those guys yelled at me like some have yelled at you, I would have run out of the room crying, but you stand your ground. It's hot," Emma says. David laughs. "What? I know you think it's hot too."

"She's like my sister," David answers. I smile at him.

"Doesn't make her any less hot," Emma mumbles. Incendia and Natalie laugh. Incendia, Logan, and Lily are all sitting in the back. Logan and Lily are really awkward around each other, but I think they're attracted to each other. They both watch the other often. Logan tries to start a conversation with Lily, but she seems to have trouble talking back to him. I've never seen her act like that before. The Lily I knew in school was very confident and not afraid to speak her mind. Logan's been like that too, so how they're acting is just plain strange. I think they're confused as to why they're feeling something, but if they don't act soon, James will intervene.

I move over to Incendia and find her glaring at the back of Bragden's head. Those two bicker like an old married couple. Similarly, neither one of them will admit their attraction. James won't intervene on that one though. I think that he's a little intimidated by Bragden's size. James is large, but Bragden is slightly larger.

"So, who's next Tom?" I ask as we back out of Mr. Thalland's driveway.

"No one right now. I have a friend in the area and we're going to stay at his house for a couple nights and train. It's been a while since any of you have trained. We can't afford for anyone to get rusty. Also, we have to help train Lily. He has a son who has been training mages and can probably help her."

"Or we could just do it," Logan suggests. Lily turns and looks at him. A warm feeling spreads through me as she looks up at him surprised. I push that emotion back into my box, trying not to read too much into it. When Logan looks toward her, she turns away, but I get another round of the feeling. I wish I knew of an off switch for these emotions.

"That sounds amazing." I've missed training. Resting my head on Colton's shoulder, I inhale deeply. I love how good he smells all the time. Colton laughs and wraps his arms around me.

"It's called soap, babe," he whispers into my ear.

"It's called soap, babe," I mimic as I move closer to him. I can feel sleep calling me and understanding my need to rest, Colton leans back a little and shifts me into a more comfortable position on his lap. I close my eyes and let myself be pulled under.

COLTON

RYANNE SIGHS AND SNUGGLES CLOSER to me in her sleep. I glance down at her. Goosebumps arise on her skin and she briefly starts shaking. The weather has taken a turn recently. It's getting cooler outside as fall starts pushing summer aside. "Logan, can you reach into my duffle and pull out a sweatshirt for me?"

As Logan reaches into the back, I ask Tom, "Who's this friend we're visiting?"

"Colin Harris. You've met him a couple times when you were younger. His power works with metal. He's able to move and manipulate anything with metal in it. It's pretty interesting. He has a...rather large home and is graciously allowing us to stay with him. We need to train and work on Ryanne's new power. Can it be combined with her magic to strengthen it? What else can it do?"

"The girl doesn't need any more strength. She can handle herself," Emma states.

"Emma, as mages we are all given our powers when we need them. She got this power because somewhere down the line, she's going to need it. You will come into your powers. Don't worry. You just have to be patient."

"I know. I know. I'm just a little anxious," she says as she leans back into David. My brother wraps his arm around her and then looks directly at me. He doesn't know how to comfort her when she brings up her lack of magic. She sighs and snuggles into his chest. "Unless you're Ryanne's size, this whole sitting on the lap thing isn't very comfortable," she mumbles.

Logan hands me a sweatshirt. I wrap it around Ryanne's shoulders. We'll have to find a way to get her some warmer clothing soon. I move the edge of the jacket over her knees when she curls closer to me, trying to get warm. "So how long are we going to stay at Colin's?"

"I'm not sure. A couple days. A week tops. Ryanne has talked with a lot of families recently. I think she needs a little break from everything for a little while. I called Colin yesterday to see if there were any mages in his area. He didn't know of any, but said that we'd be able to stay at his house until we found some more. I thought that it would be a good idea to regroup there and work out the next part of our plan."

"Well, I guess that sounds like a good idea. We could all use a break," I say. Everyone in the car mumbles an agreement. Though it's been Ryanne who's been doing the most talking recently, we've all been alert. There's always a chance that someone we visit could react violently. Some would yell at Ryanne and threaten her. Liam had to hold me back when that happened. The soulmate in me doesn't react well when I see these large mages yelling at her. She stands her ground and doesn't even flinch at their tone which usually gives her the advantage because they aren't expecting it. She's handing everything so well. Better than I expected.

"Turn your emotions off," Ryanne mumbles sleepily to me.

"Sorry," I whisper, hoping that she'll fall back asleep. How do you turn your emotions off? I try to push everything back, but I honestly have no idea how to do that. Ryanne sighs and sits up.

"This power sucks," she complains. "I can't do anything without knowing what you guys are feeling. So, even though I push your thoughts back, I can still tell what everyone is feeling. I'm a walking invasion of privacy."

"We'll find a way to control it, Ry. Don't worry."

"I don't know what I'm feeling because there are so many emotions in my mind. I can push them back into this stupid little box, but which emotions are mine and which belong to everyone else? I think they're starting to affect me personally. I feel like I'm a ticking time bomb. I have so many emotions in me that keep building on top of each other. Sooner or later, I'm going to explode," she says.

"We'll figure everything out soon, Ryanne. We'll help you," Tom says. Ryanne bites her lip and slips her arms through my sweatshirt sleeves. It's way too big on her, but she snuggles into it. I gently grab her chin and make her look at me.

"You okay?"

She stares at me, but doesn't respond. Instead, she shrugs. I lean forward and kiss her forehead. I try to push soothing thoughts out, hoping that she'll catch them. She sighs and leans her forehead against mine. "Thank you," she whispers.

"Anytime, Ry."

Ryanne settles back against me, but doesn't try to go back to sleep. I grab her arm and roll the sleeves back, revealing her hands. Lacing our hands together, I continue to push soothing emotions to her. She relaxes and buries her head into my neck. Her warm breath tickles my skin as she breathes in and out. I feel her chuckle against me after reading my emotions.

Tom stops the car in front of a large house. "Oh my sweet baby Jesus, this isn't a house. This is a freaking hotel," Incendia says. Ryanne and I turn around and give her a questioning look. She just shrugs and continues to gawk out the window. I can hear Bragden trying to cover a laugh in the front seat.

A small ball of fire shoots over the seat and hits Bragden in the shoulder. Incendia laughs, well more like giggles, behind me. Bragden hisses and turns around glaring at Incendia. When he sees her laughing, his features soften into amusement.

"These girls are going to be the death of me," Bragden says as he looks at Ryanne. Ryanne widens her eyes and smiles innocently at Bragden, which makes Incendia laugh even harder. Her mood seems to have lightened a little.

"It's because everyone else is feeling better," Ryanne whispers.

"How did you know I was thinking about that?"

She taps my nose and jumps out of the car. "I may not be able to read your mind, but I know you…and I read your emotions. You were relieved, so I guessed."

"Good guess," I mumble as I follow her out.

"Wow," she sighs as she looks up at the house. "This looks like a freaking celebrity's home. Are you friends with Johnny Depp? Chris

Hemsworth? Ryan Gosling?" Ryanne pauses for a moment, "Liam Neeson?" Tom laughs and motions for her to stop. "Tom Hanks," she whispers as the front door of the mansion opens.

I briefly remember Colin Harris. The tall man that walks out of the house looks nothing like the man I would have assumed lived in this home. In his upper-thirties or so, the man walking toward us is dressed in sweats. Ryanne covers to mouth to keep from laughing out loud. Colin stops in front of us and looks down at her. "What's so funny?"

She clears her throat and tries to keep a blank expression. "Nothing, you just aren't what I was expecting."

"Is that a good thing or bad thing, little one?" Colin asks.

"So far, it's a good thing. And little one? Never heard that before. Are all mages this uncreative?"

"Would Hobbit suffice? You do have some crazy hair." He points with his eyes toward her unruly hair. Unconsciously, Ryanne attempts to fix her curls.

"I think I like little one better," she says as she steps toward me. Colin laughs and greets Tom.

"Hey, long time no see. I was surprised when I got your call. This is quite a group you have here," Colin says as he looks over everyone. He nods at Logan, David, and me, before his eyes land on Ryanne again. I wrap my arm around her shoulder and pull her toward me. Colin laughs at me, but doesn't comment on my actions. "You must be Ryanne."

"You're one of the first to actually call me Ryanne and not say an ominous, "you're her." That gets annoying fast," she says. Colin laughs and points toward Ry.

"I like her. She's got spunk." Colin turns around, motioning for everyone to follow him into the house. Ryanne looks up at me and grabs onto my hand. I take the lead and follow Colin.

After walking through the front door, I hear a small gasp beside me. Glancing down at Ryanne, I can't help but smile when I see her gawking at the chandelier in the entrance with wide eyes. This is pretty impressive, I'll give Colin that. A large chandelier hangs down from the ceiling, casting sparkling light on every surface in the entryway. Left and right stairways divide the room into two sections, and deep mahogany flooring contrasts with the white banisters. Ryanne turns to Incendia. "This *is* a sweet baby Jesus moment."

"I sure was thinking it."

"Okay, well since you've been traveling all day, I'll show you to your rooms. If Tom's not too tired, he can catch me up on everything." Tom nods, agreeing with him. Colin heads up the right set of stairs, waving everyone up. Slowly we follow. This house is big, but is it large enough for all of us?

"I'm seeing a few couples in your group," Colin says. "I don't know how you do the sleeping arrangements here."

"I trust them," Tom says as he glares at each of us. A silent warning.

"Ok, well the Hobbit and her soulmate can have this room," Colin says as he opens one door. Ryanne glares at him after hearing the Lord of the Rings comment.

"Since you're being kind enough to let us stay in your humble Hobbit Hole," Ryanne says with a smirk, "I'll graciously ignore that comment."

With a smile, Colin motions for Liam and Natalie to take the room next to us. Natalie blushes a little, but goes along with it. Does Colin know that Liam is Ryanne's protector? He gives David and Emma the room across the hall. Colin motions between Bragden and Incendia, who are standing next to each other, asking if they're together. Incendia's eye widen as she takes a wide step to the side. Colin smiles at her reaction, but doesn't say anything. Bragden remains unmoving with a slight smirk as Colin moves on to Logan and Lily. Unlike Bragden, Logan shakes his head at the same time as Lily blushes and moves to the side. With that confirmed, Colin divvies up the remaining rooms amongst everyone left.

"I don't really know what a large group of kids like you all eat, so I guess I'll just order pizza or something," Colin says.

"You don't have to…" Ryanne starts.

"Don't tell me you're one of those girls that won't let anyone buy her stuff," Colin asks. He takes a step toward her and narrows his eyes. "Are you shy, little Hobbit?"

Ryanne opens her mouth to reply when everyone else answers for her. "I am not shy," she says as she starts to blush. I can feel Ryanne's magic crack around us as everyone laughs. That's my cue.

I start to push Ryanne into the room. "I think now would be a good time to rest." Turning to Colin, I say, "Ryanne's a vegetarian, so make sure to order something for her." I hear Ryanne start mumbling something from inside the room, but I ignore her.

Colin laughs, but nods. "Get some rest. I'll come around when the pizza is here." I close the bedroom door and turn around to face Ryanne. She's standing in the middle of the room, arms crossed, and glaring at me. Her nose is crinkled in that cute way she always gets when she's upset. I try to hide my smile, but I know that she can feel my emotions.

"I'm not shy," she says.

"You are a little," I tell her as I take a step forward. "Not as much as you used to be, but you still are."

"I'm not shy," she repeats.

I sit down on the edge of the bed and use my index finger to motion her in my direction. Keeping her arms crossed, she slowly walks to me. Standing in front of me, she says, "I'm not shy."

"Maybe," I tell her. "Maybe not. One thing's for sure though. You're cute when you're upset." I loop my index fingers through her belt loops and pull her the rest of the way. She comes willingly, but continues to glare at me. The amusement in her eyes doesn't match the anger in her expression.

"You're lucky I like you," she whispers as I rest my hands on her hips. The anger slowly fades from her face as a new expression takes over. She reaches forward and pushes my hair to the side. "You need a haircut."

I slowly move my hand up her arm, grabbing the strands of hair falling past her elbows. "Don't cut your hair," I tell her.

"I was actually thinking about shaving my head. Long hair is kind of a hassle," she says as she takes another small step. Her eyes flicker down to my mouth as she leans forward slightly.

"Don't," I tell her. She looks up in my eyes and smiles. Stepping away from me, she walks across the room and grabs the television remote. Stubborn girl. Giggling, she turns the TV on. I continue staring at her. "That's just mean," I tell her. She sits down on the bed, crosses her legs, flips through the channels, and gives me her innocent smile. "You said don't when I was about to kiss you."

I sigh and lean back against the bed, lying down beside her. I open my arms and let her scoot over. She regards me warily, but comes closer. I wrap my arms around her and pull her against my chest. She turns on her side and continues flipping through the channels.

I can tell by her steady breathing that she'll fall asleep soon. The hand with the remote falls against the side of the bed limply. With a sigh, Ryanne curls into my side. She's already asleep. I take the remote from her and turn the television volume down.

Thirty minutes later, there's a knock on the door. I glance down at Ryanne. She's lying on my arm, so I can't get up. "Come in," I whisper yell, hoping that whoever is on the other side of the door will hear me.

The door opens slowly and Tom enters. "The pizza's here if you guys are hungry," he trails off when he sees Ryanne sleeping. "Since she's sleeping, I'll put some aside for the two of you."

"Thanks Tom," I say.

"Is she alright? On the surface, she seems fine, but she's pretty good at hiding her feelings when she doesn't want attention."

"She's fine until multiple people get angry or upset, I think. She can't push all those feelings back. She starts experiencing them. She's worried that she's going to explode under all the emotions streaming into her."

"We'll see if Natalie can help her get a better handle on it."

"Thank you for everything."

He nods, understanding the meaning behind my words. Tom has basically dropped everything to help us. He originally came to us to help David and me train Ryanne. When Claire died, he attempted to fulfill her guardian-like role. Tom keeps everything and everyone in check. He *tries* to keep us out of danger. Ryanne loves Tom like a father; I can see that every time she looks at him, and I know that he looks at her like a daughter as well. We're a large family now.

Ryanne rolls over and opens her eyes. Seeing Tom in the room, she slowly sits up. "What's going on?" she sleepily mumbles.

"The pizza's here if you're hungry."

"Colton's hungry," Ryanne announces as she crawls over to the edge of the bed. "Come on, big guy. Let's go fill that tummy of yours," she says as she holds her hand out for me.

Tom laughs. "You're never going to be able to hide anything from her, Colton. She'll always be a step ahead of you."

"Yep, so don't try anything," Ryanne says as she pulls me out of the room.

"I *am* hungry," I tell Tom as we pass him. Ryanne walks out into the middle of the hallway and then stops.

Looking up at me, she says, "I actually have no idea how to get to the kitchen." I turn around and look at Tom. I don't know where the kitchen is either.

Tom laughs as he walks past both of us. "Follow me. I'll be your tour guide for the night."

CHAPTER SIX

"SO, RYANNE. I HEAR THAT you can be pretty scary when you get worked up," Colin says.

"I don't know who you're hearing these stories from," I say as Emma shoots her hands up into the air, "but I'm not scary. Do you really think some 5'3" girl could be all that scary?"

"Oh, she totally can be. Go after someone she loves and you won't know what hit you. When Dravin sent men to go after Jane and Ross, Ryanne totally…"

"Just don't go after someone I love," I warn as I smile sweetly and bite into my slice of pizza. Colin shakes his head at me, obviously amused. I hear everyone else try to hide their laughter.

"Anything else I should know?" Colin asks.

"She's too stubborn for death," Bragden says.

"How did you find that out?" he asks me.

"Well, you die twice, come close a couple other times, and live to tell the tale," I say as I take another bite.

"Oh, well you know those Hobbits were a little stubborn, so that doesn't really surprise me." I turn and glare at Colin. It'd be so easy to blast him with some magic, but he's letting us stay in his home, so I refrain myself.

"Whoa, I totally know that look," Bragden says. "You're walking on a thin line, Colin. She won't be able to hold back for too much longer."

"I'm curious to see what will happen if I egg her on," Colin says while looking at me.

"With all these emotions running through me, I don't really think you want to know," I say as I finish the pizza. Colin continues to watch me, but doesn't say anything. Shaking his head, he gives his attention back to everyone else.

"Well, if you guys are bored, there's a pool, a game room, an entertainment room. There's a music room upstairs also. I hear a couple of you are musically gifted," Colin says as he looks at me. "Just rest tonight. We'll start training tomorrow."

"Ryanne, you have to play something for us," Emma states.

I start shaking my head. "I'm not really feeling it right now," I say as I get up and place my plate in the sink. I look back behind me at Colin, who's shaking his head.

"I have someone who does that, Ryanne. Come sit back down," he says.

"Fine," I shuffle back to the table. I was hoping to waste more time than that.

"Please. Please. Please," Emma begs. "Travis, Incendia, Colin, Lily, and Mr. and Mrs. Howick have never heard you sing before."

"And I'd kind of like it to stay that way," I say.

"Girl," Emma sits up and stares at me, "I may not have any magic, but I can be very persuasive when I need to be. You know of what I'm capable of."

"You wouldn't," I say as I stand up and face Emma.

"Oh, I would."

"Fine, where is this music room?" I'd rather not find out what Emma has in mind. She can be plenty creative when something doesn't go how she wants it to.

When I move to take a step, the room starts spinning. Without warning anyone, I fall into another vision.

I'm standing in the middle of an unfamiliar room in Dravin's compound. There is a large wooden desk in the middle of the floor, cluttered with stacks of paper. Random medical supplies are scattered throughout the room. A stethoscope is strewn across the back of a chair, and a roll of gaze is located on the window sill. A box of Band-Aids is spilled on the floor, and a bottle of hydrogen peroxide is lying on a small coffee table—also cluttered with more paper. This room is a complete mess.

It's obvious that they can't see me, because I'm literally standing right beside Dravin.

"I'm doing the best I can here," Dr. Arden says. "Extracting magic without harming the individual is a complicated process. I know I said I was prepared to do it before, but I won't risk harming her. It's not perfect yet. It has to be perfect."

"You will do it when I find her whether you are ready or not. I won't risk her getting away again."

"I will not risk killing my daughter because of you. I've seen what you've done to her already. I will not stand for any more. You need me Dravin, but if you harm another hair on her, I'll quit. If I knew that Maureen was pregnant, I never would have walked away and you know that."

"Maureen is dead, so get over that. We have a blood promise, Jedrek. I keep you alive. You help me. You can't quit. You're stuck here. Do you really want the Fates to come after you? The fact that the

girl from the prophecy happens to be your daughter is just a random turn of events. It's a coincidence. It doesn't change anything. I saved your life. You owe me. If you have to repay that debt with your daughter's life, then so be it. You WILL find a way to give me her magic. It'd be a shame to waste such a pretty thing, but if I have to kill her to get her powers, I will. There's NOTHING you can do about it. Is that clear?"

Jedrek Arden stands up and glares at Dravin. I take a step back even though I know neither of them can see me, but Jedrek looks very menacing. With wide large brown eyes and flared nostrils, he says, "I will not let you kill Ryanne. End of story."

"Not the end, my friend." Dravin says as he turns to leave the room. "We're just now getting to the rising action. The climax is coming. Ryanne's a threat. If you can't extract her magic, I'll just kill her, and that's certainly not the ending you want. It's your choice," Dravin's threat lingers heavy in the air after he has left the room.

Jedrek stares at the empty doorway for a few moments before he jumps up, pushes all the paper off his desk, and starts pacing the room as the sheets rain down around him. Stopping in front of the brick wall, he brings his arm back and punches the wall. I wince and move toward him. He clenches his fist and then slowly opens his hand, revealing a long jagged scar running along his palm. He turns around and leans back against the wall. I take a small step toward him.

There's so much emotion in his expression. His dark eyes are widened and glistening with memories while his nostrils are flared, and his mouth is set in a straight line. He seems very conflicted. With a sigh, he turns and looks directly at me. "I'm so sorry, Ryanne," he whispers.

"You can see me?" I ask.

"I don't know if you can hear me, but I'll find a way out of this. I won't let him hurt you again," he says quietly. He can't see me, but he

knows I'm listening. "I promise, I'll do something. I'm so sorry about all of this."

I open my eyes and look around the room. Groaning, I sit up. My head is throbbing. I actually landed on the hard floor this time. Colton is sitting right beside me. "What? You couldn't catch me?" I tease him.

"I'm sorry," he says as he helps me stand up. I sway a little and lean back against Colton's chest. Whoa, the room is spinning. I feel hands wrap around my forearm as the dizziness fades. I blink the room back into focus and meet a pair of worried blue eyes. "Thank you," I tell Logan.

"What did you see?" he asks me.

I step away from Colton and sit back down in the chair. "I saw Dravin and…Dr. Arden talking. I think the conversation already happened through."

"What were they talking about?" Tom asks.

"Me," I whisper. I explain the vision to everyone in full detail. I don't leave out any information. I'm not sure of the significance of it all, so I need those with mage information to help me.

"The Fates are after Jedrek?" Tom asks.

"What does that mean exactly?"

Colin turns toward me and explains, "It means that Jedrek is supposed to be dead. Dravin knew that he'd need Jedrek at some point, so he made him promise his life to him. A blood promise is permanent. You can't break them without dying."

"When Dravin left the room, he said 'I'm so sorry, Ryanne.' At first, I thought Dr. Arden could see me, but I know he couldn't. He promised that he'd find a way out of this, and he wouldn't let Dravin hurt me again."

"You can't start to feel something for him, Ry. There's a chance that something could happen to him in the upcoming days," Colton says.

"You didn't see the look in his eyes, Colton. I've only ever seen that look in your eyes before," I tell him. "He doesn't want to work for Dravin, but he literally doesn't have a choice."

"Let's not think about that now. We'll worry about that later. We can try to come up with a way to save him, but with the blood promise, it's tricky. It sounds like Dravin was the one who initiated it. As long as Dravin lives, Jedrek lives. If Dravin dies, so does Jedrek."

"Does that work both ways?" I ask.

"No, if anything happens to Jedrek it won't affect Dravin."

"Why would he agree to a blood promise then?"

"He's supposed to be dead, Ryanne, but he's not. It was his time to die, but he turned away from death and found a plan B," Colin explains. "People will do anything to fight death. Immortality is very sought after."

"No one can live forever."

"That means nothing. If you could live past your expiration date, wouldn't you try?"

"I've died twice, Colin. I *am* living past my expiration date."

"No, you're not. You obviously weren't meant to die those times, otherwise you wouldn't be here. You're soulmate saved you once. You only get one healing. You were given a second chance because it wasn't your time to die. You still have time. Jedrek doesn't. That's why it's hard. His blood promise with Dravin is the only thing keeping him alive right now. If he wasn't tied to Dravin, the Fates would find him."

"What are the Fates exactly?" I ask.

"That's a lesson for another night. It's a long and complicated story," Colin says as he stands up. "Now, weren't you going to sing for us?"

CHAPTER SEVEN

"I'M REALLY TIRED OF EVERYONE making me sing all the time. I was perfectly fine being a closet shower singer," I mumble as Colton pulls me into our room.

"You have a beautiful voice, Ry. Why don't you like letting others hear it?"

"Because it makes people to look at me more, Colton. I'm already the freak with too much magic. I don't need to be the freak with too much magic who can also sing."

"I happen to like that freak," Colton says as he sits down on the bed. I try to walk past him, but he grabs me around the waist and pulls me onto his lap. I laugh as he starts tickling me and squirm to get away.

"Stop," I gasp between laughs. "Please," I whine. Colton stops tickling me. When I'm no longer being threatened, I turn around and look up at him. Standing so I'm facing him, I look straight in the eyes and just watch him for a few seconds. Because he's sitting, we're now the same height. I step forward a little and push his hair out of his eyes. His love for me cascades into my body with each movement, and I feel my smile slowly fall. I inhale deeply and push his emotions into the back of my mind. It's easier to control when there's only one person in the room with me. I lean forward and gently kiss him.

Colton moves his hands to my hips and lightly pulls me forward. I let him guide me. He removes his right hand from my hip and places it at the base of my neck. When I feel his hand move through my hair, I sigh and melt into him. Colton uses that to deepen the kiss. Running my hands up his chest, I wrap them around his neck and step closer to him. His racing heart matches mine. He moves the hand from my hips to the small of my back and hugs me to him. I can't help but shiver at the movement.

I push against his chest, forcing him to lean backward. Pulling me with him, he lies down on the bed and slowly moves backward without breaking the kiss. I feel his hands brush against the bare skin of my back, but he doesn't move them any higher or lower. I brush my tongue against his lower lip. Colton groans and pulls back.

He slowly moves me backward and sits up. I end up straddling him. "What's wrong?" I ask him.

"You're acting on my emotions," he says.

"No, I'm not," I say as I lean forward and kiss him again. He kisses me back, but ends up pushing me away again. "Colton," I groan.

He chuckles and brushes a strand of hair away from my eyes. "You're so beautiful, Ryanne," he whispers as he leans forward. "And I want you, I really do." His lips brush against mine when he talks, sending chills through my body. "But I know you wouldn't be doing this if you weren't acting on my emotions. It's very difficult to restrain myself, babe."

"Then don't," I tell him as I gently bite his bottom lip while lightly tracing the muscles on his abdomen. I can feel his heart racing against my chest. This spurs me on. Fisting the end of his shirt, I slowly pull up the fabric. He lifts his arms and lets me pull the shirt over his head. Colton leans forward and kisses me again. I press myself flush against his bare chest. His hand slowly caresses up my back. When he reaches the edge of my bra, he pulls back.

"Ryanne," he groans, "you're killing me here. I'm trying to be a gentleman, and you're seriously testing my boundaries."

I sit back and pout. "You're too much of a gentleman, Colton. It's annoying sometimes," I sarcastically tell him.

Colton gently places his large hands on my cheeks and pulls me toward him. Kissing my forehead, he whispers, "When the time is right, you'll know. You'll feel it in here," he points to my heart, "not in here." He lightly taps me on the forehead.

"Isn't it supposed to be the girl who does the rejecting?" I say as I crawl off of Colton. "Real confidence booster you are, Colton." I plop down on the bed next to him and lean back against the pillow. He turns on his stomach and faces me.

"Ryanne, will you tell me what happened to you while…"

"While I was dead?" I finish. He nods and moves closer to me—his concern and curiosity obvious in his expression. I bite my lip and watch him. His emotions continue to flow into me. He's worried that I had to do something that will affect me later on. He wants to protect me and is concerned that I'm going to act out. I sigh and look toward the ceiling, debating on whether or not to tell him everything.

Lily's story isn't mine to tell, so I bypass that and go straight to what he wants to hear. "After helping Lily, I went to my mother's grave. I cried on her grave and then she made an appearance. She told me that if I wanted to go back, I had to express my feelings. I started to vent to her, but she told me that I wouldn't get back that way. So I dug deeper. I…"

Colton moves closer to me and places his hand under my chin and turns my head toward him. He genuinely wants to help. "I admitted that I didn't feel like I was strong enough to stop this war," I say.

"And?" I watch Colton. "I know there is more than that Ry. You can trust me."

"I admitted that I didn't feel like I was good enough for you," I whisper. Colton sits up and gawks at me. I push myself up. "I was able to come back by admitting that I thought I could be strong enough someday and that maybe one day I'd be the girl that you need—that I'd be someone worthy of your love."

"Ryanne, you're crazy," Colton whispers as he pulls me to him. I stare at him. I just admitted all that, and he calls me crazy? "You're already strong enough, and you're way too good for me. Don't think you're not good enough for me. Ever."

I roll over so that I'm looking up at him. "I can't help it. You just too...perfect. A guy like you would never give me the time of day in the real world."

"Ryanne, were you not listening when I told you that I want to be stuck with you. I wanted to get to know you before the magic and before all of this happened. I saw you. You may not see it, but you're perfect, Ry. I feel like I've waited my whole life for you. I know that I'm only nineteen, but I've never felt as complete as I do with you. Now I feel like I have a purpose in life. I'm here to make you happy. I want to wake up every morning and see your beautiful face. I want to wipe the tears from your eyes and beat the crap out of the person that made you cry." I scoff as he continues. "I want to keep you safe and always cherish you. I want you to know that my love for you is true. If I have to spend my whole life trying to prove that to you, I will, because you're worth forever. Ryanne, you wouldn't be my soulmate if we weren't perfect for one another. You're literally my perfect match, and I'm yours. You need to get that through that beautiful, thick skull of yours," he says as he taps me on the nose.

I stare up into his green eyes—the same eyes looking down at me, waiting for me to speak. I lean forward and gently kiss him. Nothing I can say will top what he just said, so I pour all my love into this kiss, hoping he'll understand. I can't tell him that I'll change right away. Someday, I'll be good enough; today is not that day. Colton wraps his arms around my waist and pulls me to him. Leaning back, he kisses my forehead and rests his chin on top of my head. I lightly kiss him on the neck. "One day, I'll make you believe it, babe," he whispers to me. "One day, I'll prove it to you."

"I love you, Colton," I say as I curl into his side and close my eyes.

"Love you too, Ry," Colton tightens his grip around me. "Go to sleep."

While Colton is in the shower, I sit on the bed with Olive. I really haven't gotten to spend much time with her lately and that makes me feel like a horrible pet owner.

Comfy bed. I smile as she rolls onto her back and looks at me, waiting for me to pet her stomach. I move over onto my stomach and start petting her.

"Things have gotten crazy around here," I start to explain to her.

I know. Kyril nice.

That actually makes me laugh. Olive has taken a liking to Kyril, and he doesn't seem to mind spending time with her. It's quite adorable actually.

"And he's cute," I smile at her. Her only response is to start purring. "I'm sorry," I whisper after a few seconds. "I'm glad that everyone has been so nice to you."

It okay. She rolls over and walks over to me. Rubbing against my arm, she tells me that she understands.

"I feel really bad. I haven't gotten to spend much time with you. I've been so wrapped up in everything that's going on that I've neglected you. I really am sorry."

Don't apologize. She sits down in front of me and stares at me with her big blue eyes.

"Hey Olive," Colton says as he walks out of the bathroom, fully dressed, and running a towel through his hair. Hanging the towel on the metal rack on the door, he plops down on the bed beside me and reaches over to pet Olive. "How are my two favorite girls this morning?"

Olive loves Colton. When I first told her Colton's name, Olive told me he was cute and instantly liked him. Closing her eyes, Olive leans slightly forward, without moving from her spot, and starts purring as he pets her.

"She's definitely good," I answer for her. With a low chuckle, Colton leans back and gives me a quick kiss on the temple, but doesn't get up like I thought he was going to. Instead, he wraps his arm around my waist and scoots me closer to him.

Aww, why'd he stop? Olive whines as I roll onto my back and look up at Colton.

"She doesn't like that you stopped petting her," I tell Colton who glances away from me to Olive again.

"I'm sorry, Olive," he tells her, "but I can't give you too much love at once. You'll never come back to me." He shoots her a lazy smile and winks. If cats could blush, Olive totally would be right now. Slightly shaking, she lowers herself onto her stomach, rests her head on her paws, and looks away from Colton. I can't help but giggle as I hear Olive's thoughts.

No such thing as too much love. I glance up at Colton. *Always come back.* Those would be my exact thoughts if he was giving me that smile too. Colton's eyes move down to me and like Olive, I divert my gaze. Hearing his laugh, I know he caught me staring at him.

"What'd she say?" he whispers to me. That gives me an idea.

"Let me see your hands." I push myself up and turn my back to him. Colton wraps his arms around my back and places his hands on top of mine without even questioning what I am about to do. "Olive, think random things," I tell her.

Olive starts imaging a large scratching post. I make a mental note to get her one of those sometime in the future—when everything settles down. Concentrating on my magic, I gather up strands and push them down my arms and imagine the magic flowing through my hands and into Colton's where it moves up his arms and settles in his mind. I can feel the magic moving through and obeying me. The vibrating strands linger in my hands. Tightening my grip on Colton, I wait for his reaction. I know he'll react when the magic enters him. When nothing happens, I continue pushing.

This may or may not work, but experimenting is the only way I'll ever know.

Magic leave me. On command, my magic pushes out of my hands and enters Colton's palms. Behind me, he jumps and lets out a shaky breath as the magic slides into him. He squeezes my hands, but not tight enough to hurt me. He completely trusts me even when I experiment with my magic on him.

Olive is still thinking about scratching posts, but the visual is getting blurry as she watches us. She knows that something is happening.

He okay?

"Oh my gosh," Colton gasps in my ear and he leans forward. "I heard that."

He hear me?

"Yes, I can hear you. Why can I hear you?" he asks. "Why can I hear her, Ryanne?" As I keep moving magic between our hands, I lean back against his chest and smile up at him. His eyes keep moving between Olive and me, slightly surprised.

"I'm sharing my magic with you," I tell him. "I created a bridge between us and now you can understand Olive. Essentially, we're sharing my magic right now."

"That's amazing." His breath brushes against my neck and he watches Olive. He doesn't say anything though; he just stares at her.

What? I can see Olive is slightly uncomfortable with the attention he's giving her.

"I don't know what to say to her now that I can understand her. It's all so strange," he admits.

"Speak to her like you usually would," I say. "Don't do anything differently. Now, you'll just know how she responds instead of me telling you."

"Hey Olive," he starts.

Hi Colton. She jumps up and walks over to and steps onto my lap. Placing her paws on my chest, she looks at Colton over my shoulder.

"How are you this morning?" I love that he's talking to her like she is just another person.

Hungry.

"Well, we'll have to go get you something to eat," he tells her. Olive's ears perk up at the mention of food.

Now?

"Do you want the food now?" he asks. Olive stares at him for a few moments and then hops off my lap and prepares to jump off the bed. "I'll take that as a yes," he whispers. Releasing his hands, I pick Olive up and head toward the door with Colton following after me.

"How did you know that would work?" Colton says as he opens out bedroom door and holds it open for me.

"I didn't know that it would work, but I thought about when I transferred that vision to you before. If I was able to do that, we have to have some sort of magical connection, and since I was able to do that, I must be able to share some of my other powers with you."

Wrapping his arm across my shoulder, Colton pulls me into his side and places a small kiss on my temple. "Thank you," he whispers into my ear and guides us downstairs.

Olive leans her head back and glances up at me.

Thank you too.

Pulling my hair into a high ponytail, I follow Colin to the training room. Everyone else is already in there. I apparently slept in a little longer than the rest. "May I ask why you have such a big house? Not that I don't like it, but if it's only you and your son…"

"Why live in something so large?" he finishes. "Back in my heyday, I would let mages come into my house seeking refuge. Tom and I trained together back then and we helped train others. Because of his power, he was the best trainer I'd ever seen."

"Tom has a power?" I ask. I don't know why I sound so surprised. He is a mage; of course he has magic. I've just never seen him use any before.

"He's never told you?"

"No…"

"I don't think his power has a specific name, but I would call Tom a fast-teacher. If you're learning something for the first time and you're around him, you'll pick it up without a problem. That's why he's always around when new mages need training. He's able to push them past the beginning stages within a few hours and get them up to the level they need to be at quickly."

"How come he never told us?" How come I never questioned that before?

"Maybe because he doesn't want you to doubt your abilities. He can't teach you something if you're incapable of learning it. He may not have even used his magic on you. That's something only he knows. He can turn that power on and off with ease."

"Hmm…" I'm not sure if I want to know whether or not Tom used his magic on me when I first started training.

"Back to the story," Colin says as he turns down another hallway. "We would help out troubled mages. Give them somewhere to sleep. Feed them. Help them get back on their feet. Despite what you think, there aren't many mages out there, and we needed to make sure that our numbers didn't dwindle. I built this large house to help those who needed it. However, no one has come by in the last couple years because you're either a Gadramick or you're in hiding."

"Do mages who oppose Dravin have a name? Why are they called the Gadramick?" I ask as we start walking upstairs.

"Not that I know of. We're just mages. Dravin took the name Gadramick because he started using dark magic. For a little while, he would use witches for their magic, but somehow his power strengthened and he no longer needed them, so witches are now in hiding too."

"Witches exist?"

"Yeah, they have magic, but only those who dabble in dark magic are considered powerful. They don't usually have enough magic to do any serious damage. They're a peaceful species, so unless provoked, they'll leave you alone. I've never had any problems with one before."

"Do mages have a handbook I can read?" I ask. "There's so much stuff that I don't know. I feel so stupid when I ask everyone these questions, because apparently everyone already knows the answer."

Colin stops walking and looks at me. "Ryanne, you weren't born into this life. It was chosen for you. There's no way you could know any of this information without asking questions. Don't feel stupid for that. No one is going to judge you." He points to the large wooden door in front of us. "Those people in that room care about you. A lot. That much is obvious every time one of them looks at you. Even those ex-Gadramicks. I'd never heard of a Gadramick switching sides before. I've heard of some leaving, but no one who knows Dravin would oppose him like that. They believe in you, Ryanne, otherwise they wouldn't be here. You need to start believing in yourself if you want to accomplish anything here."

"How did that transition from a you're not stupid speech to a believe in yourself speech?"

"It was subtle, I know," he says as he opens the door. I chuckle and follow him in the training room.

"Oh my goodness," I say when my eyes adjust to the bright lights. Colin calls everyone to gather in the middle of the room. Colton, who is standing on the far side of the room talking to an unfamiliar man, turns in my direction and smiles at me. "Colin, do you think it's possible for Dravin to be stopped?"

"I think it depends on what you believe. Dravin is very confident in his abilities. From what I've heard, you're very strong. You need to use all those emotions swirling around in that pretty head of yours and let it strengthen your magic. That's why you were given that new power. It'll make you stronger if you use it in the right way. Yes, I do think it's possible for Dravin to be stopped, but it doesn't matter what I think. What you think is going to happen is all that matters," Colin says as everyone crowds around us.

"That's why you think I got this extra power? To strengthen my existing magic?"

"You're powers are emotion based, Ryanne," Tom says as he places a hand on my shoulder.

"Now, you have a ton of extra emotions coursing through you. If you can harness those, you could be unstoppable," Colin tells me. "When I instigate you, I can feel your magic moving through the air. You're powerful, but you don't know how to use all your magic yet. You put too much effort in pushing your magic back. If you would let your magic move freely around you, I think you'd be able to train much easier."

"I could hurt someone," I whisper. Since everyone is around us, I know that they are listening, but Colin is only talking to me.

"You won't hurt anyone," he confidently states.

"And how do you know that?"

"Call it intuition," Colin says as he winks at me. My mouth falls open. He's talked to Claire recently.

"So what's the plan for today?" the unfamiliar man asks.

"I was thinking that you could help Logan train Lily, Chris. Natalie and I can work with Ryanne in controlling these emotions," Colin says. I turn and look at Chris. He must be Colin's son. I can see some of the resemblance. They have the same dark wavy hair and light almost gold eyes. "Oh, Ryanne, this is my son Chris. Chris, this is Ryanne."

Chris smiles at me, and I can't help but smile back. He looks to be the same age as Bragden and Conner, which would put him in his early-mid-twenties. That means that Colin is older than he looks. Standing over six feet tall, he towers over me like all other mages. His golden eyes watch me with curiosity. I realize I don't look like a mage; he doesn't have to be so obvious about it.

"I'm not what you expected, I know."

"No, it's not that. You look very familiar," Chris says as he continues to watch me. Hmm, he actually does look familiar. Lights keep flashing before my eyes. Darkness. Sirens. I rack my brain for where I had seen him before.

"Oh my gosh," I gasp and cover my mouth. "You're the paramedic."

"I helped you before?" he asks me.

I bite my lip and look down. Colton walks over to me and wraps his arm around my shoulder. "You helped me after a car accident last year."

"Oh, yeah, I remember that now," he says, "I'm so sorry." His pity flows into me. I step back into Colton as I try to bury that emotion away. I don't want to feel that.

"Don't pity me, Chris. I can't handle any more of that." Chris nods and the pity instantly stops. He's much better at controlling his emotions than everyone else.

Colin claps his hands, scaring everyone. "Everyone else can train together. I trust that you guys can split yourself up into groups on your own," he says.

Tom pats Colton on the back as he stops beside him. "Yeah, they know who to train with. We've been doing this for a while now."

Even though everyone starts splitting up, Colton lingers beside me. "Trust Colin," he whispers to me. "He knows what he's doing. He and Tom used to work together training other mages."

"I know. He told me." Colton looks surprised, but doesn't comment on that. He nods and looks over my head and laughs. "You're being summoned."

"Come on little Hobbit. We don't want you to end up in Mordor without any training!" Colin yells from across the training room. I shake my head and stand on my tip toes to kiss Colton on the cheek. Turning around, I skip over to Colin and Natalie, trying to act more optimistic than I feel.

"Okay, little one, unleash your magic," Colin says. Natalie turns and stares at him with wide eyes.

"What?"

"You heard me. Unplug the stopper. Turn the lock. Rip off the band-aid. Whatever it is you have to do. Unleash your magic. You can keep it all down easily, but we're going to work backward."

"Liam has had to knock me out before because I can't control the magic when I let it all out."

"Trust me."

I stare at him. "Everything? The thoughts? Emotions? Weather elements? All the magic?"

"Everything."

"Are you sure you know what you're doing? I could hurt everyone in here," I start shaking my head. "No, I can't do that."

"Ryanne, you're not going to hurt anyone. You're magic will only hurt people if that is your intention. You don't want to hurt anyone in this room, so you won't. Don't worry about that."

"How can you be so sure of that? What if I do?" I whisper as I step closer to him.

"Are you angry? Mad? Upset? Frustrated?"

"No."

"Then stop worrying. You're magic is emotion based, so unless you're feeling any of those, you won't hurt anyone. Now quit stalling. Unleash the Kraken." Colin starts laughing. I can't help but join in. "Joking aside. Unleash your magic, Ryanne. All of it."

I glance around the room as I take a couple steps back. I don't know what's going to happen when I pull back the veil around all my magic. I push my magic out often, but never all of it at once. I'm always worried it is going to cause more damage than good. Everyone is training. Well, attempting to make it look like they are. Colton and Liam keep glancing over at me. I'm hit with their worry when I meet their gazes.

"Okay, whenever you're ready," Colin says.

I close my eyes as I gradually start pushing my magic out.

CHAPTER EIGHT

COLTON

"HOW ARE THINGS WITH YOU and Natalie?"

"Good. She's still really worried that something is going to happen to me. She didn't know that being Ryanne's protector meant that if Ryanne died, I would follow suit. She's kind of freaking out about that."

"That's understandable," I tell him as we both turn and look at the opposite side of the room where Ryanne is standing with Natalie and Colin. They're just talking right now, but Ryanne keeps shaking her head.

"She doesn't want to unleash all of her magic," Liam says. We both turn and look away when Ryanne glances in our direction. I get into a defensive stance and face Liam again. Neither of us are into training today. He glances back over his shoulder. The girl he's supposed to protect and his soulmate are both standing over there. We're not sure what's going to happen when Ryanne stops trying to contain her magic. We've seen little bits of it when she loses control.

Ryanne takes a couple steps back and inhales deeply. I, too, stop attempting to spar and watch her. What if something goes wrong? Could this hurt her? Shoot, I shouldn't be worrying right now. She'll feel that.

"I don't like this new power of hers," I tell Liam. "I always have to think about what I'm feeling and how it'll affect her."

"Natalie will help her come to terms with it. She's able to block others emotions; maybe Ryanne can too."

"Okay, whenever you're ready," Colin says loudly to Ryanne. Closing her eyes, she starts pushing her magic out. We instantly feel a change when a sudden breeze manifests. The air swirls around the room, causing Ryanne's hair to whip around her head. Everyone stops and watches her. The breeze becomes static as the lightning element of her powers makes itself known. I glance over at Liam who is still watching Natalie. She and Colin are taking small steps backward as Ryanne continues to push her magic out.

The lights in the room start flickering, and some of the weights against the wall start sliding across the room from the wind. I return my focus to my soulmate. Her face is furrowed in concentration. I stagger back a little as the wind intensifies. She has a ton of magic in her; even Colin seems a little shocked.

Tiny undecipherable whispers echo around us. Everyone tenses when the voices get louder. These must be from her mind-reading ability. The voices ride the wind filling in every available space, and a second later, random colors start flowing out of Ryanne. Reds, blues, grays, greens, yellows, pinks, and purples all start moving throughout the room, lighting up as they mingle with the weather elements.

She's still pushing magic out. How can someone so small have that much magic inside her? All the elements in the room intensify the higher her arms raise. When her hands are fully above her head, a white light shoots out from her body and catapults toward us. I shield my eyes the closer it gets to me, but I can't seem to look away. Following the light is all of Ryanne's magic. I fly backward from the force of her magic. With my eyes closed, I hit the cushioned mat flooring and roll a couple times before coming to a complete stop. When I open my eyes, the white light is gone. The colors and low whispers are still moving through the room, but the light electricity and the wind are starting to dwindle.

Pushing myself up, I see Ryanne trying to do the same. I get up and start to walk over to her, but Liam grabs my arm and pulls me back. "Let Colin work with her."

Colin, who had also fallen from the blast, slowly gets up and helps Natalie stand. Together both of them walk over to Ryanne, who's now looking around the room with a shocked expression on her face. "Ryanne, can you hear me?" Colin asks.

She nods and pushes herself fully up. "How do you feel?" Liam and I both step a little closer to hear them.

Ryanne looks around the room again. She seems very confused. "Umm, I don't really know. I feel weird."

I take another step forward to hear her better. "Weird how?"

"I don't know. I can hear everyone's thoughts and feel their emotions, but it's not as annoying as before. I can actually ignore them."

"You had to release the hold you had on your magic. Before, your magic was cramped inside you, building up pressure. By releasing it, you'll probably start to feel better. You won't feel the effects of keeping your magic down anymore, so you shouldn't be as tired. Keeping your magic inside probably would have been more dangerous than what you just did. You can push the thoughts out of the way and hopefully with

Natalie's help, you can control the emotions. Everything should be a little easier now," Colin says. I turn and look around the room. Everyone is watching Ryanne, wondering what she'll do next.

"Like what?" she asks.

"I don't know. I don't have all that magic coursing through me. Get creative," he says.

"Uh oh," I say right as Liam laughs. You don't tell Ryanne to get creative. She smiles and puts her hand out in front of her, palm up. A ball of electrified blue light starts forming in her hand, gradually increasing in size. Colin's smile falls as Ryanne's gets wider. Adding her left hand, she expands the ball. Looking up at Colin, Ryanne winks at him as she sends the magic toward him.

Colin throws his arms up to shield his face. When the ball is about to hit him, the wind picks up and spins around, cocooning him. The ball collides the wind, uniformly spreading out. Colin is entrapped in an electrified tornado. Thunder rolls above him as it starts pouring inside the wind cocoon.

"What is she doing?" Chris asks as he walks up beside us.

"Getting her payback," Liam answers without taking his eyes off of the scene playing out in front of us. Ryanne drops the tornado, but keeps the rain around Colin. There's a chorus of laughter around the room when everyone sees him. His clothes are soaking wet and clinging to him, his wavy hair is sticking up in every direction, and he has a very obvious frown directed at Ryanne, who is trying to hold in her laughter.

"I don't know of any Hobbits that can do that, do you Colin?" Ryanne asks through her giggles.

"No, Gandalf, I don't know of any," Colin mumbles.

"I'm surprisingly okay with that one. Gandalf was awesome," Ryanne says as she heats up the room slightly and increases the wind, drying off Colin. Tom walks over to him and slaps him on the back.

"I probably should have warned you not to tell Ryanne to get creative. She takes it very literally. You can ask any of the guys in the room."

A chorus of agreements ring out as we all shout our responses. Ryanne laughs, but apologizes to Colin. He just laughs it off. "It was impressive. Granted, it would have been funnier if it wasn't done to me, but it was nonetheless impressive."

For the next hour everyone trained. Ryanne put a shield up in the middle of the room so her magic wouldn't affect the rest of us while we worked. Both Liam and I fought with all we had, neither one of us letting the other get away with anything. If I had to pick someone, I'm glad Liam is Ryanne's protector.

"Hey, I think we've had enough training for the day," Tom says. "We should let Colin and Natalie work with Ryanne using the full room. We'll train again in the morning." Following everyone out of the room, I look behind me once more. Ryanne is moving the magic around her, weaving water in and out of the air. It's amazing what she can do.

"You don't think she'll pass out from using too much magic, do you?" I ask Tom as we walk downstairs.

"I don't think so. I believe she only passed out from the magic use because it had nowhere to go. It was stuck inside her, using up all of her energy, and making her more tired. That's probably why she was always falling asleep. I think Colin had the right idea when he asked her to unleash it. From what I've seen, she now seems able to do more. She already appears more powerful. With a little more training...I can't imagine what she'll be able to do."

"This is really happening isn't it?" Emma asks.

"Yeah, it is. The end is coming," Tom answers.

Sitting down on the couch in the entertainment room, I listen upstairs for Ryanne's movements. The training room is directly above us. I can hear people shuffling around, so I know they are still training. Chris sits down on the couch next to me, and I turn to him.

"So you were the paramedic that helped Ryanne?"

"Yeah, I was the first EMT to arrive on the scene," he tells me. "The cops cleared the area and gave us access to the vehicle. Her mom died on impact. There was nothing we could do to save her. I thought Ryanne was dead too when I first saw her. She was unconscious and bleeding a lot. If she wasn't wearing her seatbelt, she definitely would have died." Chris doesn't seem to like to talk about emergency situations.

"When we were finally able to free her from the car we found out where all the blood was coming from. She had a four inch piece of glass embedded under her ribs from the windshield breaking in. We couldn't remove it on the spot; we had to stabilize her until we could get her to an emergency room for surgery. She'd already lost so much blood. We almost lost her twice on the way to the ER. She opened her eyes once in the ambulance and stared right at me for a couple seconds before losing consciousness again. To this day, I can't get the image of her looking at me with so much pain in her eyes out of my mind. Honestly, I'm shocked she made it," he says. "I tried everything to make sure she didn't leave us. It's always hard to loose someone so young. I've seen more death than I ever wanted to, but I've saved a lot of lives, and I was so happy when I could call her a success story."

"Well thank you for saving her," I whisper. I can't imagine what everything would be like if she had actually died in that crash. At least now, I've gotten to know her. If she died, everything would be a big 'what if.' I'd never know for sure. I'd be incomplete...empty.

"I was just doing my job, Colton," Chris looks at me. He's a good guy. I already feel like I can trust him completely. We drop the conversation when Ryanne, Natalie, and Colin all walk into the room. Ryanne dramatically plops down on the couch next to me.

"I'm tired now. Goodnight," she whispers. Chris scoots over to give Ryanne more room. She smiles gratefully at him and curls into my side. Wrapping my arm around her, I pull her to me. She laughs, but lets me move her. "Surprisingly, I'm actually not that tired."

"I told you unleashing your magic would help. Now you can easily control the thoughts and emotions. The magic is always around you, so you no longer have to suppress anything. Everything should be much easier to manipulate. Come on, let me hear it," Colin says with a large grin.

"I don't know what you're talking about," Ryanne mumbles.

"Just once. I need to hear it."

Ryanne turns and buries her head in my shoulder. "You wmfh righsh," she says. Her voice is muffled by my shirt.

"I couldn't hear you. Could you please repeat that, Gandalf?" Colin asks. He's literally grinning from ear to ear. Tom starts laughing from across the room.

With a sigh, Ryanne sits up and looks directly at Colin. "Right, Colin, you were. Hmmmm."

"You sound nothing like Yoda," Chris says with a laugh.

"I wasn't trying to sound like Yoda. I was just trying to speak like Yoda," she retorts. Chris shakes his head.

"I'll take it," Colin says.

"That's probably a good idea, because you won't get anything better than that," Bragden says.

Ryanne laughs and turns toward the TV. Without saying anything, she silently gets up and walks over to Colin's DVD collection. Zeroing in on the movie, she grabs it and turns around. "Can we watch this? I'll beg if I have to," she says.

The Avengers.

Turning toward Emma, she says, "Chris Hemsworth."

"You only like him because of his voice," Emma replies.

"And everything else," she mumbles as she looks toward Colin.

"You can watch it. I don't care."

Ryanne smiles widely and then quickly hides the smile and glares at everyone, making sure that no one will argue with her. Larkin opens his mouth to say something, but a large ball of water forms in midair and falls down on him.

"Don't even try it, mister," Ryanne says.

Larkin spits out water and instantly starts laughing. No one else says anything, but everyone is trying to hide their laughter. I get off the couch and grab the movie from Ryanne. Putting it in the DVD player, I press play and grab Ryanne's hand, pulling her back to the couch.

She sits down, but her eyes don't leave the TV. Chris starts to say something, but Ryanne instantly shushes him. "She's into Superhero films?" he whispers.

"Oh yeah," I tell him.

"Interesting. I would have pegged her as a romantic comedy girl." Ryanne makes a gagging noise at his comment. "I stand corrected."

"I can stand them, but they're not my first option. Now shhhhhhh," Ryanne says as Nick Fury appears on the screen. For the next two hours we watch The Avengers. Ryanne quotes many of the lines of the movie and laughs at all the funny parts before they happen.

"This is my favorite part," she says as she lightly hits my arm. Mark Ruffalo had just shown up for the end battle sequence. "That's my secret, Captain. I'm always angry," she whispers along with Bruce Banner.

"You're too cute," I whisper to her as I lean back a little. Ryanne curls into my side and smiles up at me.

"You know who is also cute?" she asks.

"Chris Evans!" Emma yells from across the room.

"Emma is delusional, Colton. Don't listen to her. I was going to say Hemsworth. She just forgot his last name." She puts a finger out and stops me. "You're cute too; don't worry."

"It's a good thing you added that last part. I may have had to tickle you otherwise."

"I'm learning," she mumbles and she leans back against me and returns her attention to the end of the movie.

CHAPTER NINE

WE ALL TRAIN FOR THE next couple days. Now that I've released my magic, I don't feel as overwhelmed. It's much easier to contain the thoughts and emotions. I still have all my magic, but it's not stuck in me anymore. It moves freely around me, but only acts when I will it to. It listens to me completely. Natalie has helped me control the emotions. Since those are stronger than thoughts, it took a little more practice to have complete control, but I quickly got the hang of it. I can call them to the surface whenever, but I can't hear them unless I want to.

To strengthen my magic, I select a strong emotion such as anger or love and wrap it around the strands of magic. This magnifies the strength of them. With practice, I do believe that I can stop Dravin now. I've noticed a difference in my abilities and I know that Dravin won't know what hit him.

Logan and Chris have been helping Lily train. She's gotten better, but still needs some work. Considering she's only been training for four days, she's a very quick learner. Tom could also have something to do with that. It's all very encouraging, but I know this isn't going to last for long. It can't. We're going to have to go back out and find others to help us again.

"How much longer do you think we'll stay here?" I ask Colton as I walk out of the bathroom, drying my hair with a towel.

"Not too much longer," he replies honestly. "Though I wish we could. It'd be nice to relax for a little while."

"Yeah, it's like how things were before; only there are more of us now," I tell him as I step in front of him.

Colton takes the towel from my hands and tosses it lightly on the bed. Putting his arms around my waist he starts swaying. "What are you doing?"

Instead of answering, he rests his chin on my head and starts humming. I wrap my arms around his waist and lean into him. Under my ear, I can feel his steady heartbeat. I step closer to him as his arms tighten around me and start swaying with him. I love these moments with Colton. I don't know how many more moments we'll get like this for a while.

His chest vibrates under my cheek as he continues to hum. Colton always knows what I need. I've needed this alone time with him for a while now. I just want him to hold me and let me know that everything will be okay. That *we're* going to be okay.

Hearing a knock at the door, we both stop moving. With a sigh, I lean back and look up at my soulmate. I don't want him to answer it. His eyes meet mine before he gives me a small smile and steps away from me to answer the door. My heart swells with my love for him. I bite my lip to keep my girly sigh in as I watch him walk away. Opening the door, he quietly talks with Tom. I can't hear anything they are saying. I could read Tom's mind, but since they're being quiet, they don't want me to hear their conversation. Leaning against the doorframe, Colton starts shaking his head, obviously disagreeing with something Tom just said.

I let my eyes travel over Colton's long wavy hair down to his broad shoulders. Even wearing a t-shirt, I can see the defined muscles in his back leading down to a tight narrow waist. With his arms crossed, I can see the bulge from his flexed biceps—the same biceps that were just wrapped around me.

When I hear Tom mention that he'll come back later, I tear my eyes away from Colton. I need something to distract myself. I grab the wet towel from the bed and hang it on the towel rack in the bathroom. "Ryanne," Colton calls. I start to walk out of the bathroom, but the room starts to spin around me. Grabbing onto the edge of the doorway, I try to keep myself upright. I gasp as the air is pulled from my lungs. "Ryanne, what's wrong?" Colton asks as he rushes toward me. I gasp as the air is pulled from my lungs.

My body starts to shake. I fall to my knees. "He's…He's p-p-ulling me b…ack again." I manage to get out. I try to move, but my whole body begins violently shaking and I fall forward into Colton's arms. He picks me up and carries me across the room. I feel myself being placed on the bed, but I'm not longer in the bedroom anymore. I'm drifting between two places.

I'm being pulled in so many different directions, and everything spins around me. It feels like I'm thrown around the inside of a tornado. The motion is disorienting and makes me feel sick. I don't know where I'm going to be spit out, but I know that Dravin is definitely involved. Instead of gently waking up in a new environment, I'm thrown down in the middle of a cell again. I hit the hard cement floor and roll into the wall. My body instantly aches when I come to a stop. Grimacing, I move onto my back and try to sit up.

"That could have been much smoother," I mumble when I sit up and look around the room. I immediately tense when I spot Dravin in the corner.

"Yes, it could have been," he says.

"What do you want, Dravin?" I ask him as I push myself up. His tall frame is leaning against the door with his arms crossed against his chest, looking too smug for his own good. *Magic?* I let out a relieved breath when I feel the familiar tingle of my magic in the air around me. Does Dravin know that I can use my magic here?

"You know what I want, Ryanne. I need your magic."

"You want my magic. You don't need it," I correct him.

"Still as verbal as ever, I see," he says as he pushes away from the door and walks toward me. "I don't know how many times I have to tell you that it would go much better for you if you would cooperate."

"I'm not really a stickler for listening. I'm kind of a rebel when it comes to that. I like to do my own thing. Being predictable is lame," I tell him. "Maybe you should make a note of that." I throw a shield around me as I recognize the look of concentration on Dravin's face. I smile as his concentration turns to confusion. "You're going to have to do more than that if you want to get my magic."

"How is that possible?" he asks me.

"You're not the only one getting stronger," I say as I take a step toward him. "Now, I would suggest telling me how to get back because I'm starting to get mad." I call some magic to me. Not enough to do any damage, but enough to let Dravin know that I can use it here.

His eyes widen, but he doesn't say anything. "Interesting," he says as he walks in a slow circle around me. "Do you know why I became a Gadramick?" he asks me, changing the subject.

"Because you're too cool to be nice?" I guess. Dravin stops in front of me.

"My parents were mages," he starts. I mumble a *Duh*. Dravin glares at me, but continues, "They preached about how mages should work with humans. We should be equal. No one should be more powerful than another. We're supposed to work together. All bullshit, I tell you."

"What happened to them?"

"You want to know what happened to them?"

"Yes, that's kind of why I asked the question."

"They were murdered right in front of me by humans when I was five years old. Humans murdered mages because they were too weak to fight back. They had powers and could have easily overpowered their attackers, but did they fight back? No, because they thought humans and mages were equals."

"We should be equals, Dravin. Just because a few people..."

"You don't get it at all. We're stronger and smarter than they are. We're all around better people. We have powers for a reason. We're supposed to be rulers. They need to know we won't tolerate their actions. We won't tolerate their insolence and stupidity."

"Ok, let me get this straight," I say as I step toward him. "Because your parents were murdered by humans you think that all mages should rule over humans?"

"That's what I just said."

"*You* murdered people. Does that mean that the family members of those you've killed should rule over you?"

"You're missing the point. We have powers. They don't. We should rule. They shouldn't. It comes down to who has the most assets. Right now, those with money are the ones that rule. They control everything. We have magic. Money is nothing compared to our magic. We should be ahead of them in society."

"We're not in a caste system, Dravin! We shouldn't be ahead of anyone. Maybe you could rule if you would put your magic to good use. Do you really want to rule over people who hate you? I'd rather have a few loyal followers than hundreds of those who hate me. I mean really? Have you ever heard about Julius Caesar's assassination?"

Dravin moves quickly and grabs me around the neck. Apparently sometime during our conversation, I dropped my shield. Pushing me backward, he slams me against the back wall and lifts me slightly off the ground. The tips of my toes are the only thing touching the cement. I try to suck in oxygen, but his hands are cutting off my air supply.

"Let me set something straight, Ryanne. My patience with you is running very thin. At first, I thought you were cute. Short little mage with attitude. It was new, interesting even, but I'm over it. You're going to cooperate or you will die. There are no ifs, ands, or buts about it." Dravin releases my neck and drops me to the ground. I fall on my knees and put my arms out to try and lessen the blow. I hear a pop and pain shoots up my left wrist—the same wrist the Phillip recently broke. Oh, now I'm pissed. I breathe in deeply before pushing off with my right hand and standing up.

"Dravin, you really don't know who you're messing with," I say as I brush dirt off my clothing with my unbroken hand. My knees and elbows are throbbing, but I ignore the pain and face him.

"Since I was able to get you here that means your little spell is no longer protecting you. I'm going to call your farther and bring him in. If you don't fight, I'll make sure it doesn't hurt that much."

"You really think I'm not going to fight?" I say as I call my magic to me. Instead of waiting for my magic to build up, it instantly comes to me. I imagine a ball of energy similar to what I threw at Colin earlier today. When Dravin sees the energy forming between my hands, his eyes widen and he steps backward. I smile at him as he reaches for the doorknob. "I told you, you really don't know who you're messing with," I say as I throw the ball of energy. He ducks but it still hits him in the shoulder. He grunts and falls to the ground.

With his concentration elsewhere, I close my eyes and think about my room with Colton. I call more magic to me. *I want to go back,* I whisper.

My body starts vibrating. My knees give out and I fall to the ground. Instead of hitting the hard cement flooring, I start free-falling. Darkness moves around me, but I feel a slight breeze. I squeeze my eyes shut and wait for the movement to stop.

I can tell the instant I land back in my own body. I struggle to catch my breath. My throat, arms, and knees are all throbbing. Everyone, and I mean everyone, is in the room, watching me. I slowly sit up and turn toward Logan. Waving him over, I move so that I'm sitting on the edge of the bed. Without saying anything, Logan knows what I'm asking him to do.

The bones in my wrist snap back together, and I don't even gasp this time which surprises me. The pulsating pain in my knees and throat fade. Logan steps away from me. I stand up and look at everyone in the room. "I need to redo the protective enchantment."

"That's it? No explanation?" Emma asks.

"Dravin was able to call me back which means that he can get to any of you too. I need to strengthen the enchantment."

"Ryanne, what happened?" Colton asks. He stops in front of me, blocking me from everyone else. I place my hand on his cheek. He leans into my touch and wraps his large hand over top of mine.

"Nothing really," I say. "But I need to strengthen the enchantment now. I think I can put it over all of us and the house at the same time. It should be easier since I won't really be pushing any magic out. I'll just be telling it what to do."

Colton groans, but steps out of the way. His inner turmoil hits me. He's upset that Dravin got to me and angry that I got hurt. Soon after, his relief hits me. He's relieved I was able to get away without any serious injuries, and he's confused as to why I won't tell him what happened. He knows I won't reveal anything until I do the enchantment. "Thank you," I whisper to him.

Without looking at anyone, I close my eyes and feel the magic around me. "Magic come forth, I call you to me, protect our home from danger so evil cannot see," I start as the magic moves through the room, hitting every available surface, covering everything with magic—hiding the home from danger. I envision the magic coating everyone in here too. I see myself holding each of their hands as I say the spell like I did in the past. The magic flows into them. As I continue with the spell, I hear a couple loud intakes of breath. They can feel my magic covering them…protecting them. "I call you to me during this time of need to protect those within from anger and greed; protect our home from danger so evil cannot see."

When I finish the spell, I open my eyes back up and look around the room. Everyone is watching me curiously. Mixtures of awe and confusion flood into me. I mix the emotions with my magic and push them out. If I keep everything in my body, I'll start to tire out again.

Colton walks up to me. "Are you okay? Are you tired?"

"I'm fine, Colton. You worry too much," I tell him. I turn toward everyone else. "Do you feel any different? Did it work?"

"Yeah, I could feel your magic surrounding me," Chris answers. "It was amazing."

"Good, now that that's settled…what's new?" I say as I sit down on the edge of the bed.

"Ryanne…" Colton starts.

"Ugh, fine," I say as I turn and look at him. "I don't see why you want to know everything. Nothing really happened."

"Humor me."

"I was thrown into another cell in Dravin's compound. I really need to work on my entrances. They're not as smooth as I would like them to be. We talked. I insulted. You know how it goes with him. He tried to use his voodoo mind thing on me, but I threw a shield up around me. Oh, I could use my magic there. He didn't know that I could use my magic. Apparently, there was a spell on that room to stop magic use, but I broke through it. He…um, he told me about how his parents were murdered in front of him by humans. His parents were good mages, but their death caused Dravin to oppose the idea of humans and mages working together. He wants revenge, so he basically formed the Gadramicks to get it."

"How is that any different from what he's doing now?" Colton asks.

"Well, when I asked him that, he choked me, so it's not any different. He just doesn't want to think of it like that." Colton clenches his fist, and his appearance starts to fade. I jump up off the bed and walk over to him. "Hey, hey, hey. Listen to me," I grab his chin and force him to look down at me. "When he let go of me, I hit him with a ball of energy. He fell to the ground injured, and I came back. I hurt him worse than he hurt me. It wasn't that bad. I'm okay now." I hate watching Colton struggle with his power. I know that he goes invisible whenever he gets upset or angry. I don't know what specifically causes it, but it takes him a while to come back. He flickers once more and then sighs loudly. Hugging me to him, he buries his face in my neck.

"I'm going to kill him if I see him again," he whispers to me.

I pull back and look up at him. "Then, I think we better train."

CHAPTER TEN

"OKAY, HERE'S ANOTHER QUESTION. IN an epic battle of magic, which wizard would come out victorious: Gandalf or Dumbledore?" Logan asks.

"Gandalf," I say without giving it a second thought.

"Dumbledore," Chris replies. We both turn and glare at each other. We've been arguing like this all night.

"How can you think that Dumbledore would win in a battle against Gandalf?" I ask.

"How can you think that Gandalf would win against Dumbledore?"

"There would be no competition. Gandalf is a beast. Dumbledore would run away scared at the sight of the Gandalf. When Gandalf died, he found a way to come back. Can Dumbledore say the same thing?"

"How about we say that it's a tie? Both wizards are equally as awesome as the other," Logan says. We stare at Logan for a couple of seconds before turning back to glare at each other. Honestly, I like both of them, but arguing with Chris is pretty fun. "Okay, how about this one, Smeagol vs. Yoda?"

"Yoda," I say at the same time as Chris says Smeagol.

"Guys, this could go on all night. Ryanne's the prophecy girl, so her picks win," Incendia says. "Sorry Chris." I stick my tongue out at Chris and high five Incendia.

"Just because she's the prophecy girl doesn't mean that she should win all the time. I'm just as awesome on a less magical level," Chris retorts.

"You'll have to do a whole lot more to reach my level of awesomeness, Chris," I tell him. I lean against the back of the couch. Colton leans over and wraps his arm around my shoulder. I smile up at him before turning back to Chris. Colton's amusement briefly hits me before I push it back out.

"You must have to brush your teeth a lot to clean your mouth of all the crap you're spewing," Chris says.

"Ouch, Chris. That hurt," I tell him.

Colin, Tom, and Mr. and Mrs. Howick walk into the entertainment room. Tom turns toward Colton and nods. What's going on? Colton turns and tightens his grip around me, but returns his attention to the TV. "What was that about?" I whisper to him.

Colton looks down at me and feigns confusion. "What are you talking about?"

I narrow my eyes at him, but let him off for now. I'll investigate later. Curling into his shoulder, I watch the movie on the screen. I don't recognize this movie or any of the actors in it. When I see someone get shot in their head, I turn and bury my face into Colton's shoulder. I'm okay with action sequences, but I hate gore. Colton pulls me closer to him and kisses my temple.

"She loves superhero stuff, but hates violence?"

"I hate all the blood and gore," I mumble against the fabric of Colton's shirt. When I hear the shooting stop, I look at the TV.

Nothing's happening right now. I angle myself toward it and watch again.

Thirty minutes later, the lead actor in the movie is driving in a car with his wife, arguing. They have a green light, so he starts driving. She turns toward him in the car to yell at him again, but screams when she sees the headlights of a large truck coming toward them. The screen starts moving in slow motion. My mind flashes back to a year ago when I was in a similar situation. The scar on my stomach starts to tingle, and in the back of my mind, I can see the truck moving toward us—the bright headlights blinding me. I watch as my mom turns and looks at me then turns the wheel. The world around me spins and blurs together as the car flips and metal and glass debris rain in.

"I'm…umm…going to go do…something," I say as I push away from Colton and rush out of the room. I can't watch that movie anymore. Running into the hallway, I turn to the left. I don't know what I'm doing, but I can't stay in that room surrounded by everyone. I expected Colton to follow me, so I'm surprised when I turn around and see Chris standing outside of the door.

"It's not uncommon to relive an experience when you witness something that triggers a specific memory."

"How did you know that's why I ran out of the room?"

Chris walks toward me. "I was there, Ryanne. I saw the accident. I saw all the damage." He pauses and looks down the hallway. "My mom was killed in a car accident too. I was thinking about her when I saw that scene, so I knew you would be reliving what happened to you as well. Your experience is much more recent than mine." I lean back against the wall and watch as Chris stops in front of me. "I'm sorry about your mother, Ryanne. There was nothing we could do to help her."

I lean forward and hug Chris. "I know. It's just hard." I feel Chris's arms wrap around my back. "I was supposed to die in that accident. I have to live with the fact that my mom sacrificed herself because she loved me. I used to be so mad at her. I still want to be mad at her, but I'm not," I bunch my hands in the fabric of his shirt.

"Mothers always think about their children before themselves. It's a maternal thing," he says. "It shows that they love you. Someday, you'll appreciate what she did for you."

"I've talked with her," I say as I lean backward and look up at him. "I've talked with my mom. She helped me get over some of my problems. She told me that she was proud of me and wouldn't change a thing." He nods and brushes some of the tears off of my cheeks. I wasn't aware I had been crying.

"You okay?" he asks. I nod and try to smile. I know it comes out as more of a grimace. Chris looks over at me toward the door and steps away. I know that Colton is standing there, but I reach forward and grab Chris's arm. He stops and looks down at me again.

"I'm sorry about your mom, Chris." He nods and walks back into the entertainment room, patting Colton's shoulder as he passes. Colton starts walking toward me. Instead of letting him walk the whole way, I meet him halfway. Wrapping my arms around his waist, I envelope myself in his familiar scent.

"I'm sorry. I didn't realize there was a scene like that in the movie." I shake my head and look up at him.

"You have nothing to be sorry for. I don't know what came over me," I tell him.

"Come on," he says as he pulls me down the hallway.

"Where are we going?"

"You'll see."

"Close your eyes," Colton tells me as we near the back of the house. I look up at him. He's serious. I close my eyes and wait for his word. I hear the sound of a door opening and the cool night air brushes against my face.

"We're going outside?" I ask.

"Keep your eyes closed."

I do as I'm told. "This reminds me of the forest. Do you remember that? The bench?"

"Of course I remember that, Ry," he says—his voice low and husky. A warm feeling shoots through my body at his tone. Colton chuckles at my response and continues pulling me forward. "Watch out, there are two steps coming up."

Colton slows down and helps me down the stairs. "Can I open my eyes now?"

"Be patient, Ry. We're getting close," he tells me. I groan, but let him pull me forward. Where could he be taking me? I hear the sound of water running somewhere close by. Are we near a lake? I'm surrounded by the sound of crickets chirping and wind rustling the leaves of the trees. The ground below me is uneven. It feels like I'm walking on a stone or brick path. I stumble forward on a loose rock and collide into Colton's chest. "You're so graceful," he laughs as he continues pulling me forward.

"Hey, you can't say anything until you're the one walking blindly on an uneven path," I mumble. Colton stops moving, and I walk into his chest again. He lets go of my hands and steadies me. "Can I open my eyes now?" I ask.

I arch my head up toward him and wait for his response, but it never comes. Instead, I feel his lips brush against mine. Colton's arms wrap around my waist and he slowly pulls me closer. I press myself into his body and wait for him to kiss me. His breath hits my cheeks as he lingers in front of me. Oh, just kiss me already.

Colton gently presses his lips to mine, kissing me slowly. I melt into him. My knees feel weak, my heart rate increases, and I can't think straight. Colton means so much to me that it scares me sometimes. I'm slowly pushing my insecurities back everyday—telling myself that I am good enough for him. This perfect man kissing me is my soulmate. We're destined for each other. It's taken me longer to realize it, but I'm beginning to see it now. Colton pulls back and rests his forehead against mine. "You can open your eyes now," he whispers.

I slowly open my eyes and look up at Colton, getting lost in his green gaze. He's watching me, waiting for my reaction. Seeing twinkling lights out of the corner of my eye, I turn to the right. My mouth falls open as I look at the scene around me.

I'm standing in the middle of a large garden. Tall flowering plants surround me. A small fountain is located in front of me with water cascading over small ornamental stone angels, leading into a Koi pond with lights on the bottom of it lighting up the fish and giving the angels an ethereal glow. Potted plants, shrubs, and ferns cover everything in sight. A stone path leads further into the garden in front of me. Small LED lights line the path showing the way. The twinkling lights around me are fireflies lighting the night sky. Lights wrap up the bases of all the large trees in the yard and get lost under the mass of leaves.

Colton reaches over and gently closes my mouth. I draw my eyes from the garden and look up at him. Hugging him to me, I say, "It's so beautiful. Thank you for showing it to me." Colton starts walking backward. I let go of my grip around his waist and follow him. He sits down on a cushioned swing and pulls me beside him.

"While you've been working with Colin, Tom, David, and I have been coming down here to clean up the garden and add all the lights. The Howicks helped finish everything up tonight while we were upstairs."

"Why would you do that? We're not staying here for much longer..."

"Because I wanted to see that look on your face—that surprised, completely awed, totally beautiful look." I feel a blush rising on my cheeks from his compliment. "And then the blush that accompanied me telling you that," he laughs.

I lean in his side and continue to admire the scenery around me. "Thank you, Colton."

"There's no need to thank me. You've been working really hard lately. You deserve a little break," he tells me.

I rest my head on his chest and curl my knees up. My eyes follow a firefly in front of me. I reach out and catch it. Opening my fist, I watch as it crawls across my fingers, choosing not to immediately fly away. It's little legs brush against my skin as it moves onto the back of my hand. I feel Colton's eyes on me the entire time. Tearing my gaze away from the little bug, I look up at him.

"What?" I ask him when he continues to watch me. Out of the corner of my eye, I see the firefly fly off, but I don't look away from Colton. He shakes his head and looks over toward the fountain. A small smile forms as he stares ahead. "What are you thinking about?"

"Us," he answers. "The future."

"What about it?"

"I don't know. Nothing. Everything. I think about it all. What I want to happen…how I hope things play out."

"What do you want to happen?" I ask him. Colton tears his eyes from the fountain and looks down at me. He brushes a strand of hair away from my face and leans back on the swing. Using his legs, he gently starts moving it back and forth.

"I want us to get through all of this alive," he starts. I watch him as he speaks. He's trying to keep a smile at bay. "I want to wake up to you in the morning and not worry about whether or not you were attacked in your sleep. I want to watch you open your eyes and look over at me and whisper a good morning as you sit up and stretch and then try to tame your unruly hair." He laughs and turns toward me. "I love your crazy hair," he says as he grabs a curl and twirls it around his finger.

"I want to get down on one knee and propose to you and watch you say yes as tears stream down your face," I scoff at the tears comment even though I know it'll probably happen. "I want to watch you walk down the aisle in a ridiculous white dress and listen to you say I do. I want to go on a honeymoon and finally be able to love you as my wife," he says.

"You want to wait until our wedding night?" I ask.

"Call me traditional," he tells me as he tightens his arm around me. I lean back against his chest and listen to the rest of his vision. "I know that you've always wanted to wait until your wedding night as well," he whispers. It's true. I'm pretty old fashioned when it comes to relationships. "I want to buy a small house on a secluded beach, that's also surrounded by trees. A couple of years after that, I want to start a family. Two kids. Little Coltons or Ryannes running around. It doesn't matter as long as they're healthy.

"I want to watch them grow up and teach them about magic. Help train them. I want to go to all the sports events, school plays, award ceremonies, everything. I want to grow up with you and watch our children grow as well. I want to watch them walk across the stage and receive their diploma and then give my little girl off on her wedding day.

"Most importantly though, I want to make you happy. I want to be the reason why you smile in the morning and have sweet dreams at night. I want to make you laugh until you cry. If I can do that, I don't care about the other stuff. You're my life now Ryanne and if I'm with you, I'll be happy."

"You already make me happy, Colton. I'd probably be going insane right about now if it weren't for you. You're my anchor remember?" Colton removes his arm from my shoulder and rolls up the sleeve on his tight black shirt. I grab his wrist when I see the design wrapping around it.

"You got a tattoo?" I ask him.

"I told you, you've been training a lot," he says. I lightly trace the design around his wrist.

"When did you get it?"

"Two days ago," he answers. I look up at him surprised. He's had this for two days and I haven't noticed. How did I not see it during the training sessions? He wore a tank top then. "You're not the most observant person, Ryanne."

"Apparently not," I mumble. I lightly kiss the anchor and put his arm back around my shoulder. Leaning into him, I listen to all the sounds around me. It's obviously late, but I don't know what time it is specifically. I look up at the stars around me. I could sit outside all night and watch the stars. There's something so amazing about the sky. The world is so vast and each individual is so small. We're like a constellation. On our own, we're not that important. We become important when we work together to create a larger picture—the constellation.

I look toward Colton again. "I want all of that too." He looks at me confused, so I explain further. "That life you talked about…I want all of that too. I want to be your wife and I want to be a mom… someday…in the very far future," I say with a laugh.

The love in his eyes spurs me on, so I continue. "Before I met you, Colton, I had no confidence or self-esteem. I thought that no one would ever want me, and I'd go through life alone." Colton opens to his mouth, but I place a finger on his lips. "Wait a minute, let me finish. Meeting you changed all that. Whenever you look at me, I start to feel beautiful. Your gaze makes my knees go weak and my heart skip a beat." I smile up at him. "I get my strength from your faith in me. You make me feel wanted and you have no idea how good that feels. I've never had many friends and no guy ever seemed interested in me. Now, I have you—my best friend and soulmate.

"I want to wake up every morning in your arms. I love opening my eyes and looking straight into your green ones and want to do that for the rest of my life. I do want to wear a stupid big white dress and walk down the aisle toward you. I want to be able to call you my husband. I want to call myself Mrs. Colton Wagner.

"I don't want to sound clingy or anything, but I don't see a future for me if you're not in it, Colton. Don't do anything to get yourself killed, mister. I'll be very mad at you and I'll find a way to bring you back just so I can tell you how angry at you I am," I poke him in the chest. Colton laughs and kisses my temple.

"The same goes for you, little one."

I groan and lean back against him. "Not you too."

"Sorry, I think it's cute."

"That's what every girl wants to hear."

Colton grabs my chin and turns me toward him. "You're more than just cute, babe."

I smile and lean toward him. "Really?"

He kisses my forehead. "Mhmmm." He kisses the top of my nose. I let out a shaky breath as he whispers, "I think you're stubborn." I attempt to laugh, but it comes out more breathy than I wanted. "You're oblivious." He kisses my cheek. I tilt my head back as he trails kisses across my jaw. "You're funny. Smart. Amazing. Beautiful. Quirky."

"Quirky?" I whisper as he moves toward my ear.

"Mhmmm," his lips brush against my earlobe. I lean closer to him. "And I think you're incredibly sexy without even trying to be." He gently nips at my ear. I groan and melt into him. "I also think that sound is incredibly sexy."

"Colton."

"Yes?" he says as he kisses the spot behind me ear that drives me crazy.

"Kiss me," I demand.

"You're also impatient," he tells me as he moves his lips to mine. I sigh and lean into him. He slowly trails his hand from my shoulder down to the small of my back. His other hand rests on my hip and he gently scoots me closer to him. The kiss is gentler than our previous ones but filled with more love. This will be another one of those moments in our relationship that I'll always remember.

I run my hands through Colton's silky hair and stop at the base of his neck and press him closer to me. He tries to pull back, but I tighten my grip on him. He chuckles against my lips, but kisses me again. "You're also a good kisser," he mumbles to me.

"You're…eh," I sarcastically tell him. He laughs and starts tickling me. I gasp and attempt to scoot away from him, but he holds me in place. "Fine. Fine. You're the best kisser I've ever kissed." He stops tickling me, but keeps one hand on my waist. The other wraps around my shoulder again as he pulls me back against him. "Granted, you're literally the only guy I've ever kissed…"

"I'm glad," he whispers to me.

"Would you be jealous if I had kissed anyone else?" I ask him.

"I don't want to think about that," he says.

I rest my head on his shoulder again and look back out at the garden. "I'm glad you were my first kiss, Colton."

"Me too, Ry."

CHAPTER ELEVEN

COLTON

SOMETHING WET FALLS ON MY cheek. With my eyes closed, I reach up and wipe it away. Another droplet falls on my forehead. Opening my eyes, I brush the water off. I'm outside? I can't tell what time it is because the sky is covered with dark clouds from an impending storm. I look around me and see Ryanne sleeping with her head in my lap with her legs stretched lengthwise against the swing. Someone came outside last night and placed a blanket over her. When the raindrops start to fall harder, I gently try to pick her up without waking her. She sighs in my arms, but doesn't fully wake.

Carrying her back to the house, I tap on the backdoor, hoping someone is awake who can open it for me. If there's no one there, I can manage, but it'll probably wake her up. From inside, I see Tom get up from the kitchen table. "I was about to come get you both. There's a storm coming."

"Thanks for the blanket," I tell him as I walk past him and head into the living room. Sitting down on the couch, I readjust Ryanne on my lap, so she can sleep comfortably.

"That wasn't me. James brought it out for you guys when we realized that you hadn't come back in," he says.

Of course it was him.

A loud pang of thunder echoes outside, but Ryanne jumps up and almost falls off the couch. I reach out and steady her. "Ryanne, Ryanne. Calm down. It's just thunder." She turns toward me, breathing heavily.

"Oh my goodness," she settles down and looks around. "Did we fall asleep here?"

"No, we fell asleep outside, but it started raining, so I brought you in here," I tell her. I struggle to keep down a laugh. Her curls are very crazy this morning. The humidity and wind caused them to thicken. "You're having a crazy hair day," I say as I try to brush some of her curls aside.

Ryanne runs a hand through her hair and looks toward the window. The clouds have thickened. They open up and start to steadily downpour on the world below. Ryanne jumps again as more thunder rumbles. "You're a little jumpy this morning. Are you okay?" I ask her.

She ignores me and continues to watch the window; her shoulders tense when lightning strikes the ground in the distance. I look behind me at Tom, who's just as confused as I am. Reaching around, I force Ryanne to turn toward me. The fear is obvious in her wide eyes as they connect with mine. "Ryanne, what's going on?"

"We need to get out of here," she says as she jumps off the couch and runs up the stairs. I turn around and look at Tom. At the same time, we both jump up and follow Ryanne upstairs. She's banging on everyone's doors. When someone opens the door, she goes onto the next one. Tom and I stop in the hallway and watch Ryanne. David and

Emma sleepily turn toward me questioningly. I shrug. I honestly have no idea what's going on.

Ryanne stops halfway down the hallway and turns around to face me. The rest of the doors in the hallway open up to see what all the noise is about. Biting her bottom lip, she looks down and shakes her head. Her shoulders fall as she runs a hand through her hair. Looking back at everyone in the hallway, a single tear rolls down her cheek. Ry…

"Don't attack. I'll go with you!" she yells.

Who is she talking to? Ryanne walks up to me and grabs my face. Her eyes glisten with more unshed tears. She pulls me down to her and kisses me quickly. All too soon, she pulls away and moves around me, walking toward the stairs again. "I'm so sorry for what I'm about to do," she whispers.

"What's—" A large gust of wind blows through the hallway knocking everyone back a couple of steps. Tom and I are thrown backward from the force. Landing on my back, I instantly sit up and look over at Tom, who's just as confused at what just happened. "She's creating more distance between us," I whisper.

"I knew you'd finally come to your senses," Dravin says as he steps into the hallway. Adam, Natasha, and Valdus all follow after him. Large Gadramicks fill in the hallway behind them and get in a defensive stance. Natalie and Conner gasp when they see their sister. Natasha smiles and waves to her family, but the grin is anything but pleasant. I get up to go to Ryanne, but Tom grabs my arms and holds me back.

"She stepped away from you for a reason, Colton. She most likely had a vision about this," he whispers to me. I stop struggling. Just because he's right doesn't mean I have to like it. Dravin looks past Ryanne, and his eyes land on me.

"Interesting. I vividly remember planting a dagger into your side and watching you bleed out at my compound," he says as he turns back to Ryanne, "which would mean that you—"

"I said I'll go with you. Leave them out of this," Ryanne says to Dravin. The fear is no longer decipherable in her voice. She sounds confident and angry. He moves forward and walks a slow circle around Ryanne. Her body tenses as Dravin trails a hand across her shoulder blade, moving her hair to the side. Tom reaches out and clasps onto my upper arm to keep me from moving.

Liam walks over to me. "What are we going to do?" he whispers.

I have absolutely no idea. I open my mouth to tell him that when my chest tightens. An invisible hand has reached into my chest and squeezed my lungs free of any air. Coughing once, I fall to the ground gasping for breath. Nothing comes to me. Through the indiscernible noise in my ears, I hear whispers about Natasha. I already know this is her doing.

Leaning my arms on the ground, I grunt as my chest tightens further. Hearing Ryanne growl, I look up and through the clouded spots in my vision, I see her whip around and thrust her arm toward Natasha. Her concentration on me is broken when Ryanne sends her flying across the hall. Air suddenly floods back into my lungs and I breathe in, coughing as the organs try to start working again.

When Natasha lands in a heap on the floor, Ryanne turns around and faces Dravin, who also flies to the opposite wall and is pinned there by her magic. He struggles to get free, but is unable to. Ryanne's magic surrounds us as she creates a shield separating them from us. Logan puts a hand out and heals me as he helps me stand. When he finishes, I walk to the edge of the shield and push on it, trying to get her to drop the shield. We could fight if she would let us.

"I told you I would go with you if you left them alone," she says through clenched teeth.

"I did leave them alone, dear. Your little friend over there is the one that attacked them."

"You must not be a very good leader then if they don't listen to you." Dravin growls and struggles to break away from the wall again, but it's useless. Ryanne has grown stronger with all the magic training she's been doing with Colin recently.

What is she doing and why is she doing it? There must be something we can do, but Tom shakes his head. Ryanne's much stronger than us, and there's nothing we can do against her magic. I push away from the shield and start pacing. Emma runs up to me and tells me, "Ryanne must have a plan, Colton."

"No, Ryanne's like freaking Jack Sparrow," I mumble as I walk around Emma and start pacing again. She won't understand that, but those were Ryanne's exact words. She just makes it up as she goes.

Turning around, I watch as she walks over to Natasha. Helping her stand, she pulls her forward and whispers something in her ear, too quietly for anyone else to hear. Natasha's eyes widen, but she doesn't say anything. Ryanne drops her magic from Dravin. His face contorts into an expression I easily recognize as he pushes off the wall and runs over to Ryanne. He forcefully slaps his hand across her face. The force of the impact echoes through the hall that even Natasha gasps at the noise. Liam, David, and Tom all rush over to me. It takes the three of them to hold me back.

Ryanne's head whips to the side, but she doesn't cry out. Slowly, she turns back to Dravin and flips her hair back. A large red welt in the shape of a hand is forming on her cheek. I start struggling again when I see the redness.

"I said I would go with you. There's no need to be violent," she tells him politely. Dravin laughs and turns her around, handcuffing her hands behind her.

"I hope you know those handcuffs really aren't stopping anything. If I wanted to fight you, you'd know," she tells him.

"Oh, I know dear," he whispers loudly in her ear. Ryanne flinches away from his touch. Dravin laughs again and pushes Ryanne toward the stairs.

"Take me with her!" Liam yells as he steps away from me.

"Liam, what are you doing?" Natalie asks him. He walks over to her and pulls her against him, kissing her gently. It looks like more of a goodbye kiss than an 'I'll be back kiss'. Natalie must have felt the same way, because tears start streaming down her face when he pulls away.

"I love you," he whispers to her. A surprised look crosses her face, before she says it back to him. Liam turns back around and faces Dravin again. "Take me with her," he repeats.

All of the Gadramicks stare at Liam in bewilderment because he voluntarily wants to go to Dravin's compound. Ryanne starts shaking her head as she looks at him. Liam nods slightly at her. He'll die if he doesn't go with her. "Do it, Dravin," Valdus tells him. Valdus is the only one who can convince Dravin to let him go. He's the only one who understands what Liam is going through.

Dravin nods, but turns toward Valdus. "If they escape, it's your life." Valdus glances at Liam again and with hesitance in his eyes, he nods.

"I understand."

Liam looks at Ryanne who is now crying. "Drop the shield, Ryanne." She bites her lips and shakes her head again.

"They'll kill you," she whispers to him.

"Then I'll die either way," he tells her. Natalie gasps behind me. Emma goes over to her and tries to comfort her, but it's no use. I understand what Natalie is feeling right now and no amount of comfort will help.

Ryanne turns and looks at everyone, her eyes lingering on Incendia. "Don't try anything. Please," she pleads with us then drops the shield. If she's pleading with us, she knows more than she's letting on. David and Tom tighten their grip on me, but I don't try anything. I promised her that I would try to trust her. Ryanne looks at me again. She mouths, "I love you" to me, and a second later, she spins around and kicks the man holding her in the chest. When he falls backward, a thin lightning bolt materializes out of nowhere and strikes behind Ryanne, separating the metal links of the handcuffs. With her hands free, she moves toward him.

Dravin looks momentarily surprised, but quickly masks that emotion. Ryanne stops in front of him and gets in his face. Poking him in the chest, she says, "If you hurt him, I swear I will kill you."

"I don't think you have it in you to kill, little mage," he taunts. "Would you be able to watch the life drain from someone's eyes? Watch as they take their last breath, and know you are responsible for their pain? No, you're too pure of heart to end someone's life."

Ryanne takes a step forward until she's literally standing against Dravin. Looking up at him, she says through clenched teeth. "I wouldn't tempt me, Dravin. I like to prove people wrong."

Dravin stares down at her for a couple of seconds before pointing toward one of his men. The man standing in the back nods and walks toward Liam, who willingly turns around and lets the man cuff him. Another man on the left side of the room slowly starts moving toward Ryanne. I open my mouth to warn her when she spins around. "I wouldn't try that if I were you."

The man holding the vile of dormirako stops moving toward her. She must have read his mind. Dravin grabs Ryanne's hands while she has his back to him and cuffs her again. Ryanne hisses as he tightens the cuffs too tight, but she doesn't complain. Dravin pushes her toward the stairs as the man moves Liam.

Dravin turns around and looks at Incendia. Winking at her, he disappears down the stairs. Incendia glares at him and attempts to move toward the stairs, but Bragden grabs her around the waist and pulls her against his chest. She fights against him, but Bragden is a lot stronger than her.

"You can't go after him. Not yet," he tells her.

"He knew who I was," she says as she turns around and looks up at Bragden. He still has a hold of her. "He killed the only family I ever knew. I need to go after him. I can't let him get away again," she pleads with him.

"If you go after them, either Ryanne or Liam will get killed. Is that what you want?" he tells her. She sighs and leans her head against his chest, dejected. Incendia is a little under a foot shorter than Bragden. I imagine that's what Ryanne and I look like together.

A loud boom echoes from downstairs, shaking the entire house. I reach out and steady myself on the wall. "Stay here," Tom tells us as he and Colin walk down the stairs. We all turn and look at each other, confused as to what just happened.

Last night was amazing. I sat with Ryanne outside and under the stars, and we talked about our future for the whole night until we both eventually fell asleep. This morning, she's gone.

Tom returns, shaking his head. "They're gone."

"Just like that?" David asks. Larkin and Kyril both cuss. We all turn and look at them. "What?"

"While we worked for Dravin, there were these rumors swirling around that Dravin had found a mage named Zahtri. A mage stronger than all other mages. If they have him, it's not Dravin we have to worry about," Larkin says. "He'd be able to transport large groups like that quickly."

"Why haven't you mentioned this before?" I ask.

"It was just a rumor," Kyril answers.

Colin walks back into the hallway. "Well I'd say that we've got some planning to do."

Bragden reaches up and pulls his necklace off. Natalie and Emma gasp. Incendia tears her eyes from Colin and turns toward Emma and Natalie. She follows their eyes up to Bragden's hands. She instantly starts backing up from Bragden, who's still holding her. Bragden tightens his arm around her waist and hands her the necklace.

"I can't take that Bragden," she tells him.

"I already took the necklace off, Incendia. If you don't accept it..." Bragden trails off.

"You big stupid man. I'm not worth protecting!" she hits him on the chest. Bragden pulls her against him. She gasps as she collides into him and looks up at him. Without hesitating, Bragden crushes his lips to hers. Incendia tries to fight him, but when Bragden's hands moves into her hair, she stops and kisses him back.

I draw my eyes away. Natalie walks over to me and wraps her arms around my waist. I place my arm around her shoulder and take comfort in her embrace. "We'll get them back." She looks up at me. "We have to."

Bragden pulls back and hands Incendia the pendant necklace again. "Now take the stupid necklace." She glances down at the pendant and back up at Bragden—a dazed look still in her eyes. She doesn't say anything, which causes Bragden to act himself. He moves her hair aside and clasps the necklace around her neck.

Incendia pokes Bragden in the chest when he steps backward. "If I get killed and you die because of it, you have no one to blame but yourself!"

"Duly noted," he says with slight amusement.

"So, what are we going to do now?" I ask. Natalie removes her head from my shoulder and turns to look at Tom and Colin. Both Natalie and I just had to watch someone we love be carried away by Dravin.

Tom looks toward me and shakes his head. "If we stand any chance of getting Ryanne or Liam back, we need more help. It's time to start calling everyone. We'll still need more people though."

"We have to go out and find more people while Dravin has Ryanne?" I say. Natalie clears her throat. "And Liam?"

"They're not going to try anything yet. Ryanne just proved that she's stronger than he is. He'll be a little weary around her. He needs to change his plan if he wants any chance of standing up to her. The only thing that worries me is this Zahtri mage," Colin says.

"You're really willing to risk their lives? What if we get more people and this Zahtri has already killed them? Then everything we're about to do will be for nothing," Natalie says.

"We have to stop Dravin and now apparently Zahtri. Ryanne's not weak. She's proven herself so many times. She may look small and fragile, but she's not and you know that. She's fully capable of defending herself, and you know Liam will do everything in his power to make sure she doesn't get hurt. Ryanne knew what she was doing when she went with them. You have to trust her," Tom tells us.

I hate it when he's right.

Incendia turns toward me. "Colton, Ryanne's a beast. She won't take any crap from them anymore. We'll be closer to getting her back if we rally more troops. Now, quit your pouting and man up."

I can already see that Incendia's going to be trouble. Colin claps his hands. "Let's do this then."

CHAPTER TWELVE

I SLAM INTO THE WALL as the Gadramick who was guiding me throws me into yet another cell. "Esh, you don't have to be so forceful. I already said I would go willingly," I mumble. Liam is thrown into the same cell, so they obviously aren't worried about us escaping.

When I hear the sound of the lock turning, I turn toward Liam. "You shouldn't have volunteered to come, Liam. This isn't the Hunger Games. We might not make it out of this,"

"Both Peeta and Katniss made it out of the Hunger Games," Liam retorts.

"But we're not book characters…or movie characters for that matter! I highly doubt you've read the books."

"I'd rather suffer here with you than from miles away knowing that there is nothing I can do. I knew what I was…well not in its entirety, but for the most part, I knew what I was doing when I gave you that pendant. What's going on here, Ryanne? Why didn't you bother fighting? You could have taken them all."

"Dravin's not their leader. He doesn't run the Gadramick's. He's taking orders from someone else," I tell Liam as I sit down, back against the wall. I'd already undone our handcuffs. The metal is still on our wrists, but they aren't connected anymore. "I had a vision. In the vision, I fought and everyone was killed. I watched everyone be killed by something…I didn't see who or what it was, but I couldn't risk it."

Liam sits down next to me and rests his head against the wall, "Dravin's just a figurehead?"

"Yep, he's basically the queen of the Gadramicks."

"I resent that," Dravin says as he storms into our cell. I remain seated and just stare up at him. "Just because you know our little secret doesn't mean anything."

"It doesn't?" I ask him.

"No, because your little posse doesn't know about him. How can they defend themselves against something they don't know about?"

"You said you'd leave them alone."

"I'll leave them undisturbed for now, but you didn't give a timespan to follow. When the time is right, I will lead an attack. Your group has caused too much trouble for me lately. They need to be taught a lesson."

I stand up and glare at him. "I swear to you Dravin. If I find out that you attacked them, I won't hesitate to fight back. I can see it in your eyes. You're scared of me now. You know I'm more powerful than you, but you don't want your men to see it. You still need them to follow you. What are they going to do when they find out it's not even you they're working for? Hmm? That you've been lying to them this whole time?"

"Do you think they'll honestly care that it's not me in charge? Do you think they'll change their minds? They're still fighting for the same goals. Nothing has changed except for who is calling all the shots."

"I don't know what'll happen, but we can easily find out. Is *that* part of his plan?"

*You stubborn, annoying...*I tune out his thoughts when the cursing starts. I smile at him because I know I'm right. An image of him punching me is projected in my mind. I drop to the ground right as he swings his fist out. Liam jumps in front of me before Dravin can attempt to attack again.

"I wouldn't try that again if I were you." Dravin warns me, but stares at Liam for a couple of seconds, before turning around and quietly leaving the room. Liam bends down and helps me stand. "Do you always have to egg him on? Do you like getting slapped?"

"No, I don't have to, but where is the fun in that? And of course, I don't like being slapped. It hurts and makes my face swell, but someone has to stand up to him. No one has ever gone against him. He's a good leader, that's why he was chosen for this, but he's leading for the wrong reasons."

Liam leans back against the wall and crosses his arms. "You're going to be a good leader, Ryanne."

"I don't want to be a leader. I just want all of this to end," I tell him as I walk over to him and rest my shoulder against the wall next to him.

"Fate rarely calls upon us at the moment of our choosing," Liam tells me as he angles himself toward me.

"Transformers: Revenge of the Fallen," I mumble. "You know Colton quoted that to me when I first met him."

"We'll get back to them, Ryanne. You'll see Colton again," Liam pulls me to him and wraps his arms around me.

"And you'll see Natalie again," I promise him as I hug him back.

Of course he has his hands on her.

"Wow, you move on quickly," Adam says as he walks into the cell. I step away from Liam and move toward him.

"What do you want Adam?"

"Dravin requests your presence, Ryanne. Alone."

"Why? He just stormed out of here angry at me."

"Just follow me," Adam says as he turns around and heads toward the door. Liam grabs my arm to keep me from moving. "If you come willingly, we can avoid the cuffs. No one will hurt you if you behave."

"I'll be okay," I whisper to Liam. Liam looks between Adam and me, but releases his grip on me.

"And no one will touch Liam?" I ask as I step toward Adam.

"You're boy toy will be safe," Adam says with a sneer, while opening the door of the cell. As I pass through the doorway, I look over my shoulder at Liam and give him a small smile. I don't know what's going to happen right now, but hopefully Liam will remain as safe as he can get while inside this compound.

"What does Dravin want with me?" I ask Adam. I try to make a mental note of where we're heading, but all the hallways look exactly the same.

"He just wants to talk." An unfamiliar emotion moves through me. I turn and look up at Adam, trying to decipher what he is feeling. He's facial expression is neutral. *Keep your mind blank. Keep your mind blank.* He's chanting to himself.

"What are you trying to hide Adam?" I stop in the middle of the hallway and cross my arms. I'm not going any further until I know what is really going on. Adam keeps walking, but stops when he realizes I'm not following.

"I'm not trying to hide anything," Adam says as he turns and faces me.

"Liar. You keep chanting "keep your mind blank," so forgive me for thinking that you're hiding something."

"You're forgiven. Now come on." He turns around and continues walking down the hallway. I remain frozen in my spot. Adam stops midway down, hangs his head, and groans. He turns around and walks back to me. "Do you have to make everything so difficult?"

"Yes, it's kind of my specialty. Now what are you hiding?"

Instead of answering me, an emotion I recognize crashes into me. I step back and gape at him. "No freaking way." He turns his back to me and continues down the hallway again. I shake my head and follow him. There's no possible way. "You can't be serious," I say to him as I catch up.

"I wish I wasn't," he mumbles as he takes another left.

"I don't understand."

"People do crazy things when they're in love," he whispers to me as he picks up the pace. I have to jog to keep up with him.

"That is no excuse. Did you even feel any bit of guilt for what you did to me?" I ask as I run in front of him and stop. He stares down at me for a couple of seconds before looking at something over my head. I look behind me and watch as a Gadramick walks past, eyes zoned in on me the entire time. Adam takes a step closer to me and glares at him, giving him a silent warning. When he's out of hearing range, I look back up at Adam, waiting for him to respond.

"Not at first. It was all fun and games at first," he tells me with the shake of his head. I still don't understand.

"When did it stop being fun and games?"

Adam steps around me and grabs the door handle. Opening a door, he gestures for me to go inside. I stare at him for a couple seconds, before heading toward the door. As I walk past him, he whispers. "When you told me you weren't afraid of death."

I stop and stare up at him. That happened a while ago…before I healed Colton. Now that I think about it, all the confrontations after that moment with him seemed strange. He didn't seem to fight back outside of Jane's house—not enough to cause any damage. I didn't hear him when I was pulled into the dream world either. I knew he was there, but wasn't as involved as he was prior to that incident. "Well come in. Don't just stand in the doorway," Dravin says. I look away from Adam toward him. He's sitting behind a desk, watching me.

"What's going on?" I ask him. Without saying anything to either of us, Adam turns around and leaves me alone with Dravin.

"So impatient. Sit."

I heed his command. Even though I know that Dravin's not the one in charge, I know that I'm still in trouble here. There's two mages against a whole compound of Gadramicks. I can only push my luck so far. "What's this about?" I ask.

"I need to take another blood sample from you. I'd rather you cooperate with me so I don't have to give you more dormirako."

"You want me to give you permission to take my blood to see if you can extract my magic?" I ask. "Are you crazy?"

"I don't think it's possible for your magic to be extracted anymore, but we have to run one last test. Since we were able to find you, your enchantment is no longer up. For some reason, Zahtri wants you alive. Now, I'm not one to listen to authority, but he's one that even I don't want to go against."

"What if I say no?"

"Then we'll have to get creative, now won't we?"

I stare at Dravin. I don't really see a way around this. Giving them some of my blood will give me a little time to come up with a plan on how to get out of here. "Fine."

"Really? Just like that? No arguing?"

"I may be stubborn, Dravin, but I'm not stupid." Dravin watches me for a moment, before calling for Adam.

When Adam walks into the room, Dravin tells him to take me to Dr. Arden. When I don't move, Adam grabs my elbow and pulls me out of the room. I yank my arm away the second we get out of Dravin's office.

"I can walk on my own. Everyone is always dragging me places when I'm fully capable of walking myself. I'm not some helpless weak girl, you know."

"Yeah, I know," he says as he leads me down the halls again. I jog to keep up with him. I try to read his mind again, but he's repeating the chant again.

"I think I liked the jerky, aggressive, and overly cocky Adam better than this silent, brooding one."

"Believe me, I liked him better too."

"Why are you working for the Gadramicks, Adam? Honestly." Adam stops outside of two glass doors. On the other side, people wearing white labs coats are rushing around. Everyone is holding something: a syringe, needle, stethoscope, etc. It's obvious that they are testing something.

Adam chooses to ignore my question. He opens the door to the lab and ushers me inside. I instantly recognize Dr. Arden in the crowd. He's flipping through some papers attached to a clipboard. His dark curly hair is falling in his face. Adam places a hand on the small of my back and pushes me further into the room. When he clears his throat, Dr. Arden looks up from his clipboard and looks directly at Adam. His eyes quickly move from Adam and land on me.

"She's agreed to give you another blood sample," Adam states.

"You agreed?"

"Yep. So let's stab my arm and get this over with. I have a lovely concrete cell calling my name."

"You have your mother's attitude," Dr. Arden says while trying to hide a small smile.

"Don't talk about my mom. You abandoned us, *doctor*," I enunciate the doctor at the end of the sentence. This man means nothing to me. I grew up without a father and there's no way in hell I'm going to start believing that he's it.

Dr. Arden walks over to me, grabs my arm and gently guides me to a chair. "Always dragging me somewhere," I mumble as I sit down. Dr. Arden lifts my shirt sleeve up and wipes some disinfectant on my arm. I grimace and focus on the wall to my left.

"You're squeamish at the sight of blood?" Adam asks me.

I wince as I feel the needle pierce my skin. "The needle. Blood. The whole thing. It's not my cup of tea." I look at my arm and squeak when I see the blood coming out of it.

"Don't look at it, and it won't be so bad," Jedrek tells me.

"Don't tell me what to do." Both he and Adam chuckle at me, but neither says anything else. I look around the room. Nothing looks too suspicious. There are a lot of blood samples in a cabinet to my right. I wonder whose blood that is.

"Okay, you have enough. Take the needle out of me," I demand after a few minutes.

"You know, I don't like doing any of this either," Jedrek tells me as he takes the needle out. He wraps a bandage around my arm and forces me to look at him. "Some of us weren't given a choice."

I stand up and look him straight in the eyes. "Except you were. You made the wrong choice when you decided to fight fate."

Without waiting for Adam, I walk out of the room and head down one of the hallways. I have no idea where I'm going, but I don't want to be near him right now. I know that he's not actually bad, but I still have a right to be angry at him. Adam runs out of the room and grabs my arm, halting my progress. I fall backward into his chest before I can steady myself.

"If anyone sees you walking alone, they won't hesitate to attack you. Their emotions for you run from hatred, to anger, to lust. You need to stay with me if you want to remain safe. No one will go against me."

"They wouldn't know what hit them if they went against me," I tell him.

"That may be true, but some of the Gadramicks here are more powerful than you would guess. I wouldn't push your luck, Ryanne." Another surge of warm feeling hits me as Adam looks down at me. A need to protect me is written all over his face. Adam is very conflicted and I want nothing to do with it. I take a step back, creating distance between the two of us.

"Take me back to Liam."

With a sigh, he turns around and starts walking in the opposite direction. Of course I went the wrong way. I follow after him, not trying to quiet my steps. I'm frustrated and I want everyone to know it.

Adam stops in front of my cell door and looks back at me. I avoid eye contact and cross my arms, waiting for him to open it. I want to make sure Liam is safe—that they kept their promise. Adam sighs when I refuse to look at him and unlocks the cell door, gesturing me inside.

Walking through the doorway, my eyes immediately land on Liam sitting against the wall with his left arm propped against his knee. His head snaps up when I enter the cell, and I let out a sigh of relief when I see he's in the same condition he was when I left. They didn't try anything. His eyes linger on the bandage on my right arm before flickering up to Adam in the doorway with an angered look crossing his expression. I walk over to Liam as Adam closes and locks the door behind him without saying anything to either of us.

"What happened?" he asks me when we're alone. He grabs my arm and looks at the bandage before looking back at me.

"They took some more of my blood." I sit back against the wall and close my eyes. I'm not sure how long we've been here. A couple hours at least, so it's probably around mid-afternoon by now. Liam's stomach growls loudly when he sits down next to me. "I'm sorry Liam. They've never given me food here before, so I wouldn't count on it," I tell him.

"What's wrong?" he asks me. I sigh and lean my head on his shoulder. Liam can always tell when something is going on with me.

"I don't like it. Dravin and Adam are kind of being civil…it's creeping me out. They're planning something and I'm going to find out what it is before it's too late."

CHAPTER THIRTEEN

COLTON

"DO YOU THINK LIAM WILL try to contact one of us?" Natalie asks me as I throw our bags in the back of the car. Shutting the trunk, I walk around to the passenger side of the vehicle and open the door, ushering her inside. She sits in the middle and turns toward me, waiting for my response.

"I sure hope so," I tell her as I get in. Natalie leans her head on my shoulder again and sighs. They've only been gone a couple of hours now, but it's already been too long. I wrap my arm around her shoulder, attempting to comfort her. We're the only ones who understand what the other is going through right now.

"I've called everyone. They're all meeting us in Whiteshire. We'll formulate a plan afterwards. Everyone is contacting someone else, so we'll have a little more than we were expecting," Tom announces.

"But will it be enough?" I ask.

"I'm not sure." I flinch as the honesty in his voice. "We're not really sure what we're up against right now, Colton, so we don't know how many people we need."

"We're going to get them back," Bragden says. I'm going to do anything and everything in my power to make that statement true. They will not stay at Dravin's compound for long.

I sit back and stare out the window, trying to keep my mind from wandering. I can't think about what they are experiencing there...what Ryanne could be going through again. If I do, I'll go invisible, and I need to stay visible right now.

The trees outside the window blur together from the movement of the car. The yellows, oranges, reds, and greens stream together as we pass. Ryanne would love this scenery for she loves the outdoors. There were many times when I caught her just staring out a window, watching the woods. At first, I thought she was daydreaming or lost in her thoughts, and while that was the case some of the time, I realize now that she was just appreciating nature.

"How long will it take to get to Whiteshire?" I ask Tom. "I want to get this over with as soon as possible. They don't need to be there any longer."

"It'll take two hours to get there and then we'll have to spend a couple hours coming up with a plan. We won't be able to do anything tonight, Colton. I'm sorry."

I clench my first and stare out the window. Natalie grabs onto my arm and attempts to keep me calm. It's working to keep me visible, but it doesn't keep my mind from thinking about what is going on.

"Colton, we're here," Natalie shakes me awake.

I open my eyes and groggily try to assess my surroundings. When I see Natalie looking at me, everything comes back to me. I jump up and get out the car, and shortly after, everyone else follows. We're parked in another high end hotel parking lot. I go to the back of the car and take my duffle bag. I see Ryanne's duffle lying off to the side. Natalie walks up behind me and grabs her bag and Liam's. She shrugs and walks back toward Tom. I grab Ryanne's bag and follow her.

"Is everyone here?" I ask him.

"There are a lot here already. Everyone else will arrive later tonight or early tomorrow morning."

"So you think we'll be able to get to them by tomorrow?" Natalie asks.

"Let's talk with everyone and see what they think we should do. There's a lot at stake here. We don't want to rush into a compound full of Gadramicks unprepared."

"Okay," Natalie says dejectedly. I pull her after me as we enter the hotel lobby. Tom goes up to the front desk and gets our room keys. He called ahead of time and reserved rooms. We basically have an entire floor for all the mages and have the ballroom reserved for a couple nights. There's plenty of space for everyone.

"We'll call a meeting as soon as we get settled," Tom announces as he hands out the room keys. Since Ryanne isn't here, I have to share a room with Logan. Lily, Natalie, and Incendia are all sharing a room together.

Taking the elevator up to the third floor, I follow Logan slowly down the hallway. I know that I won't be able to sleep tonight, so it doesn't matter where I am. Logan unlocks the door and claims the bed near the window. I drop my stuff along with Ryanne's bag on the bed and sit down on the edge.

"We are going to find a way to get them back, man. Don't worry. We won't let them stay there for too long," Logan assures me.

"I just wish there was a way I could find out how she is doing. To see if anything is happening to her. I don't like not knowing what is going on and being left in the dark."

"Liam will find a way to contact us if something were to happen to her. You have to trust him," Logan tells me.

"I do trust Liam," I tell him. "It's Dravin and Adam that I don't trust. And now she's at that compound with some Zahtri person who's stronger than both of them put together."

"Ryanne's just as strong. You've seen what she can do, Colton. I doubt she needs us to go against him, but she can't go against a whole compound alone which is what she needs us for. If Dravin or Zahtri wanted Ryanne dead, she would be. They're keeping her alive for something. We have to get to her before that something occurs."

"Then let's start this meeting. The sooner the better."

Gathering in the large ballroom, we all help push the tables to the far end of the room. We leave the chairs out for everyone to sit in, but the tables aren't necessary. Honestly, I doubt people will sit down anyway. We all understand what is going on. As we work, no one says anything. The only sounds coming from the room are the scraping of the metal chairs against the tiled flooring.

I lean against one of the tables. I can't believe this is happening. The prophecy is unraveling right before our eyes. Everything we've ever been told growing up is coming true. I've met and fallen in love with the girl that's supposed to end all this mess. I'm more involved in this battle than I ever thought I would be. We're all more involved in this prophecy than we ever believed we would be.

Knowing what I am thinking about, Natalie walks over to me and squeezes my hand. I look down at her and do my best to smile. "I have a good feeling about this, Colton. We're doing what we're supposed to be doing," she tells me.

"Are you sure about that?"

"Have a little faith. We won't accomplish anything if we don't have faith. Ryanne believes in this cause and I do too. They wouldn't want us to sit here and worry about them. We have to have faith if we are ever going to see them again."

Hearing the truth in her words, I squeeze her hand and look around the room, watching everyone move around. Bragden and Conner are pushing the last of the tables against the wall. Logan and Lily are unstacking all the chairs, quietly talking to each other, while everyone else continues working on putting the chairs out.

I walk over to Tom as people start entering the room. I see some familiar faces in the crowd: the Prowlers, Mr. Thalland, a few distant relatives that I've only ever seen during family get-togethers. I recognize many faces from our first fight with Dravin, but there are more that I don't know. Tom wasn't kidding when he said that everyone was bringing someone else. Over a hundred people enter the ballroom. There aren't enough chairs for everyone; many mages are left standing in the back.

This could actually work. This could be the miracle we need. Dravin won't expect our numbers to be so high, and he definitely won't be prepared for us to counter an attack so soon. He thinks that he still has time, so he won't know what's hit him until it's too late.

"Did you know there was going to be this many people?" I ask Tom without taking my eyes from the still growing crowd in front of me. From my peripherals, I see Tom cross his arms across his chest and shake his head.

"I didn't, but this could work. We're already a step closer to rescuing them, Colton. We have the numbers. Now all we need is the plan."

I watch as a couple of teenage boys push through the doors and quickly scan the room. "Lucas!" Incendia shouts from across the room runs toward the doorway.

Lucas's smile widens when he sees Incendia rushing toward him and catches her as she runs into him. My eyes instantly find Bragden and even I can't help but smile when I see the scowl forming on his face. I understand that feeling.

Logan is standing near Bragden still talking to Lily. She laughs at something he says, and he smiles just seeing her reaction, but his gaze shifts to the door. His smile grows at what he sees. Lily looks away from him and towards the door as well. Logan's parents, my aunt and uncle, walk into the room and instantly look for their son. Telling Lily something, Logan starts pushing through the crowd and hugs his parents when he manages to get past everyone. Looking in Lily's direction, I catch her watching Logan. Logan says something to his parents and both of them glance in her direction, smiling when they see her. Feeling uncomfortable with the sudden stares, Lily turns away and moves toward Emma.

Natalie, whose hand I'm still holding, and Conner, who is standing behind me, both gasp as their parents walk into the room. Releasing my hand, Natalie runs toward her dad and jumps into his arms. Conner, on a much calmer scale, walks up to his mom and hugs her.

Turning toward the room, Tom shouts, "Can I have everyone's attention?" All eyes in the room turn and look in our direction. Natalie walks back up and stands beside me. The rest of our group stands slightly behind. "You all know why you are here today. We need your help. Ryanne is back in the hands of the Gadramicks and we need to rescue her. Her protector, Liam, followed her there. "

"How did she get captured again?" a girl asks from the back of the room. The tone of her voice says all I need to hear.

"Ryanne wasn't captured again. She went with them to protect all of us," I tell her. She smirks and looks down at the ground. "What is your name?" I ask her.

"Violet."

I recognize her from somewhere. "Were you at the last fight with Dravin?" She nods at me. That's where I've seen her. "You were the girl that Ryanne saved from Thomas." When the color starts draining from her cheeks, I know the answer. Violet stares down at the ground again, but nods. "Then, you should understand what Ryanne's like. She'll do anything to protect others. If any of you were at that battle, Ryanne saved you all. Doesn't she deserve that same courtesy too?

"You've all heard about the prophecy. Ryanne has proven to all of us multiple times that she's truly the girl mentioned in it. There's no refuting that once you've met her. She's everything we need in a leader. She's strong, fearless, and selfless. She puts the needs of everyone above her own. She's the most strong-willed, determined and loyal person you'll ever meet.

"Right now, that girl, my soulmate, is in the hands of the Gadramicks. She has her magic, but is way outnumbered. She's not stupid, so she won't fight her way out of it. She needs us, every last one of us, to help her. She won't ask for any help, but that doesn't mean she doesn't need it. Now, I'm going to go to Dravin's compound, with or without your help. However, we have a greater chance of being successful if you join us," I finish and look over at Tom. The room is silent as everyone takes in my words.

Natalie squeezes my arm, reassuring me and pushing calming magic into me. Why is no one saying anything? No one even reacts. They all just stare. "You said all that you could," she whispers to me. "The rest is up to them."

Tom takes a step forward. "There's one more thing you should know." Mumbling fills the room. Everyone looks around the room, wondering what Tom could be referring to. He waits until everyone quiets again before continuing. "Dravin's not in charge of the Gadramicks. They have someone more powerful calling all the shots."

Everyone starts talking at once. "What are you talking about?"

"How is that possible?"

"It can't be true. We've fought against him before!"

Tom shouts for everyone to be quiet. Hearing the harshness in his tone, the room falls silent. He doesn't yell unless it's absolutely necessary. "A mage named Zahtri is actually in charge of the Gadramicks. For some reason, he wants his identity to remain a secret until the most opportune moment. Ryanne had a vision about him and that's why she told Dravin she would go with them. She was protecting us all. The only way we can stop all of this is if Ryanne is with us. She's the only one powerful enough to go against Zahtri," Tom pauses and looks around the room, making eye contact with as many people as possible. "Will you help us on our rescue mission?"

CHAPTER FOURTEEN

I CAN HEAR SLIGHT RUFFLING around me—the sound of fabric scratching and snagging against a hard rough surface. Pulling my knees up, I try to asses my surroundings before I open my eyes. My face is resting against a hard surface, but it isn't hard enough to be the concrete flooring. Something is moving the ends of my hair. Not finding any immediate sources of danger, I open my eyes with hesitance and find that I'm lying in a cell in Dravin's compound with my head in Liam's lap and the rest of me sprawled on the cool, concrete flooring.

I push myself up into a seated position and attempt to stretch. There's not a whole lot I can do though; my body is way too stiff from sleeping on the hard floor. As I move, Liam lets go of a strand of my hair. At my questioning look, he replies, "I understand Colton's fascination with your hair."

"His fascination?" I wasn't aware that Colton had a fascination with my hair.

"Yeah, he loves your hair." He says as he wraps another curl around his index finger, staring intently at the end of my hair.

"Well, he can have it. I was thinking about cutting it anyway. The longer it gets the curlier it becomes."

"Don't cut your hair," Adam says as he enters our cell. He glances at me before giving Liam a glaring look which he returns. Honestly, if I didn't know either of them, I'd be more afraid of Liam than Adam. Liam's general appearance makes him more intimidating.

"Will you two stop being stupid? Adam, is there a reason why you barged into our lovely cell on what I'm assuming is a bright and shining morning?" I ask him politely. Liam releases the strand of hair and it bounces back into place. I catch a small smile from him at the movement, but he doesn't take his eyes off of Adam.

"I'm supposed to make sure you didn't escape during the night," he tells me.

I stare at him blankly. "Couldn't you have just done that through the window?" I say as I point to the small window in the door.

"Yes, I could have," he says. But? He's still glaring at Liam. *What does he have that I don't?*

I look between Adam and Liam again. Adam is jealous of Liam? I bite my lip to keep from smiling. This just keeps getting better and better.

"Adam, will I get killed if I ask to go to the restroom?" He stares at me incredulously. "What? Has Dr. Arden found a way to cure the need for bathroom breaks or something? I could always pull the *I'm on my period* card."

"She's cooperated so far. Take her. Then get them some food afterwards. I need her today," Dravin says as he passes our cell.

"That can't be good," I mumble as Dravin leaves. Adam glances down at me before turning around and leaving the room. I glance over my shoulder back at Liam who looks as worried as I feel.

"Are you guys coming? I wouldn't expect this kindness from him for too long," Adam yells from the hall. I grab Liam's arm and pull him after me.

"What was that about?" Liam whispers to me.

"I'll explain later." Adam stops in front of a bathroom and opens the door. He walks in and once he determines that it's empty. He signals for me to go inside. "You'd just walk inside of the girl's restroom like that?"

"Ryanne, there's literally only two other girls here, and one of them has you on the top of her hit list. Zahtri and Dravin need you alive right now. It'd mean my death if either one of them got to you."

"I can take care of myself, thank you very much," I say as I walk into the bathroom. I slam the door behind me. This is getting ridiculous. I quickly scan the room. There's no way to exit other than the door I just came through. Dang. I take care of my business, wash my hands, and join Adam and Liam again. I don't trust those two together for long.

I walk out and see Adam and Liam arguing. I was seriously gone for two minutes. What could they be arguing about?

"I'm her protector! It's my job to protect her. Not yours."

"If I weren't here, she'd have been attacked already. None of these guys will hesitate if they see her. They either think that she a killer, standing in the way of the plan, or they think she's hot. Any way will result in her getting hurt. Is that what you want? Your best bet is to let me help you guys."

I lean back against the wall and wait for the guys to stop arguing. This could take a while. They haven't even noticed I'm right here. I could stop them, but this is more interesting.

"Why the heck would you want to help? You've attacked her enough times yourself. I've had to see her wake up with cuts, bruises, and broken bones because of you. She had nightmares you were going to kill her. Is that how you want to protect her? By scaring her?"

"I've changed," Adam says.

Liam obviously doesn't like that answer. "You've changed?"

"Yeah, I have. I'm not the same guy that attacked her before."

"I highly doubt that. It's not possible to change that drastically overnight."

I look down the hallway and spot Jedrek working in the lab room that I was in yesterday. I glance toward Liam and Adam. Neither of them are focusing on me, so I quietly move down the hallway, and pause in front of the glass doors. There's no one in the lab with him. Yesterday, the room was bustling with people and now, it's practically empty.

Soundlessly, I push open the door and walk in. I still don't know how to regard this man. He's my dad, yes, but he's also the man that abandoned me before I was born. He wanted nothing to do with me, and every time I see him that thought is in the back of my mind.

He's not aware that I'm here yet, so I clear my throat. Jumping slightly, he reorganizes the papers on his clipboard and looks over his shoulder. His startled expression calms when he sees me, but shortly afterwards, his eyes widen. His gaze moves past me and lands on Liam and Adam arguing in the hall. With his mouth set in a straight line and a shake of the head, he tells me, "You shouldn't be walking around here alone, Ryanne. It's not safe."

"Did you get my blood results back?" The words come out of my mouth before I can stop them. Similarly, my feet take a few steps closer to him. He just stares at me as I move; this obviously wasn't what he was expecting at my random appearance. I think he's expecting me to yell and get mad at him.

"Yes," he answers without looking away from me. Stopping beside him, I look down at the microscope he's working on. There's a drop of blood on the slide he's examining.

"Is that mine?" With a nod, he steps back and gestures for me to examine it. I lean down and look into the microscope. I don't really know what blood looks like under a microscope, but I don't think this is normal. It looks like someone dumped glitter all over the slide. I have glittery blood. I bet fairies would have glittery blood...do fairies exist? I step back and look at him. "That's not normal."

"No, it's not," he tells me as he grabs a clipboard. He shows me a picture of a normal person's blood. It just looks like a bunch of small reddish-pink circles. He walks to the opposite side of the room and unlocks a cabinet. He grabs a slide and walks back to me. The slide has a drop of blood from a mage. It looks more like mine than the humans, but mine contains more glittery specks.

"Your blood is an enigma. Your magic is concentrated in your blood stream, but you can push it out unlike most mages. There's no way to extract it from the blood cells. It's like a magnet, except there's no way to pull the two apart." He points to the glitter. "Your blood is overwhelmed with the magic. You have more magic in you than blood, but it's not affecting you physically which is amazing. I don't know what to think of it," he tells me.

"So my blood is an anomaly?" I ask.

"Pretty much," he tells me. While he's looking down at his clipboard, I study him. As much as I hate to admit it, we do look a lot alike. We have to same dark curly hair and light eyes. We share the same straight nose and full lips. I watch as he scrunches his features when he's concentrating. I know for a fact that I do because Colton can always tell when I'm over thinking something. Jedrek tears his eyes away from the clipboard and looks over at me.

I bite my lip and look away, bringing my eyes back to the papers in his hands. The bright lights shine off a piece of glossy paper clipped in the back. As I look closer, I realize that it's actually a photograph. The familiar tingling sensation starts again in my stomach the longer I look at this photo. I need to know what it is. I reach forward and pull it out. A tiny white cat is staring back at me. Seeing the light blue eyes in the picture causes my stomach to tighten.

"What's this?" I ask him while showing him the photo.

"Umm," *How much should I tell her?*

"The truth."

"I sometimes forget that you can read my mind."

"Why do you have a picture of this cat?"

"After we started the magic extraction process, we needed to test to see if we could inject magic into other beings. If we couldn't, the extraction would be useless. We didn't want to just inject magic into anyone's bloodstream, because we weren't sure what the repercussions were going to be, so we started off with animals."

"You mean *you* didn't want to inject magic into anyone. Dravin doesn't care about what happens to anyone but himself."

She's smart. "You're correct. I didn't want to cause any harm to anyone where it wasn't necessary."

"So you injected magic from mages into this cat?"

"Yes, but the results were inconclusive. The animals didn't act any different. There were no identifiable results. They didn't react to the foreign blood in their bloodstream."

"So, you're the reason why I can read her thoughts," I mumble as I look back down at the small Polaroid.

"What?"

"This is my cat, Olive."

"And you can read her thoughts?" I look back up at him. Now I'm the one who doesn't know how much to tell. "Amazing."

I open my mouth to tell him to keep it quiet when he stops me. "I'm not going to change anything. The results were still inconclusive,

Ryanne." I let out a sigh of relief. I don't want them performing anymore tests on anyone else: animals or mages.

The room descends into silence. I hand the picture of Olive back to Jedrek. He clips it back under the stack of papers. *She's so beautiful. Reminds me of Maureen.*

I flinch and bite my lip. I thought I could handle talking to him, but I can't. I can feel the tears welling up in my eyes. "Ryanne, I wouldn't have left if I knew about you. Maureen never told me she was pregnant," he states.

"When did you find out about me?" I ask. I glance toward the door. Liam and Adam are standing on opposite ends of the hall. Both are trying to be discreet, but I know they are watching me. I look back to Jedrek.

He diverts his eyes and glances toward the door as well. Turning around, he leans against the counter and hugs the clipboard to his chest. "When you were two," he answers honestly. He's known about me for sixteen years and never once tried to contact me at all?

I can't...I try to keep the tears at bay as I turn to leave the room.

"Ryanne, wait," he reaches out and grabs my forearm. "You don't understand."

"Then explain it," I yell. "Explain why you abandoned us. Explain why my mom had to raise me all by herself. Explain why I had to watch all the other kids grow up with a mom and a dad and always wonder why I didn't have that. Why I thought there was something wrong with me because my family was different. Explain why you knew about me and still didn't want me."

He just stares at me. I can feel the tears streaming down my cheeks. Jedrek reaches forward to wipe them away, but I take a step back, not giving him the opportunity to comfort me. Sadness and confusion washes off of him, but he doesn't say anything. There's no excuse for what he did. I turn around and exit the lab, leaving him there to watch me walk away from him. I rush past Liam and Adam in the hall and go straight into my cell. I'm not hungry anymore and don't care if I don't get food anytime in the near future. I want to see Colton. I want to cry on his shoulder and feel him wrap his arms around me as he tries to comfort me, but that's not possible. I don't know if it will ever be possible again.

Liam walks into the cell and immediately pulls me to him. I go willingly, but it's not the same as when Colton comforts me. "Ryanne, talk to me," Liam says. I shake my head and let my tears fall onto his shirt.

"I miss Colton," I mumble. I hear the door close behind us, which either means that Adam is standing in the doorway or that he's just outside of it.

"You'll see him again, Ryanne." I stand back and look up at him. Out of the corner of my eye, I see Adam standing in the doorway. He's staring off in the distance, trying to look like he's not listening, but his thoughts tell me otherwise.

"No, I won't. Don't you get that? They're going to keep us here, so that the prophecy is never fulfilled. There's nothing we can do about it. Someday Zahtri is going to decide that it's pointless to keep me alive and he'll kill me, which means that you'll die as well because you gave me this stupid necklace. I've dragged you down with me," I lean my head against his chest. "I'm so sorry, Liam."

"Ryanne," Liam states and leans back, moving me so that I'm looking straight at him. "Don't you dare think like that. Ever."

"Why? I'm thinking realistically, Liam. It's about time you start doing it too."

"Have faith in our family. Have faith in Colton." A warm feeling spreads through me when I hear him mention *our* family.

"I don't want to have faith in him. I don't want him to come here, because despite them acting civil toward us, they won't hesitate to kill him. They've killed him before and you were there to witness that. I'd rather stay here and rot than know that he died trying to rescue me, because at least he'd still be living."

"Ryanne, everything will play out like it should. Don't worry."

"Worry is my middle name," I mumble.

"I thought it was stubborn," Liam says as he wipes the tears away from my face.

"I have two middle names."

I don't see how this situation could get worse. If I attack, they'll find a way to get to everyone and use them against me. Colton is probably planning some insane rescue mission. If the roles were reversed, I know that's what I would be doing. This compound is run by Gadramicks who aren't afraid to fight for what they believe in, and if Colton were to come here, he'd be killed instantly. There's no light at the end of the tunnel right now.

Wow, she's deep in her thoughts. Knowing that I just missed something, I glance toward Adam. "Would you like some food?" he repeats. I shake my head and sit down on the ground. Leaning my head against the wall, I close my eyes and attempt to tune out the slight headache I'm getting.

"You need to eat."

"Adam, I've gone a week without eating. Thank you very much," I mumble. That happened to me the first time I was at this stupid compound with these Gadramicks. They refused to give me any food or water unless I cooperated. Since stubborn is my middle name, I never got anything to eat. Adam was there, so he should know all about that.

"I would think you wouldn't want to go through that again."

"You'd think that, wouldn't you?" I retort.

"Fine, if that's what you want."

"Adam," Liam calls.

"Yeah, yeah. I know," he replies as he slams the door. I can hear footsteps walking down the hall, so I know that he actually left this time.

"We're not going to get out of here alive, are we Liam?" I ask. "I want an honest answer. I'll know if you're lying to me."

Liam sighs and sits down beside me. I lean my head on his shoulder. He moves so that he can wrap his arm around my shoulder and pulls me into his side. Before Colton, I used to sit like this with Liam all the time. It's comfortable and familiar. "I don't know, Ryanne. I'm honestly going to do everything in my power to make sure we do though."

CHAPTER FIFTEEN

COLTON

"SO, WE'RE HEADING OUT IN two days?" Natalie asks Tom; the hope in her voice is obvious.

"We're going to get them back, Natalie. If we can get everyone together in two days, then yes, we'll head out then. I don't want to leave them there any longer than necessary either. We don't know what the Gadramicks are planning."

"They've been gone for two days already, Tom," I tell him. "Two days more is all I'm waiting. I can't let her stay there for any longer. This is already pushing it. She was gone a week before and you saw what she looked like when she returned."

"I don't think they're going to hurt her this time. Something is different."

"Why hasn't Liam contacted us? That's what I want to know. He has to know how worried we are," Natalie says as she paces the room. Since our first meeting, about fifty more people have shown up. Our odds are looking much better with each passing day. However, the chance of Ryanne and Liam's safety dwindles as more time passes.

"I don't know. I'd like to know that too," I reply as I hear my phone ring in my bag across the room. I look around confused. All the people who would contact me are in this room.

I pull the phone out and grimace as I read the caller I.D. "Who is it?" Tom asks.

"Jane," I say as I answer. Jane and I exchanged numbers when she stayed with us overnight after Ryanne saved her and Ross. She's worried about Ryanne and wanted me to keep her updated…and I've neglected to do that so far.

"Colton, is that you?" I hear her say before I even get the phone up to my ear.

"Yes."

"Is Ryanne there? She won't answer any of my texts or calls. Is she okay?"

I look toward Tom. How much should I tell her? "Tell her, Colton. She deserves to know."

"Oh my god, what do you have to tell me? She's not dead is she? I swear—"

"She's not dead, Jane. Calm down."

"Then what's wrong with her? Where is she? Why hasn't she answered?"

"Dravin has her." I go on to explain everything. "We're doing everything we can to get her back. We're going to get her, Jane." I hear silence on the other end. "We are going to rescue her."

"Don't let anything happen to her, Colton," Jane whispers.

"I'm going to do everything I can to make sure she comes back to us, I promise." Jane sniffs on the other end. I know she's crying, but there's nothing I can really do to help her.

"I know you will. Thank you for telling me. Please keep me updated, Colton. I need to know."

"I will. Stay safe, Jane." She hangs up without saying goodbye, and I end the call. I can't believe none of us thought to alert Jane before this.

"We have to get her back," I mutter as I lean back against the bed. I haven't gotten any sleep the past two nights. I toss and turn wondering what's happening at Dravin's compound. Is she hurt? What's she experiencing? There are too many unknowns and I need answers before I can even think about getting my much needed sleep.

I close my eyes as Tom and Colin talk over further plans. I rest my head against the wooden headboard of the bed. I'll just rest for a couple of minutes. I feel the bed dip down beside me, but I'm too far gone to see who it is.

"Colton?" I open my eyes. I'm sitting on the small wooden bench in the garden behind Colin's house. I stand up and look behind me. Ryanne's standing behind the bench, staring at me confused.

"Ryanne?" I ask her. Her eyes widen when I say her name. She runs forward, jumps over the bench, and barrels into me. I catch her in my arms, wrapping them tight against her small waist. Her floral scent knocks into me as I bury my face into the crook of her neck.

"I've missed you," she whispers against my neck.

"I've missed you too." I pull back, but keep her in my arms. "Ryanne, are you safe? Are they hurting you? You need to tell me."

She looks up at me and sighs. "They're not intentionally hurting me. Dravin's trying to get me to use my magic, so he keeps trying to get me to fight these Gadramicks. I'm only defending myself, physically. I'm not infusing any magic, so they are able to overpower me extremely fast. Dravin stops the fight before I get too hurt, but some of the men take advantage of the situation."

I lean my forehead down against hers. She's not being beaten…so-to-say. Ryanne attempts to make herself taller. She snakes her arms around my waist and leans against me

"You don't know how good it feels to just be near you. I don't like being away from you," she whispers. She leans her head up and her lips brush against mine. "I can't sleep. I can't eat. I can't do anything because I'm so worried about you guys."

I lean forward and lightly kiss her. Ryanne sighs and melts into me. It feels so good to hold her like this—to feel her body pressed against mine, the taste of her against my lips. "Ryanne," I whisper.

"Mmmmhmmm," she says without pulling back.

I kiss her lightly once more and pull back. It takes all of my willpower to pull away from her, especially when she's pressed up against me like this…kissing me like that. "How is this possible?" I ask. "How am I talking to you right now?"

Ryanne takes a step back and bites her bottom lip. This just makes me want to lean forward and kiss those very inviting lips again. She looks up at me once more. "I don't know for sure. I was leaning against Liam, trying to sleep and I started thinking about you. The next thing I know, I'm standing behind that bench, looking at you. What were you doing?"

"I was sitting in another hotel room listening to Tom and Colin rattle off strategies. I got really tired, so I sat back and rested against the headboard and closed my eyes. The next thing I know, I hear your voice behind me."

"Maybe you have a new power," she suggests.

"Or maybe you have another power," I tell her. It's more likely that she's the one with the new power than me.

"Maybe it's a soulmate thing."

"Maybe."

"Wait, rattling off strategies about what?" she asks. I know that she won't like hearing about this. I reach forward and tuck a loose curl behind her ears. Despite this being a dream…it's surprisingly realistic. I can feel the air moving around us. The slight breeze is blowing Ryanne's hair and causing mine to fall into my eyes. The crickets and other insects are buzzing around as they fly amongst the greenery. The sound of water cascading down into a small pool emanates from the fountain behind me.

"About our rescue mission." Ryanne opens her mouth to argue, but I cover her mouth with my hand. "We know what we're doing, Ry." I slowly draw my hand away and wait for her response.

"It's a suicide mission, Colton. Please don't do this," she pleads with me. I sit down on the bench and pull her down beside me. She's always been so concerned about our well-being. Why is it so surprising that someone could be concerned about hers?

"We have plenty of mages in our group willing to help out."

"Twenty mages is nowhere near enough. Don't come for me. If they start hurting me, I'll find a way to leave. I've been looking, but it looks like the only way to leave the compound is through the back door. It's too risky, Colton."

"Ryanne we have more than twenty mages coming," I tell her. She arches her neck up and looks at me confused. I pull her closer. "We have over 150 mages willing to help rescue you."

Her mouth falls open and her eyes widen. I almost laugh at the obvious look of shock on her face. "Are you serious?"

"I wouldn't lie about that."

"How did you get that many?" she inquires. "I don't know anywhere near that many mages."

"I know some people who know some people who know some people. It doesn't matter how it happened, just that it did. We're coming to rescue you and Liam whether you like it or not."

"It scares me. I don't want anything to happen to you guys. At least if something happens to me, you all will be fine. If anything does happen, it'd be my own fault, because I don't know when to shut my mouth and mind my own business."

"Well, it scares me to leave you there. I know you have Liam to protect you, but I still worry, because you don't know when to shut your mouth and mind your own business." She laughs when I repeat her. My stomach tightens at the sound of her laugh. I've missed that.

"Just promise me that you'll be careful." She turns and faces me completely. "If you get backed into a corner, retreat and regroup, because if I find out that you got killed fighting a Gadramick, I won't be a happy camper. I still don't think this is a good idea. Don't forget about our plans," she whispers to me. I know that she's referring to what we talked about when we sat out here the other night. How she thinks I could forget is beyond me.

I kiss her forehead. "I promise to be careful."

"Thank you," she says as she leans against my chest and closes her eyes. I don't know how it's possible, but she falls asleep in a dream. I sit back and get comfortable. I might as well try and get some sleep too.

"Hey, Colton, wake up." The bed beside me starts moving. I open my eyes and look straight into the eyes of two blond girls.

"What do you guys want?" I mumble as I sit up. Emma and Natalie sit down on the bed Indian style and face me.

"Liam contacted me," Natalie says with a smile.

"Ryanne contacted me too," I tell her. Both of their smiles fall with that statement.

"What? How is that possible?" Emma asks. Everyone takes a step closer to me. I rub my eyes and sit up further.

"I don't know, but I just saw her."

"Liam doesn't think it's a good idea for us to come," Natalie says.

"Ryanne doesn't either, but why? She just said she was worried about our safety. What did Liam say?"

Natalie turns and faces Tom. "Umm, he said that they are safe, but he's a little worried about Ryanne," I instantly turn toward her. "Apparently, Dravin's had her fight against a bunch of Gadramicks and she's refusing to use her magic. Dravin attempts to stop the attacks, but some of the guys have gotten a hit on her. Liam mentioned that she has a lot of bruises. Apparently, she can't sleep and has been refusing to eat anything.

"Adam has been protecting her though. They allow her to leave the cell, but she has to stay with him at all times, because everyone in that compound has vendetta against her. Oh, and get this, apparently Adam thinks he's in love with her."

"What?" I yell.

"Yeah, Adam's in love with her, but he hasn't acted on those feelings. He's just been very protective of her. Some guy tried to attack her yesterday, and Adam beat him up. Ryanne had to pull him off the guy. Liam doesn't like it, but Adam and Dravin are the only reason why they're still alive.

"Also, Dr. Arden couldn't extract any magic from Ryanne even without the protective enchantment. She talked to him once, but that didn't turn out too well. Liam said that since that conversation, Ryanne's gotten more and more depressed. She tries to put on a brave face around him, but he knows. Ryanne doesn't think that they're going to get out of there, and she doesn't want anyone risking their life to come save her.

"They haven't come in contact with Zahtri yet. Ryanne knows that he's there. She can sense his magic around the compound, but doesn't know where he is exactly. Zahtri is the only thing keeping them alive right now. Liam and Ryanne both know that Zahtri has a plan for them, but they don't know what it is yet."

Well, Ryanne left out a lot of details. "I still say we go. Ryanne seemed shocked when I told her how many people we have. We have more of a chance than we thought."

"Liam thinks that we'll still need more people."

"Then, we'll find more," I say.

"It'll take more than two days to gather up more mages, Colton."

"I can't leave her there any longer than that. You all know her. She doesn't like others to think of her as weak, so she won't give them a reason to believe so. Liam knows what's going on in that mind of hers. If he thinks that she's depressed, she most likely is. Think about her powers. She can read minds. She can sense emotions. Can you image what being in Dravin's compound is doing to her mentally? All that anger, hatred, and negative emotions. We can't leave her there for much longer. Three more days tops. If we can't get any more, we go in there with what we have. We'll warn everyone of the dangers ahead of time, but we go anyway. I'll go by myself if I have to. I *have* to try."

"Okay," Tom says. He doesn't try to talk me out of it or offer another strategy.

"Okay?" I can't believe what I'm hearing.

"We all love her too, Colton, and Liam's part of our family as well. We miss them as much as you. I hadn't thought about what being there would be like with her magic. Even if they're not hurting her, it'll still affect her just to be there. Three days. That's all the time I'm allowing before we go there. I'll go let everyone know."

CHAPTER SIXTEEN

"LIAM, WILL YOU TELL ME more about your mom?" I ask him as I play with the flamed pendant he gave me a few months ago. "Or how you got that scar?"

"What do you want to know?" he asks me.

"What was she like? How'd it happen? Either story. Both stories. Whichever one you want to tell." I angle myself more toward him, so I can watch him as he talks. That sounds weird, but I love watching him when he talks. Liam doesn't show much emotion, but when he tells stories, he comes alive.

"She was amazing. She was the type of person who went out of her way to make someone happy. She loved making jewelry. I don't remember a day where she wasn't making something. She loved molding something beautiful out of nothing. All the girls in our tribe would come and ask her to make something for them. They always offered to pay, but mom would never accept their money," Liam smiles as he talks. He's staring off into space, reliving the memories.

"Everyone would come to her as ask her to repair their protector pendants. The mother's of all the male mages were supposed to make their sons their own individual pendants, but many women would come to mom and ask her to make them. My mom had a way of knowing people without meeting them. She could look at you and instantly know what your symbol should be. It was uncanny.

"When I was ten, she sat me down and told me the story of the flame. My great great great grandfather, Maitrec, was the historian for the tribe. He would keep the documentation of everything that occurred. The births. The deaths. The powers everyone had. Everything. He wrote it all down. Because of the time he lived in, he didn't have electricity, so he wrote by candlelight. During the days, he'd watch over the tribe, observing everything. Mom said that he was all-seeing.

"One day, a woman wondered into the tribe. We don't know exactly what happened, but she didn't know who she was. She didn't know her name, her date of birth, where she was from. Nothing.

"She was scared. The scrolls where her appearance is first documented say that she was a beautiful frightened woman with a fierceness never seen before in her eyes. Maitrec gave her food and a place to sleep. He was determined to find out what happened to her. He wanted to know why she couldn't remember—what she couldn't remember. He searched for years, but couldn't find anything. It was like she just appeared out of thin air.

"My grandfather took her in and taught her the ways of our tribe. During the days, when he used to watch the tribe, he started working on the scrolls. He had to write everything down. Our whole tribe history has been recorded because of him. From what I hear, Bragden looks a lot like him.

"Anyway, when she arrived, Maitrec took to teaching her at night. Sitting by the candlelight, he would help her in any way that he could.

She acclimated quickly. He gave her the name Rozene, which means rose. Like a rose, she was beautiful, but there was hardness underneath; she had her own set of thorns. The mystery of her past loomed in everyone's heart. As everyone grew to love her, they wanted to help solve the mystery of her past. To this day, we still don't know any information about her early life.

"Rozene came into Maitrec's life in the darkness. By the flame of a candle, she became a permanent part of his life. By the candlelight, he fell in love with her. Though it took some time, she grew to return his feelings. She was afraid of her past, but because of Maitrec's kindness and patience, she slowly grew to love him as well. We're not sure if Rozene was a mage. There's no record of any magic used by her. Maitrec said that her presence was magical though. There was something special about her. They married and had one child, Abornazine, which means keeper of the flame. Since Maitrec and Rozene, the symbol for my family has been the flame.

"During the darkest of times, her presence provided the illumination he was seeking. She brought something new to his life. Before her, he spent every day writing and documenting the tribes every detail. She broke his routine and made him live for something for the first time in a long time. She became a symbol for light. Even without knowing her past, she adjusted and thrived.

"Before her, Maitrec's flame was quickly dwindling. She brought his flickering flame to its intended brightness. The flickers left and all that remained was a strong flame burning bright. It remained bright until their deaths, but their flame will always burn bright. It's written in our town's history, where it will forever remain.

"Eventually Abornazine got married and had a daughter, my grandma. At twenty, she had my mom. Kayleena. My mom was always a little different compared to everyone else. When we're born, we're given a specific job. The elders in my tribe are pretty good at determining what each person is meant to do with their life, but my mom was a surprise. They couldn't place her in any one job, so for the first time, they let her choose. Her choice was to not choose. She wanted to try everything, and she did before she found her love for art. She loved making jewelry.

"She could literally make something beautiful out of nothing. She was stubborn, determined, and fearless. She wasn't afraid of trying something new even if it brought failure. With failure, you learn. She said that nothing could be considered a failure, because you learned one way not to do it. She was a glass half-full type of person. If you looked at something from a negative angle, she'd make you look in the opposite direction. She had a way of changing people for the better. However, the change was so subtle, that you didn't even realize that she changed you at all until later. She was incredible. I was always amazed at how well she got along with everyone and I literally mean everyone.

"She was the epitome of a flame and represented our family well. She brought brightness to everyone. She provided a constant illumination for those around her. Even those wallowing in the darkness were not immune to her flame."

Liam stops talking and looks toward me. I can see the sadness in his eyes. I lean into him and ask him to continue. "My mom met my dad, Axsher, when she was twenty. He was banished from his home tribe. She would never tell us why. In fact, I never even knew the guy. After I was born, he left. He didn't leave any clues as to his whereabouts. I don't think mom even knew why he left. One day, he just disappeared.

"Bragden knew him, but briefly. I don't think he remembers anything specific about him though. When I was six or seven, Pavander, asked Valdus to begin to work with me. He concluded that I would probably end up being a dream-walker like him. I don't know how the elders were always able to determine what our mage powers would be, but they were usually correct. Occasionally, you'd hear of a story where they got it wrong, but those were rare.

"Bragden was another one of the mages that the elders weren't sure about. They didn't give him the option to choose like my mother though. Every day while I was training with Valdus, he was training too. He was building up his strength. That's why he's so big. Since they weren't sure what his powers would be, they prepared him in other ways. Bragden became the best fighter in our tribe. People were afraid to oppose him. He was one of those people whom you always wanted to remain on their good side.

"After all of my dream sessions with Valdus, I would come home and my mom would have made multiple pieces of jewelry and have dinner prepared and ready. I don't know how she did it, but she did. Bragden would come in from his training sessions before me and would literally eat everything. Mom always made a side portion for me. I came home every night and found a small plate of food in the refrigerator.

"I remember being so jealous when mom pulled Bragden aside and handed him his pendant. Growing up, that's one of the moments you look forward to. Even though it happens when you're ten, it's one of the first steps to becoming a man. After you get your pendant, you get to start training. Bragden was already doing that. He was always one step ahead of me.

"One of the other things about my mom was that she was great with animals. They flocked to her side. Our house always had random birds with broken wings or rabbits with injured feet. She would nurse them back to health, and then release them back into the wild. We also had two horses. She rode Ava, while Bragden and I rode Ranger.

"One day while I was working with Valdus and Bragden was training, mom decided that she wanted to go out riding. She used to ride almost every day when she was younger. When she had us, she had to give it up to take care of us. I came home that day after my dream sessions and found the house empty. Pieces of jewelry were thrown about the kitchen table, but dinner wasn't prepared. Bragden was walking through the house looking for her. I came in right as he was heading out. Mom wasn't home and neither one of us knew where she was.

"The first place we looked was the barn. We instantly knew that she was out when we saw Ava missing. Bragden and I went running down the trial that we knew she frequently rode on. We found her unconscious on the trail about a mile in. Ava was nowhere in sight. I rushed back into town and got Valdus. He was…I guess, he still is, our tribe leader. He told Bragden and me to go home while they worked on mom. Bragden and I went and stayed with our neighbor.

"The next morning we found out that she was paralyzed from the waist down. There was nothing they could do about it. Our tribe didn't have any healers at the time. Healers are incredibly rare. It's a very coveted power. Bragden and I spent months after her accident helping her. Like you, she didn't like looking weak. She didn't feel like her accident was a bad thing. She looked at it as a flicker in the flame or at least she did at first.

"It was then that she fully told me about the flame. She sat Bragden and me down one night in the kitchen and turned all the lights off. She lit a single candle and told us to just watch the flame for a few moments.

"At the time, we thought she was crazy, but we listened. I watched as the candle flame danced around, casting shadows on Bragden's and mom's faces. The slight draft in the room caused the flame to flicker dramatically. A candle flame doesn't stay still for long. There's always some invisible force acting against it. After a few minutes, she started talking.

"She told us how before the accident, her flame was burning bright. It brightened with each of our births. She had everything she wanted in life: two sons on their destined paths and a love for what she was doing with her life. The accident was just a flicker in the flame. It was just an obstacle that she had to overcome in order for the flame to burn bright again. 'With each passing day, the flame will get brighter,' she said. Being seven, I didn't really understand the importance of what she was telling me.

"It wasn't until I was ten and got my pendant necklace that I started to think about everything she told me all those years ago. On my tenth birthday, Valdus gave me the day off and mom sat me down at the table and gave me a small box. I knew that my protector's pendant was inside. I ripped open that box so fast. Inside was a long necklace with a simple flame pendant attached. It was perfect. When I put on the necklace, it felt like pins and needles were spreading throughout my body. I didn't know what was happening. Mom started talking, trying to distract me from the slight pain. After a couple of seconds, the pain went away. It all exited my body and settled in the pendant. I don't know how to describe it exactly, but I knew from that day, everything was going to change. Nothing would be the same."

Liam pauses and looks off to the far side of the room. He clears his throat before he turns toward me again. I see the gloss in his gaze. He's trying to hide his sadness. I squeeze his hand, telling him that I'm still here. I don't know if Liam has ever told anyone this story before. I know how easy it is to get lost in a memory. He gives me a small smile and continues.

"Bragden and I would take turns helping mom. She would try to do everything she did before, but it was difficult. She couldn't go upstairs. At this point, Bragden was thirteen. Though he was young, Bragden was already bigger than everyone else. He would carry Mom upstairs every night and then back down every morning. I started preparing the meals. She would help me, but it wasn't the same. I remember that every night

Bragden would bring Mom into the living room and we'd all sit around the fire. I would sit across from her on the couch and read to her. I would read whatever she gave me for the night. Mom would always tell me that she loved hearing my voice. It didn't matter what I was reading, as long as she could listen to me speak.

"I could tell that she was starting to get frustrated in herself. Her flame wasn't getting any brighter. In fact, its illumination was dwindling. We didn't know what we could do to help. She tried to put on a strong face around us, but we knew. She wasn't the same. The accident changed her.

"A month after I turned ten, I was training with Tranton when I received the news that my mother had committed suicide. My strong, fearless mother took her own life. She swallowed a bunch of her pain medications and left a note explaining how sorry she was, but she couldn't take it anymore. She couldn't stand the pitied looks from the neighbors. She couldn't stand seeing us worry over her. She couldn't stand everyone wanting to help her. All her life, she'd been in control and suddenly she wasn't. She didn't know how to handle the sudden change. She even said in the note that her flame was dying and it was time to just extinguish it. Apparently, she couldn't prolong the inevitable. I've never told anyone that she committed suicide before. I always thought suicide was the weak way to go. How could I think that when the strongest person I knew made that decision?" Liam shakes his head. I can tell that right now, he's not with me. He's inside his memories. "Even now, I still don't know what I think about it.

"Besides the note, she left Bragden and me both tiny wooden boxes full of random items. Mine had this leather bracelet, my great grandfather's pocket watch, and Rozene's wedding ring. I have no idea what was in Bragden's box. He never told me, and I've never asked.

"Bragden and I didn't have any family to go to, so Valdus took us in. Valdus had previous adopted this mage, Ezra. Ezra was twelve when he came and lived with Valdus and his wife. We did not get along. I don't know what it was, but Ezra hated me and worshipped Valdus. I don't think he liked that he was no longer the center of attention all the time. He had to compete for the amount of attention he thought he deserved. As the years passed, Ezra's disdain for me grew. I tried everything I could to change his feelings toward me, but nothing worked.

"Bragden started training every day. We drifted apart. We both handled mom's death in different ways. Bragden took his anger out during his training sessions. He was always angry while I was the quiet one. I didn't express myself like he did. I trained to further my magic. Valdus and I worked on strengthening my dream-walking abilities. I hadn't come into my powers yet, but I was already showing signs. I could control my dreams. Inside of my dreams, I could literally manipulate whatever I wanted. If I imagined a certain location, I could go there during a dream. If I envisioned a specific scene or event, I would dream about it. It was amazing.

"I wanted my flame to be as bright as it could be. Just because mom's flame dwindled, didn't mean mine should. She always wanted us to thrive and she did everything to make sure that we did. I would work with Valdus in the morning, and then I would train in the evenings. One day during training, Tranton had me fighting with weapons with Ezra. I was so done dealing with all of his crap. Neither one of us were taking it easy on the other. I was fifteen at the time, and he was seventeen.

"I won't go into all of the details, but we both took our anger of the situation we were in on each other. When I felt his blade swipe across my face, I pushed even harder. I could feel the blood dripping down my face, but I continued fighting. I wanted to knock that smug look off his arrogant face.

"We both continued to push each other…almost to our breaking points. We could hear Tranton yelling at us to stop, but we both ignored him. I spit the blood that was dripping down my face at him as I swung my sword out. I watched as my blade swept out and hit him. When I saw the blood start spilling out of the wound, I stopped. I dropped my sword and left.

"I left training. I left Rockwood. I just left. I walked out of that training room and never looked back. The only thing tying me to that town was Bragden and Bragden and I had been drifting apart. I barely spoke to him. We exchanged passing glances, but that was all. I gathered up a small sack of my belongings and I walked out of that town. I needed to get away for a while.

"I got into some bad things. I was big. I knew that I was stronger than most humans and I took advantage of that. I got into drugs. Got in trouble with alcohol. I stole things. Had some run-ins with the law. I thought I was better than everyone, and there was nothing anyone could do that would make me believe otherwise. One night while I was sleeping in the park, I had a dream. Mom visited me in my sleep that night similar to what Claire has been doing with you and Colton.

"She told me to man up—to accept my responsibilities and grow up. I was seventeen at this point. I wasn't responsible for my actions. I didn't understand how my actions could affect other people. I didn't think there were other people in my life whom my disappearance would impact. Mom didn't say much to me in this dream, but she told me to remember the flame. Remember everything she told me.

"I came to my senses that night. I stopped the drugs. I became sober. I stopped stealing. I cleaned up my entire act. I walked into the first tattoo parlor I came to and got this tattoo. From that moment on, it became a constant reminder for me not look back. The future is the only thing that can change. I couldn't change what had already happened to me, but I could do everything in my power to make sure that I made the most of my future. That year was a flicker in my flame and ever since then, my flame as been burning bright."

"What happened between you and Bragden? You two are pretty close now," I ask him.

"While I was out, Bragden had inherited the house. In fact, he got everything that mom left us. I was so scared to come back. I didn't know how everyone would react, but besides a few people, everyone welcomed me back. I moved in with him. While I was away, I continued training. I grew over a foot in height. My hair lengthened and I had this jagged silver scar on my face. Most people regarded my wearily. I didn't look like the friendly boy I was before I left.

"I didn't train with Valdus anymore. Even though I was only seventeen, I had already come into my powers. Bragden and I got closer while we lived together. We realized that we just reacted to mom's death in different ways. We just needed time to let everything sizzle out. As we started to understand each other more, we pushed back everything from the previous years. I've never been as close to Bragden as I am right now. To this day, I still don't know what happened to Ezra. He left shortly after I did. Like me, he just disappeared.

"Valdus pulled me aside when I was eighteen and told me that Ezra was actually my half brother. We share the same dad. Dad apparently had an affair shortly after Bragden was born and he ditched Ezra's mother too. Mom never knew, because Dad asked Valdus to never tell her. I don't know all the details, but Valdus and my father were friends and when Ezra's mother passed, he promised to take care of him."

"Does Bragden know?"

"I think so. I'm not sure. I never spoke to him about it directly, but I think he figured it out on his own."

Liam finishes speaking and neither one of us say anything for a little while. Liam has not had it very easy. I was right with my thought that he had to grow up too quickly.

"Liam, what was your mother's power?" I ask.

He starts shaking his head. "I'm not sure exactly. I think she had premonition. I think that's how she was so good at knowing what everyone's pendants should be, but she never told us specifically. Whenever Bragden or I asked her about she would smile and say that the secret was in the flame." Hmm…the secret is in the flame…what does that even mean?

"Liam, what happens after this?"

"What do you mean?"

"You guys have been training for this your whole life. What about once this is all over? When this prophecy no longer matters? What happens after?"

"Life. Life happens, Ryanne. That's one thing you can always count on. Life goes on. Whether you want it to, whether or not you're ready for it, or whether you're even a part of it, life goes on."

CHAPTER SEVENTEEN

WE'VE BEEN IN THIS COMPOUND for too long. I've lost track of the days. I know we've only been here a couple of days, but I feel like it's been forever. It's weird how sudden my moods can change. Yesterday, I was completely fine. I sat in this cell with Liam for the majority of the day, listening as he told me his story. Today, I want to curl up into a ball and avoid everyone all together.

"Ryanne, you have to eat something," Liam says. He pushes a plate of food toward me. Surprisingly, it looks good, but I'm not hungry. "You didn't eat anything yesterday. You need to eat."

"No, I don't," I mumble as I lean back against the hard wall. Ever since Dravin tried to get me to use my magic against the Gadramicks, I've lost all appetite and desire to try and break out of here. I know he's just trying to train his men to fight against me, but I'm not going to give him anything else to use. All it results in is me getting punched, kicked, and knocked to the ground. My body is sore from all the bruises on me.

Just yesterday, Natasha came into my cell while Liam was out with Adam trying to get food for me. She pushed me against the wall and attempted to asphyxiate me. I was able to throw up a small shield, but I still felt some of the effects of her power. She laughed as I fell to the ground gasping for breath.

"Colton's not coming for you, Ryanne. He's probably moved on to the next girl by now, maybe my twin. He's always had a thing for blondes anyway." She stopped attempting to asphyxiate me the second the guard left her alone, but her glare remained the entire time.

I blink back into the present when Adam walks into the room and sits down on the floor in front of me. His emotions run into me. He's concerned, worried, and angry at Dravin for letting the men hit me. I know that he's staring at the bruise under my eye and possibly the dark one on my shoulder. "Ryanne, eat."

"Nope," I tell him.

"What's wrong, Ryanne? Really?" Liam asks.

I turn and look straight at Liam. He of all people should know what is wrong. I don't answer him though. Instead, I turn back around, lean my head against the wall, and close my eyes. Maybe I'll see Colton again.

It's been two days since I last saw him. He told me they were planning a rescue mission, but I really hope he listened to me and put that plan on the back burner for now. It's not safe. Something is stirring. Everyone is antsy. Change is in the air; that much I know. I can feel it.

I wince as someone's anger barrels into me. It didn't bother me at first, but the longer I'm here the more their feelings are affecting me. "Are you having trouble controlling them?" Liam asks me. I nod. I try to siphon the feelings through me, but have trouble. They're lingering. If I don't get a handle on this soon, I'm going to start acting out their feelings. Considering how strong their emotions are, I know it won't be good for anyone to be around me during that time.

"Controlling what?" Adam asks. Neither Liam nor I answer him. Adam may be acting nicer, but he's still a Gadramick. "Let me help you."

"Adam, please stop," I lean forward and run my hands through my hair. Placing my head on my knees, I groan. "I can't handle your concern."

"I'm worried about you, Ryanne."

"I know. I can feel that," I look up at him, "but please stop. I can feel all your emotions and being around so many people at once is starting to hurt me."

"Oh."

I wince as another wave of anger crashes into me. I can feel a few Gadramicks yelling in the hallway. Three Gadramicks run past the door of my cell, probably going to break up a fight. A sharp pain spreads through my stomach when the noises in the hallway get louder. Crying out, I curl in half, grabbing on my stomach, trying to stop the pain.

"Ryanne, focus on me," Liam tells me. "Forget everyone else; just focus on me."

He doesn't understand. He doesn't understand what this feels like. Whimpering, I lean forward and rest my head against the cool floor. "I can't. I can't, Liam. I can't do it," I gasp when the pain spreads to my head. A blinding headache lingers there and settles. Nothing makes sense anymore. "Make it stop. Please make it stop. It hurts," I cry. I feel my body shaking, but I can't control it.

A wave of coldness spreads through me, offsetting some of the pain, but it makes my body react more violently. Pulling my knees under me, I fist my hands in my hair and pull, trying to feel something else, but nothing works.

"Adam, you need to leave," Liam says. Though he's trying to remain calm, I can hear the waver in his voice.

"But she's…"

"She can feel your panic. If you can't control your emotions, you need to leave. She's only going to get worse if you stay." I can't handle it anymore. I scream. "Ryanne," Liam grabs my shoulders and pulls me up, but my eyes are closed, so I can't see anything. "Ryanne, look at me."

I hear a door close, but the pain doesn't lessen. I can't open my eyes. The room is too bright; it'll just worsen the headache. I can't do it. Shaking my head is the only response I can manage. I'm not screaming anymore, but I can't seem to form any sentences. I'm not sure I could even speak if I wanted to.

"Ryanne," Liam pleads with me again.

"Move out of the way," a deep voice says.

"No," Liam says. "This is all your fault. She wouldn't be here if it weren't for you!" he shouts; his anger rising. I lean forward and rest my head on the ground again. There's too much going on right now. I can hear Liam and Dravin yelling. I can sense the pain of the men in the hallway who are fighting. I can feel the anger pumping through everyone. I can still feel Adam's concern as my condition worsens. Someone in the cell with me throws a punch and I feel the anger rise even further as the pain spreads through someone's jaw.

I open my mouth to scream again, but nothing comes out. I don't see how this could be any worse. The pressure inside me keeps building up. A loud buzzing fills the room as if a thousand bees just swarmed the area. I can't control anything anymore. I can't do it. *Please* make it stop.

Everything continues to build up. Though my eyes are closed, it's not just darkness I see. A bright ball of white light in the distance starts flying toward me, and I can do nothing but watch.

The light overwhelms me until all I see is white…the soothing white light. The pain stops. The anger stops. Everything stops until all I'm left with is serenity. I'm alone with my own thoughts and emotions.

For the first time in a few days, I'm at peace.

The light dims until I'm surrounded by the dark again. I'm always surrounded by the dark. I can sense one other person in the room with me, but I can't pick up on anything specific which tells me that Liam near. His control of his emotions is impeccable. He's able to fully control his feelings, so it doesn't affect me like everyone else's does. Reluctantly, I open my eyes and look around the cell.

My eyes don't travel far before I meet a pair of gray eyes. I don't really know what happened, but based on the slight lingering headache, I know something did. My back aches as I try to sit up; I must have been in this position for a while. Liam shifts slightly and helps me up.

"What happened?" I groan when I'm able to stay up on my own. Liam removes his hands from my shoulder and runs a hand through his hair. Turning slightly so that I can see him, I gasp when I see the bruise along his jawline. "Who did that to you?"

"Dravin," he whispers as he reaches out and fixes some of my stray curls. "Are you feeling okay? You've been out for a few hours."

"A few hours?"

"Yeah, the pain of everyone's emotions proved to be a little too much for your body and you passed out. Dravin came in and I think he was going to try and help you, but I kind of snapped when he came in and I swung at him. I did hit him, but not as hard as he got me. His guards rushed in and pulled me back before I could do anything else."

"Liam..." My eyes linger on the bruise on his skin. I don't know what I want to say to him, but I hate that he keeps getting hurt because of me.

"I'd do it again," he whispers.

"Liam, I don't know how long we'll be here, but please don't do anything that'll separate us. When I was first thrown into a cell like this, I hated it. Being surrounded by all these Gadramicks, I'm glad I'm stuck in this cell, and I'm glad I'm with you. I don't feel as lonely, and I feel safe with you. Take it from someone who's known to push buttons: this is one situation where you want to listen. Something is happening here, and I need you with me."

I don't want to think about what would have happened to me if he didn't volunteer to come with me. Liam angles himself toward me and watches me for a few seconds. He doesn't say anything; he just stares.

"What?" I ask when he doesn't look away right away.

"Nothing," he says right as the cell door opens and Adam walks in.

We both turn toward the door. A confused look crosses Adam face as he slows his walk to a stop in front of us. "Dravin wanted me to see if you were awake," he tells me.

"There's a window," I remind him.

"I know." He doesn't do anything, but continues staring at me. The confusion remains though. Liam grunts beside me when he doesn't look away.

"Adam, what's your power?" I ask him when I start to get uncomfortable from his attention. I realize now that he's never used any sort of magic against me, so I have no idea what he can do. Even the few times I've fought him, he never attempted to use any magic.

Adam leans back and looks at me. I can tell that he's thinking about whether or not to tell me. "I can control people. Their emotions. Their thoughts. Their actions. Anything. I can control them."

I sit up straighter. "Are you serious?"

"Yep," he turns toward Liam. What he is doing? "Scoot away from her."

I turn toward Liam who has a *whatever* expression on his face, but he slowly removes his arm from my shoulder and scoots a little over a foot away from me. My mouth falls open as I look between Liam and Adam. Liam looks extremely confused.

"Oh my gosh." I turn to Adam. "Can you control anyone?"

"No. I can't control you or Dravin."

"Why?"

"Your mind is connected to your magic in some way. I can't break through the magic barrier."

"That doesn't make sense. I've met someone whose power was Persuasion and his magic worked on me."

"Persuasion and Control are two different things, Ryanne, so the magic works differently."

"But Liam can go into minds. He can knock me out if my magic gets out of control and..." I'm cut off when the cell door is thrown open.

"Ryanne, I need you to come with me," Dravin yells from the doorway. He looks anxious. He no longer has the confident demeanor he usually displays when he comes to get me to fight. Slowly, I stand and make my way over to him. Liam and Adam both stand up behind me. "Just Ryanne."

I give them a small smile over my shoulder. I know that it won't do anything because I look like crap, but it's all the assurance I can give them right now. Dravin grabs my elbow and pulls me in the hall. Adam exits the cell and glances at me briefly before walking down the hallway in the opposite direction. I watch his receding form, waiting for Dravin to tell me what is going on. When the grip on my arm tightens, I gasp and look up at Dravin.

"I've tried to be patient with you. I even tried a different approach this time, but you're pushing the limits. I can't extract your magic, so you're going to have to give it to me in other ways. You're going to fight for the Gadramicks. You're going to be our secret weapon."

I gape at him. "You can't be serious."

"I'm completely serious."

"I'm not going to fight for you. I'm not on your *team*, Dravin. You are a little messed up if you think that I'm going be your "secret weapon," and you have another thing coming if you think I'm going to let you have any bit of my magic in any shape or form. I'm not some pawn that you can just lock away until you need me."

Dravin takes a step closer to me. Out of habit, I step backward and hit the wall behind me. "If you want to see that soulmate of yours again, I'd do as you're told, Ryanne."

"I've already accepted that I probably won't get to see him again, so why get my hopes up? I know that you don't plan on letting me leave here alive. You may have fooled Adam and Jedrek with that idea, but you haven't fooled me. I'm not stupid Dravin. I know you. You're a pathological liar. You get pleasure out of deceiving people. You're smart and cunning, but easily angered—especially right now, when your perfect plan is slowly unraveling. You need my cooperation, but I'm not going to give it to you which means you're either going to resort to physical violence or tricky mind games. Either way, I'm prepared, so try your worst." Dravin narrows his eyes at me. Instead of reacting, he grabs my elbow again and pulls me down the hallway. "Where are you taking me?"

Wouldn't you like to know? You think you're so smart. Figure this out. I try to yank my arm away from him, but he tightens his grip. I stumble forward. We pass a couple Gadramicks in the hall, who step aside and let Dravin pass. Each gives me an evil glare as we make our way further into the compound. I recognize a few of them as men that Dravin tried to make me fight earlier. He stops in front of a set of doors and grabs the key ring out of his pocket. This door looks nothing like any of the other doors in the compound. Instead of the heavy metal gray doors, this one was is mahogany. Deep black swirling accents decorate its exterior.

"Dravin, what's going on?" Again, my attempts to get free are futile. His grip is too strong and while I could use my magic, there's no way I'd be able to get out of this compound alive on my own.

Instead of answering me, he thrusts an old key into the lock and turns. I try to move away, but Dravin is physically stronger than me. He forcefully pulls me forward and continues maneuvering through the compound. This section looks much older than where we previously were. Instead of electric lighting, the room is lit by candles. This was where I was when I rescued Larkin from Dravin. This is the hall from my nightmares. My airways constrict the further we go down the halls from the lack of fresh air.

Dravin's grip on my arm tightens. I bite my tongue to keep from crying out. I know that I'll have a bruise from this later. Just another bruise to add to my collection, I guess. Dravin stops in front of a door and knocks once.

"Dravin!" I yell at him. He turns and looks at me. I shake my arm out of his hand. He grabs my wrist to keep me from running away. "What is going on? Where are we?"

"Come in," a deep voice yells from the opposite side of the door. Dravin grabs the faded brass handle and pushes open the door.

If this were a movie, eerie organ music would be playing in the background setting the ominous scene. I can't see anything in the room in front of me for it is pitch black. I look back at Dravin. I have no idea what he's trying to do here. Dravin throws me inside the room and quickly closes the door. I fall to the floor, surrounded by darkness.

I cry out from the impact of the fall. My arms and legs start burning from scraping the hard flooring. I pause for a moment to collect my breath and let my other senses take over. Getting on my hands and knees, I feel the ground around me. "Really?" I mumble as I crawl forward...or what I think is forward.

I can't feel anything around me. The floor is rough. Old wood? Dirty concrete? I can't tell based on texture alone.

"You're getting closer," the deep voice warns. I instantly stop moving and turn to the right—toward the sound of the voice.

"Who's there?" I ask.

The room is suddenly flooded with light. Small flames from hundreds of candles light the room. How did that happen? I look away from the candles and look toward the right corner. A tall man, around Bragden's size is standing there, smirking at me. Without taking my eyes off him, I push myself up and stand.

Black hair, so dark the night is envious, is pulled back into a ponytail at the base of his neck. A long scar runs across his jaw line and down his neck, disappearing beneath his shirt collar. Dark brooding eyes watch me as I assess him. He's wearing a fitted black shirt and dark cargo pants. The tight shirt and the crossed arms accentuate his muscular physique. Involuntarily, I take a step back. This man could snap me like a twig if he wanted to.

"It's nice to finally meet you, Ryanne. I've heard so much about you," he tells me with a fake smile. I take another step backward when he pushes away from the wall and saunters toward me.

"You must be Zahtri."

CHAPTER EIGHTEEN

COLTON

I DUCK THE PUNCH TRAVIS throws and firmly plant my feet on the ground. When his arm stops its forward motion, I jump up and thrust my fist into his gut. He grunts, but doesn't stop fighting. If a simple punch stopped him, I'd be concerned.

I hear the sounds of the others training around me. Bragden and Incendia are working on their magic. Streams of fire are soaring over our heads, as they work on their directional commands. Larkin and Kyril are sparring together, seriously this time. Usually Larkin transports to random spots through the training room and scares everyone instead of actually training. Logan and Lily are training together, while bickering like a married couple. They still won't acknowledge their feelings for each other. If they don't act soon, James will intervene. I've noticed him watching them more often lately. His "Cupid" senses must be tingling.

I turn my attention back to Travis. I bring my left arm up to block his swing as I thrust my other fist forward. Travis easily dodges my hit. My head starts to feel fuzzy. I can see Travis's arm coming toward me, but I can't bring my arm up to block his move. They fall to my side limp. My arms and legs feel like lead. No matter how hard I mentally demand them to move, they remain frozen at my sides. Travis's arm connects with my shoulder sending me backward.

Before I hit the ground, I'm already gone.

"Colton," a familiar voice calls out. I blink and look around. I'm standing in the middle of a cement cell, similar to one that Dravin held Liam and me in. Speaking of Liam…

"What's going on?" I ask him.

"Are you guys still planning on coming?" he asks. I can hear the urgency in his voice.

"Yeah, tomorrow."

"Can you come any sooner?"

"Liam, what happened?"

He starts pacing the cell. When he grabs the back of his neck, I tense. Like me, Liam does that when he's in a situation he doesn't want to be in. "Dravin took Ryanne," he finally says.

"Took her where?" This can't be good. Last time I heard, Dravin was treating Ryanne decently…as decent as a prisoner could be kept, but I knew that wouldn't stay that way for long.

"I don't know for sure. Adam and I were trying to get Ryanne to eat something, because she hasn't eaten in days, but she refused. She started feeling everyone's emotions again, so she was trying to stay away from us, but she ended up passing out from the pain. Dravin came into the room and said that he needed Ryanne to come with him. He grabbed her and pulled her into the hallway. Adam left the cell at the same time.

"I could hear Dravin yelling at her. I couldn't make out what he was saying specifically, but Adam hid behind the corner and listened. He wants Ryanne to fight for the Gadramicks—to be their secret weapon. Well, being Ryanne, she insulted him, which he didn't like.

"He forcefully dragged her down the hallway. Adam followed them from a safe distance until Dravin disappeared behind an old wooden door. He tried to go further, but the door was locked," Liam pauses and looks straight at me. "Colton, he took her to Zahtri."

"Are you positive?"

"Where would you hide a powerful mage that no one has ever seen before? It's not easy to hide someone in a compound full of Gadramicks. People would find out. There's no other possible scenario. This is Dravin we're talking about. They're finally putting their plan into motion."

"Shit," I grab the back of my neck and look around. Ryanne has been in a cell like this for far too long. This needs to end. "I'll talk with Tom and Colin. If she's with Zahtri, she's in danger."

"Ryanne's powerful, but she won't use her magic to protect herself and you know that. She doesn't think there's a way out of this for her. She's in a lot of danger. Way more than we know."

I blink and I'm back in the woods behind the hotel. Everyone is huddled around me. "Colton, are you okay?" Tom asks as he puts a hand out. I grab it and stand up.

"No, we need to go now."

"Where?"

"To Dravin's compound. Ryanne's in danger. Liam pulled me into a dream; that's how serious it is. Dravin took her to Zahtri."

Larkin and Kyril cuss and push through everyone. "He took her to Zahtri?"

I nod. "Apparently. Adam followed Dravin and Ryanne to an old wooden door. He couldn't go any farther because the door was locked."

"I've been back there before. I've never seen Zahtri, but I could feel a difference in the air down there. It felt electric. I couldn't sense his magic specifically, but I knew that there was something there. Something powerful. Dravin never lets anyone down there. I'm probably one of two people who have ever been on the other side of that door. If he took Ryanne down there, he's very serious," Larkin says.

We can't afford to wait until tomorrow. Who we have now will have to do. Ryanne and Liam's life depend on it. It's now or never. Tom's eyes move from me as he looks at all the people around us. They're all nodding; they understand the direness of this situation.

"Okay, tonight. Tonight, we'll go and rescue them. I'll go get everyone together. You all get ready. We'll head out in an hour."

"This is it," Natalie says as she walks over to me. "We're finally going to end this."

"I just hope we're not too late."

"I SEE MY REPUTATION PRECEDES me," Zahtri says as he steps forward.

I take a deep breath. My heart is pounding a mile a minute and my palms feel very clammy. I really want to turn around and bang on the old wooden door, screaming for help, but I know that no one will come. I'm all alone.

With Zahtri.

My body really wants to step back, but I remain still as Zahtri steps toward me. I know he can sense my fear, just like I can sense his amusement. He's basically laughing at me right now, but I need to remain as calm as possible. Anything else could get me killed.

"You don't talk much," he says as he circles around me. I cringe when he trails his hand lightly across my shoulder. "That's fine. It's probably better that way." *Pretty face. Nice body. Lots of magic. She'll definitely do.*

"What do you want?" I hesitantly ask him.

"Wouldn't you like to know, darling." Why is everyone always calling me darling? "Because it suits you."

"You can read my mind," I state. It's not a question. I know he's powerful, so it shouldn't surprise me he has that ability too.

"Oh, I'm more powerful than even you can imagine." He stops in front of me. "You have a lot of magic in you too. I can understand why the Gadramicks have been having a difficult time with you, but you don't have enough. You don't stand a chance against me."

"The Gadramicks? It sounds like you're not a part of them."

He takes a step forward and grabs the end of my hair. I bite my lip to keep from saying anything, but now that I know that he can read my thoughts, the idea seems pointless. "I'm not, darling. They're weak. All of them. Those of us with power aren't meant to work amongst others. We're meant to rule over them."

"We're not meant to rule over anyone, Zahtri."

"That's where you're wrong."

"No, that's where you're wrong." I grab my hair and pull it away from him. He easily lets it go. His amusement crashes into me. I don't want to be amusing. I need to change my approach here.

"That won't work."

"Stop reading my mind!" I yell at him. Yelling at this man probably isn't a good idea, but I can't help it. All the anger in this compound is starting to affect me.

"You're able to read my mind. If you wouldn't suppress your magic as much, you'd be much stronger. I know that you recently started unleashing more and more magic, but it's still not enough. I've seen your blood results. You're magic is embedded in your blood. Only you can release it."

"I've already done that."

"You didn't release it all. You have to dig deeper than that. Break down those barriers you've erected. You're a vessel for magic, but you're too afraid to use it—to harness it. That's your weakness. If you embraced your magic, you'd be able to stand up to me instead of cowering in front of me."

"Cowering in front of you? I've been stuck in this compound for days. I couldn't leave my cell for fear of being attacked. I had to have a body guard walk me to the bathroom. I've been bombarded with everyone's emotions. Do you know what that's like? To have hundreds of people's anger and hatred move through your body? How would you react to that?"

"I didn't say you weren't strong. I can see the strength in you. I'm just saying you're not strong *enough*."

I narrow my eyes and look up at him. *A little on the short side though.*

"Why are you judging me?" I place my hands on my hips and glare at him. "What are you planning?"

Ahh, Dravin mentioned that she was smart. Zahtri takes another step toward me. My eyes flicker around the room. The only thing that could be used as a weapon is a stinking candle. "You won't find anything in here. I don't believe in using weapons."

Neither do I. It's easier to use magic.

"See, we do have something in common," Zahtri says. "I like you, Ryanne, so this can go one of two ways. Tonight, is going to be my big unveiling. It's time to step into the spotlight." He stops in front of me and smiles. "Now, the first scenario is that you come with me and stand by my side. We can work together and be unstoppable. No one would dare to go against us. You won't like the second one as much."

"I don't like the first one."

"Then, you'll hate this one. The other one is that I bring you in front of all the Gadramicks and kill you. Once they see you dead, they'll follow me. You've been a nuisance to them. You're the only person standing in their way. Dravin's been building up your ruthless reputation. If they were to watch your die on stage…they'd instantly pledge their allegiance to me. I took out their biggest threat."

"Is there a third option?"

"No. Now you can pick or I'll pick for you. You have potential, so I'd rather not kill you."

"Aww, that's so sweet of you."

"But I will if it comes to it. You're small. Like you said earlier, I could snap you like a twig."

"I don't get any other options? Stand next to you or die?"

"I think that's pretty generous. I know which I'd pick if I were you."

"Well, you're not me. I'd rather die than work for you." I take a step forward and glare at him. "The second option. I pick number two."

"If that's how it's going to be," Zahtri says. He brings his hand back and slaps me across the cheek. The force sends me flying backward into the wall. When my head connects with the dark surface, I slump to the ground and the room around me starts spinning. Zahtri's laughter is all I hear as I slowly lose consciousness.

CHAPTER NINETEEN

COLTON

PACING THROUGH THE BALLROOM, I wait for Tom to come back. Everyone is moving around anxiously. Natalie walks over to me and grabs my forearm. I halt and turn to look at her. She looks like she's ready to kick some ass. Dressed in all black, she has a sword strapped to her back and a dagger wrapped around her thigh. Dark eyeliner lines her eyes brightening her already bright blue eyes. "Calm down, Colton. Everything is going to be okay."

"How can you be so sure?" I ask her.

"I just am. If we're going to be successful tonight, we have to be sure. Ryanne and Liam are counting on us. They need us to be sure."

She's right. "Thank you, Natalie. For all of this. I would have gone crazy if you didn't help keep me calm this whole time."

"You don't have to thank me, Colton. I'm the only person who understands what you're going through right now. We need to help each other. You're like a brother to me," she says with a small smile.

"Hey!" Conner yells from across the room.

"You're like a second brother to me," Natalie corrects herself without acknowledging her brother. I laugh and hug her. Without Liam here, I'll watch out for Natalie tonight. I wouldn't forgive myself if anything happened to her after all this.

Tom walks back into the room and walks straight toward me. "I found him," he says.

"Found who?" I don't know who he's talking about.

"Vincent, I found him."

"No freaking way. He didn't want to be found. How did you find him?" Vincent is just like Larkin. He can transport to different locations without having been there before. Unlike Larkin though, he can transport many people at once. He's helped us once in the past few months. He brought Logan to the house when Emma and Ryanne were shot. His power will make transporting everyone to Dravin's compound much easier.

"I called him."

I stare at Tom. We've tried calling him countless times in the past few weeks with no success. He didn't want to be contacted, so he never answered. He remained hidden, and we remained hopeful he'd come to his senses.

"He said Claire visited him and told him that he was needed. He'll be here in a few minutes."

"Who's Vincent?" Natalie asks.

"Vincent is an old friend of mine. He went into hiding when a couple of Gadramicks tried attacking him for his power. They wanted him to work for them and didn't like his refusal, so they tried to kill him.

We've been trying to call him to see if he'd help us, but he wouldn't answer. He wanted nothing to do with this fight...until Claire talked to him. Apparently, she was able to convince him it was time to get back into the fight. To use his magic again."

"What's his power?" she asks.

"He's a traveler."

"Like Larkin and Travis?"

"Yes, except he can move multiple people, or objects, at once. He'll be able to help transport people to the compound, which means we'll be able to get there much sooner than we originally intended."

"That's great!" Natalie says. Her excitement attracts the attention of everyone else in our group.

"What's going on?" Emma asks as she skips over to us. She's dressed similarly to Natalie: dark clothes and make-up, hair up in a high bun with a sword strapped on her back and a dagger on her thigh. In fact all the girls are dressed similarly. Incendia's wearing her hair down. Her bright red hair contrasts strikingly against her black attire. Lily looks tough. It's strange to see her in anything other than her red cheerleading uniform. I'm still getting used to her being a mage.

"Vincent is coming," Tom announces. David and Logan both step forward, mouth hanging open, and stare at Tom.

"Really?" Colin asks.

"Who's Vincent?" Incendia asks. Tom explains the whole story again, this time to the entire room. Everyone quiets and listens to Tom as he speaks. Natalie starts pacing. Like me, she wants to get this over with. We're very antsy and need to get moving. The sooner the better. I don't know how much more waiting I can take.

Tom stops talking as the door to the ballroom slams open. A man stands directly in the middle of both doors. "I hear I'm needed."

"Ah, and there he is," Tom says as he points to the door. Everyone redirects their attention to him as Vincent causally strolls through the room.

"Mother of mmmphhhhmmm—" David covers Emma's mouth. Who knows what she's going to say.

"Jumping jellybeans, if Gerald Butler and Joe Manganiello had a love child, it would look like him," Incendia says. Lily and Natalie both nod their heads without looking away from Vincent.

"Dude, one of your jobs now is being their censors. You gotta be quick," David says to Bragden while he uncovers his hand from Emma's mouth, "or they'll say some crazy stuff."

"I'm just keeping things interesting," Incendia says without taking her eyes off of Vincent.

"That's what I was trying to say," Emma mumbles, "until this big bully stopped me." She elbows David in the stomach lightly.

Tom starts cracking up while Vincent moves through the room. He doesn't stop or look at anyone as he makes his way to us.

"I know I've let myself go, but I don't think it's that funny," Vincent says with a smile as he stops in front of Tom.

"It's good to see you," Tom says as he gives Vincent a hug.

"If that's what he looks like when he lets himself go, I can't imagine what he looked like before," Emma whispers to Incendia.

"It's good to see you too. It's been too long," Vincent says as he looks behind Tom. He nods at me. "You've grown since I saw you last."

"That's usually what happens," I tell him as I reach forward and shake his hand.

"I hear it's your soulmate we're going to find."

"And hers," I point to Natalie. She gives him a small smile.

"Well, congrats on finding them. We'll get them back," Vincent says.

"So when are we doing this?" I know he just got here, but I need to go soon.

Vincent turns to Tom. "Got any more snazzy outfits? I burned all mine."

"Snazzy," Emma turns to Incendia. "I like him."

"Yeah, follow me," Tom says to Vincent. Turning to the rest of the room, "Do any last minute preparations. We're going to be leaving soon."

"Okay, here's how it's going to go. Larkin is going to take Vincent out to the compound to show him where to bring everyone. He'll come back and start bringing everyone there. Don't attack until you hear my word. We don't know how to get into the compound or what we'll find when we get there. I apologize for the uncertainty, but we don't have a lot to go on. We've been there before, but didn't come across many Gadramicks. This time will be different. We will have to fight," Tom turns to Larkin. He nods, places a hand on Vincent's shoulder, and transports out of the room.

"If anyone comes across Zahtri, leave him alone. None of us are strong enough to go against him. Going against him would be a death wish. When we get to the compound, remain low to the ground. With Larkin's help, Vincent is going to bring us to a spot where we won't set off the alarms. We should have surprise on our side. We're going to need that.

"No one attacks without my say. We need to assess the surroundings before storming in. Wait for my word," Tom repeats right as Larkin and Vincent transport back into the room.

"They're gathering outside for something. I found an area where we can go without them sensing us, but we have to be quiet. If anyone says anything too loud, they'll hear us."

"Why would they be gathering outside?" Natalie asks.

"If my hunch is correct, it has something to do with Zahtri and I can guarantee Ryanne is probably involved somehow."

CHAPTER TWENTY

"WAKE UP, DARLING. IT'S TIME to go," Zahtri whispers to me. I can hear footsteps walking through the room. My arms and legs weigh a ton and despite my efforts, I can't move.

I feel my body being lifted off the ground. My head rolls back which jolts me awake. Zahtri is holding me up slightly off the ground. I try to shake the fog out of my brain. When I look at Zahtri, he places me on the ground. Since I hit my head, my equilibrium is off; I sway on my feet a little. He keeps his arms on my shoulder and steadies me. "You know for someone so powerful, you're pretty fragile."

"Did you expect that I'd just magically get up after you threw me into a brick wall? I'm still a human, not some crazy superhero."

"We should work on that," he whispers in my ear. I cringe away from him.

"*We're* not doing anything," I retort as I step away from him. Zahtri laughs. *Feisty. Hmmm, not sure how I feel about that.* He grabs my wrists and slaps a pair of handcuffs on me. I look down at the metal cuffs and back up at him questioningly. I know he can read my mind, so I don't ask him aloud.

"Do you remember that dagger that you stepped in front of?" he asks me. Of course I remember that stupid dagger. It almost killed me…for real that time. Wait…how does he know about the dagger? "I gave Enrique that dagger personally. He promised to work for me. His power was impressive. Not as much as mine or yours, but still impressive. I didn't think he'd get himself killed so easily," Zahtri says as he tightens the cuffs. I wince as the metal digs into my wrist.

"The big mage of yours has some anger issues," he tells me. I'm not sure if he's referring to Bragden or Colton. "You see I dabble a little in dark magic. I've found a way to infuse said magic with certain objects. It works best with strong metals. Go ahead. Try to get free." I don't give him the pleasure of seeing me struggle. I know it'll hurt if I move my wrists, so I just stare up at him, trying to keep a blank face. "Also, I can read your mind. You're kind of like an open book. You should try a little harder to censor your thoughts."

Zahtri starts walking toward the door. When I don't follow, he sighs loudly and walks back to me. "I like you Ryanne. It's going to be a shame to waste so much magic," he moves my hair off my shoulder. I cringe away from him, but can't do much since I'm already pressed against the wall with my hands cuffed. He leans forward. I turn to the side and feel his lips brush against my ear, "And I don't like to be wasteful, darling."

I use my cuffed hands to try and push him away from me. He leans back a little bit but doesn't step away. "Zahtri, let me make this clear." I arch my head back and point up to him. "I'm not going to work with you. Not now. Not Ever. I'd rather die first than work for a bunch of murderous Gadramicks. I've heard and felt what you all really feel. I haven't found anything here to make me sway my choice. So you can get that preconceived notion out of that big head of yours because it is never going to happen."

"We'll see about that," he says as he pushes me toward the door. The movement makes my head start throbbing again. I stumble backward into his chest. "You should have avoided the wall."

"You shouldn't have pushed me into the wall," I retort. He ushers me forward. My ears start buzzing—a low humming reverberates through the hall. I shake my head trying to clear the noise. I stop moving forward as the hall starts spinning—the candlelight swirling into the darkness. I close my eyes right as I feel my legs give out again.

COLTON

CROUCHING DOWN IN THE BUSHES, I look at the scene in front of me. Gadramicks are streaming out of the compound and gathering in the area behind it. A large wooden platform is being constructed as we speak, both with magic and physical labor. Through all the noise, it will be no problem getting all the mages here.

"Where do you think they are in there?" Natalie asks me as she crouches down beside me.

I look toward the compound door again. It's propped open because so many people are coming in and out. "Probably in a cell somewhere. I don't know. What I do know is that we'll find out soon enough."

I hear rustling behind me. I turn around and see about fifty mages crouching down behind the bushes. We need to remain as hidden as possible. Being spotted early would ruin everything. We need the element of surprise to be on our side if we have any chance of this working.

The air around me feels electric. I don't know if it is due to the magic being used by the Gadramicks or the anticipation of what is to come, but it's a little eerie. Natalie gasps as Dravin walks out of the compound; behind him are Liam and Adam—both handcuffed. There are four

Gadramicks around them. Even if they attempted to fight, with their hands cuffed and Ryanne not around, they wouldn't stand a chance.

"I didn't think Dravin would go against Adam," David says. "Even if he was helping Ryanne, I thought he was listening to orders."

I glare at Adam. He can't see me, but it makes me feel better. Adam's been with Ryanne these past few days keeping her safe while I couldn't, but I still can't get over everything he has done to her in the past—even before either of them were mages. There are some things you just can't forgive and forget.

Dravin orders the Gadramicks surrounding Adam and Liam to stand at the end of the platform. Two men stand behind them and two stand on either side of them, making sure that neither attempt to run. Dravin walks to the other side of the platform and quietly talks to Natasha and Valdus. I glance down at Natalie. She watches her twin through narrowed eyes. With a tight jaw and clenched fists, her feelings toward her sister are obvious to everyone surrounding us. Conner walks up and pats his sister on the back.

"What if we have to hurt her?" Natalie says to him. "What if she tries to kill either one of us?"

"I don't know, Nat. I don't know," Conner says as he pulls her in for a hug. "What I do know is that she's not the same girl we grew up with. She's not the same Natasha. I just have to hope that girl is in there somewhere."

Natalie nods and lays her head down on Conner's shoulder. I look behind me again. More mages are here. I'd say about half of our group is now crouching down in the field behind me, waiting for their cue to go. This could actually work. I have to keep a realistic outlook in mind. There's always a chance this could turn out way different than what we are intending.

I turn to my left where Bragden, Incendia, Lily, and Logan are all crouching. Bragden and Incendia are quietly arguing amongst each other. Incendia wants to be on the frontlines fighting as many Gadramicks as she can, while Bragden wants her to stay by his side where he can keep her safe. Lily and Logan are talking to each other in hushed tones. I watch Lily for a couple of moments. I've never seen Lily this open before. I hung out with her and other jocks while in school, but I never saw this side of her. I never realized how much people change themselves to fit in with others. This Lily is much more likeable, and I'm glad Ryanne helped save her. I'm glad she found Logan...even if they won't acknowledge it at the moment.

"Hey," Tom says as he comes up behind me. "We only have two or three more groups to come before we're all ready. I'll come back over here when Vincent and Larkin have transported everyone. It'll be a few more minutes. Do not do anything until then. No matter who or what comes out of those compound doors." Tom looks to Conner and David. "Do not let him move from behind these bushes until we're all ready, okay?" David and Conner agree.

A couple more Gadramicks come out of the compound and walk to the open area in front of the platform. "They're going to reveal Zahtri's identity tonight."

"How do you know that?" Natalie asks me.

"What else could they be doing?"

"I think you're right about that," Kyril says as he stops behind me. "Dravin wouldn't bring all the Gadramick's out in the open like this if it wasn't important. He wouldn't risk it."

"This could be the prophecy? This could be the moment that we've been told about?" Emma asks.

"I guess it depends on Ryanne. She hasn't been training the past couple of days. She hasn't been eating, so she won't have her full strength. And if she's hurt..." I trail off. I know that she has a few injuries. "We'll see what happens," I finally say.

On the platform, Dravin is saying something to Adam and Liam, but neither seems to the listening. They both have blank expressions on their faces as they stare down at the ground. Dravin's getting angry. Liam turns to him and says something. Even from this distance, I can see the anger in his eyes. Dravin reaches back and punches him in the jaw. Natalie gasps beside me and covers her mouth to keep from being any louder. Liam's head whips back, but he doesn't react. With a grunt, Dravin storms to the opposite end of the platform and yells at Valdus before rushing back into the compound.

"What the heck is going on?" Incendia asks.

The Gadramicks all quiet down and turn toward the compound doors. "I think we're about to find out."

CHAPTER TWENTY-ONE

COLTON

THOUGH ONLY GONE FOR A few minutes, Dravin walks out of the compound again, much calmer this time, and addresses the crowd. "Settle down. Settle down," Dravin states as he walks to the center of the platform. The already quiet Gadramicks turn and give Dravin their attention.

"I know many of you are wondering what is going on right now—why I brought all of you out here." He claps his hands. "As all of you know, we've had a couple guests here this week." He gives a pointed look to Liam.

"Where's the girl?" the Gadramicks shout. "Where is she?"

"Tsk. Tsk. Tsk, all in good time. All will be revealed in good time. First, we have some other things discuss."

I glance at Natalie. "She's still alive, Colton. That much is obvious. Be patient." I look behind me. Tom quietly moves toward me with Vincent directly behind him.

"We're all here, but I think we should hear what he is going to say before we act." I want to save Ryanne and Liam, but Dravin could say something we could use later. He could change everything with just a few words.

"Our goal was to bring Ryanne here and find out the extent of her magic. However, the girl is stubborn." All the Gadramicks start mumbling at once. "Her blood samples were inconclusive. Since she refused to use magic when provoked, I had to take matter into my own hands."

I have a bad feeling about this. I turn toward Natalie, who's watching the scene in front of us with wide eyes. "Ryanne's a threat to everything we stand for. She hasn't found out about our human experiments, but she knows enough to completely oppose us."

"They're testing on humans?" Emma asks Larkin.

Larkin shrugs. "I honestly had no idea about that." Kyril shakes his head, agreeing with Larkin. How did Dravin test on humans without anyone knowing about it?

"Could those be all the people reported missing recently?" Natalie asks.

"It's possible," Tom says as he listens to what Dravin is saying.

"Her magic is strong," he continues. "I've seen firsthand what she can do, but she's not strong enough to go against us. I feel a battle brewing. We're getting close, but we need someone who can stand up against any future threats if necessary."

The Gadramicks start talking amongst themselves again. They all thought Dravin was that person. "Yes, yes. I'm in charge," Dravin yells over them. They quiet and give him his attention again. "However, there's another mage stronger than me who is ready to lead. Ready to take his rightful place as the head of all Gadramicks."

Dravin turns and points toward the door. The compound door slowly opens, and I can see the outline of a large man standing there. Physically, he looks to be the size of Bragden. As he steps out of the compound and the light finally hits him, I see nothing but the small form in his arms. David and Conner both jump over to me and keep me from jumping out from behind the bushes.

"Ezra?" I hear Bragden say as he sits up slightly. Incendia turns and looks him confused. Liam freezes as he looks at the man in front of him.

"That's Ezra? *The* Ezra?" Incendia asks. Who the heck is Ezra?

Either Bragden doesn't hear her or he chooses not to reply. He glares up at the stage, body tensed and waiting. Ne needs this fight just as much as the rest of us. We all want this to end.

Zahtri is holding an unconscious Ryanne in his arms. I clench my jaw to keep from yelling out, because every fiber in my body wants me to jump up and protect my soulmate. From this distance I can see a bruise on the side of Ryanne's head. She's slowly starting to stir in his arms.

"She's as fragile as she looks," Zahtri says as he drops Ryanne onto the platform and steps over her body. The loud thud of her limp body hitting the hard surface causes anger to surge through me. David and Conner put more pressure on me to keep me down while Natalie covers my mouth to keep me from yelling out.

Liam instantly starts fighting against the mages holding him back. "You son of a—"

"It's nice to see you again, Liam. How's Bragden doing?" he asks. Bragden starts to get up, but Travis and his father stop him.

With a laugh, Zahtri turns around and faces everyone. "I know none of you know me, but a couple of you have sensed me around. I commend those of you who could do that. I'm Zahtri and I've been the one calling all the shots. Dravin's been listening to my orders and leading you. I haven't been needed until now. Until that girl," he points to Ryanne, who is still lying on her side. "came along. She's stirred up trouble where there was none. That's why I have to step in."

Ryanne groans and blinks her eyes open. "You know dropping someone while they're unconscious is a little rude. What kind of host are you?" she yells up at him. Ryanne pushes herself up into a seated position and looks at Zahtri with a sweet smile on her face. I hear Incendia and Emma snicker to my left. Ryanne stands up and walks over to Zahtri and points at him with her cuffed hands. She whispers something to him, too quietly for any of us to hear. He looks down at Ryanne amused, but pushes her behind him and steps forward.

A Gadramick walks up behind Ryanne and grabs her around the waist. She looks down at his arm around her stomach and then back up at Zahtri, eyebrow quirked. "Just as a precaution, darling. I know you could easily take him down."

The Gadramick holding Ryanne looks shocked, but keeps his arm around her. Ryanne doesn't struggle, but looks bored. I see her glance over at Liam and Adam and shake her head as she reads one of their thoughts.

"I gave Ryanne two options tonight. One, she could stand by my side and rule with me. With our combined powers, we'd be unstoppable. I'd give her everything she could ever want, but she didn't like that option. The second option was that I finally kill her in front of you all. This would solidify my position and get rid of our biggest threat. Ryanne, here," Zahtri walks over to Ryanne and grabs her from the Gadramick. Keeping a tight grip around her waist, he pulls her against his chest. David and Conner tighten their grip on me. "Well, she chose the second option. Apparently, there's another man in her life, and she'd never fight amongst the likes of me."

Zahtri reaches forward pushes her hair off her shoulder. Ryanne flinches away from his touch. "It's a shame though," Zahtri says as he looks toward the Gadramicks. "She's a beauty, isn't she?" A chorus of shouts and hoots from the Gadramicks answer. Zahtri lightly trails his hand down Ryanne's side before resting on her hip. The weight on me increases as everyone tries to hold me down. I notice Liam struggling to get away from the Gadramicks holding him.

Zahtri turns Ryanne around so he is facing him. Ryanne struggles in his arms, but Zahtri tightens his grip. Even from here, I can hear Ryanne's gasp from the pain. She's not strong enough physically to go up against someone like him. Why isn't she using her magic?

Zahtri smiles up at the Gadramicks before he crushes Ryanne up against his chest and kisses her. She squeals against him, causing the Gadramicks to laugh. All the sudden, Zahtri pulls back and forcefully pushes Ryanne onto the ground. She slams into the platform, unable to catch herself because of the handcuffs.

"She bit me," Zahtri tells Dravin.

"I warned you," Dravin says as he walks onto the platform. Liam and Adam both start fight against the Gadramicks holding them as Zahtri slowly walks toward Ryanne.

Get up. Get up. Get up. Get up. I almost jump up when Ryanne doesn't move. I can see her breathing so I know that she's alright. Zahtri crouches down beside her and smiles. Ryanne lifts her head, flipping her hair out of her face, and looks toward him. "Didn't anyone ever tell you how to treat a girl? Your mother would be ashamed of you." Laughter rises amongst all the Gadramicks in attendance at Ryanne's boldness.

"What is she doing?" Natalie asks.

"I'm hoping she has a plan," I mumble as I watch. I know that Ryanne is not known for having a plan. She usually doesn't think before she acts.

She just goes for it—no matter how dangerous. I look toward Tom. He shakes his head at me. When are we going to make our appearance?

"Still sticking with option two?"

"First is the worst, second is the best," she sings as she stands up. "Why don't you tell everyone how you really got your magic, Zahtri? Hmm? Don't you think that everyone should hear that?" Zahtri tries to walk toward Ryanne, but she apparently has a shield around her because he stumbles back a couple steps. "You're a mage, yes, but not a very powerful one. Why don't you tell them about how you acquired your magic?"

"What is she talking about?" David whispers.

"Yeah...didn't think I caught that, did you?" she asks him. "Why don't you tell everyone how the witches aren't really in hiding, Zahtri." Ryanne takes a step toward him. "You killed them off. You took the extraction process that Dr. Arden perfected and stole their magic. You decimated an entire magical race so you could pretend to be an all-powerful mage. You dabble in dark magic because that's the only magic you have. You were born into a mage family, but you never came into your powers. Instead of telling anyone, you obtained it in other ways."

Fuming, Zahtri moves forward until he's standing a foot away from Ryanne, at the edge of her shield. "Why don't you explain to everyone how you were in hiding because you don't have any magic of your own and needed someone to formulate some for you, because you're a fake. A phony. A poser."

Zahtri is seething. Why is she instigating him? The Gadramicks around us start talking amongst themselves. I look toward the doorway of the compound and see a man standing there, watching the platform. Ryanne gives Zahtri her sweet smile as she drops the shield and swings her leg around to kick Zahtri in the face. He stumbles to the side. Ryanne jumps forward and grabs something around his neck. Taking a few steps backward, she leans forward and pushes her magic out. Zahtri flies back and lands in the grass beside the platform. Dravin runs forward and attempts to grab Ryanne, but she pushes magic toward him as well. Like Zahtri, he flies backward.

The Gadramicks in the grass jump up. Ryanne gets to work on the cuffs. Making quick work, she unlocks the handcuffs and throws something to Liam. Zahtri must have had the key around his neck. Ryanne runs toward Liam and Adam and starts fighting the men behind them. She easily takes them out with the combination of her magic assaults and physical combat.

Liam unlocks his handcuffs and helps Adam undo his. Dravin and Zahtri both stand up and slowly walk toward Ryanne, Liam, and Adam.

"Now?" I ask Tom. Tom looks toward Ryanne. She throws up a shield around them and backs up. Leaning back, she whispers something to Liam who nods and prepares for the fight ahead. I watch as she leans over and kisses Adam on the cheek, causing a surge of jealousy to course through me. He looks surprised but seems prepared to fight with them.

Ryanne turns around and looks at Dravin a small smile on her face. I glance toward Logan who nods at me, knowing he has to get her. If she's going to get out of this, she has to be healed. I'm about to stand up when Ryanne starts to raise her arms. Conner and David drag me back down. The wind around us is starting to pick up. Ryanne's hair is blowing around her crazily as she calls more magic to her. All the Gadramicks trying to break down the shield are having difficulty. Even Zahtri looks stunned at Ryanne's magic. Dropping the shield, she thrusts her arms forward and sends all the wind out. The Gadramicks, including Dravin, fall backward, landing on the ground in front of the platform. Zahtri stumbles, but remains standing.

"Now."

CHAPTER TWENTY-TWO

"THIS IS IT," I TELL Liam as Dravin and Zahtri start stalking toward us. We are way outnumbered right now and the possibility of coming out of this alive is slim to none. I strengthen the shield around us and look in Adam's direction to see what he's doing. He's in a defensive stance scanning the area around us. Despite everything he's done in the past, he's really been there for me this past week. Adam gives me a small, sad smile. He knows what's about to happen.

"Thank you, Adam," I whisper to him. I lean up and kiss him on the cheek. I know Adam has feelings for me, but he never once acted on them because he knows about Colton. That's all I can give him. A look of shock crosses his face when I step back. I need to give us some time to try and get in a better location.

Magic, I need you. I don't want the magic to flow into me like I've done previously. I want it to flow around me, creating a single large gust of wind. Zahtri said I wasn't strong enough because I hadn't yet released all my magic. Well, he's about to see how strong I can really be.

While standing on the platform with Zahtri earlier, I attempted something I'd never tried before. I needed the key he had dangling around his neck, but I knew he'd read my mind and figure out my plan. Creating a shield around my mind, I projected false thoughts to him. All the thoughts were things I'd thought about previously, so I'm really surprised he didn't catch on.

Slowly raising my arms, I wait for the magic to reach its peak. I know I can do more, but right now I only need a couple seconds to move. Zahtri looks surprised that I'm even attempting to fight against so many of them. However, he should know better than that. He's been reading my mind, he knows how I think. He also knows there is no way I'm ever going to work for the Gadramicks. Now, I'm going to make sure he regrets not killing me when he had the chance.

I drop the shield and thrust my magic out as I instantly start walking back. I turn around quickly and push Liam and Adam off the platform. They know what I'm doing and instantly turn around and start running.

When I stop moving, I see all the Gadramicks lying on the grass seemingly shocked that I was able to do that to all of them at once. A few even look scared. Zahtri is the only one left standing. I throw another shield around Liam, Adam, and myself as we continue moving. Zahtri looks angered, so I know that there is going to be a battle. There's no turning back now.

I am about to drop the shield when I see Colton and Tom jump up from behind the bushes in the distance and start running toward us. I can't help the smile that forms on my face, when I see Colton alive. However, that smile is short lived when I see him making his way into the thick of the Gadramicks. A couple hundred mages jump out from the bushes behind my family and join them.

"How did they get so many?" Liam asks.

"I told him not to come," I whisper. "I didn't want to risk it. Why doesn't anyone listen to me?"

"He's just as stubborn as you are, Ryanne. You just have to accept that," Liam says. "And I told him *to* come."

I whip around and face him, totally forgetting about the fight ensuing around us. "What? Why would you do that? You know I wouldn't risk his life like that. There's a chance we're not going to come out of this alive and I don't want that to happen to him either." I point in Colton's direction, but I honestly have no idea where he is right now. I lost him when he started fighting all the Gadramicks.

"Because I want you to get out of this. Do you think he'd be able to live with himself if you died and he didn't even try to save you? No, he wouldn't. You have to think about what your death would do to him as well. You're soulmates. If you can't survive without him, what makes you think that he could survive without you?"

"Because I'm weak, Liam! Colton's not."

Liam grabs my shoulders and turns me toward him. Grabbing my chin, he forces me to look up at him. "No, you're not, Ryanne, and you're going to prove that to every last one of the Gadramicks here today. Channel their anger and strengthen your magic. Think about everything you've felt and heard since you've been here. Do whatever it takes to make it out of here alive." When I don't say anything, Liam continues, "Ryanne, Colton came out here to save you. I want you to fight so you get that life you imagined afterwards. You deserve that much."

Colton did come here to save me. The least I can do is fight. I nod and look at the mess around me. Mages are still running from behind the bushes. Our numbers look evenly matched. "Okay," I turn and look between Adam and Liam. "I'm going to drop the shield. Are you guys ready? It's about to get crazy."

"It's already crazy, Ryanne. Drop the shield. Let's do this," Liam announces. Both Liam and Adam step on either side of me, preparing for a fight. I see Natasha fighting her way through the chaos. She's asphyxiating people left and right, both mages and Gadramicks. I need to stop her from hurting anyone else. However my eyes are drawn to the area behind her. Zahtri is fighting multiple mages at once and succeeding. I'm the only one who has a chance of stopping him, but I don't think I'm strong enough right now.

"Liam," I say as I drop the shield and start fighting a Gadramick that jumped in front of me. I block his punch and Adam commands him to walk away. "I need Logan if I'm going to stop Zahtri. I need my full strength."

Another man runs toward us. Liam steps in front of me and makes quick work of him—knocking him unconscious before the man even knew what hit him. "You've got to teach me that," I tell him.

"Maybe someday," he says without even looking back at me.

The tintinnabulation of swords hitting each other echoes through the field, and my stomach tightens with each metal-on-metal pang that I hear, because I know that this could very well be the end...for all of us. Every shout and grunt I hear pierces me, weakening me with guilt. This is all because of me. These people are getting hurt because of me. I never wanted any of this to happen. I didn't want a large battle to ensue. I wanted a quick ending. A simple fight between two people where one comes out victorious. The end.

Nothing can ever be that simple.

I didn't want to be the prophecy girl. I didn't want magic. I just wanted a normal life with friends and family—people who loved me as much as I loved them. I guess some things don't come free. Through this process, I've gotten myself into some sticky situations, but I've come out of all of them stronger. Everything I've been through, everything I've done, has brought me to this moment. I gained so much through this whole ordeal.

I have a family now. I have a soulmate, best friend, and future husband all in one man. I have a dozen people who are willing to risk their life for me tonight and are now fighting with everything they have in them to stop the Gadramicks from wreaking more havoc. Their reign has gone on long enough and it needs to be stopped. All these mages are fighting for me to succeed. Each of them has a different story, a different reason for being here, but a reason nonetheless. I can't let them down.

I scan the crowd again, trusting Liam and Adam to protect me if anyone comes near. I see Emma and David fighting off to my right. Seeing fire to the left, I know that Incendia is near there and if my hunch is correct, Bragden will be fighting beside her. Larkin and Kyril are tag-teaming it and creating a lot of confusion on the far right side of the field. Larkin is transporting in and out of different areas, knocking unobservant Gadramicks unconscious. I'd like to think he's only knocking them unconscious anyway. I see Lily in the middle of a fight. She's standing back to back with Natalie, Colton, and Logan. Colin, Tom, and a third man are all standing together, fighting. Based on their teamwork, I'd say that they've worked together before.

"I see them," I tell Liam. Liam reaches forward and punches a man in the jaw. His body goes slack as he falls to the ground in pain. Liam kicks him in the chest and moves onto the next Gadramick.

She's just going to let them do all the dirty work, I see. Simultaneously, I turn around and push my magic out, sending a group of about ten Gadramicks flying into the bases of large oak trees.

"I'm going to try and push my way through everyone. Can you two handle yourself here?" I ask.

"I'm coming with you Ryanne," Liam announces. I've already moved a couple steps forward, before I turn around and face him. I throw a shield up around us again. I knew Liam would make this difficult and pull the protector card.

I look at him for a moment and then realize how much time I'm wasting just standing here. "Fine, but keep up," I smile at him as I turn around and the drop the shield. I casually walk forward into the large crowd.

That girl is crazy, I hear Liam think behind me. I shoot a smile at him over my shoulder and wink, but continue moving. With each step I take, I channel all the anger from everyone into me. Anger fuels my magic, making it more aggressive—stronger.

When someone attempts to run toward me, I point my arm out and shoot my magic toward him. My liquid lightning cascades from my palm and hits the man in the chest. Without thinking about it, I move on. I hit two more men before I think better of this idea. I stop moving and wait for everyone to come to me.

"Ryanne, what are you doing?" Liam shouts at me while fighting off another man.

"Don't worry about me, Liam," I shout back. "Just watch my back."

I bring my arms above my head all the while calling my magic to me. I don't know if this is going to work, but it's worth a shot. I can hear Liam fighting behind me, but that doesn't faze me. I know that he's fully capable of defending himself and protecting me. I trust my protector with my life.

I close my eyes and envision the scene in front of me freezing—all the Gadramicks stopping mid-motion, frozen in time, while the mages remain as they are. I need to talk to everyone for a moment and this is the only way I can think of accomplishing that feat. Still hearing the fighting around me, I push more magic out, imagining it coating each individual; lining their bodies and slowing their movements until they stop moving all together. The sound slowly decrescendos until all I hear is the breathing of those around me.

"Did you do that?" Liam asks me. Hearing the awe in his voice, I open my eyes. Everyone has frozen mid-action like someone pushed pause on a movie. It's just like I imagined.

I ignore his question and slowly weave my way through all the unmoving bodies. I don't know how long this is going to last, so I need to get to Logan fast. I can hear some people shuffling around me, but I hope they are the mages. I think some of the mages froze during the process, so I apparently wasn't as specific as I thought I was.

"Logan?" I call out. They were standing close to this area last time I saw them. I accidently bump into a Gadramick. His body teeters, but he doesn't come unfrozen. Huh, Weebles do wobble, but they don't fall down. I can't help the tiny giggle that escapes. Adam and Liam step up behind me and give me a questioning look.

"This is so cool," Adam says as he waves his hand in front of the man's face. Obviously, he doesn't respond.

"Ryanne?" I hear Logan call back to me. I turn to my left and pick up my speed. I know his voice came from this direction.

"I can see him. Keep heading forward. They're about twenty feet in front of us."

"It'd nice if I was just a little taller," I mumble as I duck under someone's outstretch arm. "Then, I'd be able to see them for myself."

Liam laughs at me, but doesn't say anything. I maneuver around all the frozen bodies. This reminds of when I was little and we'd all play freeze tag in the middle of the street—except for the fact that we never actually froze. There's not a single kid who can remain still for that long.

"So, Zahtri is actually Ezra?" I ask Liam as I duck under an extended arm.

"Apparently. I'd recognize him anywhere. He looks older now, but it's him."

"I saw that scar on him earlier and thought of the story you told me, but you didn't mention specifically where you cut him, so I wasn't sure. I didn't know for sure though until I read your thoughts. You were basically screaming them at me."

"I'm sorry about that. It just took me by surprise. All of my anger just came rushing back the second I saw him. It all makes sense though. I knew there was a reason why Valdus was working with the Gadramicks. He wouldn't just help them for no reason."

I dodge another arm before entering into a cleared area. Colton's spinning around in a circle, confused. He stops when she sees me and his eyes widen. Instead of waiting for him to come to me, I run forward and jump into his arms. My heart swells when I feel his arms wrap around my back as he catches me. I didn't realize how bad I was actually feeling until this moment. The aching feeling in my heart dissipates and the empty feeling I've been having leaves. I bury my face in his neck and wrap my arms tightly around his neck. "Thank you for not listening to me," I mumble against his skin.

"Even Jack Sparrow needs help every once in a while."

Colton sets me down and looks at me. I see and feel the anger that flashes across his eyes as he takes in my appearance. I know that I have a black eye and bruise on my shoulder. Considering the amount of throbbing in my head, I'm sure that there's an even more obvious bruise there too. "I need Logan to heal me," I whisper as I look around the small area. Everyone is here except Bragden and Incendia. Logan pushes through everyone and walks over to me.

"Well, I've seen you look worse, gorgeous."

I smile as I step away from Colton and walk over to him. Without wasting a second, Logan wraps his arms around me while simultaneously healing me. I sink into him letting his healing magic work its way through my body. "You sure do like to get yourself into trouble, don't you?" Logan whispers as he releases me. Leaning forward he kisses my forehead. "We've missed ya, little one."

"Ryanne, did you do this?" Tom asks as he points to a Gadramick on his left.

"Yeah, I knew that I wouldn't be able to stop Zahtri until I had my full strength, so I needed to find a way to get to Logan. I thought about just fighting my way through, but that would take too long, so I froze them."

"Amazing," a man says as he steps around Tom. This is the man I saw fighting beside him earlier.

"Oh, Ryanne, this is Vincent. Vincent this is Ryanne. Vincent helped transport everyone here."

"It's nice to meet you. I feel like I know you already from what I've heard from Claire and this boy," Vincent claps Colton on the back. I smile as I listen to his voice. The deep timbre of his voice is raspy yet very soothing to the ears. I can only imagine what Incendia and Emma have said about him.

"It's nice to meet you, too. Thank you for helping." My eyes widen. "Wait, Claire contacted you?"

"Yep, she said that a pretty girl needed my help and I better get off my high horse and rejoin the mage world."

"Sounds like Claire," I say. Seeing movement to my right, I bring my eyes over there. Bragden is standing there with Incendia. When he sees me he takes two longs strides and engulfs me in a hug. My feet are lifted off the ground, so I wrap my arms around his neck.

"You sure do have a way of scaring those who care for you, missy."

"I've missed you, Bragden." I say as he sets me back on the ground. "I didn't realize how much I missed our little pranks on each other until I couldn't do them anymore."

"Dude," Liam says behind me. Bragden looks over my head at his brother and smiles. I turn around right as Liam continues, "We're blood and you didn't even say hey, nice to see you again to me." He shakes his head, but can't say anything more as Natalie runs across the clearing and jumps into his arms.

"Sorry, man, missed you too." Bragden mutters, but knows that Liam isn't listening anymore. When he steps back to Incendia's side, I see the small flamed pendant around her neck. Bragden finally gave his necklace away.

I turn around and look at Colton again, but he's not looking at me. He's glaring at Adam. Liam's standing off to the side with a large grin on his face as his eyes move between Colton and Adam.

Boys.

"Colton, stop giving him the death glare."

"Nope," Colton says without taking his eyes away from Adam.

I walk up to Colton and grab his chin, making him look at me. Colton moves his head down, but his eyes remain fixed on Adam. "Colton, look at me," I demand. I wait a couple seconds and when he doesn't move, I stomp on his foot.

"Ouch," he says as he looks down at me. I can hear the mages around me laughing, but I don't acknowledge them.

"Leave Adam alone. He's proven himself to me this week and I trust him. He wants to help."

"Have you forgotten everything he's ever done to you?" Colton whispers to me.

"No, but I believe people are capable of change. Look at Lily," I tell him. Colton looks toward Logan and Lily. I see his expression change. "She used to pick on me in school too, Colton, but I've forgiven her. Why is it not possible for Adam to change as well?"

"That's different."

"No, it's not."

"He attacked you, Ryanne. Multiple times."

"And has protected me multiple times this past week." Colton stares down at me for a couple of seconds, before sighing. I can tell that I've won. "Please, leave him alone." I glance behind me at Adam, hoping that I don't regret standing up for him. Adam nods and I feel his gratefulness wash over me. He didn't want to fight Colton, because he knew it would upset me.

The shuffling around me gets louder as more mages start to make their way over to us. I hear whispers as people wonder what the heck is going on. Knowing I have to address everyone, I step away from Colton and walk to the center of the open area. I smile at some familiar faces, but there are many people here I don't recognize. My smile widens when I see Lucas and his silent posse push through everyone.

Liam walks over to me and grabs my arm, pulling me toward him. "Ryanne, I understand what my mom meant." At my confused look, he continues, "About the secret of the flame."

"What? How?"

"In this situation, you are the secret of the flame. You bring the illumination we need in this dark time. You're the light—the catalyst for the dawn." I'm the secret of the flame? "A dawn is coming," he reminds me, "but we need you."

I'm the secret of the flame.

I now know what I have to do. I look behind me and walk over to the platform. *Air, can you help me?* I ask as I visualize myself being hoisted up and gently placed on the platform. I feel my feet being lifted on the ground. I use my arms to make sure I get enough upward movement. When I'm floating above the platform, I release the magic and let myself float down until my feet are firmly planted on the wood structure.

"Look," I announce to everyone. "I don't know how long this magic is going to stay. I'm honestly surprised that it's lasted this long. Many of you don't know me and I apologize for that. I wanted to meet all of you before this time came, but plans change.

"I may be able to see the future and I may be able to read minds and emotions, but today is as much of a mystery to me as it is to you. I don't know how all of this is going to play out." So many different emotions crash into me that I have to take a step back and mentally sort through them. Determination. Anger. Sadness. Love. Respect. Fear. "I'm scared, too. I'm afraid that everything I've fought for will be lost tonight, but isn't that what life is about? Fighting for what you believe in?

"If you never had to fight for something, you've never truly lived. Life is about the unknowns. You never know where tomorrow is going to take you, but you go through the day because you want to know. Right here, right now, this is what I've been fighting for. This moment where I can finally do something good—where we all can finally do something good. We're all here for a reason. Whether it is to stop the Gadramicks," I motion toward the Howicks, "whether it is for closure, we're all here for something. I want to finally stop Dravin and Zahtri.

"They've been testing on humans, trying to see if they can create a whole new magical race. Both Zahtri and Dravin tried to keep that thought from me, but their mental barriers are not as strong as they think they are. They've been trying to extract magic. At first, I thought it was so they could give it to Dravin to make him stronger, but I was wrong. Zahtri injected himself with the magic from witches. He's learned how to use Dark Magic. Dravin's been doing some experiments on the side. They're trying to create a whole army of mages. Nonmages with powers. They've killed too many people during this experiment, and it needs to end today.

"I'm not saying that I agree with killing anyone. I've been at this compound way too many times, but since I've been here, I'm come to realize a few things. Not all the Gadramicks here are bad. Larkin and

Kyril were once Gadramicks, but now they're my family." I look toward them and smile. Both of them smile and give me a knowing nod. "Adam was once one of the Gadramicks on the top of my list, but this past week, he's been one of few reasons why I'm alive and standing in front of all of you. People can change. Please, don't forget that.

"I know that blood will be shed here today. I wish that I could save everyone here, but I can't, because I don't know if I'll make it out of this either. What happens today will be remembered for a long time, and I hope that we'll all come out of this alive, but," I glance toward the door of the compound where I know he's standing, "sometimes fate has a different plan for us. There's no more running. No more hiding. This is it." Jedrek nods and slowly walks toward me.

I tear my eyes away from him and address everyone again. I know he's still walking in this direction. "Fight for your friends. Your family. Fight for the person standing next to you. Fight for all the mages you've met. Fight for the humans who have lost their lives and fight for those we've lost. Don't forget why we're here."

I turn to my right and watch Jedrek approach me. "Oh and one more thing," I say. "Zahtri's mine."

"Ryanne, hear me out," he whispers to me. I know everyone is watching us. I bite my lip and take a step back.

"I can't do this right now," I tell him.

He reaches forward and grabs my arm to keep me from walking further away. "I may not get another chance, Ryanne." I can feel my eyes filling with tears, but I refuse to cry in front of this many people. "I was coming to see you when I got into a car accident. A semi-truck t-boned me and sent my car rolling into a ditch. I don't know if he planned it, but Dravin found me on the side of the road, unconscious. I came around long enough to agree to a blood promise. I was scared and confused and had no idea what it was, but he said that it would save my life, so I agreed.

"He needed me run his experiments. I specialize in cell research and he knew that my knowledge would be useful for his plans. I didn't know he would come after you. I wouldn't have agreed to anything if I thought you were going to be in danger. Dravin made me promise to never seek you out. To never try and contact you. That's why I never came back. I wasn't allowed to have contact with anyone I knew before.

"I've regretted that decision every day. I knew you were alive, and I knew you'd have questions, but I couldn't give you the answers you needed. I was literally bound to stay away. I've wanted to turn back time every day, just so I could see you once. I wanted to be there for you. I wanted to be your dad. I never wanted any of this to happen.

"Maureen never told me she was pregnant. I called her for months after I left, trying to apologize, but she wanted nothing to do with me. There was nothing I could do. I loved your mom, Ryanne. I know you don't think of me as your dad, but I am and I'm so sorry this is how we had to meet. I've imagined this moment for sixteen years and this is not how I wanted to tell you all these things. I didn't want to be standing here in front of hundreds of mages while you're about to fight for your life.

"If I could go back, I would choose to die in that accident like I was supposed to. I know I can't go back. I can only go forward. I know you have no positive feelings toward me, but I do love you. I regret everything I've ever done for Dravin." Jedrek turns away from me and faces the mages in front of us. "If any of you get the chance, take out Dravin. I'm ashamed of the things I've done because of this blood promise. I've escaped the fates for too long. It's time to finally stop running. Dravin's done some pretty gruesome things under the orders of Zahtri and both need to be stopped."

I can feel the tears fully streaming down my face now. Jedrek turns back to me. "Don't cry for me, Ryanne. I've accepted this and knew it was coming for a long time now. I'm so proud of everything you're doing right now. I'm so proud of you, and I'm sorry I was never there for you. I'm sorry I never got to really know you, but I'm glad to call the girl standing in front of me, my daughter. Despite what you think, I do love you and hope you find all the happiness you deserve in the world."

Jedrek looks at something over my head. He leans down and wipes the tears away from my cheek. "You're much stronger than you think. Zahtri is strong, but so are you. You can do this, Ryanne. You just have to believe in yourself as much as everyone out there believes in you." He leans down and whispers in my ear, "They're starting to stir, you don't have much longer."

With that, he leaves me standing on the platform alone. I turn around and wipe the last of my tears away. I feel a pair of arms snake around my waist. I instantly recognize his touch and lean back against Colton's chest. "I'm fine."

With a deep breath, I force myself to step out of Colton's arms, fully knowing that that may have been the last time I'll feel his arms around me. "The magic is wearing off. Get into position. It's time to finally end this."

CHAPTER TWENTY-THREE

COLTON

I HATE THAT I CAN'T make her feel better. I can see the Gadramicks stirring around me, but Ryanne is my only focus right now. I turn her around and force her to look up at me. "Ryanne, go tell him."

She sniffles and looks toward the door of the compound before returning her eyes to me. The remaining unshed tears bring out the light browns and greens in her eyes. "Tell him what?" she whispers to me.

"You know what you need to tell him." Ryanne bites her lip. I pull her forward and lightly kiss her. She sighs and nods against my lips. I pull back and tuck her hair behind her ears.

"Go," I tell her. As she moves past me, I lightly tap her on the butt. She gasps and turns around, staring at me with wide eyes. Winking at her, I jump off the platform. I can hear her laughing behind me as she walks toward her father. I'm glad I can give her a little semblance of happiness at this time, because I know in a few minutes that's all going to change.

"Is she okay?" Liam asks me while watching Ryanne. "She didn't react well when she talked to him the first time."

"She will be," I unsheathe my sword.

"Did anyone write down that speech? Because that was pretty freaking awesome," Emma says as she grabs her weapons. "That's one for the history books," she pauses. "Mage history books. Is there such a thing as mage history books?"

"I got it," Larkin says. We all turn toward him shocked. He pushes a button on his cell phone and Ryanne's voice flows out from the speakers.

"Oh my gosh, Larkin. That's amazing. Why didn't I think of that?" Emma asks David.

Everyone brings out their weapons and gets in a protective stance. Liam kisses Natalie and walks to the edge of the platform near Ryanne. Natalie frowns as he walks away again. We just got them back, and they're already distancing themselves again. Liam looks back at me. I understand what he's silently asking me. I step closer to Natalie and nod back at him. I'll watch his soulmate while he watches mine.

"Do you think we'll get out of this situation?" Natalie asks me. I bring my sword in front of me and watch the Gadramicks around us. They're all twitching; making subtle movements.

"I hope to God we do."

"Colton, I think you should use your invisibility here. Give yourself an advantage over everyone," David says. I stare at him for a second, mind reeling. Why don't I ever think of stuff like this? "Esh, you and Ryanne *are* perfect for each other," he mumbles. "She always forgets she has powers until it's too late."

"Sometimes I do forget that I have a power."

"Sometimes I remember that I don't have one," Emma mumbles. I turn and look at her but she's looking at the ground. With a sigh, she looks up, "How the heck am I supposed to fight against a bunch of Gadramicks who have powers?"

"The same way you've been doing it so far, by kicking their—"

"Hey, hey now. She's a lady, Colton," David says with a laugh.

I punch my brother lightly in the arm and turn back toward Ryanne. She's walking away from Jedrek and looking around the field. Her eyes land on mine. She nods at me. This is it. The wind picks up speed, so I know that Ryanne is calling her magic to her.

"She'll be fine, Colton. Her magic has gotten much stronger since she's been here," Larkin says. "Dravin didn't know that Ryanne's power increases with negative emotions. She's been channeling all the anger around here and she's completely pissed off. Dravin's plan has backfired."

I forget sometimes that Larkin can sense magic. Ryanne turns around and whispers something to Liam. Adam walks up the stairs on the platform and says something to Ryanne. She turns and looks over at Dravin's frozen form. Her eyes narrow, but she nods.

"What is he saying to her?"

"That Ryanne needs to watch out for Dravin. He's sneaky," Emma says, "and still very dangerous." We all turn to stare at her. How could she hear that?

"What?"

"Do you see how far away Ryanne is from us?" I ask her. "Adam whispered and you heard them. None of us could hear them from here," I say. "We'd need them to be yelling or speaking into a microphone for us to hear them." A small black microphone appears in Emma's hands.

She gasps and drops the microphone. A loud screeching noise echoes through the field. Emma looks up at David and me through wide eyes.

David smiles at her. "I think you just got your power, babe." At Emma's confused look, he continues, "You're a conjurer."

"A conjurer?" she asks. The Gadramicks around us are starting to move more often. "But how does that explain why I could hear Ryanne and Adam?"

"Hypersensitivity? I have no idea," David says. Like me, he's surveying the field around us. Normally, we'd be really excited for Emma, especially since she's been waiting for her power, but there's a lot going on right now.

I hear gasps around us and I look up right in time to see Ryanne drop to the ground, narrowly avoiding a flying dagger. Adam and Liam both whip around and face Dravin. They start to head for him, but Ryanne jumps up and shoots him with a bolt of lightning.

Dravin stops smiling as he is hurtled backward in a tree trunk. Both guys turn and look at Ryanne surprised. Seeing her lips moving, I turn toward Emma. I want to know what she's saying.

"She said she can read minds, so she knew Dravin was going to throw the dagger, and he's really starting to piss her off, so she wanted to be the one who attacked him first."

I smile. That's my girl.

Ryanne turns toward me again and places her palm over her heart. She mouths the words *I love you.* I do the same. She gives me a small smile and then does a back flip off the platform.

Without missing a beat, she side-kicks a Gadramick who had just unfrozen. Emma laughs, "I've missed her spunk."

A second later, all the Gadramicks unfreeze and start fighting again like nothing happened. A couple look confused when the mages they were fighting before are no longer in front of them, but many fight like nothing happened. I swing my sword out at the same time as I think about Ryanne being attacked by all the Gadramicks here. I think about how she looked when Zahtri first brought her out—lying unconscious with bruises on her face and body. I feel my invisibility coming out as I punch a Gadramick in the stomach. He grunts in pain as I bring my sword over my head and stab him in the same spot as I punched.

I try to not think about how I just killed a man. He's a Gadramick. This was the day I've been training for my whole life. I knew that I would have to kill. However, knowing that I would have to kill someone and actually doing it are two different things. I don't have time to dwell on this for too long, because I feel something wet start to drip down my right arm.

I didn't even feel any pain from the cut, but dark blood is dripping down my arm. I turn around and see a Gadramick grinning at me. I lunge for him, but he blocks my attack. "Your little girlfriend over there feels pretty good pressed up against me," he says. "Like we're meant for each other."

I clench my jaw. Looking at him, I see the remnants of bruises under his eyes. This must be the Gadramick Adam attacked for trying to touch Ryanne.

"How's your eye?" I ask him as I bring my sword forward again. He growls and steps back, but not far enough. The point of my weapon cuts through the fabric of his shirt and a couple layers of skin. Thick red blood seeps from the wound. Feeling the wetness on his chest, he yells and runs toward me, but I'm prepared for this attack.

Being angry, the man is sloppy. He's not balanced on his feet and he's only using his upper body to move the sword. Since he's only using his arms, he'll tire him out much sooner. I smile when I start to get the upper hand. Out of the corner of my eye, I can see Natalie fighting off a Gadramick who is nearly twice her size.

I bring my sword back and thrust it into his gut. The man gurgles and falls to the ground. I pull my sword back and turn toward Natalie. My invisibility has completely taken over. Now, no one can see me.

I walk up behind the guy and thrust the hilt of my sword into the pressure point in the back of his neck. Without letting out a single noise, he falls to the ground with a thud. Natalie looks confused at first and then she smiles. "Thank you, Colton."

THIS GADRAMICK IS REALLY STARTING to make me mad. I don't want to kill him, but he won't stay down. I've attempted knocking him out without magic so many times, but he's being stupid. I grunt as I duck his thrown punch and his laughter echoes through my mind.

He's too cocky for his own good.

Adam walks up behind him and hits his pressure point, silently knocking him out. "Why does everyone know how to do that but me?" I yell at him.

He gives me a small smile as he turns and starts fighting another Gadramick. If anyone would have told me that one day Adam and I would work together, I wouldn't believe them. Even without magic, Adam has been my enemy. Now, we're working together to stop the Gadramicks; the same people he was helping only days ago.

My eyes land on the doorway, but Jedrek is no longer standing there. I don't know where he went. Earlier, I walked up to him and apologized for yelling at him in the lab. I know that he didn't understand what he was getting himself into. I remember when I was in the car accident with mom, I couldn't think straight. I didn't know what was going on around me.

He told me to kill Dravin. "Don't think about the blood promise, Ryanne. Stop Dravin." Despite me proclaiming that he's nothing more than a sperm donor to me, I know that's not true. He's my dad. We don't get to choose who are parents are. Blood is blood. I just wish there was a way I could stop Dravin and save him. I just found him and now I have to lose him again.

I look around the field. I can't see Colton anymore. In fact, I can't really see anyone through the chaos. I laugh as I hear Adam commanding Gadramicks to fight other Gadramicks. I'm so glad he's on our side. His power is very helpful. Liam reaches past me and punches a man in the jaw. I jump back and hit Liam's chest. I hadn't seen the man standing there. I need to get out of my thoughts and focus on the task at hand.

My eyes continue their scan as I look for one person specifically. I see him standing off to the side, alone. He's not fighting anyone, and no one is attempting to fight him.

"I'm going to go after Zahtri," I yell at Liam and Adam. Both Adam and Liam knock out the men they're fighting and turn toward me. It's almost comical how both men fall to the ground unconscious at the same time.

"Ryanne, are you sure you want to do that?" Liam asks.

"Liam, I'm the only one here that can," I tell him. A man comes at me and I push a string of magic toward him without taking my eyes off Liam. He falls instantly. They both raise their eyebrows at my action, but don't say anything.

I don't like this. Colton will kill me.

She's right, but she could get herself killed in the process.

"Colton's not going to kill you, Liam. He understands that I have to do this," I tell him. I turn to Adam. "And I could very well get myself killed, but that's a risk I'm willing to take to stop Zahtri."

I walk up to Liam and give him a hug. "You're not going to die if anything happens to me," I whisper to him.

"It's not me I'm worried about," he tells me. "How do you know that?"

"It's just a feeling I have." I whisper to him as I step back.

As I turn around, Adam reaches out and grabs my wrist and pulls me back. "I'm sorry for high school."

"That's in the past," I say as I step away from him.

"I was jealous of him," he states. I instantly know that he's referring to Colton. Adam told me something similar before, but I didn't think much about it then.

"I know." Taking a few steps back, I start walking toward Zahtri. Liam looks torn. He wants to be with me during this, but I know I'm supposed to do this alone. This is what I'm supposed to do. It's him versus me. No one else. It hurts to leave him standing there, but it has to be done. I didn't get to tell him that Claire came to me while I was unconscious after Zahtri pushed me into a wall. She said that Liam was meant to protect me for this moment. Everything was leading to this. I no longer need Liam's protection, but I know nothing I tell him will make him believe that. No matter what, Liam will always be my protector, with or without magic binding him to me.

"Please remember Ryanne, a dawn is coming. Don't give up just yet," he yells after me.

"This is darkest dawn I've ever seen, Liam." I give Liam and Adam a small smile as I call my magic to me to jump onto the platform. Zahtri stands up straighter when he sees me, but doesn't move.

Two Gadramicks jump onto the platform with me: one in front and the other behind me. Simultaneously, they run toward me. I roll my eyes. You'd think these Gadramicks would communicate with each other to see which stunts work against me and which things are just stupid to attempt. I push my magic underneath me. When they're both a foot away from me, I jump and hover ten feet above the ground. The men collide into each other and fall over. I twist my body in the air and then land in a crouch on the platform. They groan and don't get up immediately. I look toward Zahtri again. He looks surprised, but still hasn't moved.

I bring my attention back to the two Gadramicks on the ground in front of me. They slowly stand up and turn toward me, angry and determined. I siphon their anger and use it to strengthen my magic. I smile as another emotion hits me. I stand up and slowly walk toward them. The men look surprised to see me approaching.

I make sure to add an extra swing to my hips. I turn toward Zahtri and smile when I see their eyes soften. Even in a fight, you can always distract a man. Zahtri looks angry when he sees my simple plan working. I stop right in front of the men and place my hands on my hips. "Hey, boys," I coo.

They look me over right as I push some magic out. I trail my finger across their chests as I walk around them. Both of them watch me, but don't do anything. They can feel my magic moving around them, but neither of them react. When I'm standing behind them, I thrust my magic out and send them flying off the platform.

I know he's there before I turn around. "Using you're feminine charms, I see," Larkin says.

"Emma always told me to flaunt it," I say. Zahtri is staring at me through narrowed eyes. Why isn't he attacking?

"I know what you're planning on doing, Ryanne."

"I'm going after Zahtri," I nod. Everyone knows that.

"You're not going to sacrifice yourself."

"If it'll stop Zahtri, I'll do it."

"Think about what your death would do to everyone. Don't do that to us. You didn't see Colton this past week. Don't do that to *him.*"

"I may not have a choice, Larkin." I put up a shield around us, so no one can attack us. A man runs toward us and bounces off the shield. "He's stronger than you think."

"No, he's not. I know exactly how strong he is and I know that you are stronger, but you don't believe in yourself, so you don't see your strength. You think that you have to sacrifice yourself to prove you're strong, but you don't. You can take Zahtri on without it resulting in your death." Larkin grabs my shoulders. "Ryanne, look at me."

I keep my eyes on the fight around us. I need to be out there. Right now, it's hard to tell who has the upper hand. I watch Natalie fighting someone. The man behind her suddenly falls to the ground, so I know that Colton is fighting with her while invisible. Liam and Adam are working together fighting off Gadramicks right below me. Liam looks directly at me, wondering what is going on.

Larkin grabs my chin and forces me to look up at him. "Ryanne, when you died, you were supposed to overcome all these insecurities. You are strong, and you are prepared. You can do this without causing your death. Would your mom want you to just give up in the end?" Harsh. Using the mom card is just mean.

"Some things are hard to change," I whisper to him.

"Not if you have faith," he whispers back and pushes my hair away from my face. I never have a hair tie when I need one. "You gave an awesome speech earlier. Fight for those you love, Ryanne. Don't forget how many of us actually do love you. No one will forgive you if you sacrifice yourself," Larkin looks toward Natalie, but I know he's actually looking at Colton. "No one."

"Larkin, we don't know if any of us are going to get out of this. I've never had to go against someone as strong as Zahtri before, and I've come close to death so many times. There's nothing that says I won't end up dead this time."

"Just be careful, Ryanne. That's all I'm saying. Don't try to be the superhero here."

"I never wanted to be a superhero, Larkin," I whisper to him as I drop the shield. "Now, go help our family. Don't let anyone get hurt." I run to the other end of the platform and jump off. Zahtri is standing by himself on this side waiting for me.

"Took ya long enough, darling."

CHAPTER TWENTY-FOUR

COLTON

"I SAID ALL I COULD," Larkin says as he transports behind me. Natalie yelps as someone barrels into her. She falls to the ground and gasps while trying to push the Gadramick off. Larkin and I both grab onto his back. Larkin stabs him in the stomach and throws him to the side. I reach down and help her stand up.

My eyes travel behind the wooden platform to Ryanne. She's tense and prepared, but she's not fighting Zahtri. I see Dravin slowly walking toward her. Ryanne suddenly turns to her right. I see Adam fighting through the Gadramicks, trying to get to her. She turns around and her eyes widen.

Put a shield up, Ryanne.

Dravin brings his arm back. The little sunlight breaking through the clouds, gleams off the metal dagger in his hand as he releases the weapon. Ryanne screams, but doesn't throw up a shield.

"Ryanne!" I yell right as Adam jumps in front of her.

The dagger implants into his shoulder. Adam falls back into Ryanne, knocking both of them to the ground. Ryanne moves out from under him. Leaning over him, I can see tears falling from her eyes. Liam runs over to them. Ryanne yells for Logan, but Liam starts shaking his head. Even from this distance, I can see the large amount of blood pouring out of the wound.

Some of their weapons must be infused with the same magic as the dagger that Enrique had. I hear thunder crack ahead. We all stop as the deep noise shakes the group beneath us. If there's thunder rolling, Ryanne is very mad.

Even the Gadramicks stop fighting when the thunder echoes through the field. Ryanne slowly stands and faces Dravin. The Ryanne standing there is not one I recognize. I've seen her mad. I've seen her upset, but I've never seen this much emotion on her before. A look of fear crosses Dravin's face as he starts walking backward.

I reach out to my left and punch the Gadramick in the jaw that was trying to walk toward Natalie. No one knows that I'm invisible until it's too late.

"He did everything you asked of him," Ryanne yells. "You killed him!"

"He slowly stopped listening every time you came here."

"You brought me here!" Ryanne screams as more thunder rolls through the sky. The little bit of sunlight that was visible earlier is no more. Dark clouds dictate the sky, creating a more suitable atmosphere for what is happening.

"Oh, he better start running," Larkin says. We all know that Ryanne's power only affects the weather when she's very upset. She has more control of that now.

Liam picks up Adam's body and drags him out of the clearing. Ryanne stops in front of Dravin and pokes him in the chest. It's strange how we can all hear her right now.

"Did you really think you would get away with all of this? Did you think you'd be able to experiment on humans? That you could just capture mages and try to take their magic? That you could just kill those who didn't give you the right results and go about your happy life like you didn't do anything wrong? Huh? Every action has a consequence, Dravin."

Dravin laughs and takes a step toward Ryanne. "Put away your magic. I'm not going to fight you."

"No, you're just going to throw daggers infused with dark magic at me. Dark magic that Zahtri told you about. Is that what you call not fighting?"

Dravin takes another step forward. He's literally standing inches away from her. Ryanne has to arch her head up to see him clearly. "You don't know what you're doing, Ryanne. Call off this attack and you and all your little friends will get out of here alive."

"I'm not afraid of death, Dravin. How many times do I have to tell you that? I'm not keeping any of them here against their will. They're here because they want to be, not because anyone is forcing them." Instead of letting Dravin say anything else, Ryanne brings her knee up and hits him in the crotch.

I bite my tongue to keep from laughing. I know all too well how that feels. Ryanne wastes no time. When Dravin grunts and bends over, she grabs the back of his head and slams it into her knee. Even from where I'm standing I can hear the crunch of his nose breaking. Taking a step back, she spins around and kicks her leg out, connecting with the side of his head. When Dravin spins to the ground, Ryanne pushes magic out and sends him flying into the tree line.

"Oh, shit," A Gadramick beside me exclaims as he starts backing up. "I'm outta here. I didn't sign up for this."

Ryanne stands there for a few seconds before turning around. She briefly glances at the crowd watching her, but doesn't react. Her eyes go straight to Zahtri again.

He pushes away from the tree he was leaning against and slowly starts clapping as he walks toward the center of the field. A steady rain is now falling from the sky—the only signs of Ryanne's conflicting emotions. She now has a blank expression on her face as she watches Zahtri move forward.

"That was an interesting little show you just put on," Zahtri says he as walks to Ryanne. I notice a few more Gadramicks leave the field. Ryanne just stares at him, but doesn't say anything. "You don't understand what you're getting yourself into, little one."

"Only my family gets to call me that, Zahtri," Ryanne says as she takes a step toward him. Zahtri looks slightly surprised at Ryanne's boldness. He doesn't know her like the rest of us. When she's angry, she pushes aside her insecurities and becomes the confident Ryanne she needs to be. She doesn't know that she does it. She still thinks she's not strong enough, but she has it in her and it comes out when she needs it most.

The wind intensifies around us as Ryanne calls magic to her. "I can read your mind, darling, your magic is going to be useless."

"Really?" Ryanne says as she pushes pure magic toward him. Zahtri flies back into the tree line and slams into the base of a tree. "Because I'm projecting false thoughts, Zahtri," she mumbles as she slowly walks toward him.

Zahtri grunts and sits up, glaring at Ryanne. She stops when she sees the smile he gives her right before he disappears.

"Where'd he go?" Natalie asks me. As soon as the words leave her mouth, Zahtri reappears behind Ryanne, grabs her, and transports out of the field.

"Are you freaking kidding me?" I shout and reach out to hit the closest Gadramick to me.

CHAPTER TWENTY-FIVE

I TRY TO THROW A shield around me when I hear his thoughts, but Zahtri transports much quicker than Larkin. One second he is in front of me, and then the next, he is wrapping his arms around my waist and transporting us out of the field.

I try to fight against him, but his grip is too strong. I slam into a large rock. My back instantly protests as pain shoots through my torso. I gasp, trying to catch the breath that was knocked out of me. Zahtri is smiling over me. It's no longer raining anymore, but the dark clouds above me could open up at any minute and shed their tears. "Get off of me!" I yell at him as I attempt to get away from him. The legs around my hips tighten and his arms pin my hands above my head.

"Stop struggling, Ryanne," he growls at me.

"Then get off of me."

"Stop trying to kill me. This would be so much easier if you'd just pick the first option."

"You're still stuck on that?" I ask. "I'm not going to work with you."

"So you'd rather let more people die because of you? They're either fighting with you or they are fighting against you. You're the reason why people are dying."

"They're fighting for or against you as well, Zahtri."

"Yes, but I don't care if anyone dies. You do," he tells me. I close of my mind, not letting the meaning of his sentence sink it. I can't over think anything right now. That'll get me killed. Liam and Larkin have both talked to me today, and I understand what I have to do.

I call my magic to me. I know Zahtri can feel it moving around us because he tightens his grips on my wrists again. The bones are on the verge of breaking when I release all the pent up anger I've gathered since I've been at Dravin's compound. Zahtri flies off of me, but he doesn't loosen his grip right away. I'm thrown into the air and land, not so gracefully, on another rock and roll a couple times before coming to a stop. Zahtri's deep grunt fills my ears as he also lands painfully against the rocks.

Since I don't have time right now to dwell on injuries, I jump up and get my first look at my surroundings. I'm standing along a cliff off the coast. Angry water crashes against the edge of the rock about thirty feet below me. I back up. If I had rolled a couple more feet, I would have fallen off. Turning around, I face Zahtri, with the knowledge that this is it. This is what I am meant to do. Claire told me I would be somewhere else during the final battle. I wouldn't have Liam and Colton around me.

Now I understand why.

I step forward, putting more distance between me and the cliffs edge all the while decreasing the distance between Zahtri and me. I can feel his magic flowing around us, so I know he'll attack soon. I push more magic out, putting it into the air. My magic works much quicker when I don't have to push it out.

I throw a shield up behind me along the cliff's edge as a precaution. Zahtri stands up and stalks toward me. "I really hoped we could have solved this civilly."

"Then you shouldn't have kidnapped me and stuck me in a cell for this past week," I retort.

"Touché," Zahtri says as he stops a few feet away from me. I throw a shield up around my mind, hoping that he can't read my thoughts. I can't read his anymore, so I know that he's doing something.

"You're smarter than I gave you credit for, dear. This might actually be fun." Zahtri's voice and constant endearments are really starting to annoy me. I'm an accent person. I love accents, but after hearing his deep almost Australian accent, I hate it. Endearments are something only those close to me get to call me. I am definitely not close to Zahtri, so he needs to knock it off.

I take a few steps to my right and watch as Zahtri takes a few steps to his left. We're now moving in a circle. As long as he's closer to the cliff's edge...

Zahtri smiles at me before running straight at me. I'm not prepared for the sudden attack, so I don't have time to move away. Zahtri's movements are much quicker than any of the mages I've fought before. He barrels into me and knocks me to the ground again. My head instantly starts throbbing and my back aches from being slammed into the hard ground. He just had to choose a cliff, didn't he? He couldn't have chosen a soft grassy meadow?

Instantly, my magic shoots out of me and pushes Zahtri off of me. *Look for weaknesses.* That's what Bragden taught me during our training sessions. My opponents are always going to be bigger than me, so I have to look for weaknesses. Zahtri stands up right as I bring my arms up. The liquid lightning shoots out of my palms and goes straight for his chest. With my hand out, I try to stand but dizziness overcomes me and I stumble to the side. He jumps to the side, but some of my magic hits him on the shoulder.

I catch Zahtri's angered look right as my feet are lifted off the ground and I'm flying backward. Time seems to move in slow motion. Zahtri watches me as I'm thrust backward and land on the hard rocks, rolling three times before coming to a stop on my back. I can't breathe and can't hear through all the ringing in my ears. It sounds like I was suddenly transported to a busy, bustling city. There's a lot of indiscernible noise around me. The world around me begins to spin as the clouds open up and rain down on me.

Everything goes black.

COLTON

"WE KNEW THIS WOULD HAPPEN, Colton," Liam yells as he starts fighting another Gadramick. There are less of them here now. A couple chose to leave after Ryanne attacked Dravin, but we're still pretty close in numbers.

I elbow the man I'm fighting in the solar plexus and kick his temple when he doubles over. "I know, but I thought she'd still be here. I thought I'd be able to know if something happened to her. Right now, she's fighting against Zahtri and none of us know what's going on. What if she's hurt? What if she needs help?"

"Trust her, Colton," Natalie yells as she ducks a Gadramick's punch. I hear someone scream to me left. I turn right as I see Emma unleash a whip on some unsuspecting Gadramicks. She sure is having fun with her new power.

Magic is flying around me in all directions. I see fire moving to my left, so Bragden and Incendia must be over there. Larkin transports in behind me and starts fighting a Gadramick.

"She has three people she can call if she needs help, Colton," Natalie says and then screams as she flies across the field. Liam whips around and zeros in on the Gadramick who attacked his soulmate. Larkin and I step out of the way as Liam runs toward him. The man's eyes widen as he tries to run, but Liam is quicker. Liam may not have Bragden's size, but he's much more intimidating and you don't want to make him mad.

I rush over to Natalie, who's still on the ground. I roll her over and she cries out in pain. At first, I don't see any obvious injuries until I see the dark blood seeping through her black clothing.

"How-how bad is it?" she asks. I slowly lift the edge of her shirt up and try to keep my face calm. There's a lot of blood coming from the wound. I look around the field. Both Logan and Liam are in the thick of the fight. There's no way for them to get to her. Honestly, I don't think she'll be able to be healed by them anyway. The majority of them are using dark magic.

"It's not that bad," I tell her hoping to keep her calm. I need to move her out of the fighting and off to the side. Dr. Arden runs over to me and crouches down next to Natalie.

"I can help her," he whispers as he looks around. He's still working for Dravin; why would he try and help me? "You're Ryanne's soulmate. I can help."

He's doing this for Ryanne. I don't know if I can fully trust him, but I do need his help on this. There's nothing I can do and I know that Natalie won't make it much longer. Dr. Arden bends down and picks her up. She bites her lip to keep from crying out. She's in a lot of pain. Dr. Arden cradles her against his chest, before turning back to me. "Cover me," he shouts as he starts walking toward the compound.

I follow closely behind, fighting off any Gadramicks that try to move toward us. I don't know how Dr. Arden knew I was there since I'm still invisible, but I'm grateful nonetheless. He turns toward me as we make it to the back door of the compound. I reach around him and open it up, letting him enter first. He rushes past me and starts running down the hallway.

Kicking open the doors to his lab, Jedrek places Natalie down on the table and rushes to the opposite side of the room. I think about Ryanne and slowly feel the invisibility melting away. Grabbing onto Natalie's hand, I turn her head so she can look at me.

"You're going to be okay, Natalie. I promise. You're going to be fine."

"I can't feel my legs," she whimpers. "Why can't I feel my legs?"

I lean down and kiss her knuckles, choosing to not answer her question. "You're going to be okay," I repeat as she starts shaking. She's so pale. I recognize this amount of paleness because I've seen it so many times on Ryanne. I look toward Dr. Arden, who's frantically searching through his cabinet.

"Will you tell Liam that I love him?" she asks me.

"Natalie, you can tell him yourself. Nothing is going to happen to you." I look toward Jedrek again knowing that I shouldn't promise her that. I said the same thing to Ryanne before she died. She's not going to make it much longer.

"Ahh, found it," Jedrek says as he rushes toward the table. He briefly glances at me before looking down at her. "This is going to sting a little." He turns toward me again, warning me. I tighten my grip on Natalie's hand. I know that I'll probably have to hold her down.

"What is that?" I ask as he uncaps the vial.

"It's an antidote I made once I found out that Dravin and Zahtri were making weapons infused with dark magic. I thought they were going to use it on Ryanne. I promised her I wouldn't let anything happen to her. I thought I could save her..." he trails off as he bends over Natalie, moving the fabric of her shirt out of the way. Natalie whimpers as the cold air touches her exposed skin.

She turns and looks at Dr. Arden, “Please make it stop,” she cries. I can see the unshed tears in her eyes. She knows that she’s dying because of this wound.

Colton, where’s Natalie? I jump and look around me, searching for Liam. Dr. Arden gives me a quizzical look before he takes the lid off the bottle and places it on the desk behind him. Beside the three of us, the room is empty, but I clearly just heard his voice.

Liam?

Where’s Natalie!

How are you talking to me?

I’m inside of your subconscious. Where is she?

I try to clear my mind. I don’t know if Liam can read my mind, but I need to remain calm. Natalie needs me to remain calm. I tighten my grip again as Dr. Arden lets the antidote fall from the pipette and onto Natalie’s skin. She tries to push away from both of us, but Dr. Arden puts pressure on her shoulders, while I lean against her legs, trying to calm her down. Her screams echo through the deserted hall, alerting everyone to our location.

She’s going to be fine. Do I just think it and he’ll hear it?

Going to be?

The wound instantly starts to fizz. It gathers on her skin until a black liquid starts seeping out beneath it. “Is that normal?”

“That’s the dark magic leaving her body,” he shouts as he puts more pressure on Natalie’s shoulders. I try to tune out the screaming. We’re helping her. She’s going to live because of this. It has to be done.

The black liquid stops flowing out from the wound, and now blood only remains. “I can attempt to staunch the blood flow, but she’s going to need to be healed.”

Liam, get Logan. Tell him to come into the compound and find the lab.

What's going on Colton? Is Natalie okay? I can hear the panic in Liam's voice.

She's going to be; just get Logan.

Natalie stops screaming and turns and looks at me. I try to smile at her and let her know that everything is going to be alright, but I know it comes out wrong. She's sweating and still looks like death has a grip on her. I lean forward and push her hair off of her damp forehead. She attempts to smile, but it comes out as more of a grimace. She winces as Dr. Arden works on stopping the blood flow until Logan can get here.

"You're going to be okay, Natalie." I squeeze her hand. "Logan's coming to heal you." She still looks so pale. While Natalie tries to calm her labored breathing, I turn and watch Dr. Arden applies gauze to the wound.

"How? I know that he hit me with dark magic."

"He had an antidote," I say as I point to Dr. Arden. Natalie turns and looks at him.

"Thank you," she whispers.

"Don't thank me. I've done nothing worth thanking."

"Despite what you think, you're a good man, Dr. Arden. I can tell," Natalie tells him. I know that she's using her powers to sense his emotions and intentions. "You have a good heart. You were just thrown into bad circumstances. Ryanne understands."

Dr. Arden applies more pressure to the wound. Natalie winces, but doesn't say anything. He briefly looks away from the gauze and looks toward Natalie. "I just wish I could have proven myself to her."

"You have. Don't worry about that."

The doors to the lab slam open as Logan rushes into the room. His eyes widen when he looks at Natalie. I step to the side, but keep a hold on Natalie's hand. Dr. Arden stops applying pressure to the wound and gives Logan some room to work.

With his eyes downcast, I finally get a good look at him. Ryanne does look a lot like him. They share the same dark curly hair, the light eyes. Ryanne's eyes are slightly larger and her nose is smaller, but it's obvious he's her father. I can see the same determination and sadness in both of their eyes. I wonder where Ryanne gets her small stature from. I don't think her mom was short...

"Thank you, Logan," Natalie says as she sits up and hugs him.

"Are you okay? Do you feel fine?" he asks her. "Liam is attacking anyone that comes near him because he has no idea what going on with you. He's worried and taking it out on everyone."

"I'm fine. Come on. Let's go."

"You should rest, Natalie," Logan says.

"No. Liam is still out there fighting and while that is good, I need to let him know I'm fine. Also, Ryanne doesn't get a chance to rest. We need to keep going for her. She's fighting for her life right now, and I'm not going to rest while she's still out there. I'll rest when she's back here safe."

I smile at Natalie, proud. I even see the grateful expression on Dr. Arden's face. "How much of that antidote do you have left?" I ask him.

"A couple more drops. I'll help where I can, Colton." I reach down and help Natalie stand up.

She looks down at her stomach. "Hmm...I didn't like that."

"Most people don't like dying," I tell her. "I wouldn't make a habit of it."

She smiles at me and starts walking toward the door. Logan follows after her. I turn around when I feel a hand on my arm. I glance down and follow the hand to a body. "Please keep her safe, Colton. Do what I can't," Jedrek tells me.

"I'm trying my best. She's not making it easy though."

"She's just like her mom," he says with a sad smile. "I'm glad she found you all. I've heard about what Dravin has done to her. Do not hesitate to kill him."

I wish there was a way to break the bond, so he wouldn't die if something happens to Dravin. I don't want to see him die, but I know Dravin needs to be stopped. Dr. Arden has already accepted that he's going to die today, so I nod. It's a shame Ryanne never got to know this man better. Based on the look on her expression when they spoke earlier, I know she wishes she had the chance. Instead of answering him, I turn to leave the room. There's nothing I can say that will make this situation any better.

Throwing open the back door of the compound, Natalie steps out and looks for Liam. I can see him in the back, taking on three men.

Liam? I have no idea how this mind communication of his works, but it's actually kind of helpful. It explains so much. Liam and Bragden would always give each other these glances and I just thought since they were brothers, they understood each other more. Bragden's probably the only person who knew about Liam's extra power. I don't think he ever told Ryanne. Natalie hasn't spotted him yet, so I point her in the right direction.

Is she okay? Liam asks as he knocks out the men he's fighting with. He turns and looks toward the compound doors. Natalie smiles widely at him when their eyes meet, and Liam starts to make his way over to us.

"You ready?" Natalie looks up at me and asks. I look at the field in front of us. Everyone is still fighting. Magic is flying in all directions. I can see Tom, Colin, and Vincent standing in the middle of the field, fighting in a circle. David and Emma are fighting beside Bragden and Incendia. They are blasting fire at anyone who steps too close to them.

We could actually do this. I look to my left, toward the platform. Dravin is using his power on mages who attempt to fight him. Natasha is standing beside him, defending him by asphyxiating people, but her eyes are scanning the crowd. If we're going to stop him, it's going to have to be a team effort. Liam punches a man and rushes the rest of the way to Natalie. He runs into her and picks her off the ground. Natalie laughs and wraps her arms around his neck. "Are you okay? You're not hurt?"

"No, Dr. Arden and Logan healed me," she says into his neck. "I'm good."

"Dr. Arden?" Liam asks as he places Natalie back down on the ground. I unsheathe my sword and look toward the field.

"He saved her, Liam. Now, let's get this over with."

CHAPTER TWENTY-SIX

I'M SWAYING. I'VE NEVER BEEN on a boat before, but I imagine this is what it feels like. My head rolls to the side, and I smell the salt from the water and can hear it crashing against the shore. Maybe I *am* on a boat. I could get lost in this feeling. I have no control of what's going on with my body at this moment, and since I don't have my anchor, I'm floating away at sea.

When my head rolls back, I jolt awake. I see the dark clouds above me and Zahtri to my right. What is going on? I groan as I grab my head.

"What are you doing?" I whisper.

"Solving our issue," he answers without looking at me.

I turn to the left and see Zahtri slowly walking toward the edge of the cliff. I'm not on a boat; Zahtri is carrying me. I gasp as I attempt to get out of his arms, but he tightens his grip, holding me in place. I literally cannot move.

"This is how you want this to end?" I shout at him.

"No, but I need to get back to the field. I need to rally my men and stop all the mages. To do that, I need you out of the picture."

"Then let's fight. Let's fight like everyone in that field, Zahtri." I say as he stops on the edge of the cliff. I can feel the blood dripping down the side of my face from a cut above my eyebrow.

"It didn't have to be like this, Ryanne. You chose this."

I try to call my magic to me, but I can't. What is he doing?

"I told you that you weren't strong enough, darling. You did pretty well for a little while. Kudos for that. But I'm done playing games."

The drop looks much longer now than it did before when I glanced down the cliff's edge. I start fighting against Zahtri again, but it's useless. There's nothing I can do against him. My heart is pounding against my chest; I'm sure that he can hear its obnoxious beat. There's no way out of this. I can't use my magic, and in a battle of physical strength, Zahtri has me beat by a long shot. I didn't see any weakness in his fighting earlier. There's nothing I can do.

This can't be it. It's not supposed to end like this.

So don't let it. I try to keep my body slack so Zahtri doesn't sense anything.

Claire?

Use your resources, Ryanne.

What does that even mean?

Zahtri stops at the edge of the cliff. The breeze is blowing my hair in all directions. Use my resources. My resources...? What the heck does that even mean?

"It's a shame," Zahtri whispers. He glances down at me and shakes his head as he throws me off the edge. I scream as I flip through the air, hurtling toward the rocky water below.

My resources. I have resources?

I have resources.

"Larkin!" I scream.

If he doesn't come...like right now, I'm dead. I feel arms wrap around my waist. I close my eyes. I hope that I didn't just get us both killed.

I stop screaming as my back slams into the ground. The arms around my waist disappear and I roll, crashing into multiple people. A large person falls on top of me, knocking any last breath I had left in me out. I don't even have enough energy in me to push him or her off of me. My eyes close and I start to lose consciousness yet again.

COLTON

I RUN PAST LIAM AND Natalie and head toward Larkin and Kyril. We need all the people out here that we can get. I step behind a Gadramick and kick him behind the knees. As he falls to the ground, I kick him in the temple, knocking him out. I step up to Larkin right as he disappears. I turn toward Kyril who shrugs, unsure of where he went. Bragden and Incendia move toward us, closing the circle we've created in the middle of the field.

I'm amazed at how much everyone has come together the past couple of days for this moment. When we needed everyone the most, they came together. We wouldn't be able to do any of this without them. Even mages who didn't know each other a few days ago are now working together to ensure everyone makes it out of this alive.

I reach out and punch a man as I hear a scream echo from behind me. I kick him in the gut and push him backward as I turn around. Larkin lands flat on his back in the grass behind me and a girl lands on the ground beside him and rolls to the side, knocking into David. He attempts to move back, but he loses his balance and falls on top of her.

Though I haven't seen her face, I know that's Ryanne. I'd recognize her anywhere. A column of fire surrounds us all, separating us from the

Gadramicks. Incendia nods at me as I bend down and pull David off my soulmate. Larkin grunts and crawls toward us.

"Ryanne?" I ask. She groans, but doesn't open her eyes. Above her right eyebrow is a giant bruise. A cut on her hairline is causing blood to drip down her face. I push her wild hair out of her face. She looks so tired.

"Logan!" I shout. She needs healed before she loses consciousness. Logan pushes past everyone and falls to the ground at her side.

"What happened?" I ask Larkin as Logan places his hands on her face.

"I don't know," he says while grasping for air, having difficulty getting any oxygen into his lungs. "She called me and I transported to her and…I don't know. She was free-falling. I grabbed her and transported back here as soon as possible. She would have been killed instantly if she hadn't called me," he says as he watches her.

Ryanne gasps and rolls to the side coughing. I lean forward and grab her chin, making her look toward me. When she sees me, she jumps up and hugs me tightly around the neck. I wrap my arms around her back. "What happened?" I whisper. I can feel everyone watching us, but I don't care.

Ryanne pulls back and stands up, shaking her head. "Stop the fire, Incendia."

"Ryanne," I start.

"I have to stop him, Colton. That psycho threw me off a cliff," she mumbles as she shoots water toward the wall of fire, creating a doorway large enough for her. Without looking at anyone again, she walks through. The fire descends back down the second she's out of sight. Logan turns and heals Larkin while everyone else just stands around, confused as to what we all just saw.

"What the heck just happened?" Emma asks.

Thunder rolls in the distance. "He just angered an already angry girl," Logan says as he steps away from Larkin. Kyril reaches down to help Larkin stand.

"Do you think this is going to be over soon?" David asks. We all glare at him. "What? I'm hungry. I forgot to eat before we came here.

"How do you forget to eat?" Emma playfully hits his shoulder. "You're always thinking about food."

"Incendia, drop the fire," I say. She shrugs and smiles.

"I'm not the one doing this," she says as she looks up toward Bragden. We all turn and look at him shocked. I didn't think he was strong enough yet to do this. He hasn't been training for that long.

"You needed time to heal Ryanne..."

"Thank you," I tell him. "Now drop the fire."

The fire around us disappears, and through the fighting, I watch as Ryanne walks up to Vincent. He looks down at her for a second before nodding and grabbing onto her wrist. Both of them disappear without saying a single word to anyone else. "Where is she going?" I ask Larkin.

"Back to Zahtri."

CHAPTER TWENTY-SEVEN

HE THREW ME OFF A cliff. Off a freaking cliff. Like really? All I wanted was a fair fight, but no, he had to throw me off a cliff while I was basically unconscious.

Vincent drops me down in the middle of the cliff edge where we were last time, but Zahtri is nowhere to be seen. I spin around in circles looking for him. "Is he supposed to be here?" Vincent asks me.

"Yeah," I point to the cliff edge. "He just threw me off of that." I look behind me. Oh no. "Take me back. Take me back!" I yell. Vincent doesn't even question me. He places a hand on my shoulder and transports me back to the area behind the compound. I knew it.

Zahtri is way too cocky for his own good. He is talking to Dravin while standing on the opposite side of the platform. Landing on it, I look behind me and see everyone fighting. Colton, Liam, and Natalie are all fighting together. Bragden and Incendia are together while David and Emma are helping Logan and Lily fight. Larkin and Kyril are tag-teaming it—still creating chaos around them. Travis is fighting with a smaller girl with his parents right behind him.

Zahtri stops smiling when he sees me standing there. "You just don't know when to stop do you?" he yells as he starts walking toward me.

"Go," I whisper to Vincent.

"Ryanne," he says.

"Thank you for helping me, Vincent, but I need you to go." When he doesn't move, I say, "Go or I will make you leave." Vincent looks down at me for a moment before he blinks away. I don't know where he went, but I'm glad he listened. Though I don't know him, I don't want anything to happen to him.

Love and anger crash into me. Instantly, I recognize it as Colton's. I put a shield up behind me as I turn around.

Colton is still standing with Liam and Natalie, but he's looking at me. I want nothing more than to go over to him and forget about everything happening around me, but I can't. I can't ignore it anymore. This is happening. This is real. Right here, right now, I have to fight. I have to fight for Colton. I have to fight for our life together. I have to fight. Without him.

I place my hand over my heart and nod at him. I can't go to him and I hope he doesn't come to me. This could very well be the end for me, and I need Colton to know I love him. Colton mimics my stance and nods back to me. He understands. I take a deep breath and turn around, quite possibly facing my imminent death.

Zahtri is waiting patiently at the edge of my shield. I don't do anything and neither does he. We just stand there. I can see Dravin moving around us. I want to stop him, but I know I'm not the one destined to stop him. That privilege belongs to Liam and Colton.

"I see you survived the fall," Zahtri says.

"I used my resources," I tell him.

"Interesting."

"What are we doing here, Zahtri? We need to stop this once and for all. No more games. Just us. No one else needs to become involved."

"I thought I was stopping this when I dropped you off the cliff's edge," Zahtri tells me with a blank expression.

"It takes a little more than that to get rid of me, Zahtri. I'm pretty stubborn."

"I've noticed."

I can hear all of the fighting going on behind me, but I refuse to turn around. I've surrounded myself with a shield, so I shouldn't have any surprise attacks from behind. I can't read Zahtri's mind because he's put up a mental shield to block me. I've surrounded my thoughts with magic, so he shouldn't be able to read mine either. I want to end this fair and square.

"How is this going to go?" Zahtri asks me. I try to keep a neutral expression on my face despite the surprise. I have no idea. I wasn't expecting him to ask me that.

"How do you think this should go?" I ask him. Zahtri starts pacing the area in front of my shield. I watch him moving back and forth. He's going to attempt something, but I don't know what.

"I think you should drop that shield of yours, Ryanne, before I make you drop it myself. Then, we're going to fight. Since you're so adamant on fighting me, I'll give you that much, but I'm not a fair fighter, darling. You better be prepared."

I take a step forward. My shield pushes against Zahtri, so he takes a step back. I continue moving toward him. I want to distance us from the rest of the fighting. I know I'll have to bring out all of my magic, and I don't want anyone to get hurt because of it. No one but Zahtri, that is.

"It's a good thing I don't plan on fighting fairly either then," I say.

I drop the shield.

COLTON

I LET MY INVISIBILITY TAKE over as Ryanne turns around and faces Zahtri again. I can't see her, but I know that she is talking to him. What is she saying? Since she's standing on the platform and Zahtri is on the ground below, they are almost the same height. I groan as I focus on the Gadramicks in front of me.

Liam won't leave Natalie's side since she almost died. I can see Jedrek fighting Gadramicks to the side. A ball of fire shoots past me. I look to my right and see Incendia fighting a Gadramick. Bragden is fighting off two, so he can't make it over to her. The Gadramick fighting her knocks her to the ground. I can see the anger radiating off of Bragden as he attempts to stop the Gadramicks in front of him. His eyes flicker over to Incendia, but he can't actually make it over to her. His arms lighten as flames erupt from his skin and ignite his body. He's literally on fire.

I punch the man in the jaw in front of me and make my way over to her. For being on the ground, Incendia is holding her own pretty well, but I can tell she needs help. When Bragden is able to stop those Gadramicks, more start fighting him.

I rush behind the man and pull him off of Incendia. Gasping for breath, she slowly pushes herself up. Since he is confused about the invisible force that moved him, it is easy to knock him out. Incendia stands, places her hands on her hips, and thanks me.

"This needs to stop," she says. Bragden is finally able to finish off the two Gadramicks that were fighting him and runs over to Incendia. He pulls her against his chest and apologizes to her. "I'm sorry. I couldn't get to you."

"Hey, hey. It's fine. Colton helped me," she says. Bragden nods in my direction, thanking me.

"You're welcome." Bragden helped Liam save Ryanne when she was kidnapped the first time. That moment feels like so long ago even though it was only a few months ago. Helping him with Incendia is the least I can do. I turn and look back up at Ryanne. Now she's talking to him. Since her shield is still up, Zahtri is taking small steps away.

I hear a girl scream behind me. I turn around expecting to see Lily or Emma, but instead I see Logan falling to the ground while a Gadramick pulls a sword out of his side. Lily is the one who screamed. I move away from Bragden and Incendia and make my way over to him

Logan can't die. I can't lose another family member. I knock down any Gadramicks in my way as I move through the crowds. Lily is crouched down beside him, tears falling down her face. Logan is trying not to let his pain obvious, but we all know what is going on.

The sword Logan was hit with was infused with dark magic. He won't be able to heal himself. "What do we do?" Lily frantically asks when I fall to the ground beside him. She grabs Logan's hands and makes him look toward her. "Logan, what do we do?" she asks quietly. James and Travis move around us, fighting off any Gadramicks who try to come close.

My eyes scan the crowd around us, but I don't see Jedrek anymore.

Logan looks at her with unshed tears in his eyes and shakes his head. There's nothing that can be done.

"Logan, you can't leave us," I tell him. "Ryanne will never forgive you if you leave us," I try to joke, but I know that it falls short. "I won't forgive you."

Lily chokes on her tears as Logan turns toward her. "Lily, if you accept Logan you may be able to heal him," James shouts from behind her. Lily whips around and looks at him.

"What?"

"If you accept him, you may be able to heal him," he repeats.

"Lily, he's telling you Logan is your soulmate." Logan gasps, and his eyes roll into the back of his head. He's still breathing but it is very shallow.

"How?"

"Do you believe that he's your soulmate?" I ask her. She looks up at me and then brings her attention back to Logan. I already know the answer. She wouldn't be acting this way if she didn't already feel something for him. They've been inseparable this week. Whether they were arguing or joking with each other, they were still together.

"I don't deserve someone like him, Colton" she says. "I've not done anything to deserve him."

"But you could see yourself falling in love with him, don't you?" Lily wipes the tears away from her eyes. I can tell that she's thinking about everything. Her brown eyes look toward me and she nods. I motion for her to come toward me.

Another ring of fire forms around us, separating us from the fighting.

Lily rushes to my side. "What do I do?"

"You have to fully accept Logan for who he is," Logan's body shudders once before going completely still. Lily gasps and more tears fall down her face. "It won't work if you don't accept him."

Lily leans down and rests her head on Logan's still chest. She fists her hands into the fabric of his shirt. I know all of this is very sudden, but if it is meant to be, everything will work out in the end. I clench my hands to keep from showing how upset this is making me. Death is never easy to see, but this is Logan. We basically grew up together. He's as much of a brother to me as David is. Lily needs me to remain calm right now.

I can hear her whispering something, but I can't hear the words. Her body tenses over his and she shoots up and looks at me, scared. "His heart stopped beating."

"Lily, you have to heal him now," I tell her. If she can't do this...I can't think like that.

"I don't know how. I don't know what to do."

"Let the mage inside you take over, Lily," I say. "You know exactly what to do."

"What if it doesn't work?" she whispers. "I don't have a lot of magic in me. I don't even have a power."

"You never know unless you try."

Lily nods and leans toward Logan again. She gasps as her hands move toward Logan's wound. She's kneeling in the blood that is seeping out of his wound, but she doesn't care. A few months ago, I never would have believed that Logan and Lily were soulmates. My cousin and the cheerleader? It wouldn't have made sense.

Lily was this stuck-up girl, while Logan is one of the most caring people I know. They are complete opposite, but since Lily's near death experience, I've found out that everything I thought about her was a lie. She's not from a rich home like she made everyone in school believe. She's not this heartless cheerleader like everyone thought. There's so much more to her. People are capable of creating a false exterior, so no one gets to know the true person underneath. She was afraid of what the truth could bring her. I'm so glad Ryanne was able to help her that day, because despite neither Logan or Lily admitting their feelings for each other, I can see the change in both of them. I've never seen Logan light up the way he does when Lily's around and she seems genuinely happy when near him.

"Nothing is happening," Lily cries. The wound isn't healing. "Logan, you can't leave me!" she shouts at him.

She doesn't remove her hands from the wound, but she leans down again and sobs onto his chest. I reach forward and attempt to calm her, but I know there's nothing I can do.

I'm about to shout for Bragden or Incendia to drop the shield when Lily gasps and jumps back. "What's going on?" she looks back toward me. I recognize the look on her face.

"You're healing him," I tell her. Logan's wound is starting to close. Lily moves closer to him and presses harder on the wound. The black liquid from the dark magic starts oozing out of the wound, but Lily doesn't move. She continues to put pressure on the wound. Once the last of the black liquid is pushed out of Logan's body, the wound begins to glow.

I try to keep my elation to myself. Logan is going to be fine. I'm not losing another family member today. Logan's body convulses once and then he starts breathing again. I lean back. I'll give them time once he becomes conscious again.

Logan is going to be fine. Oh, thank God. I don't know how I would able to tell Ryanne that. I wouldn't have to tell her. She'd know. A few seconds later, he gasps and opens his eyes. Like Ryanne did, he starts coughing and rolls to his side as he attempts to sit up. I stand up and walk to the edge of the fire barrier. I don't know if it'll burn me to touch, but I don't really want to find out.

Logan opens his eyes and looks up at Lily. Without saying anything he pulls her down to him. I turn around giving them some privacy.

"Colton," Logan says as he pushes himself up. I turn around at the sound of his voice. "Thank you." I don't need to say anything, so I just nod. He understands. Logan has done so much for all of us recently; we wouldn't be here without him. I reach out and help him stand up. He's not in any condition to fight, there's no way to avoid it. Lily stands at his side, slightly awkward, waiting for his reaction again. When he's standing, he reaches out and pulls her to him, hugging her. "Thank you," he whispers into her hair.

"Bragden, drop the fire," I yell.

The fire around us disappears. Lily has her arms wrapped around Logan's waist, helping him stand upright.

I turn toward James and Travis. "Can you help her get him off the field?"

"I can fight," Logan announces. Lily and I turn and glare at him.

"You cannot fight, Logan," Lily says.

"At least take a little time to heal yourself. If you feel well enough to fight afterwards then you can."

"Colton, I need to fight."

"And I need you to keep yourself alive, Logan. Don't do anything stupid."

Jedrek appears out of the thick of the chaos and stops in front of us. "I need a few of you to come with me," he says.

"What?" I ask.

"There are some humans locked up in the compound that Dravin was running tests on." He pulls a key from his pocket and hands Logan a key. "If you go inside and take a left at the end of the first hall there is an unmarked door. Use the key on that door. It'll lead you to the basement where you'll find five or six humans. Release them."

"There are humans here…alive?" Incendia asks.

"Yes, and I don't think I'll be around for much longer, so someone has to rescue them while I try and save those who have gotten hurt with their weapons."

Logan and Lily grab the key and start heading for the compound. Travis agrees to go with them. Bragden, Incendia, and James will continue to fight. Bragden throws up another wall of fire to allow for Logan, Lily, and Travis to get into the compound without anyone attempting to stop them.

I turn and see Ryanne flying through the air. She slams into a tree and falls to the ground limp. Zahtri is lying on the ground across from her with blood dripping down his nose.

My invisibility immediately takes over as I watch her struggle to get up.

I've noticed that the fight has almost come to a complete stop as everyone watches Ryanne and Zahtri fight each other.

Last time I saw Dravin, he was standing near Zahtri and now he's gone. I search for Liam, but don't see him. We are the ones who are supposed to stop Dravin. Claire told us that much. I look around the yard, searching for the manipulative Gadramick that has hurt my soulmate one too many times.

"Looking for me?"

CHAPTER TWENTY-EIGHT

EVERYTHING HURTS. IT FEELS AS if…I was just thrown into a tree. My body protests with each movement, but once the initial haze from hitting my head against the rough bark fades, I'm able to push myself up. I feel a lot better when I notice that Zahtri is slow to get up as well. I can feel my magic moving through the air around me as I try to formulate a plan. How can I get the upper hand here? There has to be something I can do that he won't be expecting.

I glance toward the crowd behind me. They've all stopped fighting.

No pressure there.

I stand up and throw a shield around me while I try to regain my strength. This is not going like I wanted it to. Right now, it's pretty even. Neither one of us are able to gain any leverage on the other. Zahtri pushes himself off the ground and faces me again. I can feel his magic trying to penetrate my shield, but it remains strong. I take another moment to regain my strength. As Zahtri moves toward me, I start calling more magic. I can envision what I want to happen, but if Zahtri attempts to use his magic the second I drop my shield, I won't be able to execute it like I want to.

Back when I trained a few times with Colin, he told me to get creative. That's what I need to do right now. Get creative. Zahtri has probably seen every trick in the book. He can probably assume what I'm going to attempt next. I'm creative. I know that. I can think of something he's never seen before. I can do something he won't expect, but I need surprise on my side if I plan on coming out of this alive. If he reads my mind or somehow sees my plan, we're all screwed.

I look back at the crowd again and see a column of fire ablaze off to the side. I know either Incendia or Bragden is responsible for this. Is someone hurt? I want to take more time to assess my surroundings, but Zahtri's attempts to thwart my shield are becoming stronger. I won't be able to keep it up for much longer.

Scanning the crowd one more time, I search for a specific pair of eyes. Colton has his back to me, also scanning the field. He's looking for Liam, who is standing with Natalie directly across from him. I can see him from where I'm standing, but Colton wouldn't be able to see him through everyone. Seeing Dravin moving effortlessly through the mages and Gadramicks, I gather up my anger and concern and push the emotions toward Liam. He will know it's from me when it reaches him.

Zahtri is still trying to break down my defenses. I take a small step backward as I wait for Liam to look in my direction. *Come on. Come on, Liam.* Liam jumps and looks around confused. I watch as realization dawns on him and he looks up at me. With my eyes, I look in Colton's direction. I don't have any way of communicating to him that Colton needs his help. Liam's gray eyes leave mine and move across the field. Spotting Dravin, he nods and begins to maneuver over there. At this rate, they'll both make it to Colton simultaneously.

During training sessions, Bragden told me to look for weaknesses in my opponents, but what if there aren't any? What do I do then? Zahtri is cocky, but he is rightfully so. Even though he did not come about this magic naturally, he has a lot and he definitely knows it and understands how to use it. Nothing I am doing is giving me any advantage over him.

One thing is for sure: I'm not going to back down. Even though I don't have a plan, I'm going to pretend like I do. It's worked for me in the past. Who's to say this situation is any different?

With that determined, I take a step forward. Just one step, but Zahtri looks a little surprised at my sudden move. I ignore the pain that shoots up my leg with each movement and casually walk to him. When Zahtri threw me into the tree, I landed on the ground at an odd angle. My ankle twisted beneath me as I fell, but I can't show any weaknesses. I know Zahtri is in pain too, but he's not giving me anything to use against him, so neither will I.

I take another step forward. Zahtri's footing fails as he stumbles backward. I continue my forward progression until the edge of my shield hits him. Zahtri is standing a foot in front of me, waiting for my next move. It has to be me who initiates what happens next.

The wind picks up as I call my magic to me. My magic is the only thing I have going for me at this moment. Zahtri doesn't think I'll be able to beat him because he doesn't think I've released enough magic. Magic is always going to be a part of me. Before, I had too much running through my body at once. I don't have to release anymore. My magic easily obeys me and is there for me when I need it.

Now, it's not all running through my body. It's not trying to compete with everything inside. My magic is moving through the air around me. It is still a part of me, but it is not actually in me. What magic I have in me is what I'm supposed to have as a mage. Everything else is just what I need to accomplish this task. I don't know if I'll still have all this when everything is over. I don't even know if I'll be around when everything is over.

I place my hands together and form a ball of electrified energy, similar to what I did during my training sessions with Colin. The magic crackles as the orb forms. Zahtri looks down at my hands confused as to what I am doing. I just need a little more energy.

I'm not trying to end all this right now. I just need a slight distraction and more time to call the rest of my magic to me. I need to anger Zahtri enough to get him to act. I need him to act without thinking. He needs to let his anger for everything going on take over and completely control his actions if I have any hope of being successful.

"Are you going to kill me?" Zahtri asks as he moves to the edge of my shield. I know that he's taunting me, trying to get me to react. "Are you going to watch the life drain from my eyes? Are you going to be able to live with yourself knowing that you killed a man?"

I ignore him and focus on the magic in front of me. My magic is shimmering within the shield. I spread my hands out a little further, letting the orb grow. Zahtri's eyes zero in on the magic, but he doesn't comment on it.

"Are you going to be able to wake up every morning knowing someone doesn't get that privilege because of you?" He's just taunting me. I can't listen to him. "Will you be able to go about your daily routine and pretend like you don't have blood of your hands?"

I block him out and focus on the magic in front of me. I can see his lips still moving, so I know that he's still trying to get me to react before I'm ready. It's not going to work. I can't afford to be callous right now. There's so much at stake. After a few seconds, my eyes hone in on Zahtri. He's still talking, but he's not looking at me. He's still staring at the ball in my hands. The energy cracks in my hands telling me that it's ready to be released.

I grin at him as I drop the shield and thrust the magic toward him. Before the magic even hits him, I turn around and run in the opposite direction. I visualize the magic exploding around him, and I know that I'll get hit if I stay here. A blast rings out behind me and my magic ricochets back. I push more out and attempt to create a shield around me, but the force is too strong. I'm hit with my own magic and am lifted into the air. I tuck my body in and roll when I hit the ground.

When I stop rolling, I push myself up and immediately look across to the area where Zahtri just was. Only he's not there. Throwing a shield up, my eyes move past the platform. He's not here at all.

"Looking for me, darling?" I whip around and face Zahtri again. Dang, I didn't obliterate him.

"How do you do it?" I ask him.

"I still have a few powers on you. Like the power of transport. Though, I did get hit a little bit." He rolls his shoulder, slightly wincing with the movement. I see the burnt holes in the fabric and the charred skin underneath. "Not a problem though. You'll find out that I heal very quickly. Can you say that?" Zahtri moves until he's standing along the edge of my shield. "Why the shield? Are you scared of me?"

"Not scared. Cautious. Weary. Suspicious. Yes, but not scared."

"Then drop the shield and fight me. This is what you wanted isn't it?"

Magic? This is it. I feel my magic move around me, caressing my skin with its energy. This is the moment the prophecy has been talking about. Taking one last deep breath, I step back a few steps and narrow my eyes at him.

"Let's do this," I whisper as I throw my hands up, siphoning my magic through me and drop my shield.

This is it.

COLTON

I TURN AROUND AND FACE Dravin. Everyone moves out of the way, giving us room. All the mages we brought know that Liam and I are supposed to be the ones that stop Dravin. Her two warriors are destined to put an end to the war. It has to be us. I know David, Logan, Larkin, and Bragden are really angry that they can't help. We've all seen Ryanne after she's been with Dravin. We all know what he's done to her and Ryanne has inspired us to act. I can see Liam moving toward me, but I don't look at him. I don't want to alert Dravin to his presence. Not yet.

"This could all be easily stopped."

"Yeah, would you like to casually walk in front of my sword? Or better yet, you can just take it and stab yourself. That way your blood wouldn't be on my hands."

"Tell Ryanne to stop the attack unless you want to be lowering her casket six feet under."

I feel my invisibility skimming the surface, wanting me to release it. It doesn't like the image of Ryanne lying in a casket being buried and neither do I. Somehow, I push it back. I need to remain visible.

I hope I have a good handle on it, because what I'm about to say could bring it out fully. "At least people would show up to her funeral. She's touched so many lives here. Can you say the same thing? Will anyone miss you when you're gone? These people are just followers. They don't care about you, Dravin."

Liam steps up behind Dravin and raises his sword, but Dravin turns around and faces him. "I wouldn't try that if I were you."

Liam lowers his weapon, but I move forward and kick him in the back of the knees. Dravin falls to the ground, but rolls to the side, out of the way. Getting back up, he glares at Liam and me. "This is really what you want to do? Fight to the death?" he sneers. "Are you really prepared for that?"

"You afraid to do the same thing that girl is doing right over there?" Liam points in Ryanne's direction. I briefly glance at her and watch her form a ball of magic between her hands like she did during one of the training sessions. Zahtri is talking to her, probably trying to instigate her. What I wouldn't give to be fighting alongside her right now.

"Am I afraid to lose? Is that what you're asking me?" Dravin takes another step forward. Neither Liam nor I have magic that can be used as a weapon. Dravin does. We have strength and training and I intend to use all of that against Dravin tonight. This has to stop. All this madness has to end.

"Are you afraid to go against us? Is the strong, ruthless, Gadramick leader afraid to go up against two ordinary mages?"

Dravin throws his head back and laughs. I glance over at Liam, who gives me a similar look. We're walking on thin ice right now. Instigation can go one of two ways. It can anger him enough to get him to react sloppily—to attack without thinking, giving us the advantage—or it can anger him enough to attack even more ruthlessly than he would have before. It could motivate him further, giving him the advantage over us. With Dravin, I'm not sure which way it'll go. We'll find out soon enough though.

This is the man who put a dagger into my side because Ryanne wouldn't tell him what her powers were. That feels like so long ago. Dravin knocked Ryanne out with dormirako and took Liam and me in as prisoners when we went to rescue her. This is the man who killed me.

One good thing did come out of that incident though. I was finally able to tell Ryanne that she was my soulmate. I had been battling with how and when to tell her. She had so much on her plate already that I didn't want to drop another bomb on her, but I knew she'd be mad if I kept it to myself for too much longer.

Ryanne passed out from exhaustion shortly after healing me. I remember the look on her face when she woke up and saw me alive. There was so much pain in her expression because she was seeing me getting stabbed all over again. I don't want to be the reason for putting that pain back into her beautiful eyes. We have to win this.

Will the prophecy still be fulfilled if we lose? Will all this be for nothing if we lose?

Liam and I have fought against each other many times during training, but we've never fought together. However, you can't be around someone as often as we have and not know how that person fights. Liam and I understand each other and we're working toward a common goal. We can do this. Natalie kept telling me to have faith, and now I finally do.

I have faith we can accomplish this. We can all make it out of this alive.

I face Dravin one last time.

This has to end now.

Without looking back, I brandish my sword and take a step forward, meeting Dravin. It's now or never, and I'm choosing now. Dravin pulls his sword out and deflects my attempt.

"You're going to have to do a little better than that if you want to stop me."

"Oh, we will," Liam says he joins me.

"You know this isn't really a fair fight," Dravin says as he glances between the two of us. He doesn't look scared and I know that he's not. He still thinks he's going to come out of this situation victorious. He's too cocky, and hopefully that'll get him in trouble.

"Who said anything about a fair fight?"

CHAPTER TWENTY-NINE

ZAHTRI RUNS TOWARD ME WITHOUT magic. Little does he know that all of the guys have done this to me during our training sessions, so I'm prepared. I wait until he is right in front of me and then I flip to the side while pushing my magic around me. If Zahtri tries to touch me, it'll shock him. I have my own defense mechanism. I smile as I start to feel more confident in this fight.

I was given these powers for this moment. Zahtri never came into his magic. His powers aren't real; they were produced. I can defeat him. When I died, I had to admit to my mom that I believed I could someday be strong enough to do this. Well someday is here, and I feel strong enough. I can do this. I have been captured many times. I've been beaten and broken, and I'm still here. I'm *still* standing. I came back from all of it and didn't let it affect me. In fact, all those instances just helped me prepare for this. Dravin may have helped me. I'm stronger now than I've ever been. I'm not going to give up. I'm not going to sacrifice myself. Larkin was right about that. Sacrificing myself won't help anything.

My soulmate and protector are over there fighting for the life after this. Fighting for what comes next, and I need to do the same thing. My life has barely begun. I don't want to die before I reach the middle of my story. I don't want to close the book, because I don't want this ending. This is just a chapter in my story. Just a chapter; not a conclusion. Definitely not a conclusion.

Zahtri has my complete attention right now. He turns and attempts to punch me, but I throw up my arm to deflect his blow. He's about Bragden's size, and I've fought and won against Bragden before. I can do this now; I know I can. I swing my leg out and kick him in the chest, but he thwarts my action by grabbing onto my leg and throwing me across the field. He winces when his hands connect with my skin, but he doesn't let that deter him. Twisting my body mid-air, I land on my feet and run forward without pause.

I'm not going to wait for him anymore. I don't want to be on the defensive. Besides a few rare instances, it's the offense who wins the game. I need to be on the offense right now; I want to be the one calling the shots. Zahtri seems a little shocked at my suddenness, but doesn't linger on that for too long. I jump in front of him and drop to the ground, knocking his feet out from under him. He falls, but rolls to the side, so I can't do anything else. I follow his movement as he stands up and starts circling me.

He's not using his left arm very much. His shoulder must hurt more than he's letting on. There's a weakness. I smile at him as I make the first move. I start calling my magic to me. Can Zahtri use his magic physically? He can transport and read minds, but can he do anything else? I don't think I've seen him do anything else. He's physically strong, but can he add magic into his limbs to make himself stronger?

Thunder rumbles above us as I start pulling more magic around me. Zahtri's face transforms into one of anger. I'm not going to go down easily. He has another thing coming if he thinks he'll be able to make quick work of me and move on. I can hear grunts around me of other people fighting, but I've learned from previous battles not to look. That's how you get yourself killed. I have to have faith that my family is going to protect each other. Right now, this is about Zahtri and me. That's all I can focus on.

He should look at all those times they've come to capture me. Did I cower in the corner? Maybe the first time…but I didn't after that. I fought. I throw my hands up and push the winds out. Zahtri's forward progression halts as he waits for the wind assault to end. He doesn't fall like I intended, but this is enough to give me some more time.

I hear a familiar scream echo through the field and briefly glance at the fight behind me. Dravin is in the middle of the field, fighting Liam and Colton. Surprisingly, it seems evenly matched despite the odd number. How is that possible? Colton and Liam are strong—they should easily be able to overcome him. Emma was the one who screamed though. I try to not break my concentration when I see why she screamed. She jumps forward and grabs onto Kyril as the Gadramick in front of her pulls his sword out of the middle of his chest. Larkin blinks in behind him and twists the guy's neck, breaking it. He slumps to the ground soundlessly, but it's too late. Emma falls from Kyril's sudden weight. David jumps to her side and helps Larkin move Kyril. Kyril starts convulsing. Even from this distance, I can see the tears streaming down Emma's face.

I continue pushing wind toward Zahtri. Come on, Kyril, don't leave us. I bite my lip as I continue sending thoughts in his direction. Larkin yells for Logan, but Logan isn't around. I scan the clearing, but I don't see Logan or Lily at all. Kyril whispers something to his friend and goes limp. Emma covers her mouth, turns to her soulmate, and sobs into his shoulder.

Kyril's dead.

He's gone. Kyril can't be gone. Thunder rumbles again and the intensity of the wind hitting Zahtri amplifies. I'm angry now, and I'm going to let everyone know it. I return my attention to the mage responsible for all of this in front of me. He's going to pay for this. Kyril was a good man; he shouldn't have died here. The sky above us darkens and it slowly begins to rain. The battle sounds behind me disappear. It's only me and Zahtri. Just the two of us. For this to end, two has to become one. Only one of us can survive. It's been prophesized for thousands of years. *This* day has been predestined for that long. I'm an artist and a reader, not a writer. I'm not going to rewrite history. History is going to play out like it's been prophesized. I'm going to make sure of it.

I stop the wind and run toward Zahtri, surprising him. He recovers quickly from the wind attack, but not quick enough. I stop running a few feet in front of him and transition into front flips. Zahtri doesn't move. I stop and fall to the ground and swing my foot out. With my hit and magic, he falls onto his back and grunts. I stand up, but Zahtri reaches out and wraps a hand around my ankle and pulls me down beside him.

I land on my back and gasp as the air is knocked out of me. I pull my leg up and kick Zahtri, causing him to release his grip. In getting up, he's much quicker than I am, and when I see him standing, I try to roll onto my stomach and stand, but he runs toward me before I can move. A foot connects with my stomach, lifting me into the air and depositing me back onto the ground a few feet from where I just was.

Biting my tongue to keep from crying out, I attempt to stand, ignoring the pain that radiates through my abdomen. Zahtri rushes over to me and wraps his large arm around my waist and pulls me up. Crushing me against his chest, he forces me to look out at the people fighting around us.

"Look at them!" he grabs my chin to ensure that my gaze is directed at them. I close my eyes. I don't want to see the scene in front of me. When I shake my head, he squeezes me tighter. "Look at them!" he yells in my ear.

My stomach is numb. The pain from his kick and the force he's using right now should be excruciating, but I can't feel anything. I can't get any air into my lungs and when I finally open my eyes, he loosens his grip a little. I can't help but gasp and gulp in oxygen, however, that's quickly cut short when I see the scene before me.

Larkin is fighting multiple people at once, but is completely dominating. He's definitely angry. He was very close to Kyril and is taking his anger out on the Gadramicks. Emma still has tears falling down her cheeks, but like Larkin, she's channeling her anger into her fighting. She's still brandishing a whip like earlier, but this one appears to have electricity running through it. Colton and Liam are in the middle of the clearing with Dravin. Blood is dripping down Liam's arm and Colton has a split lip. Dravin's jaw is red, but he doesn't seem to have any other injuries. Tom, Colin, and Vincent are still fighting back-to-back.

I can see Natasha fighting against a smaller girl. I recognize her as the girl I saved from Thomas a while ago. Lucas and his posse are in the back fighting against a large group of men. Incendia falls to the ground after a man backhands her. Before the man even has time to think, Bragden reaches out and punches him in the jaw. Crouching down, he helps Incendia stand—his fingers grazing against the growing redness on her face. With an angry shake of his head, Bragden turns around and searches for a Gadramick to take his anger out on.

I start to fight against Zahtri's grip again when I see a man walk behind Mrs. Howick and stab her in the side. Her back arches as he pushes the dagger in further. Hearing her cry out, Mr. Howick stops fighting the man in front of him and turns toward his wife. The

Gadramick takes this distraction to his advantage and plunges his sword into Mr. Howick's back. I cry out as I watch both of them fall to the ground. I know those daggers were infused with dark magic. The majority of the weapons here are infused with it. They won't be able to heal. Knowing that, the Gadramicks move on and start fighting other mages.

Mr. Howick uses the last of his energy to crawl over to his wife. Zahtri's grip on my stomach tightens as I try to get away from him. When he's halfway there, Mrs. Howick moves her right hand forward, and Mr. Howick grabs onto it and pulls her into his side. Even from here, I can see the large amounts of blood seeping from their wounds. Both of them start convulsing. I see him whisper something to her, but I can't hear them. I don't need to hear though. If I were in that situation, I know what I'd say.

With tears streaming down my face, I watch as Mr. Howick leans forward and places a small kiss on his wife's forehead as she stops moving. Her body goes limp under his lips and I can see his body getting weaker. He rests his forehead on hers as he stops moving as well. They're dead.

I stop fighting Zahtri. "Call off the attack," he demands, "or more people will die."

Travis, Logan, and Lily run out of the compound followed by five very scared girls. Humans. Travis calls for Larkin, and then grabs onto two of the girls and disappears with them. Logan and Lily guard the remaining three girls. Larkin blinks away from the Gadramick he was fighting and reappears beside Logan. Logan says something to him and he grabs onto the closest girl and disappears. Travis comes back and grabs the last two girls and blinks away again.

My attention returns to the middle of the field when I see Colton lying on the ground, holding his head. Dravin is making him see something. That's it. I bring my foot up and back kick Zahtri in the shins. He curses and angles down at little. I use this to my advantage and lean back, hitting the back of my skull into his nose.

When his hold on me loosens, I spin around and lift my leg up and connect my foot with his temple. He staggers to the side, but doesn't fall. Zahtri moves toward me and starts attacking. He wants this to end just as much I do, but we're both fighting for completely different reasons.

Zahtri runs toward me, growling, and using all of this strength he begins his physical assault. I don't know how my body is doing it, but I block his attacks. My arms and legs move in ways I didn't even know I could do. I don't think about what is happening; I just react. When Zahtri realizes he's not gaining anything on me, he starts coming harder. Even with drawing magic into my limbs, I'm getting sore.

I'm not going to last much longer.

Zahtri brings his arm forward to punch at the same time as his leg moves out. It was one of those moments, where I have to choose the lesser of the two evils. I chose wrong. I duck to avoid being punched and his foot hits the side of my knee. The world blurs around me as I tumble to the ground. As the grass gets closer and closer to me, I try to twist my body so the landing won't hurt, but I don't move fast enough. Landing on my left arm, I hear the snap before the pain spreads through me. I can't hold in my cry as I try to roll over and get up. Pins and needles climb up my arm with the movement and I collapse back to the ground. Zahtri moves toward me, slowly unsheathing a small dagger from the belt around his waist.

So much for a weaponless fight.

COLTON

"WELL DON'T YOU LOOK HANDSOME," my girl's voice says from behind me. I turn around and smile at Ryanne as she walks toward me wearing her bridesmaid's dress.

"You're wearing pink," I try to hide my smile as she stops in front of me. I've never seen her in pink before.

"Only because I love Emma and this is her day. I'll get back at her at our wedding," she laughs and wraps her arms around my waist. My heart skips a beat at the thought of our wedding. Ryanne and I are going to get married. This girl is going to be my wife. My life.

"You do look beautiful, Ryanne," I whisper in her ear. Her slight shiver fills me with happiness. It's been almost a year, and my touch still affects her.

"Okay, everyone get in your places. Emma's ready," Natalie says as she walks into the backyard. She's wearing a dress very similar to Ryanne's, except hers is strapless while Ryanne's is one shouldered. I let go of Ryanne and Logan, Liam, and I walk over to stand behind David at the edge of the yard.

"Hey man, you ready?" I ask him as I get into line. David is fidgeting with the cuffs on his jacket and clenching his jaw. "Relax," I laugh at him.

"I don't know what's gotten into me," he says as he releases the cuff and clasps his hands in front of him.

Before I can answer, Violet starts playing the wedding song on the piano we brought outside. Travis is standing off to the side, watching his soulmate as she plays. She grins up at him, but doesn't let that mess her up. After everything that's happened to him, I'm glad he found his soulmate.

Incendia enters the aisle and slowly walks down it, holding a small bouquet in her hand. Similar to Ryanne, seeing Incendia in pink is something that just doesn't happen. Her smile widens as she sees

Bragden watching her from one of the lawn chairs. She shakes her head and steps into her place across from us. Natalie is next.

"She looks beautiful," Liam whispers behind me. She does. I know Natalie caught that because she bites her lip and shakes her head at him. Liam laughs quietly behind me. I'm glad those two found each other too. They both deserve it. Once Natalie is in place, Ryanne steps onto the aisle.

My breath hitches and my stomach tightens at her beauty. How is this girl mine? Ryanne smiles as she takes the first step. Her eyes never leave me as she continues walking toward us. Someday she'll be in a wedding dress, walking toward me.

A couple seconds later, her smile falls and she stops walking. The crowd starts whispering at her sudden change. I glance at David. What's going on? Her eyes move from mine and land on the trees behind me. With tears in her eyes, she glances back at me as an arrow shoots out from the trees and implants itself into her chest, impaling her heart. Everyone gasps and jumps up. Ryanne falls to the ground where she stays, her bouquet landing at her side. As the wind picks up the loose flower petals, Logan and I push everyone out of the way and run to her, but I know it's already too late.

Ryanne is dead.

Logan drops to the ground beside her and attempts to heal her, but he can't bring back the dead. Only a soulmate can do that and I've already healed her once. We only get one chance. Seeing the blood soak through her pink dress chokes me up. I stand up and look toward the tree line. Who did this?

Dravin steps out from the shadows and waves his bow at me. "You should have killed me when you had the chance."

The vision stops playing in front of me. I'm lying on the ground in the middle of the field while the fight continues. I can hear grunts of pain echo through the area as punches are being thrown. I look to my right and see Liam still fighting Dravin, so I push myself up, but can't join Liam right away. Closing my eyes, I try to make the world stop spinning around me.

It wasn't real. Dravin made me see that. It didn't actually happen. David and Emma are not married yet. That was a projection... something of Dravin's imagination. As the vertigo passes, I look across the field and see Ryanne fighting against Zahtri. Alive. She's alive. She wasn't shot with an arrow. Ryanne is moving with the skill of someone who has trained their whole life. She's ducking at the right time, deflecting his advances with the correct parts of her body, and she's mentally in the zone. She's not focusing on what is happening around her.

Hearing Liam grunt in pain, I return my attention to the man who made me watch my soulmate die again. How did he know all of that? Because from the little details I know about David and Emma's wedding, that looked like it. How could Dravin have known that? I unsheathe my sword and walk toward him again. This can't go on for any longer.

Thanks for coming back, Liam says in my mind. Liam says that in my mind! Why didn't I think about that before now?

We can use this to our advantage, Liam!

What?

We can communicate to each other without Dravin knowing. We can plan something and finally finish this. I tell him. This could be what saves us.

Dravin's strong, Colton. He's not going to go down easily.

I feel the slight pain of Dravin trying to invade my mind again. Liam reaches out and punches him, distracting him. What can we do? Out of the corner of my eye, I see Ryanne fall to the ground and Zahtri stalk toward her with a dagger in his hand. She's grimacing as she tries to get up, but she's not moving fast enough.

Liam, we have to end this now.

I know. I see her.

I wonder…I know that Ryanne can feel the feelings of those around us. I try to send my positive feelings to her to help, but it's hard to think like that right now. Zahtri is standing right in front of her. Ryanne is scooting back on the ground, but she still can't get up. What happened to her?

I turn my attention away from Ryanne. I knew this was going to happen. She has to fight Zahtri. I have to be here with Dravin. Harnessing all the anger I'm feeling, I turn toward Dravin. Unlike Ryanne, emotions can't physically strengthen my magic, but they can help strengthen me. I'm not sloppy when I'm mad. In fact, it's just the opposite. My attacks are more precise.

Noticing a change in me, Liam steps to the side and lets me move toward Dravin. I don't go invisible. I want Dravin to see me. This is the man who stabbed me without a second glance. He didn't even think about it. He killed me so he could get Ryanne to tell him about her magic. He's been kidnapping and experimenting on humans and needs to be stopped. All of this needs to stop.

I reel back and land a punch of Dravin's jaw. He falls to the side, but doesn't react as much as I wanted him to. The force of my hit splits his lip, and blood starts dripping down his chin. "That's was a good hit," he says as he flexes his jaw. "But it's not going to be good enough to save your pretty little girl over there. You're going to have to try harder than that."

How are we going to do this? Liam asks me. I can hear the urgency in his voice which means that he sees something that I don't. Either Natalie or Ryanne are in trouble. I duck one of Dravin's punches and take a step back.

I have absolutely no idea. Dravin reaches out and punches me in the jaw this time, and then turns around and starts attacking Liam. I stumble backward and try to ignore the pain. I hear a small pained cry echo behind me, but I can't turn around. I have to keep my attention on the fight in front of me. Not the one behind me.

I have to focus on Dravin.

Not Ryanne.

CHAPTER THIRTY

I CONTINUE SCOOTING BACKWARD AS quickly as I can as Zahtri moves toward me. I'm trying to ignore the pain in my left arm, but I'm pretty sure it is broken. As I move, I try to push magic into my arm. I may not be like Logan, but I do heal quickly. Maybe if I concentrate all my magic into my arm, I can heal myself with its help.

Zahtri stops, and standing over me with his dagger pointed outward, he says, "Seriously, darling, this could have all been stopped. No one had to die here today. This is all your fault."

I groan and push myself back a little further. If I don't heal soon, this will all be over. Too soon. It can't end like this. It just can't.

"You're the one who kidnapped me," I remind him.

"You could have told them to stop the attack," he says.

"And how would I have done that when I was trapped inside of a cell?" I move back a little further. Zahtri follows my movement, but he doesn't attempt to stab me yet. I don't think he wants it to end like this either…However, he did throw me off a cliff, so I don't really know what he's thinking. His thoughts are still blocked from me.

"I don't know how you did it, but I know you were able to contact them," he crouches down next to me. "It was either you or Liam; one of you, if not both, was able to contact them. He's a dream walker, I know that much. He has the ability, but you don't. How'd you do it?"

I sit up, putting pressure on my left arm. A sharp pain still spreads through my arm, but I don't let Zahtri know that I'm in pain. He'd use it against me. "That's not possible," I tell him.

"Every day we prove things possible that should be impossible," he whispers as he stands up. "Get up."

"Why?" I ask him.

"Because we're going to do this your way." Using the dagger, he motions for me to stand up. Without moving my eyes away from him, I avoid putting weight on my left arm and stand.

He raises his arm and flexes his muscles, preparing to throw the dagger. I throw a shield up around my body and wait for him to throw it at me. Without my permission, my eyes close. A *whoosh* sounds by ear and my body flinches as I prepare for the possible pain. After a few seconds of nothing happening, I open my eyes and find Zahtri staring at me. Keeping the shield up, I peek over my shoulder and see the dagger embedded into the trunk of a tree.

"Are you ready?" he asks me. I bring my attention back to him. "I'm not going to take it easy anymore."

Yeah, cause he was taking it easy on me before. Cocky jerk. I keep my shield up and continue pushing magic into my arm, but I don't answer him. When Zahtri takes a step toward me, I step back mirroring his stance. I can move my arm again, so I know my magic is working. It's not working as fast as I want it to, but I'm not complaining.

"How do you think your soulmate will react to your death?" he asks me. I stop pushing my magic into my arm and start calling it around me.

He wants to do this my way. I'm about to show him what my way really means.

Zahtri takes another step forward, so I do the opposite. I just need a few more seconds and then I'll be able to fully go up against him.

"What made you change your mind?" I ask in an attempt to stall him. "You could have easily ended me when I was lying on the ground. You had your opportunity. You had a weapon, and I was injured. Why'd you change your mind?" I ask again.

"There's something about you," he says. "I like you."

"You're just prolonging the inevitable. One or both of us is going to end up dead. There's no way to change this scenario."

"You could join me," he suggests with a wide smile.

"That's not an option," I tell him. I'd rather die than work with him. He keeps suggesting that because he already knows what my response is going to be.

"Didn't think so," he says, "which is why you're going to die here. Look around. This will be the last thing you see. I'm going to be the last man you see before your eyes forever close. Not your soulmate. Not your protector. Me. You'll never see that soulmate of yours again. He's going to be so guilt ridden after your death that it'll make killing him that much easier. You'll have your own little Romeo and Juliet story. Isn't that what all you girls want? A romantic story?"

I feel my magic strengthening around me at the mention of him killing Colton. That's not going to happen. If I'm going to die here, I'm taking Zahtri with me. He can't come out of this alive.

"After your soulmate, I'll move onto his Uncle. The old man won't last very long. It'll be easy. In his heyday, he may have been a good fighter. Maybe even one of the best, but he's getting old. He hasn't been training as often. It'll be easy. One simple swipe of a blade and he'll be a goner."

My magic is bubbling to the surface. I can feel it moving around me waiting to heed my command. He's not going to kill Tom. I just need a few more seconds to gather enough magic. I push my shield around my mind. I don't need Zahtri reading my thoughts. He already knows I'm planning something, but hopefully he doesn't know what. Surprise has to be on my side for this.

"Then, I'll move onto that protector of yours. Little Liam. He's tough, I have firsthand knowledge of that, but when a mage finds their soulmate, their focus changes. He's determined to protect you and her. He can't do both. With you out of the picture, his focus will be entirely on her. Soulmates are a weakness. Hurt her, I hurt him. It's a domino effect.

Zahtri continues moving forward.

"He'll grieve her death and like your soulmate, it'll make him easier to kill. It doesn't matter how good of a fighter they are. When you hurt someone they love, they become weak. They become easy kills. It'll be a breeze. Killing Liam, I'll get my payback for this," he motions to the scar running down his face and neck. "I'll enjoy watching him struggle. I'll enjoy seeing the anger for me leave his eyes as he dies next to her. It'll be fun.

"You'll set it all off. They all love you," he says. "In the end, it all comes down to you. You, Ryanne, will be responsible for their deaths."

"You cannot pin this on me, Zahtri. You cannot blame any of this on me. If it didn't happen tonight, it would have happened eventually. You cannot say that all of this is surprising. You can't tell me that you didn't see this coming. You are responsible for all of this. You are the reason that there is a fight here. Not me."

I'm about to push my magic out when I'm hit with an unforeseen force and am sent flying backward. Sometime during Zahtri's taunts, I must have dropped my shield. My back slams into the trunk of a tree and I fall limply to the ground. I attempt to slow my fall, but the magic took me by surprise and I fall like a ton of bricks to the ground where I remain.

I need to get up. I need to fight.

But I can't.

COLTON

ANY IDEAS? LIAM'S VOICE SPEAKS in my mind. I hear a collective gasp around me, and it takes all of my willpower not to turn around and look at Ryanne. I know something is going on. I want to see that she's alright, but I can't.

Do I have any ideas? There has to be something.

I'm about to reply to Liam when a man barrels into me, knocking me to the ground. The air is knocked out of me when I land on the hard grass. Rolling onto my back, I get a good look at the man that ran into me. Jedrek rolls to the side with a grimace on his face. I push myself up and move toward him.

"What did you do?" I whisper to him.

He reaches down and pulls a small dagger out of his side. Blood starts oozing out of the wound. "You...you didn't see it....coming. It's," he gasps and lies on his back, trying to take deep breaths, "tainted with d-d-dark magi..." he trails off.

"Jedrek where is the antidote?" I can't let him die like this. He just saved my life. He saved Natalie's life earlier, and even though Ryanne doesn't know him well, she does care about him. I have to do something.

"N-no more. Used all of...it," he sputters. "Now, you can...stop D-d-ravin." He rests his head on the ground. I push myself up into a seated position. His normally pale skin is turning an ashy shade of gray—the color of death. There's literally nothing I can do to save him. Jedrek is going to die, and all I can do is watch.

"Ssssave her, Colton. Don't l-let her go," he says as his eyes slowly close. The blood is still pouring out of the wound on his side, but his breathing stops.

"Jedrek?" I stare at his chest, waiting for the subtle rise and fall. "Come on, don't do this." I hit his chest. He can't just save me and then die. It's not supposed to work like that. The good guys are supposed to survive.

"Larkin," I say quietly, knowing that he'll come.

Larkin transports in behind me. I can see the anger in his expression. I saw what happened to Kyril, and I know that Larkin and Kyril were really close. "Can you move his body?" I ask him. "I want to give him a proper burial when all of this is over."

Without saying anything to me, Larkin bends down and touches Jedrek's shoulder and leaves the clearing. Jedrek died saving my life. Ryanne's father saved Natalie and me today. Who knows how many people he gave the antidote to while we were fighting—how many people he saved. I stand up and look back in Dravin's direction. I don't know where his body was moved to, but I can't focus on that. Liam needs my help right now.

Turning around, I find Liam and Dravin very much concentrated on their fighting. Unsheathing my sword, I slowly move behind Dravin. It looks like Dravin has stopped the mental attacks and is just focusing on his fighting. Liam has a split lip and blood dripping down his arm. Even though he has a larger sword on his back, he is only fighting with a dagger. I see blood sliding down Dravin's forearm and blood oozing down his throat from a cut on his cheek. Both of them are injured, but neither one is wavering. They're not going to stop until this is finished. I can help finish it.

Liam moves forward and thrusts the dagger into Dravin's side. Dravin grunts, but doesn't stop fighting. Hastily removing the weapon, Liam steps back and blocks Dravin's punch. Blood starts soaking Dravin's shirt and spreading down his torso.

If I can move without being noticed, I may be able to end this right now. Liam's eyes quickly move in my direction, but they continue moving across the clearing as if he doesn't see me. He can't make it obvious that I'm coming. My cover could be blown.

As Liam continues to fight, I move forward, little by little, keeping my eyes on Dravin, but my ears open to the crowd around me. I don't need to get stabbed with a dagger right now. This could be what we need. Liam moves to the right and deflects Dravin's punch. He's fighting in a way that keeps Dravin's back to me, giving me the outing I need. The shot I need to finally end this. I hear another scream behind me, but it's not Ryanne's. I'm unsure of who it actually belonged to.

I take another step further. Liam ducks to avoid Dravin's arm. While down, he punches Dravin in the gut. When Dravin doubles over, Liam stands up and nods at me. Dravin looks over his shoulder at the same moment as I swing my sword around and using all the force I can muster, I sweep the blade through his neck. Dravin attempts to move, but it's too late. My sword pushes through flesh and bone and makes a clean cut all the way through. His eyes widen and mouth opens as his head rolls off his shoulders and bounces on the ground. His body falls to its knees before it lies down and blood begins pooling onto the grass beneath. Panting, Liam looks up at me and nods. We did it.

Without knowing it, Jedrek saved my life and helped us stop Dravin.

One down...how many more to go?

I turn around and look at the clearing where Ryanne and Zahtri are supposed to be. Zahtri is moving toward Ryanne...who is lying unmoving beneath a tree. The wood is splintered at the base which tells me Ryanne was forcefully thrown into it.

Without giving me any advance notice, my invisibility takes over. Seeing that, Liam turns and looks in her direction. She's supposed to be doing this on her own, but she really could use some help.

"There's nothing we can do Colton. I want to help her too, but we can't," Liam tells me.

"She's unconscious, Liam!" I can't just let her get killed while she's unconscious. I can't lose her like that.

Hearing another scream to my right, I turn and see Emma brandishing a medieval spiked flail against a few Gadramicks. She's having too much fun with her conjuring power. It wasn't her who screamed though. It was Natalie. She's fighting next to James, but James is busy with two Gadramicks and Natalie is trying to fight a man much larger than her. Liam tenses beside me and attempts to make his way over to her, but there are too many people in between us.

I scan the clearing. Larkin should be back by now. He wouldn't skip out on something like this. He wants to avenge Kyril's death. I see him transporting back and forth a few feet behind us. He's moving between two larger groups of Gadramicks. He's going to get himself killed at his rate.

"Larkin!" I call.

Larkin's eye move away from the men he's fighting and connect with mine even though I'm invisible. I blink and suddenly he's in front of me. Again, he doesn't speak.

"Can you go help Natalie?" I ask him. Liam points across the field to his soulmate. Larkin's eye move in that direction and he disappears. I look back over there and watch as Larkin appears behind the man. I don't keep watching to see what happens. When Liam relaxes beside me, it's safe to assume that Natalie is okay. I look around the clearing again looking for anyone that needs help.

I seriously hope this is almost over. I'm not sure we can handle much more. Seeing Tom, Vincent, Colin, and Chris fighting in the middle of the field, I start to make my way over to them. Liam moves to the right to try and get to his soulmate. Lucky. As I take a few steps forward, I glance back across the clearing in Ryanne's direction. She and Zahtri have disappeared. Where did they go? Damn it. Why am I always losing her?

With renewed vigor and my invisibility, I push through everyone. I wipe the bloodied sword on my black pants and push it back into the sheath. I don't want to kill any more people tonight. Too much blood has already been shed. Too many lives have already been lost.

Throwing a punch to the side, I knock an unsuspecting man to the ground and continue moving forward. Tom and his group are now only a few feet ahead of me. No one attempts to touch me as I progress the last few feet.

"Tom, did you see where Ryanne went?" I ask as I stop beside him.

"No," he answers even though he can't see me, "but she disappeared before Zahtri got to her. I'm hoping her magic kicked in and helped her. She was unconscious last time I saw and Zahtri disappeared shortly afterwards." He reaches out and punches the man in front of him. "He's probably searching for her."

Ryanne is gone, and Zahtri is searching for her. I suppress my groan and focus on the fight around me. The sooner this is over, the better. The sooner I know what happened, the better. I see Liam fighting alongside Natalie. With Dravin gone and Zahtri missing, the Gadramicks have no one to follow. I can see a few of them looking around confused. Everyone they looked up to is gone.

I try to push my invisibility away. It is helpful, but right now I want these guys to see me. I want them to see my face as I fight them. I want them to see the person they are fighting and see my anger for what is going on. I'm tired of seeing death, and I want this all to end.

Before all my invisibility has disappeared, I start to fight one of the Gadramicks who had moved toward Tom. Tom has always been there for me growing up, and I don't plan on having that change anytime soon. Like the guys around him, I've got his back.

Out of the corner of my eye, I see fire dancing around. Turning in that direction, I see two trees completely engulfed in flames. That has to be Bragden's or Incendia's work. They're creating a distraction, but for what?

CHAPTER THIRTY-ONE

UGH, MY WHOLE BODY ACHES. Keeping my eyes closed, I roll onto my back. I don't feel like anything is broken, but that doesn't mean it wasn't broken at one time. Where am I? Opening my eyes, I look up and see...trees. A canopy of tree leaves is all I can see. I'm in the middle of the forest? I push myself up, ignoring the dull pain that spreads through my body from the movement and get a good look at my surroundings. I'm in the middle of the forest. What happened to the battle? I was fighting Zahtri. Where is he?

Standing up, I spin in a circle looking for anything that can tell me what happened or where I am. There's absolutely nothing. How did I get here?

I stretch out my muscles, and I don't even try to keep in my pained cry as I move. My back is killing me. What the heck happened to me?

I pause. Zahtri. Zahtri did this to me. He...what did he do? He did something.

I was calling my magic to me. I was going to attack him, but he got to me first. He hit me with some form of magic, but how does that explain how I got here? How did I get to this part of the forest…alone?

Why do I still have more questions and no way to find answers?

Well, this just sucks. How long was I even unconscious?

I push my magic through my body, trying to heal the rest of my injuries before I attempt to go back to the clearing. I don't know what I'll find back there, so I need to be prepared. There's a multitude of scenarios that could play out or are already playing out.

I take a few steps forward. There's literally nothing but trees around me. The forest is quiet. Like so many other times I've been in a forest recently, it's too quiet. I don't hear any birds chirping or flying around. There are no animals scurrying along the fallen leaves on the ground. The sound of insects flapping their wings and buzzing through the air is nonexistent. There isn't a breeze rustling the leaves together. It's silent. A forest is supposed to be full of life. Not silent.

I walk over to a fallen tree branch and sit down, letting my magic run its course. I can feel myself being healed as I wait. I'll remain here for a few more minutes and then I'll go back. No matter what, I need to get back. I need to see what has happened while I was out.

While I heal, I continue to scan the forest. I have a feeling that my own magic brought me here, but why this spot? What is so special about this area? The ache in my body is slowly dissipating. It doesn't hurt to move anymore, but I know that fighting or continuous use will cause it to return. My eyes move to the right and linger on a rather large oak tree.

I push myself off the log and slowly walk toward the tree. As I get closer to it, I see something carved a few feet off the ground into the bark. Stopping in front of it, I see a heart. Though faded, it looks like the letters SW and LW. I wonder who carved them there…what was their story?

I'm about to step back when an unfamiliar warm feeling spreads through me. Love and…happiness? This is different from the feelings I'm usually around. This is an old feeling. I feel all the pain leave me. All the unease and uncertainty is gone. I feel confident. I feel prepared.

I don't know who those people were, but they have definitely helped me. They gave me courage. I'm finally ready to end this.

I'm ready to fight.

I'm now confident in my abilities and know that I can do this.

Closing my eyes, I focus on the clearing. I think about Colton and Liam. I think about my family. I don't know if this will work. I've never attempted to actually transport myself somewhere before. Usually my magic just…takes me where I need to be.

I push my magic out and spiral it around me. I don't know how much magic it'll take to go back there. I close my eyes and concentrate on the magic as it moves through the air. Creating a vortex around me, I start raising my hands. For some reason, extending my hands seems to work for me.

Thinking about my family, I feel a shift in the air. Pushing more out, my body tenses and starts to tighten as my magic tries to listen to me. Transportation is not one of my powers, so I have no idea how long this could take. A familiar sharpness spreads through my torso. My airways constrict as if someone has reached into my chest and squeezed my lungs. My legs and arms feel like jello and I feel myself being pulled backward. I keep my eyes closed as I move through the air. Concentrating on the clearing, I wait until I feel myself stop moving.

Hearing swords clanging together around me, I open my eyes. I did it! I'm back at the compound. My glee doesn't last for long. The burning of wood and the heat from fire infiltrates my senses. Without thinking about it, I rush out from the cover of the trees, covering my mouth and nose to avoid inhaling too much smoke.

Instantly, I start coughing and stumble as I enter the clearing. Bragden turns around and looks down at me surprised. "Ryanne?" he says as I fall to the ground unable to breathe because of the smoke. Bending down, he picks me up. Incendia throws a barrier of fire around us, but this time, it isn't hot or aggravating. I step away from Bragden and catch my breath.

"Where have you been?" he asks me.

"Umm…I have no idea actually. I was fighting against Zahtri and I remember him hitting me with some form of magic and I flew into a tree and lost consciousness. I woke up lying on the ground in the middle of the forest. Have I been gone for a while?"

"I'm not sure when you disappeared exactly, but I know that you've been gone for a little over ten minutes."

Ten minutes? "What happened to Zahtri?"

"I don't know. He disappeared shortly after you did."

"Drop the fire. I'm fine now," I tell Incendia, "The fire just caught me a little off guard."

"Are you sure?"

"Is everyone okay?" I ask before she drops it. "Colton? Liam? Emma?"

"They're all still alive…" Bragden tells me.

"But this isn't over yet," I finish for him. Nodding at Incendia one more time, I wait for her to release the fire barrier. Giving me a sad look, the fire disappears and once again I'm thrust into the middle of the chaos. Looking around, I see Colton with Tom, Vincent, Colin, and Chris. They're okay. A large arm wraps around my waist and pulls me back. I slam into Bragden's chest as a small dagger flies past the spot I was just standing.

With wide eyes, I thank him, but don't step away. That's the… second time someone had to save me because I didn't see a dagger flying toward me. Arching my head back, I look up at him and see him staring down at me with wide eyes.

"Are you sure you're okay?" he asks.

"No, but I'm ready for all of this to be over," I whisper. Bragden's arm falls from around my waist, but I still don't move away. My eyes move around the clearing looking for Zahtri. I see David and Emma fighting. Natalie, Liam, and James are all working together. Logan and Lily are fighting side by side in the back. Larkin blinks in front of a Gadramick and elbows him in the solar plexus and then leaves again. Natasha is still asphyxiating random mages as she tries to make her to way to…Natalie? I follow her line of sight, and she is definitely trying to make it over to her twin.

I briefly see Travis crouch down near his parent's bodies before he disappears. He's lost his younger sister and both of his parents in such a short period of time. I can't imagine what is going through his mind.

Without saying anything to Bragden, I start walking away from him. Throwing a shield up around me, I casually move through the chaos. I push magic into my shield, so if anyone attempts to touch me, they'll end up getting shocked.

There's something I need to do, and I'm not going to let anyone deter me from accomplishing it. Out of the corner of my eye, I see Colton stop fighting and look in my direction, but I don't stop.

Someone else needs my attention.

Walking onto the platform, I look around at the fighting around me. Many mages are staring, waiting to find out what I'm about to do. Taking a few steps back, I walk off of the platform and step into my previous spot.

Throwing my head back, I yell "Zahtri!"

I know he'll hear me, and I know he'll come.

So, I wait.

COLTON

I DUCK TO AVOID GETTING punched and while I'm down, Tom reaches out and sweeps his fist across the man's jaw knocking him to the ground. I stand up and open my mouth to thank him when I see people moving away from a girl. A girl with brown curly hair. Where has she been?

Tom sees her at the same time as I do and stops fighting. What is she doing?

Ryanne glances in my direction, but doesn't stop moving. I know she sees me, but she doesn't stop. My eyes follow her as she moves through the crowd. No one attempts to touch her. I can see the determination in her posture and facial expression. She's definitely angry.

Without pausing, she jumps onto the platform and faces the crowd. Her eyes move across the clearing not focusing on any one thing. She doesn't stop to look at anyone in particular. She's looking for something…or someone.

Standing in front of the splintered tree, she screams his name. Tom reaches out and punches a Gadramick in front of me. I'm no longer focused on the fight. I can't be. I've been trying to keep my attention on the Gadramicks and let Ryanne do her thing, but it's so hard. I want, I need, to run forward and protect her with my life. I'm not, nor have I ever been, her protector, but I've made a personal promise to protect her. She's my soulmate. It's what I'm supposed to do.

Right now, I can't protect her, but damn it, I want to. I need to be beside her. Tom reaches out and places a hand on my shoulder.

"You can't, Colton," he says. "Don't forget about the prophecy."

"Who freaking cares about the prophecy!" I yell. Ryanne looks around, waiting for Zahtri to show up. "I've seen her die too many times to care about what the prophecy states. Zahtri threw her into a tree earlier. Look at that tree!" I point to the tree she's standing in front of. "That is from her small body being slammed into it. How much force would he have had to use against her to cause that sort of damage? Huh?"

"But look at her, Colton. Look at that girl who was just thrown into a tree. Does she look weak? Does she look injured? No. She looks strong and determined. She wants this to end as much as you do. Now, let her do what she needs to do. Let her finish this. This is not your battle to fight. Ryanne has to be the one to end this. If you try and go against the prophecy, one or both of you could end up dead. Is that what you want?" Tom says.

That is definitely not what I want. I've discussed with Ryanne what I want to happen many times. We have plans that cannot be fulfilled unless we both survive.

I calm down and look at Tom. I can see how much he's struggling with this as well. I have to remember that I'm not the only one that cares about her. I look away from my Uncle right as Vincent falls to his knees. We both turn and watch as he pulls a bloodied blade from between his ribs. I look across the field and see a dark haired mage smiling at us. Phillip threw the knife.

Tom crouches down next to Vincent, who is now leaning forward, resting his palms against the ground, trying to catch his breath.

Vincent looks up and gives his attention to Phillip. Without saying anything to anyone, he disappears. "Where did he go?" Tom says as he stands up. We all know Vincent will succumb to the dark magic from the blade, but for the time being, he's going to fight with everything he has in him. With Jedrek and the antidote gone, there's literally nothing we can do about the wound.

Phillip moves out of the way and starts fighting against a different mage. Where *did* Vincent go? My eyes move away from Phillip to the opposite side of the clearing. Ryanne is still standing beneath the tree, waiting. Vincent reappears beside her and grabs onto her waist and transports both of them away from the clearing.

"What the heck?" I say as I spin in a circle. Where would he have taken her? Why would he have taken her anywhere?

Right as Vincent disappears with Ryanne, Zahtri transports back into the clearing.

"How did he know that he was going to appear right then?" Tom asks me.

"I have no clue," I say as I continue to look for Ryanne and Vincent. Zahtri's eyes move around the clearing before they land on my group. He looks straight at me and grins before he disappears again. All of us tense and wait for what is going to happen next.

When nothing happens for a few seconds, we all relax.

The Gadramicks numbers are thinning. Many are leaving. Dravin is dead and Zahtri is…who knows where. Valdus is pushing through the crowd around us working his way to…Liam?

I look over at my Uncle. He has dropped everything to help us during this time and I know we haven't shown him just how appreciative we really are. "Thank you for everything, Tom," I whisper as I start moving across the field. Tom, Chris, and Colin can handle everything here. I have to warn Liam.

Not knowing where Ryanne is makes calling my invisibility much easier. As I step away from Tom, I let it take over. No one will bother me as I make my way across the field.

I maneuver through the Gadramicks without actually touching anyone. I stop as a Gadramick runs in front of me. Mr. Prowler rushes after him. Pushing forward, I continue moving toward Liam. I see Valdus pushing his way through everyone, so I pick up my speed. He's going to get to Liam before I can.

Two Gadramicks run in front of me and stop. They can't see me, but they are in my way. Valdus starts running now, Liam hasn't seen him yet. Hitting both of the men in their pressure points, I push them out of the way before they hit the ground. I'm not going to make it.

"Liam!" I shout as Valdus pushes past a Gadramick and jumps toward Liam. He turns around and looks in my direction, but because of my invisibility he can't see me. His attention quickly leaves my area and lands on Valdus. His eyes widen, but he doesn't have enough time to move.

Valdus barrels into Liam right as Phillip's sword slices through the area where Liam just was. James grabs onto Natalie and pulls her back out of range. Valdus rolls off of Liam, but remains on the ground. Liam looks up at Phillip, but doesn't move to fight him. His attention is on Valdus.

James releases Natalie and moves toward his brother. I make it over to Liam and crouch down beside him. I can see the blood soaking the ground beneath Valdus where Phillip's sword sliced him.

"Valdus?" Liam says as he leans over him.

"I'm so s-s-orry, Liam," Valdus says as his body starts convulsing. "F-f-for ever-r-rything." Valdus turns his head and looks straight up at Liam. "Your m-mother would be proud of you," he whispers. Unshed tears glisten in Liam's eyes as he looks down at his tribe leader.

I stand up and move away from Liam giving him some privacy. I look behind me at Natalie, but see her looking to her left. I follow her line of sight and see her looking at Natasha. She's fighting against a mage, but she doesn't seem to be doing as much damage as I know she's capable of.

"I don't know what to do about her," she whispers to me. I don't know how she knew I was beside her. I grab onto her hand and squeeze. I don't know if it'll come to it, but if Natasha attempts to attack someone either one of us love, we'll have to fight her. I don't want to hurt her, but she made this decision. She chose to help Dravin. She chose the Gadramicks over us, and she has to face that decision.

Liam walks up behind her and places a hand across her shoulder. "I hope this ends soon," he says without looking at either of us. He's looking at James who is now fighting against his brother. Neither one is taking it easy on the other.

I look away and glance back at the platform. Vincent and Ryanne are still gone. Where could they have gone, and what is taking them so long?

Hearing a pained grunt behind me, I turn back around and find James pulling his sword out of Phillip's chest. Phillip is staring up at his brother in shock. I can see the sadness in James' eyes as his brother falls to his knees. "I'm so sorry, brother," he says. "You gave me no choice."

I look up at James, shocked that he was able to do that. If I was in his situation and had to fight against David, I wouldn't be able to. James takes a step back and apologizes one last time before turning away. Phillip falls onto his chest where he remains unmoving. James turns his back to us and reaches up to wipe the tears from his eyes. He doesn't want us to see his sadness, and I don't blame him.

Hearing another scream to the right, I see David gasping for breath on the ground. Emma is fighting someone, so she can't help him. I look around him looking for the Gadramick responsible and see a tall man standing in the shadows.

There's no way I can get to him soon enough. I open my mouth to call for Larkin when Natasha runs across the clearing and knocks the unknown man to the ground. Natalie squeaks beside me, staring wide eyed at the scene in front of her. Larkin transports in behind the Gadramick fighting Emma and knocks him out. Thanking him, Emma turns around and falls to the ground beside David who is gasping for breath. Did Natasha just saved him?

Even David seems a little shocked. Without saying anything to Emma, he looks over at Natasha who's fighting against the large Gadramick. He punches her in the jaw and she spins around and lands on her back. Scooting back, she attempts to asphyxiate him.

The Gadramick stumbles a little, but doesn't stop his forward momentum. Natasha lets out an earsplitting scream as her skin turns a blistering shade of red. He's a fire affinity. That's why David couldn't breathe. His lungs were literally on fire.

Seeing movement to my right, I watch Logan trying to push his way through. It looks like he healed himself enough to start fighting again. Natalie gasps beside me and starts running toward her sister. I see Connor stop fighting against a Gadramick and move toward her as well.

"Natalie!" Liam yells after her. At the same time, we both take off in their direction. Natalie doesn't attempt to fight anyone and no one tries to stop her. Natasha's screams start to die down the closer we get to her. Her skin is covered in third degree burns, and she tries to roll over, but can't move her body. Larkin appears behind the man and grabs onto his shoulder and disappears, taking the man with him. Natalie and Conner reach Natasha at the same time and both crouch to the ground beside her.

"Natasha," Natalie whimpers with tears glistening in her eyes. "Please don't go." Liam and I stop behind her.

Conner grabs onto Natasha's hand and kisses her knuckles. Coughing, Natasha looks up at them and tries to smile. "He promised if I worked with them, he'd leave you alone. He promised you'd be safe. He was going to keep coming after Ryanne, and I knew you'd become involved. I didn't want you to get hurt," she whispers. "I had a part to play. I had to play the part. There was too much at stake. Too much to lose." Natasha's head rolls to the side and her breathing slows. "I had a part to play."

"Natasha!" Natalie screams. "Don't leave me."

Connor looks over at Natalie. "Ryanne was right."

"What?"

"She told me the girl we knew was still there." He looks down at Natasha. "I love you Natasha." Leaning down, he places a kiss on her forehead.

"I still hate her," Natasha whispers as she glances at me. "Tell Madison I love her, okay?" Natasha croaks as tears fall out of her eyes and land in the grass. "I'm sorry." she gasps and closes her eyes. Her hand goes limp in Connor's. Natalie cries out and covers her mouth; tears are streaming down her face and over her hands. Liam reaches down and pulls her up to him. She stands, throws herself into his arms, and cries into his shirt. Logan finally makes it to us and drops to the ground beside her to attempt to heal her, but she's gone.

That doesn't make sense. Ryanne rescued Natalie and Conner from Natasha's attack earlier this summer...She had a part to play.

With a sad shake of his head, Logan stands up and makes his way over to David and heals him. David thanks him, but reaches out and hits me lightly on the shoulder. Without saying anything, he points over at the platform.

Ryanne is back.

CHAPTER THIRTY-TWO

ZAHTRI HAS TO COME SOONER or later. He's not going to leave me standing here alone for long. He has to want this to end as much as I do. We can't do this for much longer.

I bite my lip when someone touches my shoulder and whip around expecting to come face-to-face with Zahtri, but Vincent is standing behind me. "Wha—"

Vincent's arm wraps around my waist. All the colors around me blur and the sounds coalesce together in a vortex of meaningless noise and shades. I close my eyes to try and make the transportation process easier. When we stop moving, I lose my balance and stumble to the side. Vincent keeps a grip on me, making sure I don't fall.

When I turn around, Vincent lets go of me and reaches down to place a hand on his ribs. My eyes move down to his hand and I see blood oozing between his fingertips. "Oh my gosh," I gasp and look back up at him.

"Use his weakness," he says. I try to ignore the grimace on his face. Vincent is dying. A normal wound wouldn't push that much blood out as fast. He was hit with a weapon Zahtri infused with dark magic. "Claire said to use his weakness."

"What weakness? I can't find anything?" I look around me briefly. We're still in the forest, just an undisturbed part. Vincent takes a few steps back and leans against a tree. "I've been looking, Vincent. He's too strong. The only way I can stop this is if I take myself with him, and I'm trying to avoid that."

"Get creative," he tells me doubles over in pain.

"I've been trying. I don't know what else to do," I move toward him, reaching out. I don't like seeing him in pain. There has to be something I can do to ease the hurt.

"You're a smart girl, Ryanne. Get creative." A peaceful expression crosses Vincent's face as he stands up straight and looks at me. "You know, I was going to marry her," he whispers.

I take another small step forward, toward him. "Who?"

"Claire, I loved her." He grabs onto my wrist and I feel myself being transported again. Closing my eyes, I wait for the movement to stop. When I feel Vincent's hand loosen its grip, I open my eyes. I'm back at the clearing. The fight is still ensuing, but there is no one around us. "I can almost hear her calling me," he says with a small smile. I catch him as he falls forward, gasping.

"Vincent, please don't go." I lower him to the ground. I hope that no one shows up right now. Gently resting his head on the grass, I push his hair out of his face. "Vincent?"

"I can s-see her." The blood is still oozing out the wound. He's too far gone for anyone to help. I hope he's not in pain anymore. His eyes close, but he's still breathing. "She's so beautifu..." With one last exhale, his body goes limp.

"Vincent?" Nothing. "Go to Claire," I whisper and place a small kiss on his cheek. "Thank you."

Spotting Larkin at the edge of the clearing, I call his name. "We need to bury him," I tell as I stand up. "He deserves a proper burial."

"Ryanne..." he starts.

"Please don't," I ask him. He's going to tell me not to sacrifice myself again. I must have a look that he recognizes. After staring at me for a few seconds, Larkin just nods and blinks away with Vincent's body. I don't stray from the spot, but I move my eyes around and scan the fighting. Tom, Colin, and Chris are still fighting. Liam is with Natalie and James. Bragden and Incendia are where they were before. David and Emma are working together as well, fighting off as many Gadramicks as they can. But where is Colton? He has to be invisible, because I can't find him anywhere.

Pushing all the sounds of the fighting into the background, I bring my attention back to the small area in front of me. I need to remain focused if I'm going to do this. I need that confident feeling I had earlier. I need that feeling of happiness and love I experienced when near the tree with the initials carved into it. Running a hand through my hair, I concentrate on calling my magic to me.

When Zahtri comes, I'm not going to fight. I'm going to use all my magic. I'm going to throw everything I can at him, and he's going to wish he ended me when I was down and injured. He had a dagger and could have easily finished me off. He should have finished me off.

Hearing thunder roll above me, I push more magic out. Dark tenebrous clouds start rolling in as my magic moves around us. The sounds of fighting are completely tuned out as the whispers start materializing. I have all the attention on me, but I don't look out at the crowd. Taking a few steps back, I take in a deep breath, call out Zahtri's name, and wait.

I don't have to wait long.

Zahtri appears in front of me with a large smile plastered on his face. "That was quite the little disappearing act you just pulled. How'd ya do it?"

"Magic," I tell him without moving toward him. Get creative. I need to get creative. Vincent was right. Claire was right. Colin was right. I can do this. I just need to *get creative.* "I'll tell you about it someday."

"I hope you know what you're getting yourself into," he says as he takes a step forward. I have absolutely no idea what I'm doing, but I'm going to pretend like I do. It's kind of my thing.

"I hope *you* know what you're getting yourself into," I tell him as I push more magic around. Strengthening the shield around my thoughts, I stare Zahtri down. I can tell he can feel my magic. These games need to stop. This has to end. I'm prepared to finish this. Right here. Right now.

I feel Zahtri try to penetrate my shield, but I don't let it affect me. Without breaking eye contact, I take a step forward. Strength spreads through me as a look of shock crosses his expression. When he feels the edge of my magic brush against him, he moves back a little. I can see the disbelief in his face. I'm ready now.

Sensing that, Zahtri starts gathering magic around him as well. I can feel the shift in the air as his moves around me. Taking one final deep breath, I gather all of my magic into a giant ball and push it forward at the same time as he sends some at me. I don't visualize my magic doing anything other than just hitting him. I need to stun him long enough to do what I fully have in mind.

I'm going to get creative.

Our magic counteracts each other, and neither one of us causes any harm. This could take longer than I planned. Time for plan B. Running toward him, I jump into the air and transition straight into my flips. Usually my gymnastics stuns my opponents long enough for me to get a hit in. Zahtri sidesteps my moves, but he doesn't take into consideration that I can use my magic and fight at the same time. As I move in front of him, I push my magic out.

It cascades through the air and collides into his chest sending him flying back into the tree. Without giving myself any time to relax, I start pushing more magic out. Extending my hands, I imagine the magic creating a vortex around Zahtri. I just need him to stand up. I've created a magical tornado before, but this one will require more magic. I didn't intend to cause harm the first time I made one. This time, I do.

Zahtri pushes himself up and faces me again. I can feel his magic hit my shield, but it doesn't penetrate the barrier. He's going to have to try harder than that. When my skin starts vibrating from my own magic use, I forcefully thrust it forward. Zahtri's eyes the magic tendrils swirling towards him, but he doesn't react soon enough. Instead of barreling straight into him, I imagine it splitting down the middle and circling around, creating a magical tornado with him in the middle.

When Zahtri is fully encased inside, I push electrified magic at it. The electricity from the lighting coalesces with the vortex. The tornado lights up like a Christmas tree with thousands of twinkling lights flickering off and on. Gathering all the anger from both mages and Gadramicks around me, I strengthen my magic and continue pushing it out. Despite being wrapped in negativity, my magic glides through the air like the wind before a storm—calm and peaceful, but potentially dangerous.

The edge of the tornado bows out as Zahtri attempts to break free from the magical cocoon. Raising my hands above my head, I close my eyes and unlock my thoughts box. The thoughts of those around me swarm my senses, briefly overwhelming me. I wrap the thoughts in excess magic and push them toward the tornado. I'm hoping when they hit it, it'll confuse Zahtri enough that he won't be able to form any counterattacks.

Taking a few steps back, I continue pushing magic out and swirling it around us. I don't know what is happening in the clearing, but I can't afford to break my concentration even for a second. A second is all Zahtri needs.

Continuing to move backward, I imagine the tornado coming together at the top. I open my eyes and watch the vortex. If I can just close the vortex, I can end this. The edge of the tornado is pushed out again as Zahtri tries to get out. With renewed vigor, I thrust more magic at him.

Reaching deep inside me, I break down the rest of the barrier I had constructed around my magic. Zahtri was right when he said I had to release more magic. I had more locked up than I thought; dwelling inside of me was hidden magic begging to be used.

I'm the secret of the flame. Liam said that flames provide the illumination during the darkest of times. Mages have been living in darkness for a while now, and if I can cease the flickers in the flame and bring back its brilliant luminance once again, then I'm going to. No matter what it takes.

I feel my energy start to wane, but I continue funneling magic out. I don't know how much magic it'll take to stop Zahtri, but I'm going to find out. Starting to lose my balance, I fall to my knees and push more out. I don't think I have an endless supply of magic, so I'm sure I'm about to find out what happens when you use all of it.

The tips of the vortex fuse together, capturing Zahtri inside. Placing my palms flat against the cold earth, I push more magic out. My airways tighten with each piece of magic that leaves me. Hanging my head low, I think about Colton. My best friend and soulmate. We had all these plans together and I don't think we'll ever get to experience them now. He means everything to me, so I wrap my love for him around the magic.

I'm going to disappoint all them, but this has to be done. David and Logan's jokes echo in the background and I keep pushing. The time that

Emma and I baked a cake for Colton fills my mind. The magic strengthens as the happy memories intermingle with the strands leaving my body. I wrap my love for Liam around vibrating pieces of magic and push them out. My pranks with Bragden are pulled to the front of my mind and though my body is protesting my actions, I don't stop the flow.

I think about everyone. I think about those that came here to fight today. I think about the lives we have lost during this battle. I think about all those that died before at the hand of Dravin and Zahtri. All these emotions cascade out of me and infuse my magic. Neither one of them can come out of this alive.

All the strength leaves my body, but I don't stop. I can't stop. I close my eyes and focus on the vortex. I have to end this. The Gadramick's reign has to cease tonight. Mages shouldn't have to live in fear anymore. Humans shouldn't be at the mercy of them. The world is full of enough evil as it is. Magic does not have to add to it. Magic is supposed to be used for good. For help. For encouragement. For anything, but what they want to use it for.

Taking one last deep breathe, I gather everything I can. I can no longer see what is going on around me, nor can I hear anything, but I know what I have to do. Wrapping the weather elements, the emotions, and the voices into one giant ball of magic energy, I thrust it forward toward the vortex. Everything I had in me leaves and moves through the air. I open my eyes and watch in slow motion as my magic melds around the vortex.

A few seconds later, everything explodes. My magic release plummets back into me and surrounds me with a bright white light.

Then everything goes dark.

CHAPTER THIRTY-THREE

"RYANNE," SOMEONE CALLS OUT FOR me. I roll onto my back and try to blink away the fog from my mind. "Ryanne," she repeats.

When the haze finally dissipates, I look around. I'm in the middle of the field of dreams...only this time I'm not alone, nor is Liam here. I'm surrounded by my mom, Claire, Jedrek, Vincent, and Kyril. I'm surrounded by the dead...which means I'm dead.

I died. Again.

"Did I do it?" I ask. "Is Zahtri gone?"

"He's gone," Claire says. "You did well, dear. You did well."

I push myself off the ground. "Not well enough. I'm here. I'm not at the compound anymore. I freaking died again," I bite my lip and try to not cry, but a single tear rolls down my cheek.

My mom rushes forward and wraps her arms around me. "Don't cry, dear." I wrap my arms around her waist and cry onto her shoulder. When you tell someone not to cry, it becomes impossible to actually listen to them. Something inside me has to rebel against authority.

"Do you remember what I told you that first day in the book store, Ryanne?" Claire asks.

"Umm, you told me the town was full of unexplainable things," I reply. Before I even finished speaking, she starts shaking her head.

"I told you not everything is as it seems. Magic has a way of complicating things. You're not really dead, Ryanne. Right now, you're sort of in…between life and death."

"How is that possible?"

"You pushed all your magic out, Ryanne. Literally all of it," she says.

"I couldn't risk him getting away." Zahtri was strong. I had to make sure he wasn't going to walk away from that situation. "I had to."

Jedrek steps forward. "Do you remember how I told you that your magic was mixed with your blood?" I nod. Of course I remember that conversation. "Well, when you came into your magic, it became an intricate part of you. You need it to survive. Your magic isn't like an appendix. You can't just have surgery to have it removed and then go about things like nothing is missing. Your magic is like your heart. You can't live without a heart, Ryanne."

"So…I killed myself," I state.

"You're not dead," Vincent says. I watch as Claire looks over her shoulder and smiles widely at him. Even in death, she found happiness. Vincent glances over at her. I can see the love in his eyes as he looks at her.

"Then what's going to happen to me?" I ask to anyone who can give me an answer.

"That depends on you," my mom says. I look up at her as she speaks. She still has her arms around me.

"What do you mean?"

"When you died before, you had to overcome your insecurities to go back. You had to promise me that you'd start seeing yourself as others do. You promised to believe you were strong enough to succeed and that you were good enough for Colton."

"I did. I do. I overcame all of those things."

"Yes, you did honey," she says. "This isn't like that."

"Then what is this like?" I ask. I look between all of them. I don't really know if I like where this conversation is going. Vincent looks at me with sad eyes. My mom's grip around me tightens. I look at Claire and then focus on my mom. "Mom, please tell me."

"There's nothing you can do but wait."

"Wait? What the heck am I waiting for?" I demand as I step out of her arms.

"Whether or not your body is strong enough to heal itself."

"Well then, I'm screwed," I mumble as I sit down on the ground. "How long does it take for my body to realize I'm actually dead?"

"That's not the right attitude," Claire says. "You need to think positively, Ryanne."

"I need to think positively?" I ask incredulously. "Do you realize what you're asking of me? Do you know how hard it was for me to finally realize that I was strong enough to end this? I didn't figure that out until a few hours ago *while* I was in the middle of that fight."

"You defeated Zahtri," Kyril says. "You defeated the Gadramick that even Dravin was afraid of. You know you're strong, Ryanne, you just don't know how strong you really are. You're going to pull through this."

I sit down on the ground. How do I always get myself into these situations? *Why* do I always get myself into these situations? "I know what'll happen if I die tonight," I look up at Claire. I remember what she told me when I died in that hotel room. Dravin and Zahtri aren't alive, so not everything will play out like she previously stated, but I still can't risk it. "I can't let that happen, Claire. I can't let that path be paved. What do I have to do?"

"Be positive," Jedrek says. "Think positively."

I'm not usually a very positive person. In fact, if there was a positivity award, I would never be a recipient. Ever. Right now though, I can at least try to think on the bright side. I can think of the glass half-full.

"So how long are we talking about here? Five, ten minutes? An hour tops?"

"Only you know that," Claire says.

"Well, do you think we can get a pizza delivered here? Thirty minutes sounds reasonable. I'm starving. I've been fighting all day." I try to keep a serious expression on my face, but seeing everyone's smiles lifts my spirits a little bit.

I can do this.

But the actual question is, can my body?

"So what'll happen to you guys?" I ask moving my eyes between all of them. They're...dead. They don't have another chance. I've been given too many chances. Why don't they get one too?

"After this, we move on," Claire says. "We're here to help you. Once your body chooses, our time is done. We get to move on. I finally get to move on." I can see the small smile on her face.

"I'm so sorry," I whisper. I feel responsible for their deaths. Claire died during an explosion that was meant to kill me. My mom died in a car crash that was meant to kill me. Jedrek, Kyril, and Vincent all died in a battle that they were a part of because of me. I'm the common factor in all of their deaths.

"Ryanne, do not blame yourself for our deaths," Vincent says. "Phillip killed me. Not you."

"I chose to correct the car," my mom tells me.

"Cawtel killed me," Jedrek says, "but my death was long overdue."

"Fallon stabbed me," Kyril states.

"I chose my death," Claire cryptically says. At my confused look, she continues. "You'll understand someday. Check the books." The books? Claire winks at me, but refuses to explain further.

"Claire, what were Colton's parent's names?" I remember him telling me their story, but for the life of me, no pun intended, I can't remember their names.

"Scott and Lynelle," she answers. "Why?" I knew it. They are the ones that carved their initials into the tree. Colton's parents helped me tonight. They played a part in helping me overcome Zahtri...and I may never get to tell Colton that.

Choosing to ignore her question, I ask, "So what now?" I cross my legs and lean back, closing my eyes and basking in the sunlight. That's one thing I love about this place. It's never too hot. It's never too cold. There's a light breeze and a nice amount of sunlight. It's not blinding, but it feels good as it hits the skin.

"We wait," my mom answers.

I hate waiting.

COLTON

THE FIGHTING AROUND US HAS basically stopped. Ryanne's magic isn't just concentrated on the opposite side of the platform anymore; it's moving around us as well. She has Zahtri fully enclosed in a vortex of magic. She pulled this same move on Colin during a training session we had back at his house.

I push my invisibility back and look at Liam, who's staring at Ryanne with a worried expression on his face. Even though he's not her protector now, I know he still wants to be fighting beside her. "Something's wrong," he whispers.

I look back over at Ryanne as she falls to her knees on the ground. The vortex has folded in on itself, creating a cocoon around Zahtri. There's no way for him to escape now. Ryanne is still pushing out magic. Too much magic. "What is she doing?" She needs to stop.

"She's ending this," Liam answers. At the same time, we both start to head in her direction.

The wind begins to pick up. Increasing in intensity, it pushes against our bodies making it impossible to move forward. Voices and soft whispers fill the air. Ryanne leans forward and places her hands on the grass to remain upright. Thunder cracks above. She's still pushing out magic.

Ryanne, stop. Stop. STOP! I repeat this over and over, hoping that she'll hear me.

Lighting strikes the middle of the vortex as Ryanne shoots a large ball of magic at it. Everything around us stops as we watch it make its way to the tornado. No one is fighting anymore. Everyone is watching and waiting to see what happens next.

When the magic connects, the vortex begins to glow. Its luminance increases in intensity until it literally hurts to look at it. A couple seconds later, it explodes and the brightness shoots out across the clearing, blinding everything. My body is thrown backward and I feel myself free-falling through the air. I don't know how long I am like this, but it feels like an eternity. I can't hear anything around me. I can't see anything. I'm all alone in my quiet little universe.

Slamming into a hard surface, I'm brought out of my bubble and back into the real world. Hearing a slight ringing in my ears, I open my eyes and see pieces of wood. Leaves are floating to the ground from the trees that exploded.

Shaking the haze away, I sit and look toward the platform…or what's left of the platform. Zahtri is gone. The ground is charred and dead where the vortex was. My eyes move across from it and…

Ignoring the pain spreading through my body, I jump up and run across the clearing, jumping over bodies along the way. I don't stop to look and see who is lying down. I don't think about how many of them are dead. I don't look at anyone, except the small girl with curly hair. I jump onto the broken platform and run two steps across before going off the edge. At Ryanne's side, I drop to the ground. She's lying on her stomach with her hair across her face. Rolling her onto her back, I lean down and listen for a heartbeat. There has to be a heartbeat.

Thump.

Was that a heartbeat? *Thump.*

It was! She's still alive. "Logan!" I yell. I can't heal her. He's literally the only one who can heal her. I sit back and push her hair out of her face.

Oh my gosh.

She's covered in cuts and bruises. Did she get these before or after the explosion? I look back at the clearing. Liam and Natalie are running toward me. I can see David, Emma, Bragden, and Incendia all moving, so at least they're alive. Tom is pushing himself off the ground. Where the hell is Logan? Larkin transports in beside me. "Is she alive?"

"For now, but she needs Logan," I tell him. Larkin disappears.

I lean my head down and rest it against her forehead. "Ryanne, don't you dare leave me. We planned our life together. You can't leave me now," I say. Without my permission, my eyes start to tear up. I've seen her die too many times. I pull her body into my lap. Her head rolls to the side. She's completely unresponsive. "Please don't do this to me."

Liam and Natalie fall to the ground beside me. "Please tell me she's alive," Liam implores as he looks down at her. I can see the grimace he's trying to hide. She looks horrible, I know. She needs to be healed. She needs Logan. She pushed out too much magic to heal on her own.

Larkin transports back in beside me with Logan. Since he was in the back, his injuries aren't as bad as the rest of us. He looks down at Ryanne and grabs onto the hand that I'm not holding and closes his eyes. When the injuries are this bad, he doesn't have to find the area that needs healing the most. His power knows what to do. I watch as the bruises and scratches disappear from her skin. The swelling under her eye goes down and the cut on her lip mends itself. Her arm straightens out as the bone sets itself back into place.

Logan opens his eyes and releases her hand. I stare down at Ryanne waiting for her to open her eyes and look at me. After a few seconds and nothing happening, I look up at Logan. "Why is she not waking up?" I ask. "Why didn't that work?"

"Something's not right," he says without taking her eyes off of her. When is anything ever right? I tighten my grip on her. She has to wake up.

"Come on, Ryanne," I say. Leaning down, I listen for her heart beat again.

Thu....mp.

It's fainter now. *Thu.......mp.*

"Damn it, Ryanne. Don't you dare leave me. Wake up!" I shout and shake her lightly. Tom walks behind me and places a hand on my shoulder. We were supposed to come out of this together. Why didn't Logan's magic heal her? *Why*?

Reaching down, I rest of my forehead on hers again. This isn't the end. It can't end like this.

I know you can hear me, Ryanne. I know you're listening. You need to get back here. You need to come back to me. Jack Sparrow always found a way back, so I know you can too. You're so much stronger than this. Fight whatever it is you have to fight, just come back to me. I can't do...any of this without you. Come the hell back to me, Ry. I need you here.

I continue to push these thoughts at her. Ryanne could never read my mind, but she had a way of knowing what I was thinking. This improved with her power of emotions.

We've lost too much today. Too many lives were ended at this compound. I will not be able to bury her. Dravin can't be right. He just can't be. There's no way I can watch them lower a casket, with her inside, into the ground. I won't make it through that. I just got her back. She can't be gone.

Ryanne, please.

I move to listen to her heartbeat again. It's silent.

Her heart's not beating anymore.

I can't stop the pained cry that escapes my lips or the tears that fall from my eyes and slide down my soulmates already cold cheeks. I don't bother trying to hide any of these emotions.

I couldn't even if I tried.

EPILOGUE

"YOU READY?" TOM ASKS ME as he extends his arm out.

I take his arm in mine and smile. "I'm more than ready," I say breathily. I'm trying to keep my emotions at bay, but it's hard.

"You look so beautiful, Ryanne," he whispers. "I'm so glad you two found each other. You deserve a lifetime of happiness."

I bite my lip and blink rapidly. I can't cry yet.

Have you ever looked back at a moment in your life and realized that is the moment everything changed? That one moment had a giant impact on everything that happened later? That moment created a domino effect, and no matter how hard you tried, you couldn't slow or halt the momentum? Once everything is set in motion, there's nothing you can do. You just have to let the pieces fall where they may and hope everything turns out alright. I can't fathom how one single moment, one action, one event, one decision can be so impactful.

But it can be. Believe me.

My life has changed in so many ways. A year ago, I didn't have a large family. I lived in my own little world, completely unaware of how large the world actually was. Back then, I didn't believe in magic. I didn't know anything about powers, mages, Gadramicks, soulmates, protectors—I didn't know anything. I didn't believe anything good was going to come out of my life. At the time, my biggest goal was getting out of Stormfield, Maine. There were too many memories here. There were too many people here who knew my story…too many people judging me because of it. Now, there's nowhere else I'd rather be. I have family here. I have friends here.

I have a life here.

Walking through the doors of that bookstore changed everything. BlackMoon Bookstore was the beginning of the life I was supposed to live. That day I met Claire and Colton. Later, Colton awoke the magic inside me, bringing me into the world I truly belong in. Claire gave me her love reminding me what it was like to be a part of a family. She gave me something back I had been missing. She gave me more than I could ever thank her for. I know she's in Heaven with my mother, and they're both looking down on me, proud of everything I've accomplished.

As I'm standing here, I realize that there's nothing more I could want in life. I've endured a lot of change, but not all of it has been bad. I did go through a phase of depression. I was left alone in the world. I had no family or friends to turn to in my time of need. I was grieving, angry, and alone. I contemplated suicide a couple times, but knew that my death wouldn't solve anything. It couldn't get any worse than that.

Then, I met Colton. I met this gorgeous man who infuriated me. He was frustrating, stubborn, confusing and absolutely the sweetest, most caring man I'd ever met. I denied my feelings for him for the longest time, because I was a magnet for danger. Danger was the stalker that even a restraining order couldn't hold back and I couldn't risk it.

I erected walls around my heart after my mother's death. I wouldn't let anyone near me. I couldn't let anyone else into my heart. I wouldn't survive if something happened to them. But, like I said before, Colton's stubborn. He beat those walls until they caved in. He knocked them down and left me standing before him vulnerable. He filled the emptiness inside me and made me feel again. I wouldn't have accomplished anything if it weren't for him. I was lost before I met him. He found me on my dark, desolate path and gave me the light I needed to move forward. He stood by me through it all and never left, no matter how hard I tried to push him away.

Even today, he continues to stand beside me. The danger that followed me has diminished, and now I can fully give Colton all the love he deserves. He deserves the world for everything I've put him through. I died on him three times. I was kidnapped, attacked, bruised, broken, and bloodied, and he still chose me. He accepted me for who I was, and for that I'll always be his.

I think back to when Colton proposed. I knew it would happen soon, but I had no idea at the time. It was during the winter and I remember the snow slowly falling to the ground, creating an ethereal atmosphere around us. Colton asked me if I wanted to go for a walk and I agreed. He brought me to the gazebo and got down on one knee right there.

The doors in front of me swing open as the classic wedding music rings through the yard. Out of the corner of my eye, I can see Violet sitting at the piano playing with Travis, her soulmate, standing at her side. Her leg was broken sometime during the battle and Travis found her sitting against a tree. He picked her up and carried her around, so she didn't have to be alone, until Logan was able to heal her. They've been inseparable ever since.

I tighten my grip around Tom's arm as I take my first step down the aisle. Everyone stops talking and stands, giving me their attention. Colton stops talking to David and looks at me. His mouth falls open as he takes in my appearance, so David reaches over and closes it for him.

If it weren't for Tom, I'd be unable to make this walk. I can feel my cheeks widen from the giant smile I give to Colton. I don't see anyone else around me. The church disappears. It's just me and him.

This green eyed man in front of me holds my heart. I love him with every fiber of my being. I've never felt as whole as I do right now. Under his gaze, I feel beautiful. I feel like I can do anything. I finally feel worthy of his love. I'll never see myself like he does, but he's slowly making me forget my insecurities. I realize now that I *am* good enough.

I hear Tom chuckle beside me, but I can't tear my eyes away from his gaze. Colton's eyes never waver. He watches me as I close the distance between us. My heartbeat increases with each step. Ever since I found out that we were soulmates, I've thought about this moment. I take one final step and suddenly I'm standing beside him. I'm where I'm meant to be.

As I watch him gaze down at me in wonderment, I know there's nowhere else I want to be. This is the moment I've been waiting for. His love for me flows through me, and I smile up at him as I turn and face him. Tom releases my arm and lets me take the last step toward my soulmate. Colton's excitement and pure happiness cascades into me, filling me with warmth and love. Colton's my soulmate. My perfect half. My everything. He holds my heart just as much as I hold his. It took some time and a new power, but I know that now.

He gives me a small smile. His feelings deceive his calm and collected façade. It takes everything I have in me not to jump into his arms. Biting my lip, I stare up at him. I'm about to marry him... Colton...I'm about to marry Colton. He shakes his head as he stares down at me, but a few seconds later, he goes invisible.

A laugh bubbles to the surface when I'm no longer looking at Colton. I'm looking directly at David.

"Sorry, but I'm taken," he tells me as he flashes his wedding band.

"Colton," I whisper. I know he hasn't moved.

"Give me a minute," he whispers. I tighten my grip on the bouquet in my hands and glance at all the people who came today. There's definitely more people than I was expecting. My eyes meet Jane's and I can't help but smile at her. She winks at me, and leans into Ross's side. Lily's mom made a full recovery and gives me a small smile from the seat beside Jane. I'm glad they could all make it today.

"You look beautiful," he tells me. Looking away from the audience, I gaze up at him again. I'm amazed at the composure in his voice considering he just went invisible.

I open my mouth to reply, but nothing comes out. Colton's smile widens at my response and I hear a few chuckles behind me. My mouth literally goes dry as I fully take in Colton's appearance. His dark tux brings out the brightness in his eyes. He recently got his hair cut, so it's no longer falling into his face. He's kept the soft waves that I love so much. My eyes start to move over to the jacket he's wearing, when I feel his hand under my chin.

"You look a thousand times better than me, Ryanne," he whispers.

"You look very handsome, Colton," I tell him, thankful that my voice actually comes out.

Colton smiles at me before looking toward James. I tear my eyes away from Colton and look at James as well, telling him that we're ready to begin.

I'm so ready to marry Colton.

COLTON

THIS IS THE GIRL I'M marrying. I've known Ryanne for such a short time, but I feel like I've known her my whole life. I've felt a roller coaster of emotions since meeting her. Some people don't feel this much in their whole life time and I've felt it all in a little over a year. Since the night that I got down on one knee in front of all of our friends and family members and asked her to marry me, I've been looking forward to this moment.

It's finally here. I'm marrying Ryanne today. Ryanne Arden will become Ryanne Wagner. Mrs. Ryanne Wagner. I can see Tom smiling at me as he walks Ryanne down the aisle, but I can't tear my eyes away from the girl attached to his arm. My heart sputters at her beauty; it has dropped into my stomach and is having difficulty getting back up. Ryanne's always been beautiful, but there's something about seeing the girl you love wearing a wedding dress. Everything becomes so much more real.

Emma wouldn't let me see Ryanne before the wedding. I didn't know what her dress looked like. I didn't know what her hair was going to look like. I even had no idea what the bridesmaids were going to wear until this morning and I'm so glad for that. Ryanne's dress hugs her upper body like a second skin. Small beaded three-dimensional flowers make up the bodice before meeting the tulle skirt. Little petals are sewn onto the skirt of the dress. With each step that Ryanne makes, the petals appear to be falling down the fabric. Her long hair has been tamed and curled, and is brushing against her back and bare shoulders with the slight breeze.

Ryanne stops walking through the freshly dropped flowers that Madison put down to stands in front of me. She quietly thanks Tom, but doesn't look away. I know she can feel the strong emotions I'm currently having, but I can't control them today. All the emotions bubble to the surface when I see her smiling. My body can't handle the influx of emotions, and I feel my magic coating my skin.

Dang it. I've never gone invisible from too much happiness before. It's always been negative emotions that bring out my magic. I hear David say something behind me, but I don't pay attention to him. Come on, how do I come back if I'm already happy?

"Colton," Ryanne whispers while looking straight at me. I ask her for a minute while I concentrate on calming myself. To marry this girl, I have to be visible. She has to be able to see me. Knowing that, I'm somehow able to calm myself enough. The magic leaves my skin and dissipates into the air around me.

"You look beautiful," I can't control the smile that comes after. I'm really surprised my voice actually comes out and I remain visible.

Ryanne opens her mouth to reply, but quickly shuts it again. Ahh, I didn't think I could love her more. I watch as her eyes slowly take me in. I reach forward and grab onto her chin. This is her day. I'm just wearing a simple tux. Everyone should be focused on her beauty. "You look a thousand times better than me, Ryanne."

She bites her lip and tells me that I look handsome. I can't wait any longer. I look toward James, who's officiating, and nod. We're ready. Ryanne tears her eyes away from me and nervously smiles at James. "We're gathered here today..."

I can see James talking, but I can't hear anything. Ryanne has my complete attention. This girl I had a crush on in high school and was too afraid to actually approach for the longest time is going to be my wife soon. I have so many memories with her, both good and bad, but I wouldn't trade any of them for anything. Everything we've been through has brought us to this day—to this moment. We've been through so much together, and we've come out victorious.

Out of the corner of my eye, I watch Ryanne. She's biting her bottom lip and there's a slight blush rising in her cheeks. You'd think after everything that's happened recently, she wouldn't get embarrassed anymore, but right now there are a lot of people looking at her. Even after basically saving the world, Ryanne still hates attention.

She turns toward me briefly and catches me watching her. When her eyes meet mine, her smile widens. With a single glance, I make her smile. I want nothing more than to reach out, bring her to me, and kiss her. I just have to get through the ceremony.

Ryanne must be having similar issues, because when she looks up at me, her grip tightens on the bouquet she's holding. James clears his throat, bringing me out of my thoughts and back to the scene in front of me. "It's time for the vows," James whispers.

Ryanne previously volunteered to go first with the vows. She hands her bouquet to Emma, her maid of honor, and faces me. I can see the tears threatening to spill out of Emma's eyes. In fact, almost all of Ryanne's bridesmaids are crying or on the verge of crying. Olive is sitting on the ground at Emma's feet with her pale green rhinestone studded collar watching everything play out. Ryanne reaches out and grabs onto my hands and smiles up at me. All the nervousness dissipates and all I see in her eyes is love. Her love for me.

"Colton, we've been through so much together," her voice rings out, much more confident than I was expecting. "I won't go into all the details, because I know you already know them. Despite all the hardships we've endured, I know that I wouldn't change anything. This is where I'm meant to be. Right here, standing in front of you.

"When we first met, I was this extremely shy, depressed, lonely girl who wanted nothing more than to get away from this town. You came into my life like a raging bull and broke down all my barriers. You became my first real friend. Then, you pushed further and became my best friend. I started to develop feelings for you and that scared me to no end. Then, you became my soulmate. Suddenly, everything made sense. Everything I had been trying to push back and ignore made sense, Colton.

"You accepted me for who I was. You accepted all my flaws and insecurities. You accepted my stubbornness and my uncanny ability of attracting trouble. You accepted all of it right away. There was a reason why I walked through the doors of the bookstore that day. We were meant to find each other. I can't imagine spending the rest of my life with anyone else. We make each other stronger. You gave me the strength I never knew I had. You gave the confidence I never knew I had. You have given me so many things I never thought I'd have. You've given me so much and if I have to, I'll spend the rest of my life making it up to you. Our lives were predestined, but there's nothing more that I want this moment.

"I love you so much, Colton Wagner, that it scares me sometimes, but that lets me know it's true. We've had to fight for this moment, because nothing in life comes easy." I scoff and she smiles at me, the tears brimming on the surface of her eyes. "And I wouldn't have accepted this if we didn't have to fight. I wouldn't deserve your love if I didn't have to fight. Because I fought, I finally feel worthy of someone like you."

I suppress my groan. I should be the one feeling like that.

"Don't look at me like that, Colton." A couple people laugh behind me. "I want this. I want us. I'm so glad that I'm standing before you today. There's nowhere else I'd rather be." She reaches out and grabs the ring and turns toward me again. A single tear cascades down her cheek.

"Colton, I give you this ring as a token of my love. I promise you I'll always be here for you. I'll be the wife you deserve. I promise to be your soulmate. I promise to always stand by your side and with this ring, I gladly combine my life with yours."

Ryanne slides the band onto my ring finger and looks up at me, waiting for my vows. Another tear starts to fall. I lace our hands together and look straight into my beautiful bride's eyes.

"Ryanne, the day I met you, Claire told me that something big was going to happen, and she was right. The moment you walked through that door, I knew everything was about to change, and I'm so glad it did. We've run into a lot of obstacles along the way, but look at where we're standing today. We've overcome all of those and reached this point. Together."

Ryanne bites her lip and continues to stare up at me. I can see her struggle with keeping her emotions in control. Her hazel eyes brighten with tears that threaten to fall. "Before you, I was waiting for my life to begin. You walked into my life and completely changed everything for the better. I didn't realize what I was missing until you. I didn't realize how incomplete I was before you…how empty I was.

"Even before we were soulmates, it was my goal to make you smile. I would think about all the ways I could make you laugh. It's one of the best feelings in the world to know that you're responsible for someone's happiness no matter how short lived it is. From this day on, it's going to be my goal to always keep a smile on your beautiful face, because you deserve to be happy. You deserve the world, and I'll do everything in my power to make sure you get it.

"This is not the ending. This is the beginning. The beginning of our life together. I realize that we're young and I know it scares you sometimes, but love has no age. We were chosen for each other. We wouldn't have found out that our destinies were intertwined if it wasn't the right time. I didn't know it was possible to feel so much for someone until I met you. I love you so much that it hurts." There we go. The tears start to fall out of Ryanne's eyes. I step forward and cup her face with my hands, using my thumbs to brush the tears away.

"That means it's real, Ryanne. I can't believe this gorgeous, fierce, amazing, stubborn, frustrating, sarcastic," a round of laughs echo through the yard, "loving, completely wonderful girl in front of me is mine. You are mine just as I am yours. I've not done anything to deserve someone like you, but in this instance, I'm going to be selfish. I'm going to accept the love you're willing to give and return it back tenfold.

"You're my life now. My everything," I reach out and grab the ring. Ryanne bites her lip, trying to stop her tears. I raise her hand and look straight into her eyes. "I promise to spend the rest of my days trying to make you see what I do. All those flaws and insecurities you think you have are what make you perfect. They make you who you are and I love you for who you are. There's not a single thing about you I would change and I promise to do everything in my power to make you believe that," I say as I slide the ring onto her finger.

Ryanne chokes on her tears and turns toward James, who's smiling at us. Taking a step back, he concludes with the ceremony. "You may now kiss the bride."

I do just that.

THE END

ACKNOWLEDGEMENTS

Thank You!

That's the short and simple version. The rest of this is not that. I'd like to take this time to thank a few people who have helped me during this process.

My mom, Elizabeth, and Krista have been my biggest support system during this time. They've helped me during my crazy moments and my freak-outs during the publication process. They've all told me to go to my happy place and listen to Josh Groban. They, along with Sara W., have read through these books helping me search for errors and gave me hope that maybe these books don't suck after all. Words cannot express how thankful I am for their support, but I hope they know it. I'd also like to thank some more family members who have helped me: my sisters Rachel and Maddie, my dad, Sara Stoin, Danielle Jasperson Postnikoff, and Janet Buss. You've all been very supportive of me during this time and I thank you for that.

I'd like to give a big thank to the readers who have made this series possible. Without you all, I'd be nowhere. I have a few people that I'd like to thank personally:

Michelle Guo-you sent me my first fan email. I freaked out when I first read your message. I couldn't believe that anyone would take the time to contact me about my books. I never imagined that my books would be good enough for that, but reading that first email helped push me forward and want to continue doing what I'm doing. I'll always remember that feeling, and I'll forever be appreciative of your message.

Also, I have to give a big thanks to Taskia Choudhury, Lily Fletcher, Gina Silva, Christel Darrough, Leslie Collins, Jodie Louise Boxall, Yazmine De La Rosa, Shelly Webber, Stephenie Lammers, Cheryl Mackey, Robin Parks, and many more. I realize that's a lot of names and I haven't even come close to mentioning everyone, but you all have been very supportive during this process. I'm sorry if I didn't mention you previously.

I want to thank everyone that has downloaded and rated my books, ever sent me an e-mail, commented on my blog or social media sites, and/or told someone else about this series. You've helped me more than you know. I see all of the likes, comments, and shares you all do for me. I can't thank you all enough! I wouldn't be anywhere if it weren't for you. I hope I can continue to create works that are deserving of your amazing support.

ABOUT THE AUTHOR

Currently a student at Ball State University, Kaitlyn Hoyt is pursuing her passion for writing while working towards a Wildlife Biology and Conservation degree. Vegetarian. Proud tree-hugger. Lover of comic book movies. Avid reader. She has an unhealthy obsession for the soothing music of Josh Groban. She discovered her love for writing during the summer of 2012 and hasn't stopped writing since!

Connect with Kaitlyn:

Stay connected with Kaitlyn Hoyt at:
Kaitlyn Hoyt Writes:
www.kaitlynhoyt.blogspot.com
Facebook:
www.facebook.com/YA.Author.KaitlynHoyt
Twitter:
www.twitter.com/Kaitlyn_Hoyt
Goodreads:
www.goodreads.com/author/show/6940389.Kaitlyn_Hoyt

CPSIA information can be obtained
at www.ICGtesting.com
Printed in the USA
LVHW080840160722
723666LV00033B/1438